Rebel

Emma Ellis

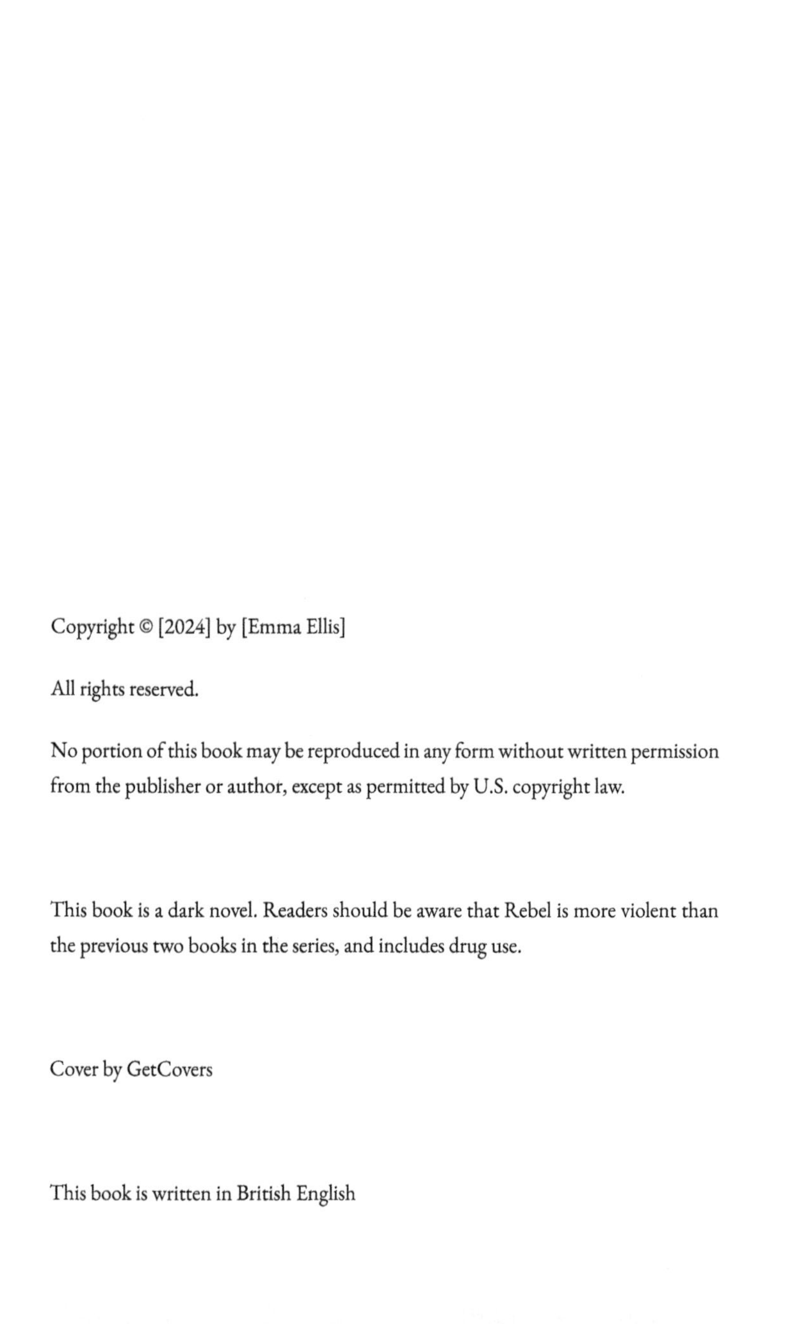

This book is a dark novel. Readers should be aware that Rebel is more violent than the previous two books in the series, and includes drug use.

Cover by GetCovers

This book is written in British English

Chapter 1
Iris

What have I done?

It's all Iris can think as she stares at the mess at her feet — innards of the beast spilled across the floor. The very essence of the Society is now nothing more than debris and detritus. Sparks. Buzzing. Humming its last tune. The final signs of life ripped apart. Funny how something so powerful, so all-consuming, is as fragile as porcelain when met with a woman's wrath.

She drops the crowbar to her side, arms now weak, rinsed of their rage. She trembles as the weapon falls and jumps when it clangs on the floor. There's so much mess. Was this her plan, to beat the thing until it exploded, to release its insides, to smash everything? A rumble comes through the floor. A building somewhere is collapsing. Another one. A bigger one. Through the small gap in the blackened window, all she can see is ash.

Is this it? This quickly? The end of everything?

'Mum,' she says.

Mae steps forward, standing among the butchery. She's glaring at the stains, the splinters, probably thinking what sort of vacuum will be able to pick this up.

'Mum, I'm sorry. Shit, I'm so sorry!'

Mae doesn't glance up. 'It's okay, dear. It's okay.' Her tone is as flat as ever. Somehow, she isn't shaking. How isn't she shaking?

'Mum!' Iris shouts now. Someone needs to take a bit of the panic. She can't keep it all to herself. It's too much. She'll burst if she does. 'Mum. Shit. What have I done?'

Mae peers at her, a rare moment of eye contact, then walks over and pulls her in for an embrace. When was the last time Iris had a hug from her mum? Ten years? Closer to twenty, probably. The hug is like rubbing salt in a cut — it draws out the sting. Iris's arms are steadfast by her sides as her mother's hold tightens, then she bends her elbows, forearms reaching up to her mother's back, fingers straight and splayed as she makes contact, reciprocating the hug and sobs. Over and over again she thinks: what have I done?

But there's that other voice, the one that was louder just now but has been silenced by panic. It's the voice that made her do it. It sounded kind, that voice, a slight vibrato, a gentle nudge.

You did what you had to do, young Iris. You did good.

Iris buries her head deeper into her mum's chest, but it's not as comforting as it should be. Her mum is too thin, too weak. Mae sways as her arms wrap around Iris, muffling Iris's ears, yet making her sobs louder. If there's enough noise, Iris won't hear that voice, that bad voice, the one that makes her do such bad things.

The footsteps come. She knew it wouldn't be long. By the sounds of it, they're taking the stairs two at a time, then closer in the corridor, through the doors, pushing them open because the electric is out and can't power the automatic function anymore. The sensor lights fail to come on. The air-conditioning is off and dripping, each drip landing in rhythm with the footsteps.

Drip. Drip. Drip.

And then, out of the corner of her eye, is Ava Maricelli. She's smaller than she appears on all the posters, but still formidable. Biceps bulge out of her fitted black T-shirt. Perhaps the gossip columns are true, and she makes her own special brand of muscle enhancer at XL Medico. Of course, for a crime of this magnitude, they send in the top Society Police. Ava is standing close now, lightly panting after her run up the stairs.

Iris should collapse to the ground, hold her hands up; but her mother's embrace is so rare, she doesn't want to let it go. Ava's lips curl into a smile. She's not pouncing on Iris, not moving to rip her away from Mae and drag her to some jail. She has no weapon. Instead, Ava folds her arms, nodding.

'Iris Taylor,' she says, and her smile broadens. Even from Iris's perspective, the twinkle in her eye is apparent. 'Well done.'

Chapter 2
3 weeks earlier

Sitting in the corner of some dingy low Score apartment party, where the floor creaks under grimy carpet from dancing partygoers, where the hand smudges on the window pre-date the Great Unrest, and soap, by the looks of it, the music blares so loudly it resounds with Iris's anger.

The guy cosying up to her and fluttering kisses over her neck doesn't help. She fans herself but doesn't edge away. It's a rare thing, her wanting to be desired, to feel the warmth of another. And an even rarer thing to crave it. Such cravings lead to more physical actions, irresponsible actions, ones that can lead to a burden being produced.

Her implant glows green. She should be safe. She should allow her body to have what it wants. Even if this guy — she can't recall his name — smells a bit like old cheese. Maybe some action in that department will take her rage away. Half an hour ago she had her first taste of Flake. That crusty burning line of narcotic has opened a channel of want inside her unlike anything she's ever known. The slippery awakening hits her like a punch in the gut.

'I get it now,' she says as he continues to kiss her collarbone. 'Why the fuck do we put up with this? Why do we do what we're told all the time, work so hard and for what? It doesn't matter. All that matters when it comes to getting your Life Score is who your family is.'

'Yeah,' he says without coming up for breath. 'Too right.'

'Fuck this. You know what I'm going to do? I'm going to take the whole God damned system down. Destroy it all!'

'Yeah. Bad girl.'

She's not a bad girl. She's never been a bad girl. She's a model citizen who works hard in her job, presents herself well, never even makes time for dating. But now, as the line of Flake fizzes through her, something in the back of her mind is unlocked, awakened, and it wants answers. Not just answers, results. Change. Her stomach cramps with yearning, a yearning for what she has never seen, never known. An abyss ahead of her attracts as if it's made of dazzling light. No more stuck in a corner goody-two-shoes Iris. She's wasted her entire life like that. It makes her angrier than anything, that she's gone along with the whole disgusting charade, that she bought into the bollocks. She's spent the last couple of days cracking her knuckles since her Life Score was revealed to be a paltry 270 despite her years of arse-kissing and overtime. Her anger boils so hot even the chilled beer can't bring her down to a simmer. It makes her last meal threaten to reappear.

As she leans in a little closer, hoping for his touches to soothe her anger, to make it productive, a voice sounds as if from behind. She snaps her head around, but there's only a wall. The other people sitting around or dancing aren't paying her any attention. The music is too loud to hear them anyway. She realises the voice is inside her. A soft voice, just a whisper, licking at her ear with more stubbornness than whatshisface sitting next to her.

You can do it, Iris. It's what you were born to do.

For the briefest moment more, she considers who said that. Perhaps it was a lyric in the song? No one else seems to have noticed. His hands are wandering now, or perhaps they have been for ages and she's only just realised. Still, it doesn't seem like the worst idea. Everything against the rules now seems like a good idea.

'Climb on top of me, why don't you?' he says, as the vibration of his fly unzipping runs through her.

It seems like the kind of party where rules can be broken. Not Eyes Forward laws, but social rules. Public displays of affection lead to Society Police having a field day. She glances around and giggles. There's no one observing, no phones held up. She's always so well behaved. Why should she be that way? Why shouldn't she break through the mould she cast herself?

She turns and hitches one leg up, straddling him, giving his hands free and easy access to the front of her. They move lower, to the area in contact with him, pulling her in closer. She glances down and tilts her head to the side. He's not the worst looking, the blue powder of Flake casing his nostrils making him appear daring, rebellious. She bites her bottom lip. She could do this, if she wants.

'Iris! What the hell are you doing?' Georgie's voice comes with a jerky tug on her arm.

'What?'

'You're dry humping some guy next to a pile of vomit. Christ, Iris. Come on, time to go.'

She shrugs her arm free, then sticks her bottom lip out in a childish sulk. 'I'm having a good time.'

'Yeah, she is,' whatshisface says, more of a slur, as he still lies on the floor.

'Put your dick away, arsehole.' Georgie spits at him.

Iris cocks her head and narrows her eyes. He's not much of a catch. The vomit on the floor splatters his front as well.

So that's what that smell is.

'Fine,' she says with a sigh and a little more lucidity than she had just now. 'Let's go.'

Georgie regards her with a tight mouth and her chin tucked in. An overly smug expression, especially considering how many times Iris has dragged her away from flat parties for misbehaving and fraternising in ways that would lead to worse consequences than just raised eyebrows. They've got their Life Scores now and can have points taken away as easily as added. Time to grow up, Iris has said to Georgie so many times before. Perhaps she finally has.

They find their jackets among a pile of clothes, not all jackets, some are clothes that should definitely still be worn. Lacey clothes. Underclothes. There's not that much flesh on display. God knows why these things are here and where the owners have skulked off to. Iris peels away a pair of knickers from her jacket sleeve, then passes Georgie her coat as they make for the door, stepping over couples in similar positions to what she'd been in just now. She's glad they're leaving. Things do seem to be getting a little wilder than usual. A tile of Flake is just by the door, propped up on an otherwise empty bookcase. There are lines already made, and she briefly considers another, then notes the heightened colours in the room, the music with notes that aren't normally there, and decides she's had enough.

They walk down the street. 'Stop staring at me like that,' Iris says. It's the best time to walk, she always thinks. This late at night, there are no lanes dictating speed. The pavement is empty enough that they can zigzag and go at their own pace.

'I can't help it,' Georgie says. 'I'm trying to figure out who you are. You've snorted that stuff. I can see it around your nose. That shit basically glows in the dark.'

Iris shrugs. 'So? Everyone does it. And so should you. I could see things. Not like hallucinating. But it gives perspective, you know?'

'Mmmm.' Georgie gives Iris the side-eye.

Iris and Georgie's lust for mischief is what cemented their friendship years ago. Not the worst mischief, just the mildly meddlesome sort. That, of course, has waned in adulthood when the repercussions became rather more serious. Although Georgie still has the twinkle in her eye that she has when she says outlandish things. It's usually Iris who's the more sensible one and when the roles are reversed, Georgie likes to hold a grudge. And Iris holds a grudge against Georgie holding a grudge.

It's gone midnight, and the flickering streetlights aren't up to the job of piercing through the night. They walk on autopilot around the piles of rubble from the latest fallen buildings. The remnants of the Great Unrest when Iris was born, just over twenty-eight years ago, are still causing havoc across Berkshire. The damaged blocks have stayed damaged. The deaths from the odd building collapsing into the streets are few and far between — not headline grabbing enough. A few quid spent on the cleanup and one more victim of the feuds. It's barely worth the staff hours to type it up. The projects to restore and renovate stall often as the population continues to decline and demand for housing stagnates. Build the houses and people will fill them, that's the worry.

That there will be more people.

They smell the body before they see it; the ghostly arm is all that's visible in the moonlight. They've seen it before. It's been here over a week. They should have taken another route home to avoid it, but forgot in the fog of booze and terse words. If any Society Police have reported the body, no one has bothered collecting it.

The body can't be anyone important, probably an even lower Scorer than them, lower than the one on St Anne's Road last month that was left for a few days. The final push to get the population to sub 100 million is not without casualties, is what the conspiracy theorists say. The Eyes Forward are hoping for murder. Georgie grabs Iris's hand and they quicken their pace, Iris holding a can of mace in her other hand.

Once the population is below 100 million, they'll make the streets safer, the Eyes Forward say.

Once the population is below 100 million, they'll give low Scorers access to the full range of healthcare.

Once the population is below 100 million, they'll take the fertility indicator implants out of women's hands.

The lies stink worse than the corpse.

Iris sees that now, feels it. That's what the Flake has done, for she can't attribute this awakening to anything else. It's given her a bullshit filter. She squints in the darkness; the reality blinding.

They make it back to their ridiculously spacious apartment that is colder than outside and wrap themselves in blankets from the sofa.

'I'll make tea,' Iris says.

Georgie shakes her head. 'Best not. We're nearly up to budget already on utilities this week.'

Iris's shoulders sag and she shivers. 'Cold drink, then?'

'Sure.'

Iris goes to the toilet first, cursing herself for not using the one at the flat party. Her piss will have to sit there all night, making the bathroom smell. They're already up to their flush tally for the day. Six lines drawn down the chalkboard that sits above the toilet, just under the sign that says: if it's yellow, let it mellow.

'It's gone midnight,' Georgie shouts from the living room. 'It can count for tomorrow.'

'But tomorrow is Saturday. We'll use more water than a weekday at work.'

'Just flush. Don't worry about it. We'll go to the park to pee — or your parents.'

As if her parents can afford any more water than they can.

'I'll leave it,' Iris decides and shuts the lid.

She collects a couple of glasses from the kitchen, then pours them each a lemonade. It's room temperature. The fridge is too expensive to run.

The sofa is too small for the space, placed close to the wall where the TV hangs. The rest of the apartment is just heat-sucking space. They wanted a smaller place, but they're hard to come by. Square footage is cheap since the declining population has left so many apartments empty. The Eyes Forward ensures a booming economy in other ways though. Soaring power and water prices keeps the low Scorers struggling. In their place. They ensure their disposable income is spent on government-controlled– and taxed goods like utilities, rather than social lives. Georgie says it's better to be cold and for the apartment to smell like piss than have no social life. Iris would normally argue but, tonight, she sees the sense in Georgie's argument.

'Who was that guy anyway?' Georgie asks.

'Don't know. Don't care.'

Georgie gives her a light punch on her arm. 'What's gotten into you?'

Iris shakes her head, then glances around the room, her vision still twinkling a little more than usual. 'I can't explain it.'

The voice returns, the one she heard at the party. It's not a song lyric, not another person sneaking up behind her, though she still turns her head around to check. It's feminine. The words are forced out with a gravelly squeak like a rusty wheel.

Try to explain, Iris. You must try to educate everyone.

She'd almost forgotten about it. She assumed once the Flake had worn off, it would go away. She's still high, that's all. She sips her lemonade, the zesty sugar snapping her consciousness back, and the voice doesn't return.

Not for tonight, anyway.

Chapter 3
Ava

Ava kicks off her shoes, then walks through her living room, pausing at the mantle to straighten the flowers. She lights a new candle from the old as its wax pools on the surface. It smells like lemon. Zia's favourite scent. Taking the picture frame in her hands, she kisses it, and then polishes the surface. Her Zia's smiling face must remain clearly visible. Every day for the past eleven years, this has been her routine, and the heartache never gets any easier. Some days are worse than others. Today is about average, a dull pain with a residual emptiness.

Mandisa arrives home moments later. They work in the same lab but rarely share their commute these days. Ava reaches for a tub of leftovers from the fridge and a spoon, then leans over the kitchen counter, eating straight from the Tupperware.

'At least sit at the table and eat.' Mandisa breezes through, still in her shoes, her swaying hips leaning heavily into each pace. Ava watches her heels scrape against the hardwood floor but says nothing.

'Your PA sent me details of the opening ceremony for the new factory,' Mandisa says. 'It seems a little sedate, don't you think?'

'I've not looked at it. If you don't like it, let her know.'

'She's your PA.'

'You're the one who gives a shit about the parties.'

'This again.'

Ava puts her spoon down and straightens up. 'Look, I've had a busy day. Working weekends is hardly fun. And it doesn't matter how much you bang on about it. I'm not going to give a shit about any damned party.'

Mandisa stops at the mirror, then pulls her forehead skin higher and sucks in her cheeks. Her endless poses, Ava thinks, are an attempt to relive the past. Mandisa never seems satisfied with the present.

'We're a couple, Ava,' she says with an air of exasperation. The frequent argument is wearing them both down. 'We have to go. As a team. You want our work to suffer? You want our Score to suffer?'

'I don't give a shit. Literally.'

Mandisa holds her hands to her mouth, stifling a sharp intake of breath. 'Ava! How can you say such things? Look at where we live, at what we've achieved, at all we've done to get our Scores so high.'

After all we've done. Ava recoils her nose at those words. That, exactly, is the problem.

Ava puts the empty Tupperware in the sink. 'I'm going for a bath.'

Eighteen years she's stayed in this relationship, so swept up with Mandisa's affections for a while, and Zia loved Mandisa's company so much that when she was alive, Ava just went with the flow. When Zia died, Ava realised how hard breaking up is. They work together, live together. Lives so interlinked don't separate easily. Between social functions and Score-climbing, and the fame that never seemed to go away like she hoped it would, she's lost any lust and feelings she had for Mandisa. She felt the rip between them, each fibre tearing bit by bit until their relationship fell like a tattered cloth. Yet still she's here. Plotting, scheming ways of how to undo the damage Mandisa has done. There's no bringing the lost lives back. No undoing the hurt.

There's only revenge.

It's been eighteen years in the making. Her plan is finally ready.

Chapter 4
Iris

Iris stares in the mirror for ages, turning her head each way, altering the lighting, adjusting the angle of her vision. She looks like the same Iris, the same unruly dark curls and pale skin, a streak of freckles over her cheeks. It's the same Iris who does what she's told, who cleans up after Georgie yet makes as much mess herself, who has no time for dating and seduction around her work hours. But she feels different. Something inside has inexplicably changed.

She stands sideways, observing her minimal curves. Her arms are toned from years of climbing and bouldering, a few bruises from this also, and thick callouses line her fingers. Her body shape appears the same, yet she swears she's several kilos lighter. It's like she's made of bubbles, like the shroud of ignorance had not only covered her but engulfed every pore. Now she's shed it, like some reptilian human, and her new skin is flexible, porous. She absorbs everything.

You're ready to see, Iris. To see what's real and what's fake.

She glances out the window and squints. She can see fine. This voice needs to go away, or at least make sense.

'It's that drug,' Georgie says when Iris's face glazes over.

It's Sunday afternoon. Iris definitely isn't still high, and even her hangover is long gone. It takes longer to rid herself of the effects of booze these days, but not that long.

'I'm fine. I've just got so much to think about now.' Too much to even articulate. Her anger has fizzled out almost entirely. She can't remember ever feeling so un-angry. The years in anger management therapy seem a waste of time when one sniff of Flake and she's more chilled than Georgie after a beer. She's no longer angry at the Society, at the Eyes Forward, but not ambivalent either. She's motivated, though clueless as to how to proceed. Her lack of initiative makes her heart sink slightly. Perhaps it is just the drug.

'I'm going to do an internet search on Flake,' Iris says.

'You going to wait till Monday?'

Iris bites the inside of her cheek. It's been years since women have been banned from using computers outside of work, but she still forgets. Yet another Eyes Forward initiative to keep women under control, to stop the gossip.

Questions are at the forefront of her mind rather than just acceptance. What's wrong with gossip? What are the Eyes Forward so afraid of?

'I'm going to my parents.'

Georgie raises her eyebrows. 'Really? You can't even wait till Monday? You're not just wanting to see if that sleaze has been in touch?'

Iris takes a moment to recall the sleaze Georgie means. When she remembers, she shudders. 'No. No, I really want to do a search on Flake.'

'Okay. Well, I'll see if Sam is free to keep me company.' Her tone is riddled with mischief.

Iris throws a cushion at her, then makes for the door. 'I'm not your sponsor. If you want to see her, that's your decision.'

'You're supposed to stop me from calling her. You know I'm weak!'

'She's not that bad.' She's really not. A little snobby, bad at keeping plans, and non-committal. But not *that* bad.

'What kind of friend are you?' Georgie says with the sort of hard-done-by attitude she pulls off so well, even when she's being sarcastic.

Iris shouts her goodbyes and shuts the door. Georgie and her rollercoaster relationships test her patience at the best of times. Georgie with a crush is like a dog spotting a squirrel. Iris has spent years concentrating on work and her Score, which seems like a waste of time now since Georgie also got a 270 thanks to her more British lineage and being prettier. Where Iris had to put in the effort to achieve her paltry Score, Georgie bothers a whole lot less with work and a whole lot more on her attractions.

Her parents' place is on the other side of central Reading along the river. Iris takes a wrong turn before remembering they've moved. Their new apartment is closer, a ground floor, larger than their previous apartment, and a whole lot more soulless. It's colder and not just in temperature. It lacks the warmth a childhood home always has. All white walls and straight lines. It's not the worst end of town. The internet is more reliable at least.

Despite a fraught night's sleep and minimal food, since Iris and Georgie's cupboards are almost bare and neither could be bothered to tackle the shops on a Saturday, Iris pedals fast, weaving past the slower cyclists, deftly dodging buses and pedestrians spilling over into the bike lanes. She grins the entire way, brimming with a joy she can't explain, like a convict fresh out of jail. Until the voice returns.

It's nice to see the country for what it is.

Iris squeezes her eyes shut and shakes her head. What a stupid thing for the voice to say. This is the Society. No one calls it a country.

Wake up, Iris.

She groans and lets go of the handlebars for a moment to slap her ears. The voice needs to shut up, or at least say something that isn't utter nonsense. She is awake. She is seeing clearly. Cryptic bullshit only makes her feel deluded again.

Iris skids her bike to a halt in the tearaway style she used to do as a kid when her dad would shout at her to be careful. She locks it up outside her parents' block, only one of six mid-rises still standing on Mill Road, the others all lost to the post Great Unrest era decrepitude. Some collapsed when the adjacent asylum fell, not strong enough to withstand the aftershock of a building that size crashing to the ground. The rubble is still there, like a mausoleum for those who perished inside. No one bothered to retrieve the bodies. No one cared enough about the Pres-X takers who went insane when it was issued to the Sub 750s. It became something of a taboo to know someone who didn't strive enough yet tried to reap the reward

Iris always shivers when she's within sight of the wreckage. The rumours of the goings on from inside are more chilling than a working fridge. Society's elders who spent their regression years in straitjackets, shackled to beds in dark and crowded dorms. The few staff that tended to them walked on tiptoes to keep the wards silent except for the patients' screams. If the insanity wore off, no one ever found out.

No one ever left.

Through the front door, the apartment still smells of fresh paint and wood chippings. The floors have been cleaned of the sawdust, and the place is immaculate as always. She pushes the internal door open. It's heavier than expected because of its extra wide size to account for her father's wheelchair. He's not using it that much yet. Just 'future proofing,' he claims.

'Dad?' Iris shouts as she enters.

Pasha's voice calls a hello from the living room, only marginally louder than the TV and the vacuum cleaner.

'Hey,' she says as she approaches, then kneels to give him a hug. When she pulls back, she takes in his slight quiver, the way his mouth struggles to smile. He's thinner than the last time she saw him. 'How are you, Dad?'

His hands cover hers, his gentle squeeze more like a brush with a feather. 'I'm fine, sweetheart.'

She eyes his uneaten lunch on the table, his coffee cup still full, and the straw sitting on top. 'You eating enough?'

'Don't you worry about your old man. How are you? What's new?'

'Are you doing your physio?'

'Iris, I am fine. Trust me. Tell me about you.'

His hair is a mess, like hers always is. His fringe hangs lower than the top of his glasses, and she brushes it back. Her mum probably left it like that so she couldn't see the smudges on the lenses. Iris takes his glasses, then rubs them clean with a tissue.

The vacuuming from the kitchen stops and Mae walks into the living room. Iris just glimpses her, yet it's enough to let her mum know she sees her.

'Hi, darling,' Mae says. 'Lovely to see you.'

'Dad's not had his lunch.'

'He had a big breakfast.'

'Yeah, Dad. What did you have?' Iris's accusatory tone isn't intended for her dad. She delicately puts the glasses back on him, keeping his hair tucked back as she does so.

'I ate more than enough,' he says. 'Now stop it, you two.' Even his rasping voice can sound hard. 'Iris,' he softens his tone, 'would you like a cup of tea?'

She stands. 'I'll make it myself.'

She walks to the kitchen, then puts the kettle on. She shouldn't have come. The mental calmness she had before is gone. He's getting worse, and her mum isn't doing enough to help.

'Iris.' Mae sneaks up on her like some insect, and she snaps around to stare daggers at her. 'It's lovely to see you.'

'He's lost weight. He seems thin.'

'He's eating plenty. I can't force him to eat more. It's hard for him to chew sometimes.'

'It's muscle wastage. You're not doing his physio with him.'

'I am, dear.'

'Not enough.' She turns her back on Mae and pours the tea. 'If he had the right medication, this wouldn't be an issue.'

'Stop it. You need to stop it, Iris. I am doing all I can.' Mae grabs a cloth, then wipes the side Iris just used. There's no spill there, Iris is sure of it. Not even a drop.

With Mae being so close, she steps back towards the doorway. 'It's not enough, Mum. He's getting worse because of you. If you hadn't dropped so many points, he'd still have his medication.'

'I know. You don't think I know that? It's complicated.'

Though the hurt is clear in Mae's voice, Iris can't soften her own. 'You were the accountant for one of the richest people in the whole of Berkshire, and you lost her as a client. All you had to do was keep her. Brown-nose, suck up, whatever it takes. That's all everyone is doing. Whatever it takes.'

'It wasn't that simple.' She has a tea towel now, drying the already dry countertop. 'Please, don't be like this. Come and have lunch with us. Can I make you a sandwich?'

'I wouldn't want to risk dropping crumbs,' Iris says through her teeth. Her mum's obsession with cleanliness is one thing she misses least about living at home, but she knows she's being cruel. It's not Mae's fault she's obsessive. Mae's expression goes from pinched to downcast, and Iris's own face falls. 'I just came to use Dad's computer.'

'Okay. Well, it's in the second bedroom, next to boxes of your stuff, if you'd like to sort through it. Take some things back to yours, maybe.'

'Sorry for creating so much clutter.'

'That's not what I meant.'

Iris walks away like a stroppy teenager and hates herself for it. But she hates her mum more. The loveless woman never showed her any affection, never consoled her when she grazed a knee, and groaned at the noise she made playing as a kid. Iris stayed living at home for as long as she could bear it to help with her dad, but their rows became too detrimental to all of their health. Watching her dad now, she regrets moving out. If she could manage her temper and her mum could stop being herself, then Iris would still be there to make sure he eats and exercises and takes care of himself. She finds it hard to visit. It's like watching one of the abandoned buildings turn to gravel.

She logs onto the computer, then clicks on the Shadownet browser, Nebula. Using her hand, she covers the monitor camera for a second until Nebula loads. She's sure the Society Police and Eyes Forward have better things to do than check for women using men's computers out of hours, like she's sure every woman breaks this law. Not that she'd ever know. No one ever discusses their law-breaking. You never know who's a snitch.

She searches for information on Flake. There are so many results, it's hard to figure out what is legit information and what is hearsay, but the reports are plentiful. Mostly consisting of short anecdotes and recommendations:

Best party ever!

Left me feeling great!

Horny as hell. Best shag of my life!

She narrows down the search: hearing voices after Flake.

Nothing. A few accounts of altered hearing while high is all. Her initial relief at the voice not being a side effect of the drug diminishes when she realises it doesn't leave her many explanations as to why she's hearing it. There is no reason she can think of besides that she's going as insane as the Pres-X takers inside the ruined building. There must be another explanation. No one goes crazy overnight.

She researches what's in the drug. The rumours say it's some cocktail of B-Well and Memorexin, both made by XL Medico. Some oversight the pharmaceutical giant never saw coming, it took a creative street dealer to do that experiment. They apparently mix in a little psilocybin from a European strain of magic mushroom. That explains the sparkly vision at least. From what the internet is churning out, from all the stories, there seems to be no adverse effects. No deaths from it. That's lucky. There's enough death already.

Searching Nebula is never complete without a dive into the darkest corners of the forums, where hackers across the Society break through the autonomous systems that block each county's internet from interacting with another. It doesn't take the most genius hacker to override the boundaries. Iris could create such a hack if she was still inclined to flex her hacking muscles, as could Georgie once. One Citizen Reform hearing is enough though, they both agreed some time ago. Iris is still convinced that the incident eight years ago cost her some Life Score points. Georgie still says it's what made them ban women from using computers, although Iris insists that's nonsense. Georgie has delusions of grandeur. She likes to think she's more of a rebel than she actually is.

All Iris wanted to do was to check out her cousin's school's press release in Scotland. Since they were in the grey area of life, too old to depend on parents, too young to have a Life Score, they were given the mundane punishment of writing essays about how great Berkshire is and a separate essay for their hometown, Reading, and received the stern warning of 'We'll be keeping a close eye on you'. The whole thing was humiliating. Humiliating, but not the level of treason that would cause Society-wide women's computer access being curtailed. Hardly a reasonable punishment.

Since when have the Eyes Forward been reasonable?

'Oh, shut up!' Iris says out loud. Perhaps the voice is an echo of Georgie from the years gone by, some memory being dredged up by a heavy night and shame of what nearly went down with that guy. It'll go away. The post-party embarrassment always does, eventually.

She continues to search the shadiest forums as a quiet Sunday leaves her with a thirst for gossip. Most chat threads are dedicated to the ruthless depopulation drivers. Conspiracy theories, mostly, saying that Eyes Forward has given quotas on deaths. Implausible, Iris thinks on first reaction, then shakes away the image of the body on St Peter's Hill last night. If there were quotas, there would be more. The odd death is hardly going to rack up to the ten or fifteen million population dent they're aiming for. It's just the usual nonsense.

The Sisters and Spies are particularly vociferous today, still moaning everywhere about women's treatment in the workplace, how women are banned from using computers. Yet they seem to use them just fine. Iris scrolls through such comments. From a young age, her mother tried to get her to pay attention, banged on about women's rights, though always chastised Iris for too much screen time. What did she expect Iris to do? Write letters? Put up posters like the Eyes Forward?

Iris was an early prodigy whose scaled-down access gave the rest of the Society a chance to catch up. Mae got what she wanted in the most backward way possible when women were banned from using the internet outside of work. Mae lost her lust for the fight for equality after that, and Iris just got angry. Silenced but angry. It's easier to exhibit rage than rebellion. Her mum is just one more thing to add to her anger list.

A few more scrolls through forums and a name comes up that she's read before: Joan Porter. It's someone linked to the madness in original Pres-X takers, some old XL Medico employee, by the looks of it. 'No one wants to be like Joan Porter,' is the gist of most sentences. Whatever. Boring. Iris wants something a bit juicier than a person from decades ago.

After she's satisfied she's not going insane from sampling one line of Flake, Iris shuts down the computer and shouts her goodbyes. Her eyes linger on her dad for a few seconds more as he laughs weakly at some corny TV quiz, then says his goodbyes with a slur.

Iris shuts the door and leaves. Her heart breaks more and more every time she sees him. If she's as selfish as her mum has said in the past, she wouldn't visit them at all. Maybe she shouldn't.

They love you. And they are more useful than you know.

That voice again. It's less rebellious now, more empathising — like a feminine version of her dad. Maybe she really is going insane.

'Piss off,' she says out loud, much to the disgruntlement of the pedestrian traffic, then cycles away.

Chapter 5
Mae

'She was using Nebula again,' Mae says to Pasha as she helps haul him up from his seat to stand. He groans, and she manoeuvres his walking frame underneath him. She glances over to the wheelchair as he turns his head the other way. There's no point mentioning that again.

'She's so much like her great-grandmother,' Pasha replies with a breathy voice. Mae can't tell if the face he makes is a grimace from his weakness or a smile at Iris's misbehaviour. 'She's a grown woman. We can't stop her.'

'You could tell her she can't use your computer.'

She's said this to him a hundred times. Why is it always Mae who has to play bad cop? It's been the same since Iris was born. Pasha instilled a desire for mischief with games and jokes and laughs, his easy grin contagious to Iris, while Mae always had to be the sensible one and reel it in. It was Pasha who suggested she take up climbing as a hobby, as a release for any mental hardships. Iris loves it, but Mae could never watch. How was she supposed to be okay with her daughter ten feet up a bouldering wall?

Pasha's walking along now, wobbly arms pushing the frame, his legs like dead weights behind him. Iris was right. He is getting worse.

He pauses to talk. Only one action is possible at a time. 'I'm not going to tell her she can't use it. She has a curious mind. And she's not daft.'

Iris's intelligence is what Mae's afraid of. She's too curious, too astute. Mae swallows, then shakes her head. 'She'll find things out. You know that. About me. About your grandmother.' And her other family. Mae doesn't add on that bit. It's implied. Pasha understands unspoken words better than most.

'So?' he says with a huff. 'It's about time we told her the truth. She should know where she comes from. She can handle it.'

Mae shakes her head and walks backwards, gesturing for him to follow. His physio will take forever at this rate, and she has a ton of work to do. He follows slowly, and she counts his steps. He's meant to do three hundred a day. She doubts he'll manage half that much today.

'It's not safe for her,' she says.

He winces as he turns around and catches his breath. 'Nothing is safe for any of us.'

Chapter 6
Iris

The voice stayed away for the rest of Sunday as Iris went climbing and pulled herself to the top of the wall to burn off some steam. There's something about clenching a fist around a handhold, hanging her weight off that one clenched fist that makes a bad mood dissolve into nothing.

Even afterwards, the voice stayed away. She was chilling in her apartment with Georgie, using up the rest of the Eyes Forward beauty credits they're paid instead of half their wages like men. It's one Eyes Forward incentive that irks Iris, yet Georgie doesn't mind at all.

'First in line for beauty supplies as a government employee,' Georgie says often when Iris moans, wishing she had the cash instead. 'You'd only spend it on this stuff, anyway.'

Georgie would. Iris, not so much. Which seems daft, as Iris definitely needs it more. One night with bad sleep looks like a week of insomnia on Iris, her skin too pale to hide the dark circles. Georgie could be awake for a fortnight and still appear stunning. Yet she painstakingly facemasks, bleaches, tints, curls, straightens, extends, and removes, depending on the body part and day of the week. She claims that's the only reason she seems so well rested. Iris knows, after Georgie's dad died and she genuinely didn't sleep for a week, that's definitely not the case.

The Life Score statistics department is on the edge of Reading, the opposite side to her parents'. It's an unassuming building. Most wouldn't even know its Life Score HQ. Probably on purpose, Iris assumes. Otherwise, there'd be hordes of people outside begging for a better Score, and they have no protocols in place to cope with a disruption like that. It's barely staffed since the software does most of it.

A couple of IT staff loiter outside, Jason included. His dad, the equally hideous Norman Bonnet, is Iris's boss's boss, and as such, Jason is as untouchable as he thinks. Jason had his dose of Pres-X-2 three weeks ago and his middle-age skin melted away into pubescent smoothness. His libido also spiked at the same time, like some fresh skin is all he needs to make him a catch. He's not, never is, never will be. He's gross whatever age he looks. He followed her down the corridor to work a couple of weeks ago, the opposite way to his. He only picked on her specifically because she's small, she's sure of it. And a low Scorer. A low Scoring woman is hardly going to press charges against a high Scoring man. The Society Police bot would reply with a 'Stop wasting our time' email.

It was a power play, Jason cornering her, pressing her against the window, his hot breath condensing on her neck. He didn't touch her, not with his hands, just his torso pressed into her shoulder blades, his crotch into her backside. At least he kept his dick in his trousers. Her forehead rested on the cool glass of her office window as he grunted from behind. The steam around them left an outline of their heads that lasted minutes longer than he would have if she'd merely touched him. That's the thing with his sort. He thinks he's the one in power, and that's what makes him weak. A cock is a feeble appendage, especially when hard with its oversubscribed blood supply. If Iris desired, she could snap that brittle cock off. The gore would be glorious.

Today, rather than hide and wait for Jason to go indoors before she enters the building and can slip by unseen, she welcomes the altercation. She's ready for it, even if her arms are half dead from climbing yesterday. He won't expect any resistance from little Iris. He won't expect someone so meek to feel powerful. She locks her bike up, smooths back her helmet hair, and grins.

The grin falters when Jason goes inside, then down his corridor before she's even made it to the entrance. Her tense muscles relax, and her knuckles crack as she unfurls her fists. Next time.

Such thoughts would have terrified her before she received her Life Score, when she thought all her good, accommodating behaviour and arse-kissing might have actually helped up her Score. Now it's clear that's not the case, she is liberated. That's what the lightness is, a void inside where ambition once was. Ambition and the dread that comes with it. Now she's floating down the river, rather than trying to swim upstream.

There are so many ways to lose points. The fall down the ladder is not only gravity-assisted, it's hammered down from the top. And when your bosses are Preserved, that hammer is more of a sledgehammer. It would turn concrete blocks to dust. Iris's Life Score is far more fragile.

What if there were no Life Scores?

The voice returns as she approaches the entrance and her hunched shoulders jolt upright like she was tapped on them. She freezes only for a split second and resists the temptation to glance around. She knows there's no one and has no desire to appear as insane as she feels. She swipes her clock-in card at the turnstiles, ignoring the trickle of sweat collecting down her neck and stares at the fancier entrance to her right, the one that Jason just went through. The 700 plus entrance. The entrance she isn't allowed to go through because of her Score. Francis's haughty voice comes from the 700 plus entrance, greeting Horace, the butler. He replies a good morning to Francis, takes her coat, then shines her shoes while Iris heaves her way through the stiff turnstile, stepping in chewing gum before trudging up the stairs, each step sticky from the mess on her sole.

What if there were no Life Scores?

It's the voice again, nagging her as she walks down the corridor to her department. It has a pitch to it that she can't place, a breathy wisdom. There's some rhythm to its patience, yet its words are nonsense. It's like asking what if there was no air, no internet, no ground beneath her feet. Some things just are. They don't need questioning.

She knits her brows, trying to remember how she felt the other night, what she said. 'I'm going to take the whole God damned system down,' or something like that. That's what she said when she was high. Now she's at work. She needs to keep her head down, not up in the clouds. It's all very well saying such rebellious gibberish, but implementing such desires is an impossibility for someone like Iris.

The walls along the corridor to her office are painted with orange stripes — warning stripes to let the rest of the staff know that an unsafe woman works there. They painted the walls that colour on her first day, six years ago, while Iris's cheeks flamed brighter than the paint. The other corridor is painted gold, to mark its safety away from the likes of her. Iris is lucky to have her job, Ella and Francis constantly remind her. A woman of Iris's status should be thankful, they say. By status, they mean Iris's implant glowing with fertility. It doesn't matter that she graduated top of her class at college and university, that she has done post grad qualifications that have given her more letters after her name than her actual name and job title combined. That green or orange glow from her implant proves her worthiness — or lack of — more than anything. She'd be done with it and get sterilised if it wouldn't break her dad's heart so much. He has enough to deal with without Iris taking his dreams of grandchildren away.

Iris sits, rolling her shoulders forward and tucks in her shirt. She pulls one side over the other to disguise the missing button and hopes no one notices the coffee stain on her skirt. She has no electricity or water budget left to use the washing machine for another week at least, so her grimy work attire will have to do. Her dark curls are as messy as ever and still wet at the ends.

Her hairdryer's wattage is too high to justify when the air will do the same job eventually.

Her inbox is full of research topics, welcoming ideas on how to even out the curve of Life Scores. In the years that Iris has worked for the Life Score statistics department, they've tried none of her suggestions, and the so-called curve has remained the same. A thick wedge at the very low end, then a dip down before the sharp climb to 700 — the Score when Pres-X-2 becomes available — a steady rate to 800 when the original Pres-X formula can be taken, and a sharp taper afterwards. 700-800 is everyone's aim and many don't care after that. Preservation drugs are their top priority. The wedge at the lowest end shows how easy it is to hit rock bottom, and it's that part of the curve that Ella and Francis bang on about the most. The way they moan about it is like people want to sink that low. It's mostly women, of course. Parents become un-Scorable when they have an unlicensed baby, and funnily enough, those unlicensed babies never seem to have a father.

It's a far cry from the smooth bell curve they're aiming for, or apparently aiming for. If it was really what they wanted, they would implement *something* instead of just talking and moaning about it. Since her dose of Flake, Iris thinks her job isn't to fix the curve, but to keep reporting the stats the press want. No one wants to make the Society more even — that's just their sales pitch.

Iris sits at her desk in her dark, windowless corner of the cold office. Bored, overqualified, and underappreciated. Last week she learned her paltry Life Score, after submitting statistical formulae that could — if they thought to use it — provide vital information as to why the lowest Scorers stay the lowest. It wasn't asked of her. She put in extra time and initiative. Francis and Ella accepted her paperwork with glazed expressions and giggled after she left the room.

'We need the stats on violent behaviours among low Scorers,' Ella says this morning. Her hair is the blackest black, pinned in a sleek up-do. She's Preserved, of course, not a Pres-X-2 taker. She's actually Preserved, one of the high Scorers who had the treatment. The low Scorers never do anymore since it was proven their minds are not able to cope. The asylums brimming with low Scoring Preserved demonstrate that, though no one has ever ascertained as to why. They upped the required Score to 800 as a safety measure and the side effects went away.

Staff shortages over the last decade have been unmanageable since there are so few people under the age of thirty, and those post-retirement are only willing to plug the gaps in the workforce if they can rule over the minions. Rule is the right word for their presence. They'd crack a whip if they could, put the staff in stocks for making a cup of tea too slowly, and have them cut the crusts off their sandwiches.

'Murders, muggings,' Ella continues. 'If anything particular comes up about the new drug that's on the streets — Flake, is it called? That's what we need information on.'

Iris makes some notes. 'Any stats needed for the high Scorers?'

Ella stops in her stride and slowly turns to face Iris. She actually makes eye contact. Her plump lips smile so widely, they thin out to a more normal size. 'Yes, Iris. Let's get some stats on how much higher Scorers contribute to the economy. The press would love to know that.' Her eyes smile with her mouth, narrow and sinister. 'With the new Life Score algorithm launch coming soon, we need to keep things up to date.' Ella paces in front of Iris for no reason Iris can tell except to hammer down footsteps and sound important. 'This is the Society, where everyone knows their place, and everyone can achieve.'

Iris mouths along with the words. So imprinted are they on her mind, it's like humming an annoying tune you can't rid from your brain, or an irritating mosquito buzzing around. The Eyes Forward slogans are an ever-present annoyance. Vacuous, yet somehow overbearing. The new Life Score algorithm has dominated the news for months, making it more representative, they say. The DNA samples everyone was strongly advised to submit seemed sensible a while ago, before Iris's mind-awakening. Now, with her mixed heritage, it seems like one more elitist load of crap, designed to purify the blood of the richest.

'So, we need to send the press the right message,' Ella continues. 'Encouragement to show that the Society is inclusive and working towards a common goal.' She doesn't demonstrate what that common goal is or how it's inclusive. Peering in close to Iris, she angles her chin to look down her nose at her. 'You're tired. Your complexion is too pale. I thought you're supposed to be young.'

Iris pulls her lips back to fashion a smile, giving a glimpse of her clenched teeth. 'I'm working too hard, obviously.'

'Ha!' Ella stands upright and holds her stomach with her laughter. 'A 270 claiming they're working hard! The jokes you low Scorers tell. Hilarious.' She walks away, high heels still slamming into the tiled floor with every footstep.

When Iris is alone at her desk again, she kicks herself. Why did she say that? She'd never normally talk back in such a way. What's gotten into her to say such a thing? Her Score is low enough and her job security precarious enough without rattling Ella's cage. She's a good employee. A good citizen.

Are you a good citizen to the low Scorers?

The voice seems so real, she can almost feel its breath on her ear. It startles her, and she drops her pen on the floor. Her heart pauses for a brief and painful moment before it starts again, rapidly making up the lag.

The voice makes a point. How is kissing high Scoring arse being a good citizen? Being a good citizen would mean supporting her own people, empathising with their troubles instead of fanning and peeling grapes for the Society's most wealthy. She replays Ella's lecture and mouths the slogans again. Does Iris really believe such crap? She thinks perhaps she did once, and letting go of that belief is like carving out a piece of her soul. Her faith is now shattered. She's lost in the Society. Aimless, ambitionless, truthless.

She looks up the stats. More than just the stats. She investigates. Violent crime is up, murders are high, so many are reported, but with zero investigations into them, they're just allocated a likely perpetrator number based on their neighbourhood: Mr X killed in an un-Scorable street, so an un-Scorable killed him. Mr Y killed in a Sub 300 block, so a Sub 300 killed him. Mrs Z killed outside a Sub 200 café, so a Sub 200 killed her.

No points were awarded for any of the murder reports. Since they were reported but not witnessed, and no face was filmed. Not a single violent crime reported in any high Scoring neighbourhoods. Why would anyone report it? The citizens there don't need the points. No high Scorer is a snitch.

Iris sucks her teeth and leans back in her chair. The stats seem bad, but are they at the heart of it? Society Policing and offering points to do so is a bribe for the poor, for the hungry living on powdered rations, the un-Scorables who commit the heinous crime of having an unlicensed child. For the high Scorers, it's protection. The un-Scorables are nearly all women, the fathers never named since they say it would be best to keep the father's name off the birth certificate, then only one of the parents becomes un-Scorable. They say that they'll be able to help financially then if they keep their Score, to provide food. That, of course, they'll stick around. Some women really are that gullible. Her old neighbour, Nancy, was. Iris never saw her again after she moved.

You see now, don't you? You see what's wrong?

The voice is making more sense now, pulling at the curious bits of her brain. Iris resists the urge to answer out loud. Instead, she nods, subtly, then necks the last bit of her tea.

She checks the time. Ella will be over any moment and ask for these numbers. Her hands hover over the keyboard, her arms not coordinated. It's as if there's a devil on one shoulder and old Iris on the other, a contradiction of whispers guiding and misguiding her. She could just lie. A simple lie, though not really a lie, a non-divulgence, like the real stats they feed the public are a non-divulgence. Only her idea is tipping the scales the other way, against the usual trend. Her idea means backing her fellow low Scorers.

She itches her palms, wipes some sweat from her brow, then tries to slow her quickening breath. It would be so simple. They know her as a good employee. They'd never suspect a thing.

She types the stats, her own take on them, omitting every violent crime she had the time to investigate that never had a guilty conviction or even a suspect. Iris believes her time investigating was longer than the Society Police ever spent investigating the crimes themselves, so she leaves out their assumptions.

It's not a lie, she repeats in her mind over and over. Yet the difference in results is stark. Taking out the assumptions and unsolved crimes makes the low Scorer crime rate lower. A lot lower. Low Scorer crime rate is a third of what it was before. Including the assumptions makes some prejudiced figure based on that damned mysterious algorithm. She doesn't buy into the Life Score's algorithm's speculations. It's just some stupid secret formula the Eyes Forward decided decades ago should summarise a citizen's worth.

Fuck it.

Yes, the voice says. *Fuck it.*

She smirks. The voice at this moment is more like a friend than insanity trickling in. It has her back. She emails the stats to Ella, sure she couldn't pull off such a deception face-to-face, and melts into a puddle of sweat.

The news plays on a loop from a TV in the corner of the office, large enough that Iris can read the subtitles from her corner desk. It takes mere minutes for her stats to be reported. Well, what she's always considered to be her stats. They never misreport. But her latest stats show violent crime among the lowest last month. The news report does not.

The puddle of sweat turns into a lagoon, and that voice cackles in her ear.

You see, don't you, Iris? Now you really see.

Chapter 7
Ava

Watching the Memorexin come off the factory line gives Ava goosebumps. The drug that gave her Zia much happier final years is now used by so many, and the refined Memorexin formula that Ava helped to create has made a difference for so many of the Society's elders. It slowed Zia's dementia to a manageable level until her cardiovascular system gave up. It gave them the chance to build more happy memories.

Now Ava is using the drug for another purpose.

Syphoning off a little excess stock isn't too hard, especially since she works in research. That and a kilo or two of the antidepressant, B-Well, is easy enough to come by for someone in her position. The joy of having a high Life Score isn't all about eating in the best restaurants.

That level of wealth is immunity.

Ava's latest research is into psilocybin. XL Medico gave her the okay to dredge up century-old research into how ancient magic mushroom hallucinogenic properties have motivating and antidepressant effects.

But Ava has other ideas.

The psilocybin opens up neurons from dormant bits of the brain, parts of the mind that the endless Eyes Forward propaganda have deadened over the years, snuffing out any mental liberty and turning citizens into parrots, repeating their mantras without the slightest idea of what they are talking about. But not all citizens. That was an oversight in the Eyes Forward's plan. They assumed that any rebellious thoughts would come from low Scorers, from those who get the worst deal in the Society and have the least power. Give someone enough wealth and they conform — stretching their legs with the strong strides that the extra power brings. When it's only the low Scorers who consider the government to be wrong, no one listens. No one cares about a low Scorer bleating about unfairness. It's white noise. As long as the rich stay rich and the occasional poor person becomes rich, then the illusion of possible prosperity is maintained, and everyone keeps their head down. Everybody strives to Score.

That's why they've made such an example of Ava. Poor second-generation immigrant. Look how well she's done!

When Ava thinks about her own past, her own arduous climb up the Score ladder, she notices the arthritis in her fingers. There's only so much knuckle-cracking and punch bag training those joints can put up with. The novelty of Mandisa's charms wore off a long time ago. There's nothing in the 900 plus club that appeals, nothing except the camouflage it offers against prying eyes and suspicion. No one would suspect her of any wrongdoing. No chance a 900 plus would question the system.

The mixture of psilocybin, Memorexin, and B-Well blends easily and doesn't even need distilling. The centrifuge incorporates it all to perfection, leaving a crystallised pale blue powder ready to be ingested.

When the next two kilos are made, Ava leaves, walking down Friar Street, past the signs stating, *Berkshire is the best county there is! Keep your money in Berkshire. Boost Berkshire economy! There's no place like Berkshire. Want an adventure? Explore Berkshire.*

Ava keeps her gaze straight ahead. She knows what the billboards say. They're all the same, repeated on every street. When it's not the Berkshire posters, it's the Eyes Forward reminding all citizens to *Strive to Score,* or *All Eyes Are Our Eyes*. Occasionally, there's her own picture, arms folded, like her image will force good behaviour and conformity. If the stats are to be believed, it works. *Behave and you too can end up a 900 plus, just like Ava Maricelli!* one TV advert says. Her position as top Society Police is the stuff of legend around Berkshire.

She meets her associate in a café and hands him the suitcase. He dresses better than most 400 pluses. At first glance he appears more like a 700 plus, people would assume Preserved, since his baby-face makes him look younger than even his twenty-eight years.

'Hi Angus,' Ava says. 'You staying for coffee?'

He nods, then grins his easy grin. 'Cappuccino.'

She passes him the suitcase. Boldly. No one would suspect a drug deal.

'How's distribution?' she asks.

'Good. Catching on. You think it's helping?'

'It should.' She leans in closer. 'The whispers on Nebula are beginning. People are waking up.'

The coffee comes, and he takes a sip. There's a darkness in his eyes, a fear that Ava lacks. She's motivated by what has happened before, and he, of what is to come. Fear of the future is less intense than that of the past. He was born during the Great Unrest and was just a kid when Pres-X made people go mad. He hasn't seen chaos with his own eyes. The trauma isn't burned into his nightmares.

'I need to see it work for myself,' he says. 'To attend a party or something.'

'No. You can't risk it. You need to be seen to be a hundred per cent behind the Eyes Forward. We both do.'

He nods. 'And what about Lloyd Porter?'

Her lips twitch, and her knuckles crack as she tightens her fists. 'We don't need to worry about him. He'll be taken care of.'

Chapter 8
Iris

The corpse has now rotted so much, one arm has detached. A grey and sinewy mass of flesh and exposed bone lies limply across the gap between the pedestrian lane and bike lane, the rest of the body hidden under rubble except for what Iris assumes to be what's left of the shoulder. She only spots that because of the rotten cabbage smell attracting a swarm of flies that are congregating there, feasting on what remains. Still, no one has come to clear it up.

Iris's heart aches as she cycles past, and it's more than just chest pain from holding her breath while riding uphill. There must be someone missing this person. A couple of Eyes Forward representatives walk past in the pedestrian slow lane. They always walk slowly — purposeful step at a time so everyone can see them. They sport identical black suits and wide-brimmed hats with the same haircut neatly clipped underneath. Somehow, even their build is similar.

Iris stops in a lay-by and just watches. Their faces have the same blank expression as the Eyes Forward logo that is pinned on their lapel and glints in the early evening sun. They're close to the corpse now, but instead of noting it or paying it any attention, they follow the pedestrian lane on its wider course around it. Like a dead, rotting body is just what they expect to pass on their walk. What are they even doing in this part of town? It's so rare to see them anywhere except in the town centre.

Iris continues watching, trying to appear like she's tending to her bike. They walk up St Peter's Hill about halfway, cross the road, then rejoin the pedestrian traffic back down. Perhaps the Eyes Forward have a steps quota. They have no devices in their hands, so they're not Society Policing, just out for an amble as if that's normal. No one else seems to notice. Some pedestrians give them a bit more room on the pavement, that's all.

Behind Iris, the Eyes Forward billboard displays the walled-in eye design, *All Eyes Are Our Eyes* written underneath, along with the new Life Score-hype posters: *The Society. Where everyone knows their place, and everyone can achieve!* The picture that supports it is of two young, beautifully made-up women smiling, their skin smooth like burnished metal as their implants glow gold, showing their sterility. Desirables, clearly, the name given to Pres-X-2 takers where the women are always infertile.

Across the road, prints of the government walled-in eye are draped across piles of ex-buildings. More and more, that logo is everywhere, on every corner, every bus stop, every public building, as if their concerned citizens haven't been indoctrinated to their ideals enough already.

Iris gets back on her bike and pedals, then pulls over and stops again, staring, unblinking, at one of the Eyes Forward posters for a moment. A closer glance, and it's clear the vandals are not without their counter decorations. Graffiti, more than Iris has ever noticed before, has been painted across the side of buildings, both standing and ruined, some even on Eyes Forward posters. *ETC* repeated on every design. As in, etcetera? Iris frowns and shrugs it off. Vandals are hardly the brightest.

Open your eyes, Iris.

Okay, the voice is annoying now. Her eyes are obviously open, as open as that damned government logo. Or how else would she read the bloody signs? The voice seems to flip between commending her for seeing and chastising her for being blind. She huffs and dismisses her thoughts as a symptom of being tired and cycles again.

Rather than go straight home, she opts to turn around and stop by her parents'. Visiting twice in as many days is more than she can usually tolerate, but something is telling her to visit, calling her, in a way she can't explain. Is it that graffiti? She thinks maybe. Maybe she has seen the acronym ETC before, or perhaps it's her mother's passive aggressive text earlier, reminding her to come sort out her boxes of stuff that still litter the spare room.

'Iris, what a nice surprise,' Mae says when she answers the door. 'Are you staying for dinner?'

'How's dad? Where is he?' She goes to the living room, but Pasha isn't there. Mae has been hanging photos on the wall, family photos of them smiling, and ones of Iris as a baby. There's a ruler and leveller on the coffee table and every picture is perfectly straight and aligned. Iris fights the urge to knock a photo off a few degrees.

'He's gone to see Rolan. They're starting a photography course or something. You should visit them.'

'Why? Moira is horrible and Angus is just weird.'

'It would be nice if you and your cousin were friends.'

Iris ignores this, having no desire at all to befriend the family that hates her so much. 'Can I use the computer?'

Mae lets out a slow exhale and stands to the side. 'Sure. You know where it is. It's in the same room as all your boxes that still need sorting.'

The boxes are piled up with *IRIS* written neatly in black marker on each side. In their old place, her bedroom was still made up. Posters of old study guides and now-forgotten celebrities still hung alongside pictures of her and Georgie pulling faces, on graduation day, on birthdays. A lifetime of childhood knick-knacks cluttered the shelves and dresser, so much so that Mae refused to go in there. It was too much of a jumble for her to stand.

This new room is a bed and a load of boxes. The filing cabinet in the corner reminds her this won't be her bedroom anymore, but an office. She left home two years ago, but being kicked out stings more than she thought it would. Stupid sentiment. She shakes away the hurt. There was another bedroom, but they knocked the wall down to make the living space larger for her dad's mobility aids, so she can't complain. She'll put a few photos up when she gets around to it and take the rest of the stuff back to her place when she can be bothered. Or when her mum's nagging gets too much to tolerate.

After pulling out a few photos and stuffing them in her bag, she's done all the unpacking she feels like doing for the day. The rest is all childish stuffed toys and old college bits, stuff that should be thrown away if she just lost an ounce of sentiment.

There's a framed photo of her great-grandmother as well. Iris's namesake, who she never knew. That smiling face haunts her, fills her with the survivor's guilt that's so common among children born during the Great Unrest, when being born required the need of a life donation to free up space for the extra burden on the Society. Murderers at birth. Iris's survivor's guilt is worse than many, less bad than some. The legacy of bad government decisions doesn't end when the policy stops. The effect lingers on longer than the supposed economic benefit.

Georgie, like Iris, exists today despite her impoverished beginning, though Georgie's mother was not so lucky. Her lagging post-birth baby bump had her executed on the street a week after giving birth. Should have known better than to be seen in public so soon after giving birth, said the papers. Georgie keeps the clips in a scrapbook under her bed. 'To remind myself of how shitty the Society is,' she says when she's being overly outspoken.

Her mother had a government-issued bracelet that showed her pregnancy was 'neutralised,' the term the press used. Georgie's tattoo is still visible in its outgrown deformed state as Iris's is. The tattoos that show they had a life donation to legalise their births. But the killers didn't care. They thought Georgie's mum was still pregnant and did what they must to ensure the kid would never be born as baby Georgie slept in their apartment across the street.

Georgie thinks she inherited part of her grandfather's soul when he was euthanised, newborn Georgie screaming in his arms as life left him. She claims this every time she prefers whisky to gin, or a stray hair appears in unladylike places. 'That's a Grandpa Eddie hair, that one,' she says. The nanotechnology linked the pregnancy with the donor and the tattoo ink was mixed with the donor blood. The conspiracy theorists say their souls are connected.

Iris closes the box on the photo, shutting the guilt away. Where Georgie has a photo of Grandpa Eddie on her bedside table, Iris prefers to remain more detached. The kindness in her great-grandmother's face doesn't feel like the bond that Georgie claims to have. It only serves to make Iris's guilt worse.

With the boxes closed and re-stacked in neat enough piles that Mae probably won't moan about for another day or two, Iris gives into the computer's beckoning. She sits at the desk, covers the camera as she switches it on, then loads up the Shadownet browser. She's simply curious, she tells herself. She's not expecting anything, but she types *ETC* into the search bar.

As soon as she hits enter, the entire screen goes black. She pulls her chin in and blinks a few times, then rubs her eyes. It's still a black, blank screen. She's about to click the mouse somewhere to find an escape icon when the black screen gains a circular border that looks like rocks. They whizz past as if she's in a tunnel. Nebula glitches often, but this seems too professionally done to be a glitch. The movement continues despite her clicking the screen and pressing the escape key until it finally stops. There's a light at the end, just outside of the tunnel, and across the screen the letters *ETC* form. They hover there for a second, then morph, spreading out until the words *Escape The Cave* appear.

Huh?

It's some hack. It must be. She hasn't dabbled in such things for years, not since her Good Citizen hearing, too focussed on beginning with a high Life Score to risk such trouble. But now, trouble seems enticing.

Her eyes glint as her fingers hover over the mouse. She shouldn't be on a computer at all, let alone messing around with some hack. She should turn it off. She doesn't know what this hack is about. It's probably some crappy video game. Yeah, she should definitely turn it off.

However much her brain is telling her limbs to do the sensible, law-abiding thing, her tense hands will not comply.

A muscle unused withers. Now, hers want flexing.

She remembers when the announcement was first made shortly after her Citizen Reform hearing. Women were encouraged to learn other skills, to focus their studies on 'subjects that ensure the safety of women', not to muddy their minds with unscrupulous forums. Such topics are best relegated to cafés and bars, public settings where others can observe. There was little argument. Arguing means risking your points if you're deemed to be causing trouble. And no one wants to risk their chances of getting Pres-X-2.

Is Iris fussed about Pres-X-2? At twenty-eight, it's hard to gauge. She's got a couple of decades before she'd become eligible, regardless. That's a lifetime away.

Now though, that withered muscle begins to wake. Her fingers fizz with life as they brush over the keyboard, her wide eyes glow with anticipation for what can happen next. She wets her lips as she waits. A text bar appears blank at the bottom, and she types her question: *What cave?*

The words disappear and others reappear one letter at a time.

P

L

A

T

O

'S

Plato's Cave.

She scrunches her nose and scratches her head as the screen disappears in front of her, the usual forum dashboard replacing it.

Is that it? Her shoulders hunch as disappointment overtakes, and she leans her elbows on the desk. She waits, hoping for something more to happen, for at least an explanation as to what Plato's Cave is. Nothing. She bites her lip and taps her feet for a bit until she decides on another source of information.

'Mum—' Iris switches off the monitor before Mae appears in the doorway. She's the best one to ask. Her mum, awkward and reclusive as she is, may be mostly unhelpful and loveless, but she has a worldliness about her. A wisdom others seem to lack.

'Yes?' Mae asks from the doorway.

'What's Plato's Cave?'

'Excuse me?'

'Plato's Cave.'

Mae pauses a moment, then folds her arms with the kind of stern parent vibe she used to give off when Iris was little. 'Where did you hear that?'

Iris shrugs. 'Saw some graffiti somewhere.'

Mae nods, slowly. 'Well, from memory, Plato was an ancient philosopher. His cave theory, well, it was a way of saying that people only know what they're shown. The world outside the cave is imperceptible. Quite an old-world way of thinking. Not the Society way of thinking.' She raises her eyebrows at this in the sort of disapproving way she does when Iris leaves a mess.

'I see. I'll just be another fifteen minutes, and then I'll have to head home.'

Mae backs away, keeping her gaze on Iris for longer than would be natural from her position. When Mae has turned and is out of sight, Iris switches the monitor back on and searches the forum. She doesn't want to type ETC in case it interrupts again, but it's given her a clue as to what to search for around the forum. Is that what the graffiti means? Plato's Cave? It sounds like the sort of anti-oppression message enshrouded in subtlety that someone who's due a stint at a Good Citizen hearing would write. The forum is glitchy, stuttering often on a grainy screen. The search function is rudimentary, poor-quality graphics and a font from a century ago. She searches: *what is Plato's Cave?*

An image comes up of a sculpture, one that was once up in London but was destroyed when the Eyes Forward took over. She reads the story, all of it. The theory the philosopher Plato had, his way of explaining, well, brainwashing, is the only word Iris can put on it. A group comes up quoting it several times. It's the SAS. Iris has a sharp intake of breath when she sees that. The Sisters and Spies. She's not sure why she's surprised, probably because they tend to limit their ramblings to women's rights and that word they always bang on about — feminism. It's the sort of word that makes you spit foam when you say it.

She clicks some links and finds her answer in a forum that has recent posts as well as ones from years ago. The group her mother used to encourage her to follow is still going strong. Somehow, learning this ETC business is something they're touting, makes it feel less credible and more like nonsense.

Iris winces as she reads, almost afraid the screen is going to jump out and bite her. The sort of things they're saying are the kind of thoughts she's been having since the flat party. Why bother with the Score system? What purpose does it serve? *Discrimination* — another word that causes unwanted saliva to gather and eject. She shouldn't be reading this. She shouldn't be reading about people who hate the government, who disagree with the Eyes Forward.

She squirms, an itch radiating down her neck, but keeps reading. This particular forum isn't even limited to Berkshire. From Nebula, she's connected to other counties, all across the Society, more wide-reaching than the hack that got her in trouble years ago. She may feel enlightened, but is she ready for trouble again? Is she ready to be stripped of the few points she has? Georgie could be un-Scorable and just accept it, make do with her lot and not give a toss. She'd wear it like a badge of honour or use it as a chat up line. Iris sweats at the thought.

Nebula is safe, she reminds herself.

Posts come up naming some Eyes Forward representatives, the worst ones, the ones with the bad ideas who cause the most trouble. Ken Wicks, Kylan Morris, and Lloyd Porter. Porter? She's seen that name somewhere else before. She doesn't have time to ponder as another name appears. The screen glitches, snow replacing the forum for a moment before it pops up again. She doesn't read the post. The name just jumps out at her like a wasp. Her own.

Iris Taylor.

The browser shuts down, and she is booted off Nebula. All that fills the screen now is the happy family photo that is the usual wallpaper of her father's computer.

Chapter 9
Iris

'Your father will be home any minute,' Mae says as Iris makes to leave. 'Rolan is bringing him. Won't you stay and say hello to your uncle?'

'Not today.'

She's avoided Rolan and his family since they moved back down from Edinburgh. It seemed exciting at first, to be related to someone who had visited another county, and such a faraway one as well. But Rolan's wife, Moira, made it quite clear that young Iris is a poor substitute for Rolan and Pasha's beloved grandmother.

'Do you remember those lovely pies Iris used to make? Grandma Iris, not young Iris, obviously,' Moira would say, as if that needs clarifying for the rest of the family. 'Such a shame Grandma Iris can't be here right now.' And even, 'The world is just a sadder place without Grandma Iris, don't you think?'

She wasn't even Moira's grandmother. That's perhaps what irks Iris the most. And even if she hadn't volunteered to donate her life, she'd still be dead by now or Preserved, the thought of which makes Iris shudder. The Preserved have been around her whole life, but the thought of having a grandparent visibly her age still sits as comfortably as a soggy T-shirt.

Her life donation tattoo itches when she thinks of them, of Moira's disparaging remarks towards her. The tattoo is stretched and warped now, a dusting impression of that walled-in eye design, tinged a blackish-red from her life donor's blood. The idea of that was to make the nano detectable by scans, to prove it's not fake, though it feels gross and morbid to Iris now. It burns hot when she feels the guilt, her arm flushing with shame along with her cheeks. She never chose to have a life sacrificed for her, never chose to be conceived during such perilous times. As a foetus, she had no say in the matter. Try explaining that to Moira and her son, Angus, who was born weeks before Iris and required no such sacrifice.

It's dark by the time Iris cycles home. That's how long she stood staring at the blank screen. Nebula wouldn't reload, no matter how much she glared at the computer and fiddled with the wires and restarted the damned thing. The internet signal was fine, it just glitched out. Not uncommon for the Shadownet, though always immensely frustrating when it happens.

Iris cycles home past the Eyes Forward posters with the Society Police slogan still ever-present, but taking a more minor role alongside the new Life Score algorithm hype. *The Society: Where Everyone Knows Their Place, And Everyone Can Achieve!* It's been spoken about in the press for months, adverts with annoyingly catchy jingles and the kind of light shows normally reserved for arcade games. Iris bought into it a while back. The way the adverts blare on gives the impression that everyone will be jumping up a few points. There's never any mention of a possible fall back down. All citizens may strive to Score, but it comes with a caveat: break your back trying or else you'll have fuck all.

Iris is starting to think it's not so nice being enlightened. She was happy enough when she was blindsided with a little glimmer of hope. Now it's hard to imagine the new algorithm could send her 270 in any direction but down.

Her bike has developed a squeaky chain, and its tyres are half deflated. She forgot to service it over the weekend. It's a cheap thing. The battery runs out too quickly, and she can only afford to charge it a few times a month. She saves those charges for days when the headwind is brutal, or she has a hangover. The rest of the time, the electric motor is a dead weight she has to lug around. Her parents offer her some electric for it sometimes when she visits, but she can hardly use up their scant funds. Besides, cycling unassisted has given her strong legs. Perhaps she'll be as tough as Ava Maricelli one day. Perhaps she'll have a decent enough kick to cripple Jason if he tries anything again.

The bike lane isn't busy, rush hour long gone, so she goes at her own pace, grinding the pedals, wondering the entire way why the hell her name would appear on Nebula. She's a nobody. No one in the SAS knows her. She's never interacted with anyone. There must be another Iris Taylor, some reprobate with more stints at Good Citizen reform hearings than her.

Yet, as she rides, she has the crawling sensation of eyes on her, licking their way over her body, cold hands grasping and stroking up the back of her arms and shoulders. She shudders so violently, she almost tips the bike. She stops a moment to reset her mind, to force herself into acknowledging that there are no limbs or eyes on her, besides that ever-present Eyes Forward logo that now adorns almost everywhere. Lit up billboards show the eye rotating in the same way it does on TV. No left, no right, it looks to the future. Only, right now, that eye is staring directly at Iris.

From the side of a house comes a rustle, the sort that stems from clothing snagging on brickwork. She snaps her head around. In the darkness, it's hard to make out the shapes. The pathetic streetlights barely light the road, let alone the shady corners. It's probably some dealer, just some low Scorer seeking easy prey.

She pushes on the pedals to cycle away, but there's no momentum, only the sound of metal on metal. Her chain has come off. Dammit. She crouches down, not caring about the oil smudges on her fingers — not that there are any anyway since she's let her chain get too dry. She yanks at it, then remounts it on the sprocket.

Another rustle followed by a footstep lightly scuffing the tarmac.

Iris, go! Now!

The voice is only marginally louder than the footsteps, but it grabs her attention. She stands, then glances back in the direction of her flashing red bike light. Around the flickering light is the blackest black, but in the beam, there's a silhouette, and hanging by its side is the glimmer of metal.

Shit!

She mounts her bike and cycles away, using all her weight to push on each pedal stroke, praying her desiccated bike chain doesn't snap. Her heaving lungs suck in the coppery smell of fresh blood mingled with the ever-present decaying bodies. She swerves to miss a dismembered limb strewn across the road. The same one as before? She can't stop to check. In that slower moment, as she steadies herself, she spares a split second to glance behind at the figure. A large outline, dressed in black, and hanging from its hand is a long metal knife.

Chapter 10
Iris

Iris arrives at her block with her heart not only hammering in her chest but her temples too. Sweat stings her eyes, blurring her vision. She locks her bike with shaking hands, staring over her shoulder once before running inside and up the stairs with every bit of energy she has. When she bursts through her front door, she slams it behind her, then leans on it, her breath heaving its way in and out as tears stream down her face.

'Christ, Iris. What happened to you?'

Through panting breaths she tells Georgie, or tries to, but she begins to dry retch and cry.

'Fucking hell,' Georgie says when Iris manages to explain enough. 'You're serious?'

'A sword. A massive knife. Something like that. Another body. I almost rode into a leg or arm. I don't know. Christ, Georgie. There's some slasher out there!'

'Probably a Sub 750 Preserved.'

Sam's voice from the sofa sends Iris's heart rate spiking again. She hadn't noticed her there. Hadn't expected to see her since she and Georgie ended things a month or so ago when Sam suggested she take on a second job to strive to Score more.

'Oh, hi Sam,' Iris says, trying not to sound more flustered.

'They all went crazy,' Sam continues, turning the volume down on the TV. 'Not all of them got locked away. A fair few still roam the streets, and I'll bet not all of them died when the asylums came down. Quite a few asylums fell since they were all in really old buildings, but not all. How many years ago was that. . .eighteen years? We were kids. I reckon those Preserved are in their prime right now. They'd look about our age too.'

Iris eyes Sam, wondering if Sam is hinting at her own age. With her cropped hair, shaved on one side, and sturdy physique, she doesn't appear to be Preserved. The Preserved make Georgie's level of glamour seem half-hearted. Sam's a 500-something, a mid Scorer. Pres-X takers were never that low. The side effects were too well documented by the time the Sub 600s had a shot.

'Thanks a lot, Sam,' Iris says. 'That's really reassuring. Exactly what I wanted to hear.' She makes no attempt to hide her sarcasm.

'Georgie, since when were you seeing Sam again?' Iris goes to the fridge and takes out a tepid beer. The fridge is just for storage these days, which seems pointless, as it's not like the other cupboards are full. They can never afford to do a big shop. Iris opens a cupboard and steps back, taking in the view. Actually, the cupboards are full.

'Sam got us some groceries,' Georgie says. 'Isn't she the sweetest?'

'Erm—'

'Just doing my bit for the low Scorers,' Sam says, her smugness making Iris want to dry heave again. Sam is hardly a top Scorer. She always acted like Georgie was punching above her weight being with her. But she's snobby and nasty and has a face like a cat who ran into a lamppost. Iris remembers why Georgie told Iris to stop her from contacting Sam. Wealth is too easy to settle into, too easy to get used to.

'Where were you anyway? Why are you home so late?' Georgie asks. Her hair is a mess, all splayed out on one side and stuck on the other. Seems like a good thing Iris is late. Georgie's just-fucked face is much better to walk in on than her being-fucked face.

'My parents'.' She doesn't know where to begin or how to explain what she saw online, her own name included in the nonsense. She struggles to even picture it now. That was a near-death experience ago. A run-in with a fresh corpse ago.

Iris walks to the bathroom and checks their shower minutes' tally. There are three minutes she can use up. Georgie will likely want some after her night in with Sam, but Iris doesn't care. She needs to scrub, to take the crawling feeling from her skin. Three minutes won't be enough. She runs the water scalding hot, hoping that will help burn off some of the sensation. Showering vigorously, she uses her nails to work the soap into every inch, red scratch marks criss-crossing over her skin. She washes her hair even though it doesn't need it, like somehow a thorough clean will cleanse her tainted mind and memories. As she dries herself, the chills she felt before have barely dissipated, the minor relief fleeting as she feels guilty for using so much water. She crosses off the minutes on the tally, now in debt for the week. She'll have to forgo some showers later to make up for it.

Georgie knocks, then comes in before Iris tells her to, the steam escaping as she does.

'Sorry about the water,' Iris says. 'I'll cut my share for the month.'

'Don't worry about it. Shit, Iris. You look awful.'

With the steam gone, the mirror clears. Awful is being kind. She's as pale as that corpse. 'This forum online. They knew my name. My name was written all over some site bad-mouthing the Eyes Forward. What if the Eyes Forward are now out to get me?'

Georgie glares at Iris like she's as insane as she feels, and she hasn't even mentioned the voice yet. 'Maybe it's another Iris Taylor.'

'How many Iris Taylors can there be?'

'There must be more than one. There's over a hundred million people in the Society. If the Eyes Forward were after you, they'd be here, at the door, taking you away. Sending out some slasher isn't their style.'

She's right. Iris knows she's right. Yet she also knows what she saw, what the voice warned her about. They may not be after her, but there is someone out there. Someone bad, doing bad things. And another body, another murder that will probably never get investigated because it was in a poor part of town.

'Sam's theory sounds more likely,' Georgie says.

Iris shoots her a look. It's so like Georgie to back up Sam's ideas now that Sam is back in her life.

'You've probably been spending too much time online, on the Shadownet,' Georgie says before Iris can muster any sort of defence. 'You know we're not supposed to. It's probably flagging up.'

Iris blinks, halting her tears. 'I've not. Just a bit. But loads of women do, not just me.'

'They don't though, not many. Not really. It sucked when they took our computer rights away, but everyone has kind of adapted now. Gotten used to it. It's just the way it is. And it's not that bad, not for us. At least we're lucky enough to live in Berkshire, the best county.'

Georgie's words make Iris bristle. The voice returns like a feather tickling her ears.

Is it really the best county?

Iris shudders, yet the voice repeats, and she has to question Georgie's rationale. Why do they always say that? Why do so many posters state that with no comparison or reasoning? They all repeat it, nearly every day, and every citizen is meant to feel honoured they live in such a place.

Iris tightens her towel and tenses her arms. 'Why?'

'Why what?'

'Why is Berkshire the best county to live in?'

Georgie does a one-shoulder shrug. 'Everyone knows it is.'

'Have you ever been anywhere else to compare?'

Georgie grimaces. 'Ew. No. Of course not.'

Iris raises her eyebrows, then walks out of the bathroom, her hair leaving a trail of splashes on the floor behind her. 'Sam, you ever been to another county?'

Sam takes her attention off the TV and turns to slowly face Iris, eyes wide, almost horrified. 'God, no. Why? Berkshire is the best place to live.'

'That's what the posters tell you. It's what the Eyes Forward tell you to think.'

Iris goes to her room before Sam has time to argue, wrings out her hair, then puts on her pyjamas. They're thick, fleecy ones, comforting and warm. Georgie says goodbye to Sam down the hall, and Iris relaxes a little. She closes her eyes and pictures some of the nicer bits of Berkshire: the pretty patch of river in Pangbourne, the holiday chalets in Aldermaston, Broad Street shop fronts with more high Scoring eateries than anywhere else in the Society. Not that she can go inside, but they're nice to dream about. They promote some ambition. Everywhere else must be ramshackle dives, squalor and grey. Berkshire is the best county there is. She knows this. It must be true.

She pats her hair with the towel and takes a few deep breaths. Adrenalin. That's what's wrong with her this evening. Fight or flight hormones are messing with her brain.

'Anything on the news?' Iris asks.

'No. Loads of stuff about the Life Score algorithm. I've had that jingle stuck in my head all day. I hear it at work so much it's beginning to drive me insane. Oh, and some story about Flake causing havoc.'

Flake. Was what she saw a hallucination? Some delayed after-effect? Is she actually going insane?

'Perhaps you could listen at work tomorrow?' Iris asks. 'Maybe there's a story they're not running. They haven't even reported the bodies recently.'

'I'm only HR at the newsroom. It's pretty rare I hear anything.' Georgie turns, and Iris makes her most pleading expression. It's nothing on Georgie's usual sulking face, but it does the job. 'But sure. Yeah, I'll listen and ask questions if I can. Come here.' Georgie pulls Iris in for a hug and Iris leans in, letting Georgie take some of her chill away.

When they were kids, Georgie always said she envisioned herself being a news anchor with a makeup artist tending to her during commercial breaks, barking questions at some politician or activist while smiling with ruby-red lips and staring down the camera with sultry thick lashes. Such prime jobs are, of course, impossible to get for a Sub 300.

'I lied about some stats at work,' Iris says. Her adrenalin is wearing down, leaving her deflated in such a way that makes confessing seem like a good idea.

Georgie pulls back, her eyes wide. 'Bloody hell, Iris. That's a bit risky, isn't it?'

'They lied anyway. They just reeled off what they wanted to say. Is that my boss lying or the news?'

'Probably both adding their own embellishments.'

Iris walks to the sofa, then sinks into it, hugging her knees. 'What do they even employ me for? There's no point to my job if they just make up whatever stats they want. I have two bosses. Two! And a big boss for the whole building, Norman dickface Bonnet. It's like a prison.'

Georgie takes a couple of biscuits from the cupboard, then sits next to her, handing Iris the unbroken one.

'Because you're brilliant, and they don't want you working anywhere else.' She takes a bite and crumbs spill down her front. A vast dislike of crumbs is the one trait Iris gets from her mother's compulsive tendencies. 'You don't see it, do you?' Georgie continues while chewing. 'You coded the entire statistics software. Your firewalls made your department impenetrable to even the best hackers. You built the entire security network for the Eyes Forward headquarters. Alone. You know everything about Life Scores, and they want you where they can keep an eye on you. They're afraid of you. Think about it. You're the smartest person in Berkshire, yet they've stuck you at that desk. You're more powerful than you know.'

Iris takes a bite of her biscuit. Sod the crumbs. 'I'm poor. I'm female. I'm fertile. I'm trash.'

'Maybe they gave you a shit Score because they don't want someone as brilliant as you having power. You thought of that?'

'They gave me a shit Score because my dad's a quarter Greek and I went to a shit school.'

'Yeah, that too. I just mean. . .you may not get into trouble anymore by breaking rules, but that doesn't mean they don't want to keep an eye on you. You're still a genius, Iris.'

She's not, Iris is sure. Maybe when she was a kid and was studying advanced coding from the age of five. She was the sort of kid who could understand computers but struggled to put her T-shirt on the right way. Her gifts annoyed her parents more than made them proud. Less screen time, more reading, they'd say again and again. Try to engage in conversation face-to-face rather than just online. She went along with her parents' demands as a desperate attempt to fit into a world where so few people her age existed to befriend. Her parents, both being orphans, made her covet the child-parent relationship as if it were something sacred. That is, until she didn't.

Georgie gives her a peck on the cheek. 'Don't be afraid. They're not sending anyone to kill you. You're too important to them. The entire Life Score system is in your hands.'

'Hardly. I don't even know the algorithm,' Iris says, snorting a laugh.

Georgie brushes the crumbs onto the floor, then grabs the remote control. 'No one knows the algorithm.'

Chapter 11
Ava

From the funeral home, Ava can see the Society Police building. Her photo flanks the entrance. Her head is tilted down in it but not enough, meaning her eyes are like little dagger-cut slits, the angle taken from below to make her seem like she's peering down on people with her artificially enhanced biceps. She always hated that picture. To portray her as some formidable strength is a lie. Sure, she's martial arts-trained and can stand up for herself, but she's not the confrontational, hard, tough person that photo implies she is. And it's everywhere. Every time she meets someone new, they remark on how much smaller she is in real life. As if they expected her to be the size of the ten-foot poster.

Despite the mental torment that came with the job, it's worked beautifully. She's the poster woman for the Eyes Forward. No one would ever suspect her of being anything else.

She takes out her phone and loads up Nebula. She spends way too much time scrolling through the Sisters and Spies forums still — it's nice to have company and companions. They offer reason in the madness. She sends a message, telling them of XL Medico's part in the Pres-X homicides, that the B-Well only worked for the high Scorers, that the Pres-X was always meant to go bad and make its users psychotic and suicidal. For years she's been sitting on the evidence, waiting for just the right time. Now, she turns on the faucet, flooding the Shadownet with the truth. And the truth is powerful, beautiful. A butterfly emerging from its chrysalis.

Ava looks over her shoulder, then the other. The staff all went home a while ago. She knows she's alone in the building, but it's impossible not to be paranoid when committing such treason. The Eyes Forward have a constant presence. All eyes are our eyes, but that's not to forget the other senses. The streets listen. They can smell, and they have a taste for blood.

The Society Police building is as dark as ever. No light escapes the gaps in the boarded-up windows. Eighteen years she's been the top Society Police, branded as such. Yet she's still never been allowed to see inside the Society Police building. Her request for access is always replied with an 'invite only' and 'not necessary' message. Whoever sends those messages tells her to give self-defence lessons to the 800 pluses, to host a fundraising gala, to give a speech at an event. Yet there is never a face to the name.

Ava has her suspicions.

She's borrowed an Optical Gas Imaging camera from XL Medico. In the dark, it works perfectly, with few people outside to interfere. Through the reflective glass across the front of her own business, L.M. Funerals, she erects the camera on a stand, then points it to the other side of the road. It's as she suspected, yet no amount of previous suspicion can take the knot of surprise from her gut. The reality is like a punch, and she exhales sharply.

Oxygen. All the oxygen is being extracted from that building. The windows on the side are blacked out except for the odd small gap on the top floor where the boarding up was shoddily done, the old building's angles a mismatched array of acute and obtuse. And in those little gaps on the top floor, is not the telltale blue of the oxygen on the OGI, but instead, the more purple shade of nitrogen and carbon dioxide. A cool gas mix. A non-combustible mixture.

Ava shivers at the sight despite sweat collecting across her hairline. Her suspicions confirmed, nerves shake through her.

Without breathing gear, no one is going into that building. The keycard pad on the thick steel door down the alleyway shows someone goes in sometimes. Ava knows. She's been watching. It's what roused her suspicions over the lack of oxygen. Once a month, an Eyes Forward representative puts on breathing apparatus, then goes in to tend or service whatever is in that building. And whatever it is needs to be kept cool. Fireproof.

A new month is fast approaching. She's ready.

With the new Life Score algorithm set to launch, the Eyes Forward representative that will want to ensure everything is hunky dory inside that building is obvious.

Lloyd Porter will be doing the rounds on the first of March.

The hypothesis she began the evening with is the only reason she can think of. There are no humans working at the Society Police headquarters at all. Just computers. Lots and lots of heat-producing computers and all the precious data they collect. It's an information treasure-trove for the Eyes Forward.

Chapter 12
Iris

Iris leaves for work early, just as daylight breaks. The night before left her with non-existent sleep, and she jolted awake every few minutes, the moonlight slicing through the blinds reminding her of metal spikes. Her building isn't as bad as the un-Scorable dorms, hardly any external cracks and the windows and the doors nearly all close properly, but the pipes creak and footsteps from other residents' apartments shake every floor and every tiny bit of movement kept her awake.

Cruising down the hill, she earns a few bell rings and angry grunts as she keeps her hands on her brakes, taking it too slow for the morning rush, looking out for the body that was in the road the night before. From the smoothness of the flow of traffic, it's clear there's no obstacle to contend with. Another building fell down to the right, spilling bricks and concrete across the ground with a trickle making it into the pedestrian lanes. No one looks twice at the collapsed building. It wasn't some un-Scorable dorm but a Sub 100 block — homes for people not at their worst, but those who have only just clawed their way out of the grimiest gutter. No one worth bothering with, most seem to think. The building adjacent has some more steam at its windows, boxes and belongings piled up outside, mostly kids' toys by the looks of it. Whoever was in that building has just shifted over one block.

It's hard to pinpoint exactly where she was when she saw the body, but from her adrenalin-spiked hazy memory, in line with the collapsed building seems about right. She slows down further. Her brain is working too hard for her to cycle efficiently, and her bones turn cold. Was that what she saw? Some victim of the collapse, a person with some metal tool trying to save people? Did she flee instead of help?

Great. Guilt on top of paranoia. That's all she needs.

The pedestrian lanes are less busy than they used to be. Iris can remember them being so squashed, it was impossible to see outside of the horde from the middle. These days, it's easy to see slits of daylight peeking through the gaps in the steady stream. Over twenty million off the Society's population total in Iris's lifetime, though apparently that's still not enough. Her fertility indicator implant glowing around the clock never lets her forget that, despite the Great Unrest and the licensing needed for babies, and the number of elders who died from reacting badly to Pres-X, the Society is still behind its global population commitment. A global target is hard to fathom for most citizens. Non-Berkshire targets are even difficult to comprehend. Iris suggested at a work meeting a while ago that perhaps since all the stats are devolved locally, population targets should be too. Francis and Ella had been none-too-impressed with her input. 'The likes of you should be seen and not heard,' one of them said.

The likes of you.

The voice accompanies her on her ride, reminding her of what she'd soon walk into. Is she insane or is it welcome company? Iris isn't sure. A wingman, backup. A haunting? She no longer snaps her head around when she hears it and accepts it's inside her somehow. A dormant part of her brain reignited, maybe. A friend.

Yeah, she thinks. Insanity is about right.

The quarterly update from the Prime Minister is expected any day now with the latest tally, total, and demographics. It seems so pointless since the new Life Score algorithm is coming out soon and that could make all their results different. Her suggestion at delaying the update was met by Ella's usual huff and Francis's tut that's so audible, Iris is surprised she doesn't rip the roof off her mouth. So, Iris must put the data together, same as every quarter. It makes it a more stressful time at work, as Ella and Francis nag Iris even more than usual. She normally pores over this with the kind of precision Georgie applies to her eyebrows. Now, though, she's already decided she'll just write down anything and sit back twiddling her thumbs.

Jason is hovering at the entrance, vape in hand, the mist obscuring half his face, but his menacing grin is still visible. Being creeped out once in twenty-four hours is plenty, and Iris hesitates after she dismounts her bike. Ella and Francis won't be in for a while. She's surprised Jason is, to be honest. Perhaps his dad is working him hard, making him prove himself. Iris laughs at the thought. He's the son of an 800 plus, that's all the proof of his worthiness he needs.

A couple of months back, before Jason's advances and during a particularly bad cold snap when she and Georgie had no funds left for the extra heating required, she plucked up the courage to ask Norman Bonnet for a pay rise. His office smelled like sweaty bacon, and he was picking the fat from his teeth. Iris had to force herself not to heave when he pulled a long, stringy white thread and its adjoining spittle from his gob, then placed it on his desk.

Iris said she was willing to do extra work, said she is due a promotion. She listed her achievements, which made it abundantly clear she's significantly overqualified for the job she does. Mr Bonnet, as he likes to be addressed, replied by studying her appearance, a slow look up and down and criticising her dress. It wasn't fitted enough, apparently. It didn't flatter well.

'You're not striving enough,' he said. 'Be a shame if a pretty little thing like you never gets Pres-X-2. It would be a shame for you to age-out. You need to dress better. Do your face better. Get your priorities right.'

Pretty is an exaggeration, Iris thinks. Perhaps being so close to Georgie and her eternal glamour makes her feel that way. She's no pig, she just doesn't put in much effort, as Mr Bonnet rightly points out. She doesn't even extend her eyelashes. Perhaps that's why the old perverts like her. They think she's innocent. Pretty girls get the better jobs though. Beauty over brains in the Society, always. For the women, anyway.

Iris squared her shoulders. 'I deserve a promotion, sir. I am better than this job.'

He smacked his lips and wiped the corner of his mouth with his tie. The ketchup residue left a stain on the cloth. He probably has hundreds of ties. 'You are a woman,' he'd said, as if Iris was unaware. 'A fertile one at that. What sort of message does that give off if you were to be handed promotions like sweeties.'

As if a promotion after six years is like handing out sweeties. Iris didn't cave or buckle at his remark. 'And if I were gold?' she asked. A pointless question. It'll probably be twenty years before her fertility indicator implant glows gold with sterility.

'Look, up your Score, and I'll think about it,' he said.

Sterilisation is a guaranteed 50 point boost, but Iris doesn't want to be sterilised. Why should she? Part of her mum's Sisters and Spies lessons she heard repeatedly as a kid had sunk in: why don't the men get sterilised instead? There wasn't much she took away from those lessons, but that one really stuck. She braced for more ridicule. 'I need a promotion to up my Score, sir,' she said.

'And that is the great conundrum of life. Shame for you, but there you have it,' he said with a dispassionate tone before clearing his throat and leaning over his desk. He's a heavyset man, and the wood groaned as he did so. 'There are, of course, other ways to up your Score. My son, Jason, would be pleased to help. As would I, for that matter.'

She left his office after that. Better to keep quiet than to argue. Better to run away than vomit on his desk.

Jason's heavy breathing and body-pressing might as well have had a certificate of authorisation. From her half-hidden position around the corner of the building now, Iris watches Jason fill his lungs with his vape, lift his chin high, then lick his lips, and she feels the need to vomit again. Suddenly she's very aware that getting in early leaves her alone in the building with him and his rancid breath. Horace, the butler, is just arriving to welcome the 700 pluses at their entrance. He won't pay any attention to Jason's perverted nature. Iris's implant glows green. The punishments for sexual assault on women outside of their orange time is minimal. She's easy prey right now.

There are a few cafés across the street, and she decides that would be a safer option than being alone in the building with Jason and his freshly Pres-X-2-fuelled intentions. She locks her bike, then walks to the first café but keeps walking. It's a 400 plus. Farther down the street, the Life Score requirements remain stubbornly high. Now she remembers why she never bothers to go to a café and drinks the foul staff room coffee instead. She loiters in the street a while, folding her arms across her chest as the wind picks up and cuts right through her thin, cheap layers. Then, when her shivering spreads to her jaw and her teeth are making as much noise as the bus lane, she turns and heads back to work.

Across the sea of heads in the pedestrian traffic is the dark hair of her cousin, Angus. He slicks it back so much that it straightens the curls she knows he has. She ducks her chin down lower, rolling her shoulders forward, trying to make herself small and invisible among the throng. She's not seen Angus in months and has no desire for pleasantries now. She's only ever met him a handful of times, but he looks so much like her dad she can't miss him. He may resemble her dad's side, but he gets his personality and attitude from his mother, Moira. He nods along with her jibes towards Iris and harks on about his Life Score like he's some 900. Moira recently had her Pres-X-2 and the brief moment Iris saw her, it was as if she'd won a battle. 'Ageing is the enemy. We must never surrender.' She actually said that. All the while, Angus stood there wearing his usual smile, which is somewhere between smugness and pity.

He's closer now, and the slow lane is not slow enough. She glances left and considers jumping into the fast lane, but it's clogged with so many people, she can't see an opening. Angus is now but a few people away and inching closer. Perhaps he'll move into his fast lane, but her heart sinks a little when he doesn't. Iris hunches her shoulders more, bends her knees a little, imagining she's tiny — an ant, a flea, a worm.

'Iris,' he says, as their paths cross, and he jumps out of his lane to join her. 'Great to see you.'

Dammit! 'Hi, Gus.' She plasters on the best smile she can manage.

'You want to go for a coffee? The place up here is pretty good. I can get you in with my Score.'

'How generous of you.' Iris glances at the entrance to her work. Jason is still outside loitering like some rat waiting for scraps. It's also still freezing cold. Angus and his eternal smugness seem like the least threatening option, so she nods. 'Thanks.'

Angus shows his Score app to the barista, then signs to say he's responsible for Iris. Like Iris is some minor or reprobate. She nearly walks out when she sees the disclaimer: I take full responsibility for the actions of. . .

Iris folds her arms and sucks her teeth as they make their way to a table. The place isn't as fancy on the inside as she expects, although having never been anywhere 300 plus, let alone 400 plus, she's not sure what she expected. The staff mostly act bored. Perhaps a 700 plus café is needed before the coffee is served with enthusiasm. It smells divine though, and it's a lot warmer than outside.

Iris's latte comes served with an ornate leaf pattern, so beautiful she feels bad drinking it.

'So, what's new with you?' Angus asks. 'Saw your dad the other day.'

'He's worse, I know.'

'My dad offered to get his meds, but he refused. Said he'll figure it out.'

'That sounds like Dad.' She bites the inside of her cheek. Pasha's pride is his worst trait. He'd rather suffer and risk Iris losing him than admit he needs help. 'So,' she says, steering the subject away from hurt. 'How are you liking being back down this way? Missing Edinburgh?'

'A little. I like it here though.'

'Because Berkshire is the best county there is?'

'Well, Edinburgh is in Midlothian County, and Midlothian is the cleanest county in the Society, and is the safest county.'

Iris smirks. 'Is that what it says on the posters?'

'Yeah, it does. Everywhere.'

Iris sips her coffee and wonders for a moment what posters say in other counties. Do any say that they're crap, the least safe, the worst? She forces the thought from her mind. What's the point of even thinking about other counties?

'I think Dad mentioned you've got some business thing going on down here?'

'Yeah. I'm helping project-manage the new XL Medico building. We're renovating an old shopping centre into the factory. Have you seen the development? It's almost finished now, and it's state-of-the-art.'

'Nice.'

'They're going to be making Pres-X-2 there. I've been working with Ava Maricelli. Can you believe it? A real celebrity.'

Iris puts down her coffee a little too firmly, and it spills over the rim. 'When did you start working for her?'

'Maybe six months ago,' he says, too nonchalantly, like he doesn't even care.

Iris's body thaws in seconds, and her temperature spikes to boiling. 'You know she fired my mum as her accountant, and that's why her Life Score was halved. That was about six months ago.'

'Oh, I'm really sorry to hear that.'

'Bit of a coincidence, don't you think?' Iris says through her teeth. 'What did you do, recommend someone else?'

'No. Iris I wouldn't—'

Iris rolls her eyes. 'Yeah, right. You high Scorers are all the same. You watch over each other and don't give a shit about anyone else. I'll bet she has some higher Scorer friend of yours doing her accounts now.'

'Really, Iris—'

'Save it. This coffee tastes burned by the way.'

She leaves half the coffee behind, then walks out, Jason and his vape-breath seeming like less of an inconvenience than her arsehole cousin.

At least the entranceway to the Life Score statistics building is empty now. Hopefully Jason's crawled back into his hole and will stay there for the rest of the day. Iris pushes her way through the turnstile and walks down her corridor, her implant turning orange as she does. Good. At least being at her most fertile time should keep Jason's advances away. She's as unfuckable as it gets.

She makes herself a mug of instant coffee in the kitchen and half regrets not finishing the cup Angus bought. Even if he is an evil shit, there's no point in blaming the beverages. It didn't really taste burned. Pride before the fall comes to mind. She's too much like her dad, she thinks.

A week of bullshitting statistics has left her unmotivated at work. Glancing around her office, everything feels overbearingly oppressive. The clock ticks loudly. Its digital display has no hands, the tick is added in just to send shrills of panic over timekeeping. The kettle is set to eighty-five degrees, making it okay for coffee, but her tea is always tepid and poorly diffused. She must rush to drink it. There's nothing to savour. The air temperature is kept cooler than anyone likes, the barrier around her cubicle is obtrusively high. There's no window. It's like she's in a hole. A cave. Every furnishing and decoration she now sees as a way to crush any spirit and to enforce expected behaviour.

She's not allowed to stretch her legs and explore the building. Such a change of scenery is permitted only for men or safe women. Especially with Iris's implant now orange, she'll have to deal with tuts and grimaces everywhere she goes. The few staff that work there are well-practised in displeased facial expressions, and Iris being the lowest Scorer and the only unsafe woman is the way they usually choose to direct such attitudes. She always put up with it before, wrote it off as a part of life, that being her age and gender, it's to be expected. But why? Why should it be that way? She rolls her shoulders back, stretches out her arms, filling all the space she can around her. She's no longer willing to accept the sensation of being shrivelled and insignificant, no longer just seeing herself as a potential burden-maker. If anything to this department, she is less. Her thoughts and reasonings are expanding. She has broken out of the cave.

On every wall, posters state Eyes Forward slogans: *Strive to Score, All Eyes Are Our Eyes*, peppered with the Life Score statistics department's own brand of brain-numbing crap: *The Society Relies on Us! If we report, they will achieve!* Even the chairs are dictators, suppressing comfort and making their users sit upright and uncomfortable. Iris has been experimenting with ways to slouch, a little lean off to the side, sliding her butt further down. Nothing feels natural. It's all forced, like formality is teased out of her.

It's not long before Ella and Francis arrive, preceded by their perfume and complimenting each other's outfits as they discuss their social plans and which important people they've met.

'It's the most exciting thing we've had in the calendar for such a long time,' Ella says, her voice more squeaky than usual.

'Wonderful incentive,' Francis says, accentuating the 'wonder' as if she's blowing out candles. 'And all tracing back to this department.'

'We're making such a difference here.'

'Oh, I know, Ella. I feel like a pioneer — saving the Society.' Francis fist-bumps the air.

'And dressed like that. Perfect.'

Their loud and egotistical voices continue to echo after they've made their way to their office.

Iris scratches her head. This department? Perhaps they're finally implementing one of Iris's suggestions. Her chest swells a little at the thought before she remembers she'd never get any credit for it. She attempts a slouch again and folds into the corner.

You don't care, she reminds herself.

'Iris, my office.' Francis's lofty voice jolts her upright.

Iris's slouch experiment has left a twinge in her back, and she stands slowly, cracking her shoulders as she rights herself, then walks towards Francis's office, dragging her feet. She's getting called up on her attitude, she's sure of it. She should have seen this coming. As enlightened as she may be, being enlightened isn't going to earn her a better income or help her Score. The whole Score thing is bollocks, this she is sure of. But her initial Flake-inspired bravado, saying she's going to fuck the entire system, has been replaced with reality, and with reality comes dread and depression. She still needs to pay for food and heating. The system is fucked, and she's powerless to stop it. What can one woman really do?

Anything you want.

The voice's encouragement is tenacious, though currently uninspiring. Without instructions or ideas, that sound of madness lacks substance in the same way the Eyes Forward slogans do. Buzzwords, that's all. Empty and useless.

'Shut the door behind you, Iris,' Francis says, a sharpness to her voice. 'Sit down.'

Francis and Ella are both present, in their own padded, comfortable chairs.

'We need to discuss something of a delicate nature,' Ella says. 'The curve. It is still too steep, even after years of us trying to work on it. As you know, the strive to Score mantra is the basis of the Society, but the bell curve of wealth distribution we're aiming for is still too steep with that ghastly wedge at the lowest end. Our quarterly ideas briefings haven't brought up anything useful.'

'The Eyes Forward haven't implemented any of the ideas though,' Iris says. 'For example, making Pres-X-2 more universally available—'

Francis holds up a finger. 'There have been no reasonable ideas. The fact is, we need to make that climb harder. It's too easy to climb and too difficult to slip back down the Score ladder.'

Iris flinches and grips one fist tightly in the other hand. Her parents' Score was halved when she was born, then after years of striving, halved again when her dad had to stop working due to his health. Then halved again when her mum lost her most lucrative client. The journey down the Score ladder seems plenty easy enough to her.

'The Eyes Forward and Society Police are aware of a new drug that's being abused by the low Scorers,' Ella says. 'Especially the young low Scorers.' She scrunches her nose, and Francis copies her. 'So we're presenting you with an opportunity to add a considerable number to your Score.'

A crease forms between her brows. 'Right. . .'

'We understand you asked Mr Bonnet for a promotion. Well, here is your opportunity. We want you to monitor Flake's use. You'll have a special login for the Society Police app, a senior log in. And if you find the source of this drug, its distributors, its makers, then you can dig yourself out of the Score you have currently and rise above these backward low Scorers. This could be very lucrative for you.'

Iris takes a moment to comprehend what Ella's saying, and when she does, her breath catches for a moment. 'You want me to snitch?'

'That's an immature term for doing your bit for your Society. This drug is a menace. It causes all sorts of treasonous thoughts, not to mention the unknown health implications. You would be doing the Society a great service.'

'If it simply killed off the low Scorers, this wouldn't be such an issue, you understand? Is that clear?' Francis says with a pinched face.

'Crystal,' Iris says flatly.

'And young people climbing the Score ladder are taking it. If we cut the points from those, that would certainly help the curve in Berkshire.'

'It might make that wedge at the lowest end bigger,' Iris says, almost regretting her smartarse tone.

'Well,' Ella says with a giggle, 'we have a plan for that later.'

Iris narrows her eyes at them, then folds her arms. 'And what about the top end?'

Ella and Francis purse their lips. 'Excuse me?' Francis asks.

'Well, punishing Flake distributors may make a difference on one side of the peak, but what are you doing for the 700 pluses to flatten the curve there?'

Francis sucks her teeth. 'Well, we are softening punishments and have a new incentive for the high Scorers to earn more points. Not that it's any of your business, but it should sort the curve that end.'

Iris suppresses her scoff. 'I see. So, what you want is for the graph to flatline, then a step.'

'If you don't wish to help, or don't have anything insightful to say, you may leave. Go back to your desk,' Francis says, more snarky than usual. 'But this assignment comes with privileges. Internet privileges.'

'You will need internet access around the clock,' Ella says. 'So, the out of work hours cutoff on your phone will be disabled, meaning you can keep up with the news and internet gossip.'

Iris's folded arms slacken. 'And a home computer?'

'You'll be allowed to purchase one on credit, if you wish.'

Iris thinks about it. Around the clock internet access would mean she can research freely why her name was on Nebula. She could research Flake without worrying about getting caught. She'd have the sort of freedom men have. Well, not entirely, but a lot more than she has now. And she only has to say she's going to *try* to snitch. She never actually has to do it. She could do this. She could play this coin.

She smiles her sweetest smile and nods. 'Very well.'

Chapter 13
Iris

A snitch. Can Iris really bring herself to do such a thing? She ponders this as she cycles home, hoping for the wind in her face to give her some perspective. There are some newly un-Scorable women with screaming babies strapped to their chests, moving into an un-Scorable dorm just off Gosbrook Road. But louder than the cries are the heckles from a few people walking past.

'Serves you right for making a burden!'

'Slut!'

'Whore!'

'Burden-maker!'

Iris keeps her eyes on the lane in front, her mouth shut and jaw tight. There's nothing she can do to help. She's a paltry 270 unsafe woman. A no one.

Her chest tightens as she tries to imagine having the Society Police app live at a flat party, of being caught by a low Scorer. The heckles directed at her would be worse than those of the un-Scorable women. She'd be branded a snitch, a traitor.

A traitor to your people or to the high Scorers?

The voice is pointing out the obvious. It's a soft voice, but its cryptic nagging is giving her a headache. Clearly, she doesn't want to be a traitor to her own people, but crossing the high Scorers has dire consequences. There's a version of her consciousness sitting on her shoulder, her hands attached to the strings they hold, trying to move her in whatever way they want, to make her a good citizen, to fit the Eyes Forward ideals.

She shakes her head, then rubs the back of her neck, her back knotting with tension. No. She can't do what they ask. Even old, pre-Flake Iris wouldn't have done that.

The tightness in her muscles eases as she reminds herself that all she has to do is pretend she's going to snitch. Deceit is getting easier for her. She barely even sweated when she bullshitted about the latest stats. She can nod and smile along with whatever awful ideas Ella and Francis have for her, since it's not like they really gave her a choice. No doubt her Score will be lowered even more if she doesn't seem to comply.

Why does your Score matter?

It's a stupid question from her vocal insanity. It's all very well saying she's done with the whole Life Score crap, but she still needs to eat. She still needs to heat her flat. Her narcotic-induced ideas were just that. Inebriated bravado. Rebellion is a luxury for the rich, and why would they want to rebel, anyway? That's why the entire system is screwed. The poor are oppressed into towing the line. The rich can do whatever the fuck they want.

Iris stops by the shops after work and gets some quick-cook pasta for dinner. She discovered a while ago that quick-cook pasta can be soaked in cold water and it becomes soft enough to eat — eventually. Saves the electric. That and some mixed vegetable sauce, which only takes a few seconds in the microwave, and it's her usual budget-friendly dinner. Not the sort of dinner that's in any way satisfying. The takeaway next door to the shop makes her salivate in a way her own food won't.

Riding up St Peter's Hill, the bikes ahead bottleneck, then come to a halt. There's an angry chime of bike bells ringing, a few aggro expletives as the cyclists are forced to wait, then walk their bikes as the pace is too slow to pedal. The smell tells Iris why long before she sees it. The sweet yet stale scent of damp concrete from a building collapsed isn't enough to disguise the tang of copper or the musty mothball aroma of a fresh body. Fine dust particles from the wreckage fill the air and clog Iris's eyes with grit as she gets closer. By the time she's alongside the building, she's like a dog and guided by the stench alone.

Bearing slightly left, away from the smell, she avoids one body, then banks again a few paces later to avoid another. It's only the top halves visible, the rest are under brick and render.

But there are more.

When Iris's eyes have watered enough to clear her vision, she remounts her bike and skids as her front wheel rides over a stream of blood flowing down the hill, meandering its way from a pile of bodies. Not near the collapsed building now. They're not crushed bodies from falling bricks. The wounds that score their skin are from being hacked up and mown down in the streets, like the weapon she saw. That long, glinting metal would do exactly that sort of damage.

Iris's stomach churns, the street spins, and her arms tingle. She sways on her bike, so much so, she puts her foot down. She manoeuvres herself out of the bike lane, away from the angry traffic but close to the bodies. Their eyes are still open; a deathly stare of a prayer never answered

Iris glances away, a cold sweat inching over her. This is a bad part of town. Un-Scorable dorms and Sub 100 blocks line this part of the street. These bodies could be here for ages before they're cleaned up. These are more deaths that will never be investigated.

She swallows back the lump in her throat, and for the first time, she loads up the Society Police app. With shaking hands, she holds her camera close to the faces, the ones she can see without moving limbs and torsos. The closest woman's face is so young, but the blood that's collected in every crease of her skin, mixed in with dust, makes her complexion grey and mottled, adding an illusion of age she'll never have the chance to experience. Her bright blue eyes are motionless, yet petrified, old tears crusted on her cheeks. She appears to be about Iris's age, and based on her attire, clearly un-Preserved.

That could be Georgie.

Iris uploads her photos to the Society Police app. It's all she can do. Maybe someone is missing these women and knowing what happened to them will give them closure. Though it's likely no one will look for them. No one wants un-Scorables as friends.

With her internet access now around the clock, she checks the news, but there's nothing. The only story the news bothers with is about the looming release of the new Life Score algorithm, about how the whole of Berkshire is on tenterhooks. Footage shows bunting being put up across the highest Scoring establishments, some interview with an 800 plus saying how, due to his long lineage back to Britain, he's sure he's going to top 900. Iris groans. Nothing at all about the body count in the low Scoring neighbourhoods. No one cares.

She arrives home to find Georgie alive and well, not that she was really worried one of the bodies would be Georgie. She's not un-Scorable or even a Sub 100. Surely, no one would mean Georgie harm, though the mental anguish is torture enough.

As soon as Iris walks in the door, Georgie runs to her and they hug.

'You saw it too?' Iris asks.

Georgie nods and tightens her hold. 'It stinks. I'm so glad you're okay.'

Iris grabs two bottles of beer from the fridge, passes one to Georgie, then swallows half of hers in one gulp. Georgie's just had a shower and her platinum pixie-cut hangs in a sheet across one side of her face. She always alternates sides every few minutes when her hair is drying. Claims it gives volume.

'All those poor people. And the traffic chaos.'

Iris nods. How like Georgie to point out the practicalities.

'Why is no one clearing it up at least?' Georgie asks. 'It's undignified.'

'I reported it. Maybe someone will.'

'What? On the Society Police app?'

'Yeah. Thought might as well.'

Georgie lets out a long, loud exhale. 'Well, I guess that's at least doing something.' She drinks some of her beer, then makes a face that shows just how bitter it is. 'Sam's invited us to a cocktail bar opening tonight.'

Iris almost chokes on her beer, and her eyes stream from the effort to keep it down. She double checks the date on her phone. 'I'm not sure. It's Thursday. I've got work tomorrow.'

'Oh come on,' Georgie says, bending her knees like she's about to beg. 'Just a few cocktails. I need this. I need to get that image of the bodies out of my head somehow. We need cheering up.'

Playing third wheel to Georgie and Sam sounds like possibly the worst way to get a horrible sight out of her mind. 'I don't know—'

'And we won't be late. It's a 500 plus place. We've literally never been anywhere so fancy.'

Iris's taste of high Score life doesn't seem to be ending with a half-drunk coffee from Angus. A bar, an actual cocktail bar. She wets her lips, the room-temperature beer now tasting sour and old. She's seen those cocktails with their multi-coloured and ornate garnishes. Better than a coffee served by a grumpy barista.

'Sure. Okay. Why not?'

Chapter 14
Iris

Iris rifles through her closet to find her most glamorous, or least plain, outfit. It doesn't take long, so few are her clothes. Just something that doesn't have a stain on it, or she doesn't wear to the climbing wall would be fine. She slows her rummaging as she feels giddy, the distance from her head to the floor varying more than it should. Just excitement, she tells herself. Or dread — they manifest in the same way physically. Or maybe it was necking the beer so quickly, or the fact she hasn't eaten dinner yet. Or maybe it really is excitement coupled with the heavy guilt of trying to enjoy herself after what she just witnessed.

You can put an end to the suffering, Iris.

She snorts a laugh, glad Georgie isn't close by to ask what she's laughing at. Stupid voice, saying nonsense things. There is always suffering. Wiping out the human race is pretty much the only way to put an end to it, and she is fairly sure that isn't what the voice is suggesting.

She draws the curtains, trying to retain what little heat there is in the room, leaving her with just the dusky glow of the old lamp on her desk. Sitting on her bed a moment, she stretches out her neck and arms, the sort of stretches she normally does after a stint on the climbing wall, but the way she was gripping her bike handlebars earlier has left her just as rigid. With looser muscles, she relaxes and allows her excitement to return. It's okay to be excited, albeit with undertones of apprehension. She shouldn't feel guilty about wanting to enjoy herself. Survivors' guilt resurfaces at the oddest of times. She had nothing to do with the bodies she saw today, yet she's breathing, and they aren't.

A high Scoring bar! Closing her eyes a moment, Iris tries to picture it, to encourage the excitement to take root. Perhaps she can meet some high Scoring people, not Preserved, but actual people about her age. They can't all be like Sam. She gets out her makeup bag. Such plans deserve the full works. Perhaps even some association with a high Scorer will help her Score. Berkshire really is the best place since it has so many high Scoring bars and has more high Scorers than any other county. That's why it's the best county there is.

What does Score matter—

'Oh, shut up!' she says to the voice before it pops her bubble. She needs to let her hair down a bit, to have a little fun, and the raspy incessant nagging is prohibitive. How can she know that Score doesn't matter if she doesn't get to see what all the fuss is about?

She applies blush and a second coat of mascara, grateful that Georgie always ensures their beauty supplies are well stocked. As she dusts her cheeks, making herself look like the sort of woman Norman Bonnet thinks she should present herself as, she realises she's well and truly back in the box. Plato's Cave is deep and climbing out takes too much effort. There are no grips like the bouldering wall. It's like its sides are made of glass.

There's something comforting in the familiar. Wipe the dust away and it still collects again in the same old places. The windows always smear again, however new and shiny you make them.

The shackles of normalcy attach to her ankles like heavy chains pulling her back. She's dragged them around for this long, she might as well keep them. No longer light and impulsive with her awakening, her shoulders sag as she realises Georgie was right. It's better to just accept and get on with life. Her brief interlude of treasonous thoughts was just that. A footnote in the big picture. She's drawn a line under it. She doesn't want to end up as some dismembered un-Scorable. There's safety with a higher Score and safety in the pursuit of it.

Her sense of ambition has received a renewed push. Perhaps such an opportunity is what she's been lacking. A break from the same old grind at work and the same old flat parties on weekends. It's likely not so bad being a high Scorer. Of course, Sam began with an absurdly high Score thanks to her parents' lineage. She barely has to strive at all.

'Everything I try on looks shit,' Georgie shouts from her room before walking to Iris's. 'And my eyelashes. They've all clumped together.' Georgie, of course, is gorgeous. Her sleek hair reflects the light like a mirror and her eyelashes clumping is just not true. Sometimes, Iris thinks Georgie has some trickster mirror in her room, one that shows her lies.

'You look great,' Iris says. 'Seriously great. Stop worrying. Sam will still fancy you with or without eyelash clumps.'

'I might meet someone else though, someone even better. We're not exclusive.'

Iris rolls her eyes and turns her attention back to her own appearance. 'Whatever.'

'Cheer up, Iris,' Georgie says as she sits on the bed. 'It was awful, those bodies. But you've done all you can.'

Iris's attempt to exude nothing but excitement isn't kidding Georgie. Her best friend knows her too well and can sense any malaise like a dog can sniff out a biscuit. Iris can't tell her about all her troubles, about her job offer to snitch on the low Scorers, that being back in the box is a little stifling, airless, that breathing in this circulated air is musty and getting her down, that she's betraying herself by being excited to fraternise with high Scorers. Her emotional contradictions are eating away at her. Being awakened, then resolving to conditioning is like being pulled in two different directions, and she's ripping down the middle. Like she was about to get a leg up, and now she's been hammered back down.

'I just can't get it out of my mind. All the death,' she says. A simpler explanation.

Iris finishes the last of her makeup. It's going to take a little more than eyeliner and an up-do to make her look like she belongs in a 500 plus bar. She turns to the side, stands straight, and inspects her negligible curves, then slouches again.

'Are you worried about that slasher guy?' Georgie asks. 'It's like you said, probably just some poor soul wanting help.'

Iris is regretting telling Georgie about that. Georgie would have stayed and helped. She wouldn't have been all paranoid and bailed. She would have at least asked instead of listening to the weird voice in her head. Georgie would have shown kindness instead of insanity. But she wasn't there. It was creepy as fuck.

'You got your mace?' Iris asks.

'It won't fit in my handbag.' Georgie holds up her dainty clutch. It looks like it wouldn't hold much more than the few sequins that adorn the front.

'So, take a bigger bag.'

Georgie cocks her head as she inspects her bag, then lets it hang to her side. 'No, this is the best one. You've got mace though, right? It'll definitely fit in your bag.'

Iris nods and grabs her larger, more practical bag — a linen thing with stripes, more suitable for a trip to the supermarket than a swanky bar, but it'll do. After several outfit changes to find the best mix of alluring, clean, and comfortable enough to cycle in, they leave and head into town, taking the smaller roads to avoid the bodies and letting their brakes go down the hill, allowing the wind to add the last bit of volume Georgie claims she so desperately needs.

The bar has security at the door, checking their names as they go in; huge guys who Iris assumes must have day jobs clearing piles of bricks from fallen buildings. Iris stumbles over her name as she stands jittery, like someone who needs to pee. Georgie fares little better and lets out a little squeal as they walk through the doors.

They're greeted with the smell of vanilla, and music at a volume where it's still possible to hold a conversation. Ornate light fittings bejewelled with crystals shine soft light over inviting chairs and a floor that ripples with colour like flowing water.

Sam sits in a booth with some other people who must be her colleagues. Cosmetic dentists always seem to have the same toothy smiles and well-fitted clothes, gesturing in such a delicate way, it's as if they're explaining crowns and veneers. Sam flashes them her own dazzling display of pearly whites and waves them over.

'Hi, Georgie. Oh, Iris, you came too. Wasn't sure if it was your thing.' Sam's voice is etched with a disappointed tone that makes Iris's back itch.

'Well,' Iris attempts to sound casual, 'I was invited.'

'This place is great, isn't it?' Sam says. She's directly facing Georgie, and waves at a barman who walks over with a tray of cocktails and places them on the table. Tall, elegant glasses that sparkle under the lights. Iris takes one and sips. Her eyes widen with delight as she tastes notes of flavours so exotic, she doesn't even know what they are.

Across the bar, she sighs when she spots Angus. Of course he's here. There are so few people under thirty in this town who can enjoy such a bar. Only nine other people in the whole of

Reading received their Life Scores when Iris and Georgie did. In the *entire* town. Iris and Georgie being the lowest, of course. Most of the pregnancies that survived the Great Unrest were from parents who could afford to buy a life, and so had the high Score to fund the credit. Iris and Georgie being alive is something of a miracle.

Iris sips her drink again. Divine.

'I hear you work in the stats department?' The question comes from a cute brunette with the sort of dark eyes Iris could get lost in. Kira, she introduces herself as. When Iris faces her, she flicks her hair over her shoulder in a way that makes Iris think she's flirting.

'Yep. Just analyse data, really.'

'Well, you must be clever to understand all the numbers.'

Yeah, definitely flirting. Iris's invite now seems more explainable. She's here to keep Sam's friend entertained.

'You're at the dentist's with Sam?' Iris glances up through her eyelashes, sipping on her straw. She could do a lot worse than hooking-up with a high Scorer like Kira. And she certainly seems a lot more charming than the guy from the other night.

'Oh, no. I know Sam through friends of friends, really. You know how it is.'

'Sure.'

'So, you must run all the numbers for the Eyes Forward quarterly population update.'

'Yep. It's all go, go, go in the office at the moment,' Iris says. She takes another sip of her drink, maintaining eye contact. Just because she rarely flirts doesn't mean she's bad at it.

Kira leans in closer. 'Any inside scoop? Have we flattened the curve? Gotten rid of that nasty step at the un-Scorable end?'

Iris bites her bottom lip and lets out a girlish laugh. 'Sorry. Confidential until the announcement.'

'Iris won't even tell me the work stats,' Georgie says and gives Iris a nudge. 'She's a pretty good secret keeper.'

'Well,' Kira says, 'my parents are 800 pluses, and they're saying there's some big announcement on the way. Something about adjusting the imbalance, some incentive.'

800 plus! Iris wets her lips. 'Well, I wouldn't know anything about that, I'm afraid.'

They believe it all. Don't you see? That's why you have to tell the truth.

The voice comes back so suddenly, Iris chokes a little on her drink. Kira smiles and politely gives Iris the space she needs to cough as her cheeks flame with embarrassment.

'Strong, aren't they?' Kira smiles.

Iris nods and tries to laugh it off. Why is the voice back now? She inspects her drink. It's pale pink with gold glitter, no frosting of blue Flake in it or on the rim. Why won't the voice just go away? She's definitely not high.

I'm not going away, Iris. You need to see. You need to make them see.

Iris mumbles an apology, then makes her way to the toilets, walking slowly, fighting the urge to run. Despite spending so long applying makeup, she splashes cold water on her face and neck.

Iris. Your fear isn't me. It's the Society. It's what's happening.

'Go away!' she says into the mirror. She's alone in the bathroom. At least no one else will know she's insane. She leans closer to the mirror, her stare boring into her own eyes. Leaning in close, her breath fogs the glass and her eyes blur into black pits.

She's not insane. Impossible. She's a good citizen. She works hard and likes climbing. These are the things that make Iris herself, to remind her of who she is, not this voice, not some nagging demon telling her to think bad thoughts.

'I am Iris Taylor,' she says to herself. 'I am Iris Taylor. I am Iris Taylor.'

'Iris?'

Georgie's voice makes Iris snap around. Georgie is there, wide-eyed with an upturned mouth. 'You okay?'

'Sure,' she says, breezily, well, as breezily as she can manage. 'Just needed to cough. The drink irritated my throat.'

'All right. Well, another one, maybe? Kira's getting a round in. I think she likes you.'

Iris clears her throat, ruffles her hair, then checks her makeup for smudges. She's not often attracted to women, but a little recklessness with Kira might be just the distraction she needs to clear her mind. 'Great. Let's go drink.'

Chapter 15
Iris

Another cocktail isn't enough to make Iris relax. She flinches when Kira strokes her arm, glances over her shoulder when she hears other voices, and finds Sam's constant talk about the new algorithm tedious, that and whatever the new rebalancing incentive could be. Iris stifles a yawn whenever the conversation meanders towards Life Score statistics. She came here to enjoy herself, not to talk about work.

Angus being there is a distraction. He spots her and waves and she turns away. He's probably thinking she's trying to sleep her way up the Score ladder, which, judging by the way she's trying to flirt with Kira, could be true.

After a couple more cocktails, Iris tells Georgie they should call it a night. However alluring Kira is, and however much she wants to enjoy herself, they still have work tomorrow. Iris and Kira swap numbers and enjoy a brief hug, a kiss on the cheek, and their heads linger close for a few seconds before Iris pulls away. Any more and Angus will probably tell the family and before she knows it, her mum and dad will be wanting Kira round for Sunday lunch.

Iris and Georgie leave, staggering slightly as they collect their bikes, both mounting the wrong bike initially, before giggling and swapping back.

They cycle through the busy town centre, and the crowds mingling on the streets, waiting to go into bars or just looking in longingly. Pickpockets, most likely some of the lowest Scorers. When you have so few points to lose, why not? Iris shortens her bag strap and keeps a hand on it as much as she can.

The cycle bridge over the Thames is deserted, strangely so. It's never that empty. They pay it no regard and carry on to Gosbrook Road to the foot of St Peter's Hill. Iris's bike wobbles slightly. Is that the booze or some tremble in the ground? She slows and listens for the telltale rumble of a building giving way, yet hears nothing but the wind whooshing past. Georgie doesn't seem to notice anything.

'So, Kira. . .' Georgie says, the intonation at the end adding a tone of mischief.

'Yeah.'

'She seems nice.'

'Yep,' Iris says, flatly, like a door closing.

Georgie peeks over. In the darkness Iris can tell she's making her sad, pouty, tell-me-all-the-gossip face. Iris laughs and shakes her head. Georgie creates enough gossip for the pair of them and always craves more, whereas Iris rarely has any desire to know or to share.

Some lights come on behind them and Iris turns around. They're blindingly bright, not just the usual hazy streetlights but more like floodlights, moving towards them on bikes with far better power than theirs. They're past the highest Scoring residences now, getting close to their shitty end of town. Such bikes aren't seen around here often — no one has the electric allowance to charge such a thing. Stolen maybe, or they're high Scorers who're lost.

Iris and Georgie are riding side-by-side and they exchange glances, give a little shrug, then instinctively pick up speed. Instead of putting some distance between them and the dazzling lights behind, the glare is getting brighter. The bikes behind are getting closer, lighting their way. Iris turns again, but the dazzle bleaches them out. She can see nothing but the light, and when she turns back to face the front, the afterimage leaves her vision even darker than it was before. She blinks to clear the blotches, relying on Georgie's outline to the side of her to guide her way for a moment.

The bikes are closer now. Much closer. Their riders pant breaths as loud as their own. They could just pull to the side and let them pass, but there's something telling Iris not to, some instinct fighting its way out of her gut, telling her to ride faster. Iris looks over at Georgie, squinting the eye that is closest to the lights and the two of them lock eyes, Georgie's instinct matching hers.

Digging deeper, they push on up the hill. In the corner of her vision, in that squinting eye, Iris sees it: that long glint of metal in the light.

Iris. They're coming for you.

The voice is warning her. In her heart, she knows this, her intuition agrees.

'Georgie, shit!'

Iris's tone is enough to tell Georgie they need to hurry away from the light, away from whoever it is on those bikes, away from whatever that long metal spike is. They pedal faster and faster, their bikes groaning and clanging as they do. The other bikes are on them now, a rub from their tyre behind almost destabilises Iris, but she tugs on the handlebars and rights herself, gaining an inch or two. She swerves and Georgie reacts, veering further into the road.

The air rushes past the metal as it swoops down next to Iris. She hears the whoosh, feels the wind brush her cheek. Her coat catches the blade, and it rips at the elbow. A clean cut, razor-sharp that doesn't even snag. The blade comes back up again.

'Georgie, duck!'

Georgie, eyes wild with panic, banks to the right, then careens across the entire road as she attempts to steady herself. She screams Iris's name as she topples off the road and into the grassy bank.

One bike screeches to a stop behind as the other is side-on with Iris. She turns hard right, puts her foot down to skid her bike around a 180 switchback, then rides right into the person approaching Georgie. She has no time to acknowledge the size of him, the thick tree trunk of his torso, his height more than a foot taller than she or Georgie. But such comparisons don't enter her mind and her wheel slams into his leg. His knee buckles, and he tumbles, curses, and the other bike catches up. His brakes grind as he stops right next to her and takes a swing with the blade. Iris ducks as the metal skirts past her. She reaches for the mace in her handbag, then sprays him in the face.

There's a throaty grumble from the face, mostly covered in a tight hood, but his eyes and mouth get doused in a cloud of mace. He cries and reaches for his eyes as the other one stands, then takes his own smaller blade from his belt. Iris is ready and quick, spraying him too, and he collapses to the ground with a whimper, landing on top of his partner.

Iris grabs Georgie by the hand, yanking her up from the bank, and they ride. With all their strength, they ride.

Chapter 16
Iris

'Oh my God, Iris,' Georgie says as they make it through their door.

It's the first thing either of them has said. Iris's lungs are burning from the exertion. She's never cycled so hard in her life. Everything hurts now that they're safe, and she sits on the floor by the front door, legs too weak to even make it to the sofa. Her heart hammers so much it might burst out of her ribs, and she shakes worse than a collapsing building.

Iris faces Georgie. She's fared no better. Her face is ghostly white, a contrast to the pinkish rims of her eyes. 'Let me look at you.' Iris crawls to her, then pulls up Georgie's muddy sleeves before checking her neck and brushing away the debris from the grassy bank. She pulls her feet gently and manipulates her arms. A few grazes from gravel, that's all. Nothing broken. No big wounds.

Iris's jacket wasn't so lucky. The rip from the knife-sword, or whatever it was, goes right across, and the padding is coming out. She inspects it, then pulls at the padding. That could have been her arm. Her flesh. That padding could have been her blood. Or Georgie's.

'Let's. . .' Iris's voice shakes. Words seem far away and out of reach. She swallows, tries to still her heart. 'Let's have a hot drink. Some. . .some chamomile tea. . .with sugar.'

'The electric—'

'Fuck the electric.'

While the kettle boils, Iris helps Georgie strip off, then puts her under the shower. She marks off the entire next day's flush tally to make up for the water. Their piss can stew for the day. That's not important right now.

They could have killed Georgie, could have killed both of them. Whoever *they* were. That thought goes around and around. Iris can't shake the image of Georgie cut up and bleeding onto the tarmac. It's so real in front of her eyes, it's like a premonition. Her friend, her best friend since they were kids, the friend she grew up with, got in trouble with, gossiped with. . . They could have killed her.

She makes the hot drinks, then sits on the sofa. Her balled fists press into the side of her head, and she tugs on her hair as she cries. Then she grabs a pillow, buries her face into it, and screams, the same way she used to when she was a kid and was so full of rage it had no other way out. She screams and cries into her pillow until it's too wet to use anymore.

Use that rage, Iris.

She doesn't dismiss the voice now. The voice isn't her insanity; it's her guardian angel. And it's right. Her anger burns hotter than ever. She clenches her fists so tightly her fingernails cut her palms and her knuckles release a dull crack. She grits her teeth and gets her breath under control, long and steady in and out against tense chest muscles and through a tight mouth. Anger is too soft, too ambivalent.

She is seething.

She loads up the Society Police app to report the encounter, though she knows without video footage, without facial recognition, it'll go nowhere. Just another statistic.

Sounds familiar.

Georgie's shaking has abated a little when she comes back from the shower. Both dressed in their warmest pyjamas, they sit on the sofa and Iris hands her a cup of tea. Iris's hands are still, not even a slight wobble. Her wrath has steadied her.

'Thank God you had the mace,' Georgie says, staring into her cup, the steam collecting around her.

'Yeah. Used the whole bloody can. I've got another in my room. You should carry some too.'

'Somehow my handbag choice doesn't seem so important.'

Iris puts her arm around her, squeezing her shoulders, forcing the fear from her. 'You're okay, Georgie. We're both okay.'

Chapter 17
Iris

Iris wasn't planning on attending the flat party at the weekend. Thursday was traumatic enough, going outside seems unnecessary. A cosy Saturday night nestled indoors is what she needs. Sober, recovering, being safe. Keeping Georgie safe.

But then Georgie says, 'I want to try it.'

'What?'

'Flake. You seemed so different afterwards, like all your trauma had gone. Like you understood things I didn't.'

'Well,' Iris scoffs. 'It wears off.'

'No, it doesn't.' Georgie inspects Iris's face, gazing at her in such a way only best friends can, friends that know each other's every freckle and blemish. 'You have some weird perspective. Not bad weird. But you're different.'

Iris turns her face away, feeling shame under the spotlight. Her sample of Flake led her to be disappointed with the state of things, then disappointed with herself for not changing anything, then disappointed she gave up on that view. There was nothing about it that was good. 'I have no idea where to get it,' she says.

'You know it'll be at Marny's.'

Marny's flat parties serve up every narcotic going. When Iris attends, she usually spends the night with her hand covering her glass in case of any wayward doses, while avoiding people that stagger around with sweaty green faces, seeking the nearest corner to throw up in. Georgie thinks they're fun and a place to meet other fun people, but Iris usually finds them a headache-inducing nuisance. They're the sort of parties where Iris's indiscretion the week before would have raised more glasses than eyebrows. And it's not like she ever wants to see Marny again. She's been avoiding her for months.

Georgie hasn't heard anything useful around the newsroom at work regarding deranged slashers roaming the streets, nothing about some breakout at a Pres-X asylum. Plenty of idle chitchat about Flake-usage though, and of course, Life Score algorithm hype, but not a whiff of the real news. Decoy politics, Georgie calls it.

'If there was a real danger, more so than usual, there would be some gossip somewhere. Decoy politics can only cover up so much,' Georgie says, in the sort of whiny begging voice that makes Iris want to say no just to be mean.

'I dunno. It just doesn't seem sensible this weekend.'

'Marny's is only a few streets away,' Georgie says, 'not at the bottom of the hill.'

'But right by some un-Scorable block. And I'm orange.'

'So? We'll stay till morning, so you won't get caught being out. We always stay till morning anyway. It's only a five-minute ride. I want to try it. I need to.'

Iris thinks about her new job assignment, about her call up to snitch on Flake suppliers. She'll find some there for sure. Avoiding the dealers seems like the best way to not be tempted to turn Judas.

'Please, Iris. After Thursday night, I need this, and I don't want to go without you.'

The thought of Georgie going out makes Iris's stomach roll. Iris wants her within sight and earshot, somewhere she can grab her if needed. Iris doesn't crave the high of Flake, the enhanced vision and dissipated anger were nice but not something she needs. What she does need is a kick up the butt. Her thoughts have festered into a pool of nothingness the last few days, enlightenment morphing into inaction. Perhaps a little line would give her some ideas about how to handle her predicament at work. Albeit, that predicament is centred around Flake-usage. She certainly doesn't want to end up grinding some tosser on the floor again.

Georgie's face is all big eyes and a pouty bottom lip. Her pleading face is near impossible for anyone to refuse. Iris dips her chin and her shoulders drop, her fight waned. With a heady mix of tiredness and restlessness, she thinks, what the hell.

Chapter 18
Iris

The party is dingier than most. The smell of urine and unwashed armpits mingles with aftershave that stings Iris's throat but doesn't cut through the miasma of the other stenches. The flat is heaving. The entire block is. Marny is in the 300s, and the block is all Sub 400. By the appearance of the clientele, every resident has invited their lower Scoring friends. Iris and Georgie arrive with a crate of bargain beer and wade through the merry crowd, well, some merry, some already involved in alcohol-fuelled heated debates, and they find their way to Marny's top floor.

'This looks fun,' Iris says with a subtle hint of sarcasm that Georgie doesn't seem to notice.

'That guy over there,' Georgie says. 'He looks just like some man I shagged last year.'

'Georgie, I think that's him.'

'Oh!' She giggles and puts her hands over her mouth. 'I think you might be right.'

Georgie drank an entire bottle of wine before they left their apartment and bumps into the handrail with every other step, laughing as she does. Iris, sober and alert, eyes every face they stumble past. She has no clue what the men looked like on Thursday. Their balaclavas kept them well hidden, but she might recognise their cough if she maced the same guys again. She couldn't even say with certainty they were men, their stocky physiques being her only clue. But maybe the mace has left their eyes red and their skin raw. Maybe they'd recognise her and Georgie and flinch at the sight of them. With one hand, she supports Georgie, the other holds the can of mace in her bag.

'Shall we find you some water?' Iris asks as they make it to Marny's apartment.

She bats Iris away. 'You're always so sensible, Iris.'

Iris gazes around the room and thinks that turning up at this party was definitely not sensible. It's barely past eight, and the music is pumping, the baseline coming through the floor and tickling right up to her nose. A couple of chairs break just next to her when three people try to sit on the same one, and someone else is throwing up into the sink.

'Oh, don't worry about the chairs. I'll get more on credit and maybe up my Score enough to escape this prison.' Marny's voice carries across the crowd before she appears, her sparkly top creating a glitter-ball-effect on the wall next to her. She looks at Iris and Georgie a while before greeting them. 'Hi, Iris. How are you?'

Marny seems like the soberest one there, next to Iris. She hugs Iris, then pulls away, running her eyes up and down Iris's body with a half-smile. Now Iris remembers why she's avoided Marny for a while.

'Good. Thanks, Marny,' Iris replies. 'You?'

'All the better now you're here.' She's shouting over the music someone's just turned up another notch or two. Marny's glance goes to Iris's hand at the orange implant, and Iris flinches under her gaze. Marny now knows she's unlikely to be hooking up with a man tonight.

Iris's cheeks flush, and she has no response. Making small talk at the top of her voice seems so much more difficult than mumbling something. She shifts her weight on her feet and avoids Marny's come-to-bed eyes for a moment until the awkwardness fills every crack and crevice in the room and gooseflesh prickles up Iris's arms.

'I'm just going to grab a drink,' Iris says and turns her back on Marny, then pours a large vodka coke from the stash of booze on the counter and necks half of it, just as Marny gets pulled away to some spillage emergency.

'Wow,' Georgie says. 'That was so awkward.'

'Yeah.' Iris downs the last of her drink.

On the rare occasions she has a desire for anyone at all, Iris usually prefers men. Men are simple, she'd explained to Georgie one night, whose own preferences are split the other way. Just feed them and fuck them and they're happy. Women are too complicated. They require time. She'd said this in such a way that implied she has the experience to back up such a claim. Both her and Georgie know that's not true. Several months ago, she'd indulged in some female company, and Marny thought there was more to it than a drunken, late-night fumble, and Iris has been dodging her ever since.

It's an hour later when Georgie reminds Iris she wants to try Flake. Iris watches her sway to one side, then overcorrect and stumble the other way, laughing like a kid who's been caught stealing biscuits. She doesn't seem any more drunk than she did earlier, or perhaps Iris is, and so the comparison is the same. There's a mirror with a blue pile of the crystal powder next to the microwave that no one seems to be claiming.

'Well,' Georgie says, 'loads of people here are on it and everyone seems okay.' She hiccups at least three times as she says that.

Iris takes a swig of her beer, holding it in her mouth a while before swallowing, hoping that'll get rid of the dryness. 'Well, that's probably okay then.'

Georgie grabs Iris's hand and squeezes. 'How much did you do before?'

'I can't actually remember. Let's just have a small bit.'

Iris spots some people with the telltale dusting around their nostrils, so she checks. 'How much is a dose, like, each?' She realises her drug lingo must show her as the ignorant novice she is. A man nods and obliges in making them a line each, smiles at them, then hands them a small cylinder to sniff through.

'You first,' Georgie says.

Iris declines the cylinder. Reusing someone else's snorting device seems a step too far. She rolls up a receipt from her pocket and inhales a line. It burns all the way up as if it's made of crushed glass, but the hit is instant. She grins and hands the receipt to Georgie.

Georgie stands upright, her eyes widening as big as teacups, her mouth parted in an O. She says nothing for a while, just gazes around the room, her head rotating slowly side-to-side. The effect on Iris is no less dull, just less of a surprise. The fairy lights that hang from the window dance along with the music, more of them, each choosing their own part of the rhythm. The vibrations through the floor feel seismic, and Iris and Georgie both grab the table for balance.

Each conversation pierces the music in waves: the bitching, the dismay, the laughs. Their features are clear now in the half-light, like she can see every contour of their faces. The lowest Scorers are so obvious from their tattier clothes, their less made-up faces, standing in their own groups away from the 200 and 300 pluses. Despite cross-Scoring friendships being common, en masse, people still congregate with their own. The Eyes Forward labelling system is sheepdog to the sheep.

Women's fertility implants glow through the dim lights, displaying their status, the absent glow on the men's hands standing out like black holes.

They could talk to some Sub 200s in the adjacent corner, but Iris doesn't want to seem offensive or overbearing to them. They could talk to the 300 pluses congregating in the middle of the room, but they'll probably take one look at her and Georgie and treat them like easy pickings. In the corner, some people who look about Iris and Georgie's Score are sitting talking, and Iris feels a pull to join them. She takes Georgie's hand, and they duck and dive through the crowd.

Iris is only vaguely aware of who's talking. The voices are clear; tracking the speaker is the challenge. Each conversation is like the background music, a hum with the odd crescendo and diminuendo. She strains to hear, leaning in, wanting to home in on every word and ignore the other distractions around: the laser light, the smashed glass, the man tripping over, all such things snap her focus and invade her senses. She leans in more and puts her hands behind her ears to deflect the sound, then shimmies in closer to the group. The conversation is centred around the bodies. No one seems to know any of them, reports and rumours of some loved ones unaccounted for.

'They're the bodies we can see. What about under the rubble, in the Thames?'

'I haven't seen a significant building collapse in days, so they can't use that excuse.'

'It's a mad slasher, or maybe a gang.'

'It's the Eyes Forward culling the low Scorers. It's what they want.'

It's not right. You know it's not right.

The voice startles Iris, and she jumps, her heart freezing for a second. It must be the Flake. It's been minutes since she took it and the voice has returned, louder than the droning music, louder even than the heavy baseline pumping through the speakers. She can feel it in her temples, her chest, her throat. It's like the voice is inside her, whispering to her bones.

Think about it, Iris. Think about how wrong everything is.

It is wrong. The bodies. The lack of reports. The warped statistics. It's wrong but knowing something is wrong changes nothing.

You could, though, Iris. You are more powerful than you know.

Georgie had called Iris powerful just a few days ago. A compliment from a friend, consoling her. That was all it was. But Georgie isn't speaking now. She's distracted playing with a lighter, entranced by the tiny flame.

Iris is so focussed on the voice, she barely notices the hands creeping up on her from behind. Thick fingers and dirty nails. She turns and recognises the guy, some leach from a flat party last year. She'd elbowed him in the guts then and does much the same now, not at all interested in another telling off from Georgie. He tries for a second fiddle, and as tantalising as his touch is, she pushes him away, making sure her implant is visible.

The gossip is rife through the group. Everyone has an idea, an opinion. Iris cranes her neck and leans forward, but when their arguments get repetitive, she gets up and moves to another group, flittering from gossip to gossip. She wants to hear it all, every opinion and every tidbit. She craves information.

'They don't give a shit about this end of town. The bodies, so many now. No one does anything.'

'Strive to Score? We're just striving to survive here!'

'I overheard some Preserved, must have been a 900 plus, saying there's going to be some big step to address the imbalance.'

'You're laughing if you think that'll help us though. I wouldn't be surprised if all these people were killed by the high Scorers just for kicks, knowing nothing will be done. They get a thrill and bump a few off the population.'

The group all speak with animated enthusiasm, throwing up their hands and shaking their heads, though they have sad faces. It's clear in their hollowed-out eyes, their drawn-down mouths, like their smiling muscles have never been used. There's no joy here. Only struggle.

Iris sits, rubbing her arms, chilled to her core. The fact the Eyes Forward do nothing about the killings is bad enough. The thought that they could be sanctioned makes her last drink threaten to come back up. It's just gossip, she reminds herself. The sort of slanderous stuff she would have ignored weeks ago and found more interesting subjects to converse about: work, dating, decor, who Georgie's screwing, the new Life Score algorithm. Now she hangs off every word, wishing she could write it all down, describe this feeling so when Flake wears off later, she'll have some evidence.

Listen, Iris. Listen to it all.

She's lost Georgie between groups somewhere but spots her still with the first crew, enthralled, leaning in and nodding along. Iris returns to sit with her, cosying up next to her and a purple-haired woman on the other side. She's hearing this all for the first time. That feeling Iris had a week ago is returning. That first awakening was blinding. Now it's more like a constant glare, migraine-inducing and sickly. Her heart is like a flutter, rippling through to her stomach. Excitement and nerves are so similar. Which one is she feeling?

'I wonder if the same thing is happening elsewhere — in other counties?' Iris says.

The group all turn to face her, like flowers turning to the sun. All their brows are knitted in mimicking faces of alarm.

'Other counties?' one woman says, her eyes the colour of Flake.

That idea seems a step too far, even for this free-thinking group, and Iris retreats a little, shifting back into the shadows.

'You know, I reckon that's worth investigating,' one man says, younger than Iris, maybe just in his twenties, unburdened with having his own Life Score to maintain and improve.

'We're penned in here,' one woman says, the loudest of all, venom in her voice. 'They never tell us about the rest of the Society. Hell, I don't even know anyone who's been to other counties.'

'My cousin has,' Iris says. 'He lived in Scotland.'

A hush descends over the group, all eyes on her again.

'Really?' the purple-haired woman asks, a whisper, really.

'Yeah. He says it's the fairest county.'

'Well, it can't be as good as Berkshire,' the young-looking one says with an air of wisdom older than he should have at his tender age. 'Berkshire is the best county to live in.'

Iris sips her drink. 'That's just what the signs say.'

Another hush. A stupefied silence. If the music wasn't so loud, Iris is sure she'd hear cogs in their brains cranking.

'I never realised. You're right!' The biggest guy spits when he talks, then pushes back his dark blond hair that's almost as long as Georgie's, though a lot less sleek. 'All we're doing is reading signs.'

Georgie pulls Iris in closer and puts her face right by her ear. 'Iris, you tried to tell me. I didn't get it before, but I do now. It's not right. The entire Society. It's like it's not even. . .I can't describe it. . .it's not even a Society. It's an idea forced upon us. The Society isn't real.'

'Iris?' the angry woman says. 'Is that your name? Iris *who*?'

'Taylor.'

The woman blinks hard, wipes some of the blue crust from her nose, then her eyes dart side to side. 'Iris Taylor. I know that name.'

Iris remembers her name on Nebula, and her mouth runs dry. She sips her drink and backs away slightly. 'It's probably just common.'

The angry woman doesn't push it but rejoins the rant on the Eyes Forward-advertising. The guy opposite is staring at her breasts, a glazed expression on his face. He's clearly had Flake, and Flake affects some people differently.

Iris sits up straighter, adjusts her top to conceal more skin, and notices Marny hovering next to her only a few feet away. Shit. She's trapped. Breast-starer is still leering, and at that moment, he seems like the obvious solution. She shuffles to him, then takes his face in her hands and kisses him. That'll get rid of Marny and, well, the kiss is quite nice actually.

'We're going to take the whole fucking system down.'

Not Iris speaking. That sentence breaks through Iris's lust, and she moves away from his lips, turning her head to scan who said that and to gauge reactions. It doesn't appear to have been said by any of her group, but she's said such words before. Was it the voice, or are there others who share her vision, who want to collapse the entire hierarchy that is the Eyes Forward and their Life Score system?

She grabs Georgie and gets up, pushing through a group, then another, until she finds a small group sitting on the floor, nostrils crusted blue, joints in hand. Beer bottles lie to their sides, tipped over and trickling onto the lino floor.

'Whatever it takes,' a woman says. Through her thick spectacles, her eyes are full of wrath. 'This shit has to stop. Everyone needs to escape the cave, like the graffiti says.'

'I agree,' Iris says. 'Let's fuck up the entire system.'

'How?' Georgie's voice is small but comes through clearly, like a headlight in the fog. 'You keep saying this. But how?'

'Burn down the Eyes Forward building,' one man says. His shoulders are twice the width of Iris's. He looks like he could dismantle a building with his hands alone.

'We are just one county,' one man says with a voice higher pitched than Iris expected from his buzzcut. Across his dark skin, the glitter-ball light shines like diamonds.

'Maybe there aren't these issues in other counties.' This woman has blue hair, and her voice smacks of the kind of naivety Iris wants to laugh at.

'There are. I speak with some SAS members in other counties,' Spectacle-Wearer says.

'Sisters And Spies?' Big Shoulders says with a scoff. 'That group is about as legit and useful as the Eyes Forward.'

Despite his rebuff, a warmth spreads through Iris at the mention of the SAS, dissolving her chill to nothing and a grin spreads. She edges closer to the woman who mentioned them, a little starstruck. Maybe this woman is one of the Sisters.

'You wait. It's not just us.' Spectacle-Wearer speaks slowly, hovering her stare over each of them individually. 'People are getting more and more pissed off. *ETC* has been painted in other counties too. Sometime soon, everyone is going to revolt. I'll reckon then all we'll need is a baseball bat and ten minutes to take down the entire shitshow.'

'It all starts with the Society Police.' Big Shoulders recoils his lips when he says this, punching one fist into his other hand.

'Not much we can do about them,' Buzzcut says. 'All eyes are our eyes isn't an understatement. I got 10 points deducted the other day from someone filming me putting cardboard in the wrong recycling bin.'

'Bloody Life Scores,' Big Shoulders says, punching his hand so loudly this time it makes Iris jump. 'If they weren't a thing, if people weren't so worried about their chances of getting Pres-X-2, we could disrupt everything. Easy.'

Spectacle-Wearer nods along. 'It's a bribe from the Eyes Forward. A ransom, even. They control everyone with that drug.'

Are you listening Iris? Keep listening.

Iris's knees bounce up and down. She is listening. She's never paid so much attention to anything before.

'So that's where we start,' Buzzcut says, only now his voice is lower, more determined. 'That's what the SAS should be doing. Fuck with the Life Score system; cause chaos there, and the rest will follow. People won't bother Society Policing when there are no points in it for them. Without points, Pres-X-2 distribution will have to change.'

'The new algorithm is out soon. Maybe that'll change things for the better.' Blue-Hair's innocence makes Big Shoulders belly laugh.

'I work for the Life Score statistics department,' Iris says, then holds her breath as her stomach sinks to the floor. She never tells strangers what she does for a living. But her tongue is loose, and she can't stop it, and. . .well. . .this lot seems harmless enough. 'Whatever I do, they still bullshit figures.'

'Sounds about right,' Spectacle-Wearer says. 'Nothing real matters. All the Eyes Forward care about is control.'

Georgie nods. 'Who invented that bloody algorithm anyway?'

'Lloyd Porter, I heard,' Big Shoulders says.

'I heard from SAS it was someone called Percy Greyshot,' Spectacle-Wearer says.

Buzzcut scratches his head. 'I heard someone called Bruce Clarke.'

'Well,' Iris says, her voice coming out jittery with her eagerness. 'It seems that's the first bit of information we need.'

Chapter 19
Iris

Iris peels the man's arm off her sometime early Saturday. The sun isn't out yet and outside bears the hazy mist of a day not yet begun. The man protests and reaches for her again, but she shuffles away. His brows lower in a confused or hurt expression, Iris isn't sure which. She's just pleased they kept their clothes on.

She checks her phone; it's five a.m. At least it looks like she didn't load up the Society Police app. They took some selfies, that's all. With her mouth feeling like old carpet, she goes to find Georgie. She steps over fellow passed-out partiers, her shoes making scratchy noises like Velcro across the floor. A small mirror of leftover powders is on the counter, and she briefly wonders if that would assist or hinder her walk home. She settles on the latter and pours herself a glass of water instead. As she gulps it back, she peers in the glass and realises how filthy it is. What looks like ash floats inside, and the cloudy imprint of several lips stains the rim. She puts the glass down. Marny is thankfully in someone else's embrace, still half awake, hands roaming, and Iris averts her eyes in search of Georgie.

Marny's apartment is syrupy sweet, like gone-off orange juice mixed with cola and the eye-watering tang of spirits. She leaves through the still-open door into the corridor where the smell switches to old cabbage and lumpy vomit piled in the corner. Where the dirty glass failed to rile her delicate insides, that smell does, and she leans against the wall as heat rises up her neck. She holds it together, swallows back some chunks, then finds Georgie in much the same position as she was, with a woman Iris doesn't recognise, whose arm is significantly harder to move out of the way than the man's was. Georgie groans as Iris gently shakes her awake, rubbing sleep from her eyes. A sticky trail of saliva traces across her chin, which her hair is stuck to. Iris ducks into the nearest apartment to find a damp cloth, then wipes Georgie's face before fetching her a glass of water.

'Come on, G. It's time to go.'

Georgie kisses the woman firmly on the mouth as she mutters her goodbyes, then she and Iris stagger out of the apartment.

The pre-dawn dimness is garishly bright with the Flake still enhancing Iris's vision. The moonlight bounces off windows and pavement, scattering in starbursts. Iris screws up her eyes, regretting she doesn't have her sunglasses. From the looks of it, they're not the only low Scorers just leaving various apartment block parties to shuffle home, though the bike traffic is mercifully light, and they can amble along in the slow lane without too much dodging and hassle.

'I had such a fun night,' Georgie says, sounding more asleep than awake. 'You?'

Iris rubs her forehead, struggling to remember most of it. 'Yeah, I think so.'

There was talk about anti-Society stuff, dangerous talk. No Society Policing, she's sure of that. Though they did swap numbers. Did she say anything stupid? Probably, though she hopes not too stupid. She doesn't think she was that drunk, though based on how much her head is still swimming, maybe she was. She yawns as she tries to remember. Someone had said something about Life Scores or Society Police. She'd introduced herself, and they acted like they knew her name. Was that real or some fake memory? She can picture a haze of colours and hear their raised voices over the music, blurred and distorted.

Dangerous being in such a state. Dangerous and dumb. She could have said something she shouldn't. Can she trust these people? She looks up at the road ahead, and her legs ache before she's even put any real effort in. It's all uphill on the way home, and at their sleepy pace it'll take another ten minutes at least, but Iris isn't sure if she has the strength. Georgie appears stable enough to turn her head without swaying her bike. She's faring much better and puts her hand on Iris's handlebars.

'Come on,' she says. 'I'll get you home and make us some food.'

The sliver of moon and flickering streetlights are unhelpful as, just a few seconds' cycle away, they collide with a mass blocking the bike lane. For a moment, Iris is transported back to Thursday night, but there's a stillness to the early hour. There's no one lurking in alleyways, no blinding bike lights after them.

The early morning is inert. Iris overcorrects the collision, and her bike tips the other way, then she tumbles off and braces herself to hit the tarmac. Instead, her landing is soft. Too soft. Squishy.

'Iris!' Georgie shouts. She's staring straight at Iris, and she speaks slowly, enunciating every syllable like Iris is deaf. 'Take my hand. Don't panic. Don't look down. Just take my hand.'

Iris stiffens at Georgie's tone but reaches for her hand. She grasps, realising it's the same softness as the mass below. She swallows, her mouth even more parched than it was a moment ago. 'Georgie!'

'Don't look, Iris. I've got you.' And she heaves Iris to standing.

Iris dusts off her backside and elbows, keeping her eyes on Georgie. It doesn't feel like gravel and dust that coats her clothes though. It's sticky.

'Look at me, Iris. Okay?' Georgie is stern. There's no uncertainty, no room for argument. 'Get back on your bike. When we get home, close your eyes and strip your clothes off and jump in the shower. Okay?'

Iris's head trembles into a nod. Georgie never speaks in such a way. The tone of her voice is like a captain instructing a crew on a sinking ship, but Iris doesn't want to see, doesn't want to know what's made Georgie react in such a way, and certainly doesn't want such an image burned onto her mind. Georgie passes her bike to her, and they ride as Georgie tells Iris to keep looking straight ahead.

Don't look back. Don't look down.

It's not long before, under a dim streetlight this time, they come across another such mass, spotting it this time before either collides with it. And another.

And another.

Iris's instincts had known what she'd fallen on, but seeing it makes her taste bile. The chunks she swallowed back earlier are fighting their way back up. Despite the chill of the early hour, sweat stings her eyes and the street spins around her.

'Oh, my God, Georgie.'

The streets smell like metal, not the rotten stench of an old corpse. These are all fresh, blood still pumping, limbs twisted and contorted in fight or flight. In the stillness, the gurgling sound of escaping fluid trickles down a drain. The streets are otherwise quiet. Too quiet.

There are too many bodies to count. They're piled up, fleshy mounds of death, panic still on their faces, clawing to get over each other, to flee — a futile attempt to cling on.

Georgie sniffs back tears. 'What the hell happened here?'

Swallowing is no longer sufficient to keep the vomit down and Iris's throat gives in. She throws up onto the pavement, washed with more guilt than nausea as some splatters onto a body. A young woman, tattered clothes, thin, likely un-Scorable. Her eyes are still open, her mouth frozen wide in a silent scream.

All of them look like the lowest of Scorers. Poor. Disposable in the view of the Eyes Forward. The conversations of the night flood Iris's memory. With her hangover gone, their voices replay with perfect clarity. Snapping her head around, one way, then the other, the freshness of the blood, still liquid and trickling, is what makes her realise.

Whoever did this could still be out here.

They listen for cries or screams or some sort of commotion. There's nothing. It's like this was an ambush, some killer coming from the shadows and massacring the lot in seconds.

'My parent's place is closer,' Iris says.

'Let's go there.'

They race on their bikes like they never have before. Weaving around bodies — hitting a few, they both stumble more than once. There's no point checking any for signs of life. Whoever did this was thorough.

They arrive at Iris's parents' and hammer on the door. It's five-thirty a.m., not the usual time for visitors. There's no answer, and Iris curses their new place. She had a key for the old one. They probably think it's some drunk or hooligan. Iris calls her mum's phone.

'Mum! It's Iris. Open up.'

Mae comes, slowly, riddled with sleep, to open the door. 'Iris. What time—' She gasps. 'My God, what happened?'

Iris and Georgie run inside, then slam the door behind them, panting ragged breaths. They're safe.

For now.

Chapter 20
Iris

Mae tells them both to have a lie down, but they don't sleep. Sleep eludes them, as every time they close their eyes, all they see is death. They shower, using up a precious amount of Mae and Pasha's water, washing their hair and scrubbing themselves raw. Mae gives them clean clothes, and they curl up together in the spare room, holding each other, not wanting to let go. Iris can tap out the beat of Georgie's hammering heart, suspecting hers is just as hard.

They try to explain to Mae, but they have no words for the horror. Words don't exist to describe something so awful. There was so much death. A rancid carpet of gore.

There's nothing on the news. Not a word.

When dawn breaks, Iris switches on Pasha's computer, loads up Nebula, then searches through the Shadownet. She finds forums that break through autonomous systems where she can speak with people in other counties.

It's the same across the Society. Mass murder of low Scorers. Bodies. . .so many bodies and nearly all women. Un-Scorable women, some with babies still tied to their chests. Hard to identify, as their phones and devices were taken or broken.

It's been years since Georgie's browsed the Shadownet, and she reads with her mouth agape, her limbs trembling so much, she can't type. Iris's fingers brush the keyboard, searching for the questions they're not sure they want to know the answers to.

'What the hell is going on, Iris?'

Iris doesn't reply but keeps searching. She finds mentions of other topics first, some leak about the Pres-X problems years ago, about how the Sub 700s went insane. She takes photos of that article with her phone in case she can't find it again, then keeps scrolling.

For answers, for an explanation, for some justification.

There are patrols on the Shadownet. The usually safe space for people to air their concerns is no longer some secluded chatroom. Forums are being taken down. The Eyes Forward cyber security are ramping up their efforts like never before. They usually leave people to gossip on the Shadownet, but now, forum after forum is gone. The words fizzling out quicker than Iris can read them. Search results pop up, then are replaced with error messages and that damned walled-in eye logo seconds later.

Even the Sisters and Spies have been silenced.

Iris sits back, biting her nails, then scratches her head. Next to her, Georgie hugs her knees, silent tears tracing her cheeks.

There is no answer, no explanation, no justification, just a wall of silence like that damned Eyes Forward logo. A cave.

Iris peers at Georgie, her glassy eyes like mirrors reflecting her own anguish. What do you do when there is no one to help? No one who cares.

But you care, Iris.

The voice lights a spark inside. She hadn't realised she'd been missing it, but with the Shadownet silenced that voice is the friend she needs. The voice of reason, of encouragement. Where her thoughts were spiralling from dark place to an even darker place, that voice makes all her thoughts converge into one straight line, to one single focus that's pinpoint sharp.

Iris scrolls her phone contacts. She got some numbers last night for the people they were talking to, the people who want to take action. She can't talk to them online, but they can meet face-to-face.

Her dad is awake now. His wheelchair squeaks through the hallway.

'Iris, sweetheart?'

'Yes, Dad.'

'Come here.' He opens his arms for a hug and Iris rushes to them. She cries and cries. Georgie gives them a minute, then joins in, all of their arms enveloping. Mae watches from the corner. Iris glances over as the sunlight reflects off a tear Mae's yet to shed.

'What's happening, Dad?'

He holds on tighter. 'I don't know. But you're safe, okay? You'll stay here—'

‘No.’ Iris pulls back. ‘I have to go out. I have to meet some people.’

‘Absolutely not,’ Mae says, as stern as Georgie sounded earlier. ‘Please, darling. Stay here where we know it’s safe. Your friends can come here if they like.’

Georgie nods. Mae and Pasha’s place is as good a meetup place as any.

Iris calls the people she spoke to last night, shaky fingers struggling with the touchscreen, but she manages, not wanting to text, not wanting anything detectable. Woozy, hungover voices answer, those who are still passed out at the party. They haven’t even left yet. They still have the tranquillity of not knowing, of thinking their hangover is the worst part of their day. Others answer with the quiver of panic, those who made it home. Those who saw the massacre. Iris tells them the address. Some say they’ll come.

Blue Hair arrives first. Skylar’s hair is bluer in daylight than it appeared at the flat party. She’d cycled home alone and had much the same experience as Iris and Georgie.

She sits in the living room, sinking low into the chair, her legs tired more from shock than her cycle. Her eyes are red, her face almost as pale as a corpse. ‘They’re gone. The bodies. Did I imagine it? There were so many.’

‘Really?’ Iris and Georgie both say.

‘Honestly. The streets are clean. I feel like I’m going insane.’ She gives the impression she could be. Her eyes are wild, and her body shakes like she’s the one who did the killing. If Iris hadn’t seen it for herself, she wouldn't believe Skylar. 'Did you take photos last night?'

'No,' Iris says with a hint of regret. 'God, I didn't think to. We just fled.'

'There's some blood stains,' Skylar continues, wiping her eyes. 'But even those bodies that have been there for ages have gone.'

Big Shoulders and Spectacle-Wearer arrive next. Johan appears angrier than Iris has ever been. Iris backs away from him as he comes in, worried he'll explode.

'Who the fuck is doing this? We just left the party but loads left and came back. All saying what they saw. I went for a peek and came straight back for Tash.'

Tash seems like she can handle herself, as well as Johan. She's almost as broad. Even her spectacle frames are robust. 'What the hell? It's not on the news. Nothing.'

Ezra, the man with the high-pitched voice and buzzcut arrives last, face tear-streaked. He can barely get his words out through his panicked breaths. 'My sister. I can't get in touch with her. She's un-Scorable. She had a baby. My little nephew. I haven't heard from them.'

'You reported them missing?' Iris asks.

'Of course. But just a standard reply. I sent their ID for facial recognition. If any Society Police take a picture, they'll let me know. That's it. I've tried to call their friends, other un-Scorables. Nothing. I went to their dorms. There's normally tons of people holed up in there, kids screaming. The place smelled weird, like, I dunno, like some sort of solvent. I can't describe it. Not clean, like some gassy smell. And it's empty. They've all gone. I couldn't stay long. The building was creaking. I know that sound, we all do. It's about to fall down.'

Georgie rubs his arm, though he doesn't seem to feel her touch. 'Maybe they've gone to find a new dorm,' she says, her voice soft with sympathy. 'There's a few empty one's closer to town. I'll bet they've gone there.'

Ezra doesn't reply. Georgie's voice doesn't penetrate his fear. It's like she never even spoke. No one else says anything. No words of comfort or reassurance. The sinking feeling lodged in Iris's gut tells her what she knows, what she's sure they all know. She doesn't need telling, but the voice returns anyway.

You know what happened to them, Iris. And you know who did this.

Chapter 21
Iris

The six of them search the streets all Sunday afternoon. Pasha and Mae's pleas of asking them to stay indoors land on deaf ears. They walk out, all holding hands, a chain of fear and determination. And Skylar was right. The bodies have gone. All of them.

They leave bikes, opting to walk instead, worried they'll miss something if they move too quickly. A clue, a cry for help, some evidence of what happened.

Georgie holds Iris's hand so tightly it cramps. They link arms instead, the sides of their torsos touching, seeking every bit of comfort they can. Occasionally, Georgie pauses to blow her nose, to sob, for her knees to go weak. Iris doesn't let go. Georgie's screams from the other night haunt her as much as the massacre. She can't lose Georgie. She'll never let her go.

The streets are still quiet, desolate compared to the usual hubbub. The breeze is normally blocked by people, bikes, the traffic of life. Now the wind howls with abandonment.

The Eyes Forward posters and billboards still hang everywhere. They all walk up to one with a smear of blood across the bottom, smudged across the *ETC* graffiti. Iris glances at Ezra, and he takes a tissue from his pocket to wipe some of it.

'DNA,' he says. 'I might be able to send it somewhere. We all sent our DNA in for the new algorithm, didn't we? Maybe they can test it.'

'Good idea,' Iris says in her softest voice.

Whenever she's seen a dead body before, and it's been clear it's an un-Scorable, she's assumed no one cares. Since no one collects the body, it's never investigated, there's nothing in the press. But that's part of the illusion, she realises. Ezra is proof of that. Even the poorest have people who love them. It's not only the high Scorers that matter.

Most citizens don't know. Around the shops and bars people carry on about their day like normal, like Berkshire still has a beating heart. If they hadn't been on the streets in the brief window when the bodies were visible, if they hadn't been on the Shadownet before the forums were taken down, if they hadn't spoken to anyone, they'd never know. The news still reports nothing except the new Life Score algorithm hype, the bars that are putting up bunting to celebrate, and the Eyes Forward's jubilation at the coming upgrade. A very excitable anchor reports on the update that second doses of Pres-X-2 will soon be available and isn't that just the most marvellous thing for the 700 pluses? Nothing about any massacre anywhere. A bubble of ignorance. Decoy politics. Surely, if the news isn't reporting some massacre, it didn't happen. If the government isn't acknowledging it, it can't be important.

The only clue is the emptier pedestrian and cycle lanes and the lack of screaming kids, crying out their worries from the un-Scorable dorms. The only evidence is the lack of volume.

They haven't found Ezra's family. They wander the streets, search the un-Scorable powdered rations centres, then check other dorm buildings. There's gossip among lower Scorers, hints of concern, but no one speaks too loudly. Again, the lack of volume is the most disconcerting thing. Mere whispers against the shouting of normalcy.

If no one else had seen it, Iris would assume it was a hallucination, another aftereffect of the Flake.

I'm not a hallucination, Iris. Nor were those bodies.

She nods a response to the voice. Its breathy tone has a desperation Iris feels, like it's fuelled by her fear.

By the time they make it back to Ezra's family's building to see if they've come home, it's gone, collapsed into nothing. A shower of dust hangs over it in a halo of loss. Another pile of rubble to add to the others.

Ezra drops to his knees, his hands on the ground, and howls the sort of howl that the others feel in their stomachs, the sort that pulls tears from your eyes. A haunting sound of despair. They all sit beside him on the tarmac and cry too. They cry for his loss, for the loss to the whole Society. People walk around them, giving them a wide berth instead of care. The onlookers don't need to speak. Their faces say it all: no big deal. It's just what happens. They should have known better than to create a burden. They probably think it's some un-Scorables who've lost their home. They probably think their burdensome child was in the building when it fell.

'They should strive more rather than rely on old buildings,' one pedestrian says.

Iris doesn't bother to see who said it. She has no strength to retaliate. One hand holds Georgie's, while the other slams her knuckles into the pavement. Her blood stains the ground. One more citizen's blood.

The smell hasn't left Iris's nose. It scorched her senses. When she hugs herself in the cold, her flesh feels like their flesh. When she looks at people's faces, it's their eyes she sees staring back. When she glances at Georgie, she's as pale as the bodies.

She receives a message from Ella: *If you are out at your low Score parties this weekend, don't forget your assignment.*

Her shoulders tense, her neck cracks, and she pockets her phone. Her vision clouds over. She doesn't see what's in front of her, doesn't see the ground or the people. All she sees is Ella and the other highest Scorer's faces when she destroys the system.

Somehow, she will destroy it all.

The Flake is well out of her system, but its impression remains. Her determination lingers and cramps. It hasn't waned into inaction like last time. She can't shut her eyes nor deny what's happening.

Fuck this. Fuck this whole system.

Use that anger, Iris.

The voice is the only thing that makes sense. The only logical sound in the madness. She doesn't try to shut it away. She listens and nods like it's an old friend.

In the others, she sees the motivation, the heartbreak leading to a desire for action. Iris's anger is shared, multiplied.

One person inciting a riot is nothing more than a tantrum. A group, that's a rebellion.

They haven't said another word about their idea, fear stapling their mouths shut. But she feels it in the air, sees their cheeks rippling over grinding teeth. As Iris is about to mention it, a siren blares through the street, so loud they all cover their ears. It dulls after a few seconds and is replaced with every phone and device ringing and vibrating. Iris, like everyone, grabs her phone. The message fills the screen:

Criminal activity concerns. Every Sub 400 must go home. Curfew implemented immediately.

Chapter 22
Iris

Back in their cold apartment, Iris and Georgie huddle together on the sofa, sharing a blanket and allowing themselves one cup of hot tea between them. The news announcement takes forever, and Iris loads up her phone, remembering her new internet access.

'How come you can get online?' Georgie asks.

'My boss said I could. Because of the quarterly update coming, she might need me to work.' The lie comes too easily. Yet next to the horribleness of the weekend, one small fib seems like nothing.

She doesn't have the Shadownet browser on her phone but checks the normal news sites: *Announcement coming soon. All Sub 400s to stay at home*, is all it says. At least they're doing something, Iris thinks. At least they're taking action.

Iris looks at the forum photos she saw earlier that she didn't get time to read properly. Some leak about Pres-X being poisoned by XL Medico, another way the Eyes Forward tried to eliminate the less well-off, to try to create their utopian Society of no one but the rich. The leak seems legit, with evidence and science that Iris can't really understand, but goes to much greater lengths than any trivial gossip.

Before that, there's the selfies they took the night prior. Smiling, drunk, oblivious of what was to come. In the background of one is something Iris didn't expect to see. She zooms in, sure she must have it wrong, but the bigger image confirms it. Angus. What the hell would he be at a flat party for? And looking at what's in his hand, he's passing someone a large quantity of Flake.

Angus is a Flake dealer?

The idea is so preposterous, Iris can't fathom any reasoning. She doesn't have time to either as the news start-up tune blares through the TV and pulls their attention. Like Tash and Johan and Ezra and Skylar, and all the other low Scorers who know, they're expecting to see a news story about the massacre, to explain where the bodies went, that the curfew is for their own safety as someone's targeting the lowest Scorers. For some warped assumption of fairness and empathy, they expect to hear the Society Police and the Eyes Forward are investigating with all their resources, that they promise to find out what happened, that their thoughts are with the families.

The news reader hands the spotlight straight over to an Eyes Forward representative whose face is as deadpan as ever, his eyes half-hidden under the shadow of his hat. His black suit is the only part that indicates he could be mourning, but they always wear that.

'An evil and terrible tragedy has occurred in Berkshire,' he says, his voice lacking any variation in pitch.

Iris and Georgie brace themselves for the story, for the details they witnessed, for the full tale of the horror.

'A senior Eyes Forward representative has been murdered. Lloyd Porter was a valued member of the Eyes Forward and has been instrumental in the Society's function over the past decades. His murder has shocked the core of the Eyes Forward.'

In the pause he takes for dramatic effect, Iris and Georgie exchange glances, their comprehension is muddled, it must be. Perhaps he's building up to the worst bit, easing them into the most awful news.

He continues. 'Understand that this murder will be investigated with all the resources we have. We believe it's linked to the new street drug, Flake. Anyone caught in possession of this drug will be stripped of all their points. Any un-Scorable found in possession will be imprisoned.'

Iris rubs her eyes with the balls of her hands while Georgie massages her temples. Did he just say that?

'All Sub 400s will be under curfew until we have a lead on the murder. Between the hours of seven p.m. and seven a.m. weekdays, and all-day weekends, low Scorers must be at home or have a permit signed off by an 800 plus explaining their reasons for being out. We are appealing to witnesses to give evidence for this most appalling of crimes. Rest assured we shall leave no stone unturned—'

Georgie mutes the TV and stares at the picture of the murdered man that now fills the screen. 'They're kicking off about the murder of one of their own? One. One murder. What about the entire un-Scorable block that's disappeared?'

Iris's mouth hangs open, taking a while for her to form words. 'They don't care. They literally don't care.'

'But we saw it. It wasn't just the drug, was it?'

Doubt seeps into Georgie's voice, as it does in Iris's thoughts. They did see it. She's sure, isn't she?

'Come on, G,' Iris says, stamping some assuredness into her tone. 'We saw it, touched it, smelled it. Our clothes were covered in muck. They just don't care.'

That's the painful truth, an old wound re-ripping, never healing, like an infection that is never tended to.

The un-Scorables don't matter. The low Scorers don't matter. The Eyes Forward think a massacre of poor women matters less than the killing of one rich man.

Chapter 23
Mae

Mae hasn't moved from her seat since the news announcement. She didn't jump up to clean the drink she knocked over in shock and hasn't even snapped at the ever-present band on her wrist. Her knitting lays idle on her lap, a dropped stitch or two that she hasn't noticed.

'How are you?' Pasha asks, his tone etched with concern. His hand reaches for her, but she doesn't reciprocate any affection. She can't feel his warmth.

'I'm fine,' she says, as if on autopilot. It's what he always says, so why not her?

'Mae-bug. Talk to me. Your father just died.'

She hears the worry in his voice. Emotion, what's that like? She feels nothing. There's a vacuum where feelings used to be, like her father's death has killed her senses.

'I haven't seen him in years. I wasn't even sure he was still alive. What is there to say?'

'How you feel about it.'

He'd love her less if he knew how she felt, that as the shock wears away, she's fighting off a smile. If she was a higher Scorer and allowed out, she'd go and buy some champagne. Although, thanks to her father and the Life Score system he devised, she can't afford champagne.

'I feel nothing,' she says. She's being half truthful. She just doesn't finish the sentence. Nothing but joy. . .nothing but relief. . .nothing but distrust. It's hard to believe he's actually dead. Such evil people don't expire so easily. Evil just keeps on living.

At least Iris doesn't know who he was, and she'll never know. They opted to keep Mae's family a secret from her. There was no sense in telling her that her genome is threaded with such wickedness.

'Does my lack of sadness make me immoral?' she asks. 'Perhaps deep down, I'm as bad as him.'

His shaky hand tightens its grip, and she places her other hand on top, squeezing, trying to convey her strength and resolve, to be his sturdy rock in a rushing river, then she releases his hand, picks her knitting back up, and fixes the dropped stitches. 'I'm fine. Really.'

Chapter 24
Iris

The messages come as soon as the news finishes.

Tash: *What the fuck? One man!*

Johan: *Fuck that guy.*

Ezra: *Still no news from my sister.*

Skylar: *Who the hell is Lloyd Porter anyway?*

Similar expletives and disbelief circulate between them for hours, the tension rising. Iris's fingers slam into her phone harder and harder with every message, and Georgie breaks two nails but doesn't even care.

They want action, Iris. You are not alone.

In the week since she first took Flake, she thought she was alone, unable to articulate exactly where her unease came from. Nothing externally had changed. The Society was what it had been her entire life. The walls of the cave never changed. She changed though, and explaining that was like trying to explain eyesight to a worm. It's like she's discovered a whole new colour, and now Georgie sees it too. Iris doesn't have to think of the vocabulary, it doesn't matter. Once it's there, it's entrenched, the feeling, the knowledge that the way the Society is, isn't how it's meant to be.

The palpable anger on the message thread is heating up. It's not just empty words now, Iris is sure of it. There's a wrath that can't be contained, a thirsty vengeance that needs to be quenched. After the bitching and rage has sizzled on for long enough, Iris plucks up the courage to ask the question, the one she hopes they're all itching to ask: shall we put a stop to this?

The replies come through from all four straight away. A simple answer: yes, combined with a fuck yeah from Johan.

They formulate a plan — an aim, at least — take on the root cause of the Society's injustices, and they're all in agreement about how to go about it.

The plan is simple enough: disband the Society Police, dismantle the classist Life Score system, and overthrow the Eyes Forward.

'Yeah, really simple,' Georgie says, her voice dripping with sarcasm. She's not lost any enthusiasm for the cause. She's just like Iris, still fairly clueless about how they're going to implement such a plan.

Perhaps if Iris keeps thinking it's simple, she'll begin to believe it. The task, in reality, seems impossible, although they're not without ideas. Tash, especially, is keen to flex her hacking muscles, and Johan is keen to flex every other muscle. If passion was enough, they'd achieve everything they're hoping for and more.

The team: Iris, an ex-genius coder and hacker. Georgie, an average coder wannabe TV presenter. Tash, an extremely good hacker — the more they get to know her, the more useful she sounds. Johan, an angry guy whose skills are limited to physical fighting. Ezra, a puddle of grief. And Skylar. . . Iris isn't sure what she'll be useful for.

A dream team.

If only that team was also armed with state-of-the-art hacking gear and weapons.

Iris doesn't sleep much on Sunday night. She doubts any of them do. What they may lack in resources they make up for in determination. Somehow, they're going to do it. They're going to take the Eyes Forward down.

***

The atmosphere at work on Monday is jovial. Iris's body is like a dead-weight, and she drags it to her desk, the weekend bearing down on her as if she were under the rubble.

The Preserved and other high Scoring staff are beyond excited, laughing over their coffee cups, the usual array of compliments towards each other only peppered with the odd mention of the tragedy that is Lloyd Porter's death.

Iris sits alone in her dark corner, her computer hiding her face, for which she is thankful. They can't see her snarling at their every joke and laugh, can't see her face turning beetroot-red with rage.

She half wishes she could shut her ears like she can her eyes. The other half of her wants to listen in. The main subject of their excitement is some big meeting for the highest Scorers tonight at the old church in the centre of town. Some local celebrities will be in attendance, much to the delight of Ella and Francis. Even Ava Maricelli is giving a speech.

'It's so exclusive,' Ella says to Francis. 'And this will be my first meeting as a 900 plus.'

'Got a few points over the weekend too, thanks to the Eyes Forward incentive.' Francis leans in like she's trying to be subtle, but her voice lacks the dulcet pitch of modesty.

The mention of an incentive lurches to Iris and grabs her attention. Kira, from the bar, had mentioned some incentive, and there were similar rumours at the party as well. She pauses her typing to lean in a little.

'Can't wait to see that curve in a few days,' Ella says, rubbing her hands together. 'When the tallies are in.'

Iris may have been slacking at work last week, but she wasn't completely vacant. She scratches her head, trying to think if there was something she's forgotten. Perhaps they've finally implemented one of her ideas, although an incentive that only benefits the highest Scorers doesn't ring any bells.

'Such nasty business, this Lloyd Porter murder,' Francis says. 'Still, at least that means the low Scorers are under lock and key. Keeps things simple.' She glances Iris's way, and Iris diverts her gaze.

Their chortling laughter makes Iris's blood boil. How can anyone be so delighted? Don't they see what's happening? Don't they understand? One high Scorer gets killed and they implement curfew. Hundreds of low Scorers get massacred, and there's not a whiff of concern anywhere.

Use that anger, Iris.

How? What is she going to do? Punch them in the face? She'd sure as hell like to knock their teeth out, dent those plasticky preserved complexions forever. Ella and Francis are so vacuous they'd cave right in after one blow. Iris straightens and curls her fingers, stretching out the limbs she wants to use, to slam all her hate into one fist.

Ella and Francis walk to their office, Ella dropping her phone on the way. She bends to pick it up and her back cracks so loudly, Iris startles. Ella's hand flies to her mouth, while a tremble ricochets down her arm and her eyes glisten with tears.

'Francis,' she says, so quietly. If Iris wasn't paying attention, she'd miss it. 'It's happening again. It's too soon!'

'Oh, Ella. It's just a crack. Even kid's joints crack.'

Ella grabs some paperwork and peers at the words, moving the page closer, then further away. 'I can still see to read. Thank God!'

'There, there.' Francis rubs her shoulder. 'You're all right. Let's get you some tea.'

'Caffeine? No! No more. It's ageing. I can't. Oh, God. I'm ageing too quickly again!'

Iris's lips twitch into a smile, and she angles herself to hide behind her computer more. This spectacle occurs in one form or another most days, and it's Iris's most entertaining part of her work life. Her Preserved and Desirable bosses seem to forget the preservation drug turns back the clock but doesn't stop it dead. They still age, they just start over. Now Ella and Francis are panicking about the odd wrinkle creeping in, how tired they appear if they miss a night's sleep.

Iris bites her lips, trying to stop her laugh as she sips her tea, free of the dread that consumes her Preserved bosses. They glare at her often, even pinch her cheeks sometimes, and comment on her tired eyes. They appear to be mid-thirties but scowl when they see Iris looking fresh-faced. Are likely to point out any blemish, such as her lack of makeup, nitpicking their way through Iris's faults in a poor taste attempt to validate their own minor aesthetic flaws. It's only jealousy, Iris is sure. They both must be about a hundred and twenty years old. Iris can see the naivety of youth has long gone from them. That's what they envy, not Iris's skin or hair or eyesight. But she has the sheer bliss of cluelessness of what is to come. Nothing delicious ever tastes as good as it does the first time you eat it. Their old Preserved lives have the bitter taste of experience.

Iris smiles as Ella and Francis's joviality warps into worry. There's something sadistic about taking pleasure in other's troubles, but Ella's back cracking is hardly trouble. In lieu of physical violence, a chuckle at her boss's minor ailments is the best she can manage.

***

Iris stays at the office later, not doing much, just dreading going home. She doesn't want to get home before Georgie, doesn't want to worry. Sure, Georgie will worry about her, but she can handle that better right now. Georgie is far more pragmatic. She won't panic over a few minutes like Iris.

When there's only half an hour before curfew, Iris makes to leave. Ella and Francis are in the ladies room, staying late to go straight to their exclusive meeting at the old church rather than go home and back again. Through the window to their office, Iris watches them touch up their makeup and tidy their hair. On the desk just outside the office is Ella's phone. It's been there all day since she dropped it before her back-cracking panic.

Iris pauses. There's no one else around, as always, no one paying her any attention. It's just her, and the phone of a 900 plus.

You know what to do.

The voice is sinister in its instruction, a steady certainty. Iris glances around again, then her arm moves, making the decision before her brain catches up.

Fuck it.

She swipes it, putting it in her pocket before she changes her mind, and makes for the old church.

Iris cycles hard and fast into town. It's not far, just a couple of minutes, and she pushes through the fast lane all the way. She parks her bike a little way away so she doesn't arrive looking like the low Scorer she is, then walks the last hundred metres or so. Across the checkerboard paving slabs, weeds poke up through the gaps. Such small plants, she thinks. So weak. They're nothing really. But there they are, pushing up and rising above the concrete. They make entire buildings out of concrete and the spindly things can still take hold. Even the strongest substances are brittle if the opposition is determined enough.

She flashes Ella's phone with her 900 Life Score shown on her way in. She doesn't look Preserved, she knows this. She looks exactly like a twenty-eight-year-old low Scorer, scrawny and badly dressed, but in the sea of other arrivals, she's disguised behind flamboyant coats and handbags and somehow goes unnoticed.

She hovers at the back, alone, trying to blend in with the shadows. The church hasn't been used as a religious building in decades, but inside still has the damp scent of old incense and candles. The stained-glass windows remain in some walls, though the religious scenes have been repainted with the Eyes Forward logo on some. The walls crumble like so many old buildings, but joists have been erected internally to save the top Scorer meeting house and its precious attendees. Iris chances her luck and grabs a few hors d'oeuvres from a silver platter, then eats them, trying not to groan. Fresh soft cheese on flaky pastry, topped with fig. Real fig, not dried. It's the sort of high Scorer food only available at the more exclusive delis. For a moment, she thinks she should strive to Score more if it means food like that.

But everyone deserves good food, Iris.

Yeah, yeah, she replies to the voice, mouthing the words without making a sound. I know.

She takes in the room, the who's who of Berkshire, all chatting and laughing. Mostly Preserved, some still have the rosy glow of a recent Pres-X-2 treatment. She counts four Eyes Forward representatives, although, since they're walking around and all look the same, it's hard to be sure. Ava Maricelli is mingling among the crowd. She appears so much smaller than her many photos. They must digitally enhance her muscles. Her biceps are big, but nowhere near as bulky in real life. Her face is less mean too, less stern, more solemn.

Norman and Jason Bonnet are walking around the room, slapping the backs of the other men, giving slow and seedy looks to the women. Norman takes an hors d'oeuvre from a plate and licks his lips before eating it, though Iris thinks the lip-licking has more to do with the woman he's staring at in front of him. She shivers, like she feels his eyes on her, like his drool is trickling down her neck. The rest of the hors d'oeuvres she has in her hand are no longer appealing.

Across the hall, she spots — of all people — Angus. Her bratty cousin converses with the top Scorers. Iris picks at some pastry between her teeth as she watches him cruising around like he fits in. He's maybe a 500, nowhere near an 800 plus. What the hell is he doing here? More Flake dealing? She turns her eyes, employing her childhood logic — if she can't see him, he can't see her. Yet her scalp prickles with unease, and she tucks herself deeper into the corner.

She messages Georgie, telling her she'll be home late. She's still got Ella's phone, so she can get away with being out past curfew if anyone catches her, as long as they don't use facial recognition software. It's a risk, a big one. But what's she got to lose, a few measly points? She has knowledge to gain, and that is far more valuable. She wants to know what this incentive is, what the high Scorers are so hyped up about.

Through the doorway, her breath catches as she spots Francis and Ella, and she tucks herself a little deeper behind the tall velvet drapes that line the room. Ella's face is flushed, likely from explaining her way past the guards in the absence of her phone.

Shit.

Iris angles away from them and pulls her shirt up to cover as much of her hair as she can. It's not like she has her mother's fiery red locks, but her tight curls might prove distinctive.

Ella's shrill whisper edges closer. 'I know someone here has it. I can track it on your phone. Some low Scoring skank has taken it.'

'Shh, Ella,' Francis says. 'You don't want to be known for losing your phone.'

Iris leaves the phone on the nearest table and finds another corner, closer to Angus, Francis and Ella creeping up behind. This was a stupid idea. What did she think would happen?

The room is full now, stalling Ella and Francis's walk around as they bump shoulders and chat and plaster on smiles for all the high Scoring citizens. The lights dim across the space and spotlights brighten the stage. The room quietens down, those still chatting get hushed by others, and Ava Maricelli steps up to the microphone. In the spotlights, Iris finds it hard to believe she's the demon Society Police they say she is, the most well-known Eyes Forward stooge. She stands with rounded shoulders in a black linen suit, her long dark hair plaited with loose wisps flying free.

'Thank you all for attending tonight,' Ava says in a voice that makes her seem softer still. 'The events of the last few days have been dramatic, but the Eyes Forward want you all to know that your Society Police are here for you. The early start to the incentive caught a lot of us off guard. It seems there was a hack, emailing some of you to begin the cull early. We apologise for this, and the hack is being dealt with. Rest assured your points will still be counted, but the incentive is still on hold for now until we can work out all the technical glitches and ensure the safety of all participants. For the next couple of weeks, kills will not count towards your Score.'

There's a resounding groan from the audience while Iris is so still, she struggles to draw breath. Gooseflesh coats every inch of her. An incentive. A cull. Her stomach churns at the word. Points being awarded. Each realisation chimes in her head like a grandfather clock.

Ava continues. 'I know that will disappoint some of you. But with the tragedy of Lloyd Porter's death, your safety is our first priority. Lloyd was an important member of the Eyes Forward, and this couldn't have come at a worse time. The Life Score algorithm update must happen in his absence, and the work he has been doing now needs to be redistributed. The Eyes Forward are finding a replacement as we speak, but it does mean Life Score-tracking for the next few days will be less accurate than usual. The algorithm is a living thing, it is not as simple as keeping a computer running. Let us have a moment's silence for Lloyd Porter as we remember his great achievement.'

The crowd all dip their heads, giving Iris a chance to have a clearer look around. This is the incentive Ella and Francis were talking about. Her right hand is balled in a fist, and she squeezes it with her left. Those rumours she dismissed at the flat party were spot on. All those people killed were part of some incentive.

A firm grip on Iris's arm and a breathy, 'Come with me,' sounds in her ear.

If she wants to protest, she can't. The grip is firm, fingers bite into her bicep and she's yanked past a doorway into a hallway, carrying on right into the men's bathroom.

'What the hell are you doing here?' Angus asks when he releases his grip.

Iris rubs her arm where his hand was, the bruises already forming. 'I could ask you the same.'

'Past curfew. How the hell are you getting home safely?'

Safely? As if Angus cares about such a thing as low Scorer safety. 'I think my questions are much more important than yours. The Eyes Forward are actually incentivising this massacre? You know about this, don't you? Why? You're only a 500.'

His mouth forms a thin line, and he barely moves his lips to speak. 'I'm taking you home,' he says as he grasps her arm again.

Iris pulls free. 'Jesus Christ, Angus. I knew you were a snob, but this. . .this! You're pure fucking evil. Not surprising, given your mother.'

'Shut it, Iris. You don't understand.'

She spits in his face. 'Fucking murderer. Fucking scum.'

Iris makes for the door, then runs to her bike, sprinting as hard as she can, her heart already elevated, the burning in her lungs satisfying. She keeps her hands up, covering her face in case of any facial recognition software. She's way past curfew now, not that she cares about losing points. Fuck the points. But if anyone confronts her, she's going to slam her fist into their skull. When she cycles, she pedals as fast as she can, out of the saddle, pulling on the handlebars as much as pushing on the pedals. She should have punched Angus, should have punched them all. Should have burned that building down with all of them in there.

Soon, Iris. All of this you will do soon.

Chapter 25
Ava

Ava leaves the stage, pleased to be under normal lighting instead of the garishly bright spotlight that blinded her to the crowd's reactions. She smiles at those who wish to speak with her while stepping widely around groups of people, keeping her distance. She's learned over the years that's the best way to avoid engaging in conversation. She's a busy woman, they all know this. Eccentric, maybe. It's not a crime to be unsociable. One of XL Medico's top researchers, and she has her funeral business all on top of her Society Police duties. As a celebrity for the cause, everyone knows how packed her schedule must be, for that's what comes with her achievements and her devout service.

People will believe anything.

She nods, waves, and thanks them for coming. Some want to ask her about preservation drug advancements. When can they get their second dose of Pres-X-2? Can they halt ageing altogether? Surely a 900 plus shouldn't have to experience creaking bones and stiff joints, and surely there should be a vaccine to stop grey hairs by now. She's heard it all before. Hundreds of times. The highest Scorers are too important to get older. The economy relies on them being Desirable. No one wants to do business with a crone.

The wisdom of age with the aesthetics of youth, that's what they all demand. Although wisdom seems in short supply.

A few other utterances follow her this evening. They're getting even more sinister these days. Over the years, the entitlement of the highest Scorers has become laced with venom. Around the time of the quarterly population stat updates, this venom is at its most toxic.

'What are we going to do about the scourge of un-Scorables? Will the cull be enough?'

'Hasn't XL Medico found a way to enforce sterilisation of the burdensome low Scoring women yet?'

'Why should un-Scorables get a choice when the Society has no choice but to put up with them?'

'Surely the Eyes Forward can just let them starve. Punishment for Lloyd Porter's murder.'

'You know, if they were starving, that could make the incentive safer for us. Weaken their resolve a bit. We'd be doing them a favour.'

'Who do these low Scorers think they are? They do nothing for the Society.'

Ava bristles at their words, smiles through gritted teeth, and does her best to make her expression look like their words are worth considering. She glances past them, to the stained-glass windows with the Eyes Forward logo and imagines smashing their heads through it.

Ava's smile gets tighter and more pinched as she tries to maintain it. The soft, empathetic eyes she has mastered over the years from running the funeral home have hardened into narrow slits. Mandisa will tell her such expressions give wrinkles. She can say such things with an air of superiority. It's been nearly two decades since her Pres-X-2 treatment, and her skin is as smooth as it was the week after treatment. Mandisa's glossy hair is like a sheet of black diamond, although Ava knows she's dyeing it these days. Mandisa is always radiant despite her hectic time at work; trying to contain the recent leak about the Pres-X issues years ago hasn't been easy. The poor lamb. The press still hasn't run the story thanks to Mandisa and XL Medico's level of influence. Ava doubts the story will ever make the mainstream news.

Mandisa converses with the other high Scorers with ease and no tightness in her neck or facial muscles because Mandisa is one of them. Eighth generation British, she glides around the room full of supremacist snobbery. Ava can hardly stand to look at her these days. As beautiful as she is, it makes her skin crawl. She maintained some affection for her while Zia was alive, but her death put an end to the charade. It's like sucking on a sweet. It tastes nice, but at some point, you know it's going to rot your teeth.

Ava watches the egotistical gesticulations, combined with the cries of appreciation, 'Well, at least the Eyes Forward are finally taking action!' and finds a quiet place to stand. She definitely doesn't want to join in with conversations this evening.

Ava makes her way to the corner where Angus stands. He's been staring at her for ages, beckoning her with panic in his eyes, his brows lifting into a tense forehead before jutting his head back like he's trying to reel Ava in on a fishing line. She feels sorry for the kid. He knew what he was signing up for, but a whiff of danger and he crumples like a handkerchief. He's too young for this. Perhaps he wasn't the best choice for a business partner.

'What's wrong?' Ava asks.

'Iris. You know, Mae Taylor's daughter — my cousin — she was here.'

'She's an 800 plus?'

'No. God knows how she got in. Is this bad?'

Ava ponders this for a minute. She's not seen Iris since she was a kid, but if she's anything like her parents, this isn't a bad thing at all. She remembers her as a brilliant coder at a young age. No doubt Mae introduced her to Nebula and Sisters and Spies. Ava would be surprised if Iris is an Eyes Forward supporter and if she is, there's still no harm in her knowing anything. She makes a mental note to tap Iris's phone; keeping tabs on her might be the most cautious thing.

It dawns on Ava that Iris might not even know who she really is. Ava only discovered Iris's lineage information due to her excessive hours on Nebula. Iris Taylor's name comes up so often, she did her due diligence.

'No,' Ava says. 'She'll spread the word, I think, but I'll make sure. This could be good. Very, very good.'

Chapter 26
Iris

Iris messages the group as soon as she's safe in her apartment and not about to be busted for being out after curfew. With shaky fingers, and blurred vision from sweat and tears, she types: *They're killing them. It's true. It's a government-sanctioned massacre. Starts again in two weeks.*

She looks at the photo again of Angus and the Flake at the party, then uploads it to the Society Police app, but feels no better. It's not enough. She still wants to punch his face in.

Iris breathes out slowly, like she's pushing all the badness out of her, all the toxic air she inhaled in that room. She holds her stomach and pushes further, exhaling it all, all the tension and hate and doubt. When she inhales, it's with reality. They really are doing this. They really are going to kill the low Scorers. And they really are excited about it.

She goes to the bathroom, then throws up, using the final day's flush to get rid of that. No way can she leave a basin of puke to ferment until tomorrow.

It's a while before she gets a reply. Such news takes time to sink in. And when they do reply, it comes in the form of curse words and shock. Iris wishes she had proof, wishes she wasn't the only one who heard it, that it wasn't just her job to spill the bad news. It's the final nail in the coffin for Ezra's family. He'll know now their deaths were nothing more than a sick game.

Georgie messages to say she's spending the night at Sam's. Iris is alone in their flat, with no one to console her, no one to tell her she's doing the right thing by warning them. She paces and bites her nails until her fingers bleed. She needs to warn more than just those guys. Everyone should know what she witnessed tonight. But then, what can she do about it? She's still powerless. She sits, closes her eyes, then rubs them. The sight of the massacre is still so fresh in her mind. She can still feel the softness of the body beneath her. She shivers and almost throws up again.

If they can't find a way to stop it, is there any sense in telling them? Has she just filled their hearts with dread ahead of another massacre?

Shout it from the rooftops, Iris. Tell everyone.

The voice is right. If enough people know, they can defend themselves. If she spreads the word, maybe more have a chance to find safety. Once she's sure the nausea has passed, Iris eats some pasta and sauce leftovers, but she pushes it around her plate, her hunger quashed by her worries. For she knows, the rich and powerful get what they want. What chance does the will of the poor have up against the clout of the rich? The poor are fragile, brittle, easy to snap. The rich might as well be made of steel.

At least she and Georgie aren't the lowest Scorers. She takes some comfort in that. At least Georgie will be okay.

Chapter 27
Mae

It's been a long time since Mae's seen a dead body. She lives close to work, so she avoids the ones that crop up in the streets. The last body she saw was when Iris was born, and they were on that beach as Pasha's grandmother passed away. It was so peaceful for her. A pain-free end was the one silver lining of the government-enforced euthanasia from the times of the Great Unrest. She looked like she was sleeping as she cradled baby Iris in her arms. Grief came instantly in the sea of emotions that hit Mae after giving birth. Pasha's mixture of disbelief and joy ricocheted through him as his body shook with tears on top of his lack of medication. Mae was overwhelmed with love, for the tiny baby she'd been originally so reluctant to have and for the elder who gave her life. She'd never known such warmth inside her.

She hopes the dead body she's on her way to see now suffered a more harrowing end. A man who has enforced so much misery doesn't deserve the peace Pasha's grandmother was given. She hopes it hurt. That his last moments were full of fear. She hopes his eyes bulged in fright, and that he choked on his own blood, tinged with regret for all he had done.

It's funny. A lifetime of ambivalence towards the man, writing him out of her life, not knowing if he was alive or dead. Now she knows he's dead, she hates him.

Mae didn't expect to get the email naming her as next of kin. She didn't know her father was aware she was still alive. It seems silly to think he wouldn't have known. The Eyes Forward must keep tabs on everyone. There are no secrets in the Society.

She walks to the funeral home from her office, not wanting the speed of the bike. A slow journey preferable, delaying the inevitable. L.M. Funerals is the only place that caters to a high enough Score to tend to her father. It also happens to be owned by her ex-client and ex-friend, Ava Maricelli. She pauses, moving to the loitering area at the edge of the pedestrian lanes when the funeral home is in sight. She can catch her breath, cool off a bit. The pedestrian traffic is rife with body heat and stale air, or perhaps it's just her nerves.

She hasn't stepped foot on the premises in years, hasn't seen Ava in such a long time, not since Ava suggested going further than Mae was willing to for their cause. Their friendship struggled when Ava rose to greater heights. With power comes great ambition. It's easy for Ava. She has no one she cares about to endanger. Mae has too much to lose.

Mae takes a breath, squares her shoulders, then walks the final few paces.

As soon as she enters the funeral home, the smell of flowers is overpowering, and Mae's eyes take time to adjust in the low light. It's probably supposed to be soft and calming. Mae finds it dark and confusing. She knows her sight is failing early. It did last time she was at this age.

'Can I help you?' The man at reception wears a pained expression, oozing sympathy that Mae doesn't need.

'I'm Mae Taylor, the next of kin for Lloyd Porter. I believe his body is here.'

He clasps his hands in front of his chest, then offers a slow nod. 'My sincerest condolences. He's in the viewing room. Can I take your coat, and I'll show you through?'

Mae hesitates, takes a step back, then tugs on her sleeves. Does she actually want to see him? What benefit would that serve? At least she'd know the bastard is really dead. She looks at the door, then back at the receptionist, snaps the band on her wrist, then hands him her coat. 'Very well. Is Ava Maricelli on the premises?'

'No. Not today. She doesn't come in often.'

Her shoulders relax, and a little wave of relief takes her sweat away. At least that's one less person from her past she has to see today. 'No problem. Thank you.'

She follows him through to the viewing room, twenty paces to the door, then enters alone. She doesn't look for a while, opting to stare straight ahead at the wall instead until curiosity overrides all else.

Her lips retract at the sight of him. She never resembled him before he was Preserved. She was her mum's mini-me, all flaming hair and pale freckled skin. That's probably one reason why he had such distaste for her. It was only her intellect she inherited from him.

The body is lying flat, still wearing that goddamned suit. The blackest black with the walled-in eye logo embossed on the front lapel. It's all they ever wear. His hands are intertwined at his chest, as if clutching the heart he never had. She walks closer, right up to him, staring down at the man who gave her life, yet took everything from her. On the little adjacent table is a box of tissues. She won't be needing those. A chair, also, for if her knees give way to grief. She stays standing.

The coroner's report says he had seven slash wounds to his abdomen, though Mae can't see that through his suit. She fights the desire to check, to make sure the wounds are really there, that he's not about to spring back to life. The Preserved appear no different, dead or alive. His eyes are closed, but his complexion still has colour, and his collagen hasn't shrunk away. She reaches one hand out and pinches his cheek. A firm, sharp pinch, trying to bruise. A living person would flinch, but this corpse just lies there.

He is really dead.

He must be a hundred and forty years old now, though he seems the same age as Mae, a few years younger even. The signs of middle-age have crept in over his preserved skin. A slight off-colour under his eyes, fine lines across his still-plump skin, some furrow above his nose and across his stern forehead. No laughter lines. No surprises there.

Mae tilts her head to the side, and there's recognition. Though the angles of his features have blurred into the standard Eyes Forward visual mantra — a stronger jaw, lower hairline, steely expression — if she didn't know for certain it was her father, she would have dismissed him as any of the Eyes Forward representatives, so alike they all are, yet not like the father she knew. His black hair is unvaried in its tone, even at his stage of life. Unlike Mae, who seems to sprout a new grey hair daily, lightening her mass of red. He must have dyed his hair to match his suit. A smattering of grey wouldn't do. They'd be distinguishable.

Mae tries to think when she last saw him. When she gained grant funding to come up with the hypothetical formula. She was better than him. Smarter. He needed her. Then he ran off with her work, twisted it, and made the Society the elitist hellhole it is today. Her stomach heaves, and her throat burns as she thinks of all he's done, of how destructive he has been.

God, she hates him.

She should find words to say, but her tongue sits idle, her lips too tight to form words. What is there to say? Anything at all? To the man who created her yet never nurtured her. The man who gave her life yet never loved her. Some last utterances to the man who destroyed her and her country. But her mind is blank. She has no words for such hatred. Instead, she counts the floorboards, the flowers, and times the beat of the softly playing music.

She gazes at him a moment longer and the corner of her mouth lifts into a smile. She takes a deep breath, her lungs inflating fully, easily. A weight that has been pushing her down for so many years is gone.

He's gone. He's really gone.

She turns on her heel, then walks out.

'Again, condolences Mrs Taylor,' the receptionist says, his expression so pained she thinks he must have an injury he's trying to conceal.

'I assume the funeral finances are taken care of by his estate?' she asks.

'If that is your wish. I can speak to a probate lawyer. Do you have any requests for the service? I have some leaflets here.'

She disregards the leaflets. 'Keep it cheap. The most basic coffin. A mass cremation. No grave. No flowers. Let it be the most miserable shit show you can possibly put together.'

'Oh, erm. . .right. . .'

'Dispose of the ashes in the dustbin. Thanks very much.'

Mae fetches her coat before he has a chance to hand it to her, then exits the funeral home. The temperature has lessened. There's a cool breeze finding its way to her through the heavy pedestrian traffic, and she inhales the freshest air she has in a long time. Inflating. Light. Like a balloon. She glides back to work with a smile on her face and a fuck him on her lips.

Chapter 28
Iris

Iris drags herself to work the next day, out of habit more than care. Muscle memory gets her out of bed in the morning, puts on her clothes, then has her sit on her bike and glide down the hill. She doesn't instruct her limbs to do anything and feels nothing when the fabric of her shirt wraps around her body. The wind on her face is nothing. She's numb all over.

The streets are clean, quieter, no stench of rotting corpses today.

She scuffs her feet along the floor in the corridor, not concerning herself with creeping in as quiet as a mouse. What's the point of being demure and polite in the Society where all they care about is your Life Score? Jason and Norman aren't around — a small bit of good news.

Ella and Francis arrive, and for a split second, Iris sits up straighter and puts her hard-at-work face on. But only for a split second, again muscle memory guiding her. A moment later, her posture falters and she prefers an uncomfortable slouch and twinging back to looking enthusiastic about work.

'A great man was murdered,' Ella says, standing ostentatiously close to Iris's desk. 'Perhaps if you had discovered some

Flake dealers and helped the Society deal with these villains, Lloyd Porter would still be here today.'

Iris exhales loudly through her nose and continues tapping away at her keyboard. She's not typing anything legible, just faking it. They obviously aren't following up on the Angus-lead. No doubt they want a Sub 200 to be caught instead.

'The press needs the stats on Flake-usage. How many of the diabolical lower Scorers are using it, and its effect on violent crime and treason.'

Iris stops typing at this. They're asking for fairytales. 'There are no stats. No one is testing for Flake consumption. Violent crime rates are the same as always.'

'Well,' Ella says in a pitch akin to scraping nails on a wall. 'We'll see about that.' She walks away, her skinny legs stamping out each footstep, muttering something about how unhelpful low Scorers are.

Iris is no stranger to such comments, and she resumes her pretend typing. After a few minutes, Francis turns the TV up, her face full of glee as the reporter takes on their false sombre face. The expression they make appears firm and earnest, whereas Iris knows from Georgie, that particular newsreader bursts out laughing as soon as the cameras switch to commercial break, no matter how serious the story. He also likes to pass wind when interviewing people, just so they make their bad smell face at the time of his choosing. Quite the professional.

'We have heard from our statistics department that Flake is rampaging through the low Scorers, with violent crime up two hundred per cent as a result.' The person sitting next to the newsreader recoils his nose at the stat. He must have just let his gas rip.

'The new laws regarding Flake-usage seem ineffective as, so far, they have failed to curb its use. A reminder to all that being caught using Flake renders the criminal un-Scorable. Un-Scorables using the drug will serve prison time.'

Iris swallows and tries to remember the party at the weekend. No one was Society Policing, she's sure of it.

'The Eyes Forward and Society Police fear more heinous crimes, such as the tragic murder of Lloyd Porter. As a result, we have this message.' He lifts a piece of paper, then taps it on the table, as if he's reading from that instead of the autocue. 'The Society Police app will auto download on every device, and reporting crimes is no longer an option but essential. Anyone found not to be reporting a crime will be convicted of that crime. The app even works on women's phones when offline, so there is no excuse. Drastic times call for drastic measures, so it has been decided that women with Scores over 800 will now have internet access around the clock as men do, so they can keep an eye on the news for their security. This initiative will be closely monitored to check for any security irregularities. These changes are effective immediately.'

Francis turns the volume back down and faces Iris. 'Well, at least someone is doing something about all the low Scoring criminals.'

Breathe, Iris. Breathe. You'll put an end to this soon.

The voice calms her in a way that anger management therapy never did. It's almost as effective as being on a climbing wall. She's soaring above it all, rising above it. Their pretence is theirs alone.

Ella nods with Francis, 'Anyone not reporting it must be taking it, I think. And I'm sure that all those low Score junkies will be found out.'

Iris keeps her gaze on her computer screen, dodging eye contact, then she picks up a pen and jots down notes, or at least it looks like she's making notes. Doodling is what she's doing, doodling and avoiding the stares of the Preserved. She's a shitty liar. Her face always gives her away. She flushes too easily. It's something she can thank her mother for.

The newsreader's sombre expression is replaced with one of excited glee. 'In other news. Second doses of Pres-X-2 for the 700 pluses are to be rolled out of the factory soon! The refurbishment is on schedule thanks to Ro Developments. Here's Rolan Taylor to tell us all about it.'

That piques Iris's attention, and she looks up. Her uncle's face fills the screen. Her dad's brother looks so much like him, only with a squarer jaw, and his hair styled to straighten his curls.

'Here at Ro Developments, we have worked tirelessly to refurbish what was once the heart of Reading's community.' Iris is sure Rolan is using a different voice. He sounds deeper, huskier. Below Rolan's face are old photographs from decades ago, when the centre was once a shopping mall, then when it was nothing but a wreck. 'This old building is now being put to an exceptional use, to provide the Society with Pres-X-2. The new factory has been finished to a high standard with all the latest equipment.' The footage now leaves Rolan and shows the inside of the factory, smiling staff waving at the camera. 'We are breathing life into Reading town, and Ro Developments has many other projects lined up. The parts of the county most damaged during the Great Unrest are finally getting the attention they deserve. Ro Developments, the beating heart of Berkshire.'

Iris snaps her pen in half. It doesn't matter what the voice says now, she's so mad, she must have steam coming out of her ears. Fucking Rolan, her own uncle, profiting off the carnage. For every building that gets destroyed, every collapse of an un-Scorable dorm, he's going to be there to take the cheque for the rebuild. No wonder Angus is such an arse. Iris always thought Rolan was all right, and Moira was Angus's only elitist parent, but Rolan is just as bad. How is it he and her dad are brothers? Pasha would never have such an attitude.

Rolan is building the cave they all live in and plugging up the door.

All day, Iris sits in her corner, keeping herself to herself, plotting instead of working. She craves the climbing wall, some fresh air, to get away from the crappy office atmosphere. She watches her Preserved bosses parade about, chat and laugh, all the while a headache brews across her temples and her jaw aches with rigidity. Occasionally, they remind her to get on with her work and threaten her with points deduction. No doubt they're hoping to make her un-Scorable just so they can kill her in a few weeks' time.

Kill. That's actually what they want to do.

Her bones run cold, but however chilled she is inside, she burns hot with anger on the outside. She snaps two more pens before she tempers her rage. What did her anger therapist used to tell her? Count your breaths, imagine your anger filling a balloon and just letting it go.

What a load of crap.

When she gets home, she's just as angry. She locks her bike and slams her feet into each stair as she stomps up towards her flat. She opens the door, then slams it shut, kicking it afterwards and groaning from her stubbed toe. 'Fuck!' She grabs her foot with one hand and punches the door with her other. 'Fuck!' Now her hand also hurts. Is there no pain-free release for anger? No productive way?

Revenge, Iris. Revenge will help.

'I don't know how to get revenge! I don't know how to stop them!'

'Who you talking to?' Georgie appears from the bathroom. Her face is as red as Iris assumes her own is.

'Fucking high Scorers. Murderous scum,' Iris shouts.

Georgie sniffs and wipes her eyes on a tissue, then starts pacing and biting her nails.

'You thought of anything?' Iris asks. 'Have you got a plan? We need to do something. You know my uncle is profiting from the carnage too? He and his hideous 800 wife are going to rake it in for every low Score block that gets demolished.'

'That's awful. I'm sorry.' Georgie's voice is quiet, breathy. The low volume grabs Iris's attention as much as a shout.

'What's wrong?' It's then she notices her eyes are also red, pink streaks underneath from tears. Georgie never cries beyond the odd sniff. She's always the optimist, the calm one ready to tackle anything with practicalities and a touch of glam. Crying just isn't in her DNA.

Georgie proves all of that wrong and sobs, the sort of breathless crying children do when they are so inconsolable, it's as if their entire world is ending. Iris runs to her, then pulls her shaking body in for a hug.

'Hey, we'll think of something. We'll get these bastards. You hear me? We're not giving up.'

'It's not that, Iris. I mean, that's so awful, but that's not why I'm crying.'

'What? How can it not be? What's worse?'

She pulls away, swallows, then takes a shuddering breath. 'I'm pregnant.'

Chapter 29
Iris

'Whose is it?' Iris asks, her tone maybe too harsh, too condescending. She puts her arm around Georgie again and tries to be more supportive, to not give a lecture right now, although that's what she really wants to do. How could Georgie have been so stupid? Georgie's hand implant glows blue. Such a pretty colour for something so awful.

Georgie continues to cry, staring at the floor. 'Some guy from a flat party a couple of weeks ago.'

'Who? I don't remember some guy. You're like, ninety per cent gay.'

Georgie gives a one-shouldered shrug, then blows her nose. 'Yeah, but that ten per cent bites me in the arse sometimes.'

That's an understatement. Iris purses her lips and bites back her judgement, not all that successfully. 'Fuck's sake G. Were you orange? You screwed some guy during your orange time?'

'My implant only went orange the next day. I thought I was safe.' She walks to the sofa, then plonks down, lifting her knees up to hug them.

Iris sits next to her more delicately. 'Well, you know what you have to do.'

'I know. Believe me.' She wipes her nose, then looks at Iris with those pleading, impossible-to-say-no-to eyes. 'Come with me? I don't want to do it alone.'

Iris puts her arm around her and kisses her forehead. 'You know I will.'

***

Abortion clinics are more common than corner shops, and their local one boasts 24-hour appointments 7 days a week. It seems pointless at the moment when the low Scorers are all under curfew. They leave straight away and make it there for six p.m., pulling their jackets up high to conceal their faces as they walk in. The last thing either of them want is to be spotted and become the subject of gossip.

The waiting room is whitewashed and uncomfortably bright. It smells like the sort of pine-scented disinfectant they use in schools and other underfunded buildings. Hard plastic chairs that creak, yet refuse to give. There are no magazines, no TV or radio. Silence and boredom frees up all the brain capacity for worrying and regret. Footsteps echo, every whisper can be heard. It's only the two of them, luckily, besides the receptionist who has all the bedside manner of a scorpion.

Georgie isn't crying anymore. Her red eyes have a faraway glaze. 'I wouldn't mind a baby, one day.'

'Well, maybe wait till you have a licence.'

'Or you take the Life Score bollocks down.'

Iris snaps her head round to glare at her. 'Shh!' she hisses.

'Sorry.'

Despite the empty waiting room, they wait nearly an hour before Georgie is called through. She takes Iris's hand when she stands and Iris goes in with her, into the doctor's room where the chairs and lighting are equally uncomfortable.

They don't give pills anymore, the doctor says. He has a stern face, one riddled with disapproval, as if Georgie is the first knocked-up woman he's seen. He never says she should have known better, but it's implied by his tone and by the way he recoils his top lip and glares down his nose. Iris feels guilty even though she's only there for support. She squeezes Georgie's knee, feeling her muscles tense.

'It's a procedure,' he says. 'More reliable this way.'

Georgie agrees with an air of disinterest that Iris knows is as fake as her eyelashes. She just wants it gone, she says. 'Let's get it over with.'

Georgie signs the forms, then goes through to another room, while Iris waits outside. Iris taps her feet, cracks her knuckles, then closes her eyes as if she can sleep. When that fails, she paces, sits again, then drums out a rhythm with her fingers on the adjacent chair until the receptionist's steely gaze shrivels her into silence. She checks the time. Forty-five minutes.

A groggy and woozy Georgie emerges shortly after. Her speech is slurred, and she struggles to hold the paper bag of pills and condoms she has in her hand.

'For any pain,' the doctor says as he tells Georgie she is free to go. He hands them a note, excusing them for being out after curfew like a bloody school prefect.

They walk home, in the slow lane, Georgie propped up against Iris, the two of them zigzagging along the way. When they get to their building, Iris puts her arm under Georgie's armpit and half carries her up the stairs. 'Just a few more steps,' she says as they near the top, her arm and back aching from the strain.

Georgie replies with just vowel sounds and a bit of dribble. When they arrive home, Iris helps her into bed and tells her to sleep it off, then leaves a drink and a snack on her bedside table. Says for her to rest up. She'll feel right as rain in a few hours.

'I'll bring you a hot water bottle.'

'Eleeetic,' Georgie mumbles, and Iris is sure she's telling her to watch the electric, but she ignores that and puts the kettle on. Georgie's recovery is more important than whatever else they need the electric for.

Iris puts the hot water bottle on the bed and tucks Georgie in. She's already asleep and her nose is whistling little snores. When Iris turns out the light, she does a double take as she sees her implant glow. No longer blue, but not green either. Georgie's implant has turned gold.

The colour of sterility.

Chapter 30
Iris

Iris thought Georgie might sleep right through until morning, but it's ten p.m. when Georgie mumbles a greeting and walks to the bathroom. For a few minutes, Iris waits, listening to the shower, to Georgie humming as she washes. She watches the steam escape the bathroom and fog up the window above the door. Wrapped in a towel, Georgie walks back to her bedroom and Iris braces for her to realise. It's then that Georgie screams. Iris runs to her, and she collapses into her arms.

'It's gold! What have they done to me?'

Iris finds biscuits in the cupboard and sits Georgie at the table. She wraps a blanket around her shoulders, but her shaking doesn't stop.

'It's probably gold because you've just had a treatment,' Iris says, trying to convince them both. 'It'll turn back to green soon.'

'You know that's not true. Gold means sterile. Totally infertile. They've sterilised me, Iris. I know it.'

Iris puts her arm around her. Despite the blanket, she feels cold. Iris checks her forehead for fever. 'Can I get you something? I'll go to the shop. Anything you want.'

Georgie shakes her head and pushes the biscuits away. 'I wish my mum was here. Or Grandpa, my dad even.'

A best friend is no substitute for family, Georgie has claimed before, when Iris moans about her mum. It's a thoughtless moan, dissing the thing she has that Georgie covets most.

Georgie's mum was killed during the Great Unrest, a few days after Georgie was born. She still had a baby tummy. She had a bracelet that showed Georgie's birth had been neutralised, Grandpa Eddie had given his life to allow Georgie to be born, the tattoo made partly of his blood was etched across Georgie's forearm the day of her birth. That didn't stop the Enough thugs. They saw a woman with a tummy and beat her to death in the street when she went out to buy nappies while Georgie slept in their apartment above. Georgie scratches at her tattoo, the mark that proved ineffective in keeping the violence and tragedy away. Two people died so Georgie could live. Iris's one murder on her shoulders is bad enough. She can't imagine how bad it must be for Georgie. Her guilt rages with her sadness.

Georgie makes little sniffs as she struggles to keep her tears back. Iris can count on one hand the number of times she's seen Georgie cry, and two of those have been in the last few hours. 'I wish I'd kept it,' she says. 'At least then I'd have a baby.'

'You don't want a baby.'

'But never? *Never?*'

Iris doesn't answer. She'd always assumed never. No one has babies anymore. Well, no one who doesn't want to end up un-Scorable. The talk of standing up to the Eyes Forward has gotten them questioning so much, yet Iris never questioned her own maternal instincts, or lack of. Some things are drummed in so hard they never change. Conditioning that can't be undone.

Georgie goes back to bed to sleep away her nightmare, to curl up and hope for the pain to go away, both physical and mental. Iris makes her a hot water bottle again, then leaves the flat to go for a walk but quickly realises she's under damned curfew and can't even do that. She stands at the entrance to her block instead. The night is cold, and the chilly breeze prickles all over like needles. Physical discomfort to take away the mental.

The streets are quiet. Most people in this part of the town will be under curfew. The wind carries litter and debris, swirling in eddies across the abandoned pavement. A little way down the hill, candles flicker from outside one of the collapsed un-Scorable dorms. There's still been no press, no officials investigating the carnage, no Society Police.

A few less babies, a few less irresponsible women, that's what most people will be thinking. These deaths were for the common good of the Society.

Iris's insides bubble, rage fizzing through her. She has no outlet for her wrath, and it wants to burst out, to be unleashed and rampage through the streets. She holds her mouth in her hands, falls to her knees, then screams. She screams and screams until her throat burns.

You know what to do with your anger.

'I don't!' she yells, not caring anymore if people think she's insane. She *is* insane. She is mad with rage. 'I don't know what to fucking do!'

An eye for an eye, Iris. Take them down.

Chapter 31
Mae

For someone who prefers routine and order, who enjoys the predictability and rules of arithmetic over the ambiguity of conversation, Mae has learned to deal with the randomness of life exceedingly well; she thinks so anyway. Even though Iris still sees her as an unaffectionate oddball, it's not for lack of love for her daughter, it's because she has too much. Mae being near anything spoils things. She's tainted. Look at Pasha. Iris was right. His decline is all her fault.

Visiting the corpse of Lloyd Porter — the term father just doesn't sit right, she thinks of him by name, or title, an Eyes Forward representative — has disrupted her week enough. The relief of his death was short-lived. She still has a struggling accountancy business to run, a sick husband to care for, a house to clean, and food to source on their pitiful Score. It's the kind of Score that allows non-perishables only and cleaning products made of ninety-nine per cent vinegar and smell as such. Dwelling on joy is a luxury for the wealthy, both in Score and in time.

The Eyes Forward representatives turning up at Mae's office is therefore another disruption she can do without. They march in without warning or pleasantries. Thank God her receptionist is at lunch.

'Mae Porter?' the one standing in front of the other two asks, his voice so flat it's almost robotic. Was her father's ever that monotone? She can't even remember him saying a word to her, but her mother's voice is stamped on her memory in the form of gin-scented slurs.

She winces at her maiden name. 'Taylor. Mae Taylor.'

'Daughter of—'

'Yes,' she says. She doesn't need reminding.

'Come with us.'

The three representatives turn around without even checking if she follows, so sure they are of obedience. And of course she obeys. She's no match for them. She stands on stiff legs — she's been sitting too long — and shuts down her computer, then leaves a note on the desk for the receptionist and follows them. It's thirty-six paces from her desk to their car that's parked, obstructing both bike and pedestrian lanes. Those inconvenienced make no remark. It's clearly an Eyes Forward car. Instead, they stop a few seconds to stare at Mae as she leaves her office and gets in. She keeps her head down, eyes to the floor, lifting her handbag in front of her face to cover her reddening cheeks.

They drive five minutes down the road. If it wasn't for the bus traffic, the drive would have taken thirty seconds. It would have been quicker to walk for sure, though Mae's grateful for resting her legs and for the blackened windows that keep her hidden. Her heart races when she realises where they're going. She knows the building well. It's where Iris works.

'Is my daughter okay? Has something happened?'

They don't respond. They alight the car when it's parked and give minimal instruction. 'Follow us this way.'

At the building, they go through the corridor painted blue and gold — men and women of safe age. Mae's heart slows a little as she thinks at least Iris won't be this way. They arrive at a sparsely furnished office with Venetian blinds, which one representative shuts, an empty table, and one chair, which Mae assumes is for her, so she sits.

The three representatives stand close, mountainous compared to her on a chair. Their near identical faces peer down, towering above wide shoulders. Their chins are massive, their nostrils huge holes.

'Your father's death has left a gap in the workforce,' one of them says. 'We understand from conversations some of us had with him that you are quite brilliant, even more so than him, apparently.' He smirks.

Mae leans back, a futile move to gain space since one of the representatives is standing directly behind her. 'I. . . I'm just an accountant.'

'Going back through data from a few decades ago, it seems clear that you were instrumental in developing the Life Score algorithm.' He spits when he talks, the spray landing on Mae's face.

'It was hypothetical,' she says quietly, hoping they don't hear her voice quiver. 'I was interested in the arithmetic, not discriminating against people.' She flinches at her words, yet her candour goes unnoticed. She shifts her weight, crosses and uncrosses her legs, then sits on her hands.

'The Life Score algorithm is no longer fit for its purpose, as you know. The new algorithm launch is due soon as I am sure you have seen on the news. Lloyd Porter's work needs to be finished. You are here to help us overhaul the entire system.'

'I-I—' Mae stutters, her mind reeling.

'Your father's Life Score is inheritable.' The one behind her is talking now. She cranes her head to glance around. 'You are aware that only Eyes Forward representatives' close family can inherit their Life Score?'

'I. . . I am aware.' Her tremulous voice makes her sound uncertain, but she's an accountant. Of course she knows this.

'Well, we shall extend this rule to you, as a courtesy, if you help the Society through this transitional period. I'm sure you would enjoy a Score of 900. Your husband's health would certainly benefit.'

Mae's fidgeting ceases and she sits rigid. Pasha. With a Score like that she could get him the best medication there is. He could walk again, run, get his strength back. And all she has to do is finalise her father's work, to create a new algorithm they're no doubt hoping will make the Society even more unfair than it already is. But she would be a 900.

In the Society, that matters.

Chapter 32
Iris

Iris visits her parents after work a couple of days later. Perhaps Georgie's yearning for her own late parents has rubbed off. Georgie's losses give perspective on what should be cherished. Or perhaps it's the idea that parents are meant to be there for you when the world goes to shit, to iron out that knot in your stomach and tell you everything is going to be okay. There's something in a parental hug she craves even though visiting them usually causes more stress than it eases. Her worries aren't going away on their own.

She cycles back past the un-Scorable dorm vigils again, and the mourners are still attending, although fewer. So many still walk past and don't even notice. Grief isn't contagious, it's a lonely state of mind. Some can brush it away like dust.

'Iris,' her mum says when she opens the door. 'Come in. We need a chat.'

'Is Dad okay? Whoa.' She stops just past the doorway to take it in. 'What's with all the new gadgets?' There's a new hoist that hangs from various points of the ceiling, CCTV cameras outside showing images on wall mounted monitors, and speakers in the corners. Then, through the doorway to the living room, there's a reclining chair in its upright position. All appear brand new, expensive — the latest stuff always is. How have they afforded this?

Pasha walks to Iris without crutches, smiling fully, his whole face working. Iris's jaw drops. She hasn't seen her dad so mobile in ages.

'Come give your old man a hug,' he says. She runs over and he holds her tightly, with almost the strength of a healthy human.

'What's happened?' Iris asks, her head buried into his shoulder. It's the best hug she's had in years. 'You doing your physio? Mum finally looking after you?'

'I got a new job,' Mae says.

'Good. About time.'

'Careful, he's only been on the medication a day.'

'Darling, I'm fine,' Pasha says. 'Better than ever. The medication works wonders.'

Iris steps back and just looks at him. Sure, he's still thin, and he lost a lot of muscle mass, but his limbs work, and he's not shaking at all. She holds her hands to her chest, her heart full to bursting.

'Listen, Iris,' Mae says. 'We need to talk. Come and sit down.'

Mae's voice dips, quieter than usual, and Iris's joy is diminished as suspicion claws its way through her gut. Her dad being healthy, all the new stuff, it's like a different house to the last one she visited, with different people. Mae's tone doesn't convey delight in their fortune. It smacks of something different, more sinister. Is it guilt? Shame?

Iris follows them through to the living room where the display of pricy credit-purchased items carries on. Physio equipment, a treadmill, weights, and a new TV remote with bigger buttons designed for shaky hands. There's even a shiny new vacuum cleaner standing in the corner, and a beautiful new chess set on the coffee table mid-game. The place smells like polystyrene packaging. This stuff must all have just arrived.

Iris sits on the new sofa. Its velvety cream surface is so clean, she fears messing it up. No springs dig in; instead it's perfectly comfortable with its orthopaedic pillows.

Pasha sits next to Mae, their fingers interlocked. They're staring at their feet, shoulders rolled forwards as if cowering from Iris. She sits, watching her parents struggle to find words for a while.

'Are you guys going to tell me why you're being weird? What new job can possibly give you the Score that can get you all of this stuff?'

Mae nods, then clears her throat. 'My new job. . .' She pauses again and takes a deep breath. 'I'm working for the Eyes Forward. We're concerned about your safety. With this Lloyd Porter killing—'

Iris tuts and waves her hand dismissively. 'I'm more worried about the low Scorer killings.'

'You shouldn't be. Your Score isn't that low. But Lloyd Porter, well. . . You should know. . . I've taken over his job.'

Iris's eyes bulge. That's a huge job, the sort the Eyes Forward will scrutinise your every move for. The sort of job that has a high profile within the government, especially with the new algorithm launch. It's way above her mum's usual occupation. 'You're doing the Life Score algorithm? How? How the hell—?'

'There's a lot I need to tell you,' Mae says. She's speaking so slowly, like she thinks Iris is a child. 'We wanted to shield you from all of this. We only ever wanted to save you the burden of knowing this. But now, well, it's safer for you if you know. Please understand, it was a long time ago. Years ago. I was stupid. I never thought it would be used in this way. It was hypothetical, that's all. It was my thesis, just a theory.'

Iris lifts her shoulders and eyeballs her mother. 'What was just a theory?'

'The Life Score algorithm. It was my thesis. I helped develop it.'

Iris flinches, her pulse throbs in her head, and her brain repeats what Mae just said. Her mum helped develop the Life Score algorithm. Her mum made the algorithm that ruins people's lives. But that was developed years ago, the exact date she can't recall. School history classes went over it. Her mum was probably a child genius. The weirdos are usually the smart ones. Her chest swells slightly with a little glimmer of hope. Maybe this is a good thing. Maybe her mum can help. 'So, you can make it better? Fairer? You can fix it?'

Mae snaps the band on her wrist. 'That's not really the aim. I just need to make sure you're safe.'

'Safe?' Iris almost laughs. Her mum always has her head buried in the rubble. She has no idea what the world is really like. 'Do you know what they're doing to the un-Scorables? Do you even understand?' Iris's desire for less stress by visiting her parents seemed like a long shot a few minutes ago. Now, such a luxury is a million miles away.

'Watch your tone with your mother, Iris.'

Iris shoots her dad a look. He's usually the one she can rely on for backup, to take her side against her mum's gripes and moans. Have they forgotten when she and Georgie turned up after the massacre? The comfortable sofa now feels less so, the forgiving cushions suffocating rather than supportive. She glances around at all the new stuff — possessions bought with dirty credit. A comfortable life replacing common decency.

'None of us are safe until the Life Scores are fixed,' Iris says, over-enunciating every word to hammer it home. 'We're all one wrong turn away from becoming un-Scorable ourselves. You know they're planning another massacre? A bigger one!'

'You and your dad have to be my priority,' Mae says. 'I can't change the whole Society. This job means your dad can get his medication.'

'Dad will be fine if you just do your original job properly. This is greed.'

'No, Iris—'

Iris can feel her cheeks heating and tears welling up as she nearly boils over. 'You didn't see their faces. The fear they must have felt. All those people being killed just because they have a shitty Life Score means nothing to you? You can fix it. You can make it fair.'

'Your dad—'

'Mae,' Pasha says, a sharpness to his tone. 'Iris is right. We're being selfish. You could do more here.'

Mae shakes her head and leans away from him 'No. Listen, Iris. You have to understand. You two are what's important. I need you to stay at home. Be extra careful. Lloyd Porter, well, he was my father.'

Iris's breath catches, her hands go to her mouth.

'Estranged,' Mae adds, as if that somehow makes it okay. 'We hadn't been in touch for a long time.'

Iris does the crude maths in her head. She doesn't have her mum's level of arithmetic ability, but the sum is straightforward. Lloyd Porter was old. Really old. 'But he was, like, over a hundred and fifty.' She knows what that means. She just doesn't want to say it. A silence passes while she finds the courage to say the words out loud, to hear her own voice confirm it. 'You're Preserved.'

The evening sun casts half the room in shadow, and Mae's red-rimmed eyes glint from glassy tears in the half light. 'There's so much you don't know. I've been trying to protect you from all of this.'

Iris tries to bite her tongue, to keep her tone soft and temper her rage, but she snaps. 'Preserved! You? And what about dad?'

Pasha shakes his head. 'No. just your mum.'

Iris stares icy daggers at Mae. At the woman she thought she knew as her mother. 'Fucking cougar.'

'It's not like that.'

'Yes, it is. You're one of them. Some Eyes Forward lover. Working for them, ramming this algorithm into people's lives, *ruining* people's lives. You literally ruined the country just to have the power over who lives and who dies, who ages and who doesn't. You might as well have been the one to kill all those people! And now you think it's all okay for you to play along with their sick games because you like all the fancy new gadgets.'

'Your dad's medication—'

'Find another way! Speak to his dickhead brother. You're too proud to accept help from him, but not to turn your back on everyone else? Or don't. Keep your shitty Score and just wait. I'm going to take the whole goddamned system down. Somehow. I'll burn the whole fucking Society to the ground before they can hurt anyone else.'

'No! Iris. You have to be safe. Please—'

'Piss off telling me to be safe, Mae Porter.' Porter. She knows that name. Not from Lloyd Porter. Not from her mum. Iris stands, panting with fury as she tries to recollect through the vertigo of her temper. 'Porter. There was a woman. Another Porter. I saw that name. . .'

'Sit down, Iris.'

Iris stamps her foot. 'No. The other Porter. Who was that?'

Mae sighs, then briefly makes eye contact before she stares back down at the floor. 'Joan. Joan Porter was my mother. You might have seen her name crop up somewhere. Nebula, probably. She wasn't well known, but every now and then her name comes up.'

'Why? Who was she? Why would your mother's name come up?'

'She invented Pres-X.'

Iris sits down then. Her knees weak, the room spinning. She feels her mother's shame. 'All those people going mad and dying in asylums. That was you.'

'No. That was my mother, and no. I had nothing to do with it.'

'Except you took Pres-X.' Iris glares at her mother now, her middle-age skin that's actually over a hundred years old. Her awkwardness, her bizarre wisdom. She's an old woman in the wrong decade, in the wrong life. It's so damned obvious now that she knows. She never saw it before because she was stuck in the bloody cave. 'You're as bad as all of them. I don't believe this.'

Chapter 33
Iris

Iris empties the contents of her boxes into a large bag before leaving her parents' place, and now hauls them back to her apartment, dragging the bag across the ground, letting it thump over each bump and kerb. Clearing out all her stuff will please her mother, which annoys her more that she's taken it, annoys her more than her aching muscles from each tug and pull. But this cuts all ties. She wants nothing to do with those people, wants no essence of herself in their house.

Preserved, her mother. She just can't believe it. Well, she can. But beneath all her mum's weirdness and coldness, she still really thought there was a good person. Not some sell-out for a longer life.

The bitch.

They've been lying to her forever. Her own family are Eyes Forward supporters, cosying up with them now, working on the algorithm that will continue to discriminate, that will lead to the death of so many. How could they? How could she?

She itches, and she wants to scratch until she bleeds, to rid herself of her tainted blood. Their blood. Those people are what she's made of. Bile burns her throat, and she vomits just outside her apartment block. It's not enough. She can never rid herself of what's inside her.

They love you, Iris. They're just trying to protect you.

Shut up, she tells the voice, silently this time. Her neighbours don't need to know about her being crazy. It's clear the voice is back to speaking nonsense again.

When she's lugged the bag through her apartment and into her room, she tips it upside down and spills its contents. Memories of her scant years litter the floor, and she smiles. Her mother would hate the mess. Among the clutter is the framed photo of her great-grandmother, not the Eyes Forward family on her mother's side. Her namesake. Old Iris.

Iris Taylor.

She itches her tattoo, and something clicks in her mind, but the cogs turn too slowly, stalling with her anger. She squeezes her eyes shut and searches the back of her mind for the memory just out of reach. She needs to search the internet, and she remembers her new access. She takes her phone from her pocket and instals the Shadownet browser, Nebula. It takes an age to download and when it does, the forums are sparse. Anything relating to the SAS has been shut down. Somehow, despite Nebula's promised anonymity and safety from the reach of Eyes Forward, they've intercepted it and censored what they like. It's old tech these days, most likely. The graphics appear the same as they always did. No one ever thought to update it.

Code words are being used in the place of the initials to beat the bots. Bizarre expressions like familieS Among Seekers, capitalising the acronym. Easy for a human to spot when they know what they're searching for.

There's nothing useful that she can find, just the usual rants about women's rights and anti-Eyes Forward control stuff. A lot of anti-Society stuff. A phrase that Iris heard before at the party: the Society isn't real. It doesn't make much sense, but it rings true. Then, after a spark of ingenuity that makes the computer screen glare brighter, she searches her name. Her great-grandmother's name.

Iris Taylor comes up everywhere.

Nebula is unstable. She recognises the signs of a glitch in the making, and her phone screen is frustratingly small to read what she needs to as quickly as necessary. But it's enough. She gets the gist. She doesn't dare even blink in case she misses something as she chews the inside of her cheek, staring at her phone, scrolling and scrolling.

For all the evil her mother's side has done, her father's side fought against it.

There are accounts going back years of how Nebula was founded to allow people — women primarily — to have a space to speak freely, how the SAS hacked a government building to find out about covert deals with big money companies, how they tried to stop the rollout of Life Scores decades ago, how they sourced fake IDs for pregnancy refugees to get across borders, and how they exposed bribes and deals that reeked of cronyism designed to line the fattest wallets.

And her great-grandmother was at the heart of all of it.

There are posts of thanks from women dating back decades. Thanking Nebula, the SAS, and naming Iris Taylor specifically for facilitating their escape with their baby and finding them safety during the Great Unrest. Older posts too, much older, whistleblowing posts about when the Eyes Forward shut off counties and came up with their slogans promoting each county to stay contained: *devolved is evolved!* Whatever that's supposed to mean.

The SAS told stories of how deprived certain parts of Britain are as a result, not that the Eyes Forward care. They abandoned those places because the Eyes Forward, the founding members, were from Berkshire. Berkshire really does have more 800 pluses than any other county. They've hoarded the wealth here.

The SAS broke past the autonomous systems with their hacks, enabling families to keep in touch when travelling became harder and harder, and then impossible. When communication was cut, the SAS found other ways.

Thank you, sisters. Thank you, Iris. Thanks to Nebula, I can speak to my daughter.

Thank you, Iris. With my new ID, I was able to emigrate to another county.

Thank you, sisters and Iris Taylor. I can now afford groceries.

Thank you, Iris and Sisters. I now see the Eyes Forward for the monsters they are. My partner does too.

The thanks continue, on and on until it becomes clear. Iris Taylor wasn't just a member of the SAS. She founded it.

Iris Taylor didn't just use Nebula. She invented it.

Then the condolences. For her husband, Angus, who Iris's cousin was named after. They suspect he was murdered by the Eyes Forward as punishment for Iris's crimes, that Iris had a target on her back, and that the effort was ramped up when she and her SAS friends fought against the rules that caused the Great Unrest. Ninety years old she was then, and she was still fighting. In the end, she opted for a more peaceful death than what the Eyes Forward would have afforded her.

Iris being born gave her great-grandmother the opportunity for the Nan-E euthanasia. Her namesake's life donation was a blessing in many ways. Her birth was a kindness.

Iris sits back, wipes her sweaty forehead on the back of her hand, then takes deep, controlled breaths. Her desire to rid herself of her blood has gone, for it's not all bad. She's part Iris Taylor, and Iris Taylor was a legend.

She's a cocktail made of both sides, a hybrid of the Eyes Forward and those against them.

The Porters don't define her.

She's not tainted. Diluted, maybe, but the Taylor blood is more dominant in her. No way is she going to be like the Porters.

Iris puts her phone down, then goes to the window. Their apartment overlooks the hill that leads to the town centre. The building opposite is a Sub 200 block. Adjacent is an un-Scoreable dorm. She sees the mothers with their babies tied to their front leave to collect their powdered rations twice a week and hears the kids playing inside, rarely outside. Displaying children is akin to flashing your privates. Grotesque. Unseemly. Like airing your dirty laundry in public.

Except it isn't. These are the sort of people that Iris's great-grandmother tried to protect. And now, with her blood marking Iris's arm, the baton has been passed to her.

Iris's mouth forms a stern, straight line, and she clenches her fist. She needs to finish what her namesake started.

Chapter 34
Ava

'What the fuck is this, Ava?'

Mandisa so rarely swears, it spikes Ava's attention as soon as she walks through the door. Mandisa holds the bag containing two vacuum packed packages of compressed pale blue powder. There's no denying what it is. Photographs of Flake have been all over the news.

'It's Flake,' Ava says. She's a master of keeping emotions out of her voice, and she speaks without a hint of fear or surprise. 'I'm top Society Police. Confiscating drugs is kind of one of my main duties.'

Mandisa dumps it on the table, next to the bag where she must have been snooping to find it. Ava tenses and swallows. She should have been more careful.

'Then why did you bring it home?' Mandisa asks, her pinched face clearly not buying Ava's excuses.

'It's late.' Ava adds a yawn for effect. 'You're cooking tonight, and I didn't want my food to go cold. I'll deal with it tomorrow. I've got a lot of work still to do.'

Mandisa narrows her eyes, then recoils her lips as she pushes the bag away. 'Horrible to have such things in my house.'

Ava cocks her head a little and thinks for mere seconds. Such thoughts should take longer. They require more preparation, but the idea comes to her so suddenly it's as if the universe has aligned. An opportunity to be seized. She wishes she had time to process the idea when she's filled with less hate, is less tired and has longer to plan and think it through. But this opportunity doesn't play by those ideals. Ava's years of anger cloud any rational thought.

This is what Mae warned her about, that she was going too far, that she's lost her morality to the cause. Ava argued that the ends justify the means. The idea she's having now, well. . .she can justify it a hundred different ways.

'Okay, okay,' Ava says with a smile. 'I just wanted to spend time with you. But it doesn't look like you've started cooking yet. We can go drop it at Society Police HQ now, if you want? I have the key with me.'

Mandisa perks up at this, as Ava knew she would. To see inside such a building is unheard of. It's the most exclusive offer Mandisa has ever had. Mandisa's pinched face softens, and her eyes sparkle. 'You have a key — to the headquarters? I thought no one but top Eyes Forward representatives see inside that building.'

'I am top Society Police. They deemed me important enough.'

Mandisa's eyes flash with awe and envy. To be important enough. . .that's what she always craves. She wets her lips then puts on her most coy voice. 'Sure. Well, okay then. It'll be nice to see inside that building.'

Mandisa changes into a smarter suit and touches up her hair and makeup. Ava watches her with a physical yearning she hasn't felt in a long time, but she shakes it away. Now is not the time. It's too late. It'll only make the next part of her idea harder.

As they leave, she eyes the picture of Zia. The candle next to it has finally burned out. It's as if Zia isn't watching this bit. Her back is turned, her wholesome goodness has gone. Probably for the best. There's no way she'd approve.

They cycle into town, the bags of Flake in Ava's backpack. Part of their route takes them past an old asylum where Sub 700 people ended up when the expired Pres-X drug they took poisoned their minds. When they were denied the cure for the formic acid that built up in their systems, which drove them to suicide and homicide.

Mandisa cycles ahead of Ava, her glossy black hair flowing behind. Ava grits her teeth, remembering Mandisa's part in it. She was part of the team that allowed the elders to suffer so much, that denied the less wealthy elders the cure. Millie. Erin. Just two horrific deaths that Ava witnessed personally; their guttural cries of fear at the end still echo in her mind. So much suffering and death in the name of the Time's Up movement that Mandisa helped propagate. When you inflict such pain and suffering, it should be repaid with interest.

After thinking about that, Ava's pleased she didn't make an advance on Mandisa. She probably would have strangled her, and that would have been far messier.

Thanks to curfew, the streets are quiet enough. There are a few 400 pluses milling around, but not enough to cause any sort of commotion in Ava's direction. All the same, Ava is pleased the key she's acquired is for a side door.

They park the bikes a way away, Ava's suggestion — a more secure bike rack, she claims — not to draw attention to themselves entering a rarely visited building. 'Protocol,' she calls it.

Mandisa laps it up, eagerly nodding at the procedure's particulars, for only the most exclusive would know such a thing. Mandisa doesn't suspect it's so her bike isn't seen anywhere near the Eyes Forward building, that Ava doesn't want her presence there traced. Not that anyone would suspect such a thing. Ava is a 900, not the sort to commit a crime according to the statistics and the Society's model on how citizens behave. And, as Ava knows, no one goes in or out of this building. It doesn't even have any oxygen.

Ava opens the thick steel, windowless door using the copy she made of Lloyd Porter's keycard just after her knife sliced his abdomen for the seventh time. That's their weapon of choice on the low Scorers. For him to meet such an end seemed fitting. She'd smiled when the blood bubbled up his throat as he lay on his back, choking as the claret trickled down his chin and gushed from his wounds. Even the Preserved show fear. They fear death more than anyone, for it's the thing they thought they'd escaped.

Cheats never prosper, so the saying goes.

A rush of cold air comes out as the door opens, and before Mandisa can blink, Ava pushes her inside. Mandisa stumbles and spins around as Ava kicks her in the stomach, then swipes her handbag off her shoulder, her phone inside. Mandisa exhales winded air, grabbing her stomach, and strains to draw breath.

'Ava,' she rasps. 'What the fuck—' Her mouth makes the words, but the volume is nothing. No scream. No pleas. Ava shuts the door on her, then locks the bolts.

She hasn't even worked up a sweat, yet her heart beats so fast it's like a hum. She rests her forehead on the door, squeezes her eyes shut, and a lump forms in her throat.

'Sorry, Mandi,' Ava says to the door. 'For everything.'

Chapter 35
Iris

Iris doesn't dodge Jason at work today, although thankfully his advances come at the end of the day as she's leaving. He waits at the turnstiles by the exit, blows her a kiss, then gives her a wink. When she doesn't respond, he stands in her way and makes a comment about her chest, how she could do a lot worse than hooking up with a Desirable.

Desirable. It's not just a noun to Jason, the awful word Pres-X-2 takers named themselves. He believes it's true, that it describes him accurately.

Iris shivers thinking about it.

She ducks past him and makes it out of the building and onto her bike without so much as a grope. She can't even complain about him. She was by the entrance, a communal area for men and unsafe women. Such clashes in behaviour are to be expected, so the mantra goes.

She grunts with every pedal stroke, trying to sweat out the memory. The fast bike lane isn't fast enough. She considers hopping into the bus lane but thinks better of it. She doesn't want to be deducted the points if she gets caught.

Why do you still care about points?

Worrying about her Life Score is instinctive. It's hard to unwash a brain after a lifetime of conditioning. She grips the handlebars tighter and swerves across the bike traffic, into the empty bus lane, enjoying a minute or two of open road. No one in front of her, the breeze on her face. She can see far ahead instead of just the back of the head of the person in front. She feels free.

A bus comes up behind, beeping its horn, and Society Police get their phones out. Freedom was brief.

But her taste for rebellion remains. She's a rule-breaker now. Lying about stats at work, stealing Ella's phone, riding in the bus lane. She's back in the bike lane, panting as she catches her breath, yet her face wears the widest grin.

Freedom's easy, Iris, when you're out of the cave. You just have to grab it.

***

Her shoes splash in a puddle when she walks into her apartment. There's a pool of liquid across the kitchen floor with shards of broken glass next to it. It's whisky, by the looks of the bottle.

'Grandpa Eddie wanted a whisky,' Georgie says when Iris glares at her. By the looks of the new bottle that's open on the table, Grandpa Eddie wanted several whiskies.

Iris grabs a dustpan and brush, then cleans up, since it's clear Georgie isn't going to. Georgie shouldn't be bending over much anyway, and shouldn't be drinking either, probably.

'Fifty fucking points,' Georgie says, necking the last of her current glass.

'What?'

'That's how much they've increased my Score for sterilising me against my will. I'm a 300 plus. Whoopee!' She hiccups as she talks, then pours herself an extra measure and slams the bottle on the table. 'And guess what? I'm being promoted. My dick-head boss took one look at my gold implant and congratulated me — *congratulated* me! Then said I'm now safe to work on the newsroom floor.'

Iris tips the broken glass into the bin. 'Oh, well. Silver linings.'

'All I ever wanted was to be a newsreader. Not that I'm getting that job, but I'll be in among it. And all because they tied my tubes. Like I wasn't any good before. But I'm the same. I'm still me.'

Iris grabs herself a beer, then sits at the table.

'And that anchor,' Georgie continues, swilling her fresh glass. 'You know, the one with the voice he puts on to sound all husky, but he sounds like he needs to cough up phlegm? He made a move on me, blatantly, the twat. He said, "Nice to have some new safe meat around here. Let's go for a drink sometime." Can you believe it? I told him I prefer girls, and he shrugged like my preferences don't matter. The prick.'

Iris shakes her head as she listens. Georgie can handle herself with perverts. She would never have just faced the wall and kept quiet like Iris did with Jason. Georgie would have kicked him in the bollocks and punched him in the nose. Iris never told her about that incident, she would have received a lecture about standing up for herself in response, and Georgie may have done something reckless.

The TV is on, the news channel on a loop. The Lloyd Porter story is now second to the excitement over the new Life Score algorithm. Iris takes several large swigs of her beer when the Life Score launch jingle plays, then clenches the bottle so hard she's surprised it doesn't crack. More broken glass is not what she needs to be dealing with.

It's launch week for the new algorithm. The news is blasting out that obtrusive theme jingle every ten minutes to remind everyone, in case the bunting across the streets and the posters on every street corner aren't enough of a reminder. The whole of Berkshire is saturated with it, as if excitement can permeate like osmosis.

The newsreader is so excited now, his usual husky voice sounds like he's had a dose of helium. 'To further extend the marvels of the new algorithm, your Life Score app has a new feature. It will be able to instantly tell you someone else's Life Score. Just hold your phone up, and it will use facial recognition as well as device location — or implant for women — and tell you the Score of anyone you see! You can also set it to group assessment, so in any room it can tell you how many there are in each Score bracket. Just so you can check you are in the best and most appropriate company. So, everyone, keep striving and be proud! Because this is the Society where everyone knows their place, and everyone can achieve.'

'For fuck's sake,' Iris says. She untucks her shirt and flaps it, fanning herself, her anger simmering and threatening to boil over. Her mother, her own mother, is behind this.

'The whole bloody newsroom has that bunting,' Georgie says, slurring from the whisky, rearranging the hot water bottle on her tummy. 'Little flags with that stupid walled-in eye on it everywhere. It's gross.'

If the news reports are to be believed, the new algorithm is going to be wonderful. Fairer, they say it's going to be — more inclusive. The TV plays out the same slogan again: This is the Society, where everyone knows their place, and everyone can achieve.

Yeah, right.

Iris chuckles at the voice, sounding more like her own. It's usually easy to tell the difference. The voice wobbles, not with uncertainty but with gusto, a vibrato of wisdom. Unlike Iris's own voice, which to her mostly sounds moany and crass. But now and then there's overlap, like maybe the madness is going away and the voice has been her all along, her conscience, her inner mentor.

She gets up to turn the TV off just as her phone rings. Tash is calling.

'Iris, I've figured it out. The hack. I know what to do.' Tash sounds frantic, stumbling over her words, her pitch wavering all over the place.

Iris gasps, her hand goes to her mouth. 'Okay,' she says. 'Let's get everyone together. Meet here in an hour.'

She hangs up and takes a second to process what she just heard. Tash has a plan. A hack. They're actually going to have a plan.

Georgie glances up from her drink. 'Who was that?'

'Tash. They're all coming over.'

'Cool,' Georgie says, then whistles. 'Go look in the cupboards. I stocked up on snacks from that corner shop. Quite nice stuff too. The perks of being 300 plus.' She laughs over her last words.

'Good.' Iris takes the bottle off her and Georgie pouts. 'You need to sober up. This is important.'

Chapter 36
Iris

'We don't know the exact date,' Iris says to the group when they've all arrived and are sitting. Drunk Georgie hastily arranged an assortment of mismatched snacks on the table and is working her way through most of them, as well as the glass of water Iris put in front of her. 'But it's a fair enough bet to assume it'll be next weekend. That's what Ava Maricelli said at the meeting, and it gives time for the new Life Score algorithm to work out any kinks. I reckon a ton more people will be a low enough Score to be prey. That's got to be their aim with this, to tank more people's Scores.'

'I'm only a 120,' Skylar says. 'If they're going for Sub 100s, that could be me. I may lose 20 points with the new algorithm.' Her blue hair lacks the volume it had at the party. It looks as drawn as her face.

'No fucking chance,' Johan says. His biceps tense through his T-shirt while he sits with balled fists on his thighs, reminding Iris of an alpha gorilla. 'They're not going to lay a finger on you. We won't let that happen.'

Iris puts her hand on Skylar's shoulder. 'We'll keep you safe.'

'The hack is going to be easy. Tash has it all figured out. She's a goddess at this sort of thing,' Johan says.

His skills are limited to punching and grunting, so his assurance of a hack isn't overly convincing. Iris curses herself that she's not more useful. She was a decent hacker once and can code better than most. She's inherited her innate abilities from old Iris apparently, the one who gave her life for her, the one family member that Iris longs for. But she let it slip. Tech moves on, and Iris didn't.

'What if the new algorithm makes us all un-Scorable?' Ezra says. 'We could all be hunted before we've even helped anyone.' He still appears ghostly with grief. None of them ask if he's heard any news of his sister. The answer is clear.

'It won't. I'm certain we won't all be un-Scorable.' Iris really is sure of that, not that she can tell them why, but there's no way Mae will make it so Iris suffers more. Iris hates her, but she's still her mum. She knows her well enough to see that. 'Tash, you're a 300 plus, so's Georgie now. So, you two are a safe bet, I reckon. Make sure Georgie knows everything about the hack. I'm a 270, probably okay too, so I'll also make sure I know it inside out. That's three of us who probably won't be hunted.'

Probably. She's hardly offering much confidence. In fact, she's acutely aware of how pathetic she sounds. But she's not about to give empty promises. Blindsiding is the government's job.

Skylar has the kind of face that morphs from fear to sadness, with little in between. Even her smile is the sort you'd have when remembering the good times you shared with a dead relative. As she listens to the plan, her watery blue eyes stare straight ahead, vacant. Johan stands next to her, arms folded, playing the big brother and tells her it's all going to be okay. From the look on Ezra's face, nothing will be okay ever again.

'Johan was right,' Tash says. 'The hack is simple enough. I mean, I can't hack the Eyes Forward, no one can. Their firewalls are a fortress.'

'Yeah, we know,' Georgie says with a hiccup. 'Iris created those firewalls.'

Everyone turns to face Iris now. Tash's jaw is on the floor.

'Iris, seriously? Can you break through it?'

'Nope. I did a good job, sadly.'

'Dammit,' Johan says.

After a second, Tash waves her hand at Iris. 'It doesn't matter. I have a plan. We may not be able to hack the Eyes Forward, but we can hack everyone else.' She glances around at everyone's faces, all but Johan appearing quite confused. 'It's brilliant in how simple it is. I've called it Plato. Get it?'

Iris half smiles, Georgie doesn't. Iris makes a note to explain Plato's Cave to her later.

'So,' Tash continues, 'we have to initiate it on the day the hunt starts. The Eyes Forward have helped us with this one. You know every phone has the Society Police app and it's running all the time. They've made it law that everyone is Society Police, so that app has auto downloaded on every device, and it's live all the time. They said it's because of the Lloyd Porter murder, but really, it's so they can track us. But I can intercept that. I can make it so everyone escapes. Plato is going to get everyone out of this cave.'

Chapter 37
Iris

With Berkshire having the highest concentration of 800 pluses, that means there's a ton of Preserved and Desirables who are expecting to make the most elite 900 plus group. There are even some 900 pluses who expect to top the Score ladder and reach the coveted 1000. Iris doesn't think she's ever even met a 1000. The Prime Minister must be, she thinks. Maybe there's only one.

Who cares?

She smirks. The voice is talking sense again.

At work, Ella and Francis seem to have mixed views about the whole thing. Where Iris usually inwardly laughs at their ridiculous pomposity, she now grinds her teeth and cracks her knuckles. She needs to get to the climbing wall to work off steam, to find an outlet before she screams like a teakettle. She watches their pained sympathy with each other. Their biggest fear is that their status could be less exclusive, while low Scorers fear death.

'What if a pitiful 750 ends up 900?' Ella says. 'It might ruin it.'

'Trust the system, Ella,' Francis says. 'You know it serves us well.'

Iris rubs her temples and stares at her computer screen instead, blocking them from her view before she eyes up the boiling water in the kettle, the bread knife, the glasses, or anything else she could batter them with.

Norman Bonnet has shown up at work today and by the way he parades through the office, everyone should be grateful and awestruck in his presence. There's obviously not a high Score luncheon to attend, a gap in his busy schedule of schmoozing and lobbying. He marches through the corridor, chin high and belly out, grunting with every step. Iris cringes. Ella and Francis fawn in his presence, laugh at his not funny jokes, and agree excitedly with everything he says. They may both be 900, but his late 900 Score makes their knickers wet.

'With the big event coming up,' he says, voice booming. 'I've been studying the psychology of the low Scorers.'

'With a brain like yours, that must be easy,' Ella says.

Iris scrunches her nose. When he's not around, they both say what a brute he is. But here he is now, and they're lapping him up like they're kittens and he's the milk. Brown nosing for points is all they care about.

'And I am quite confident I will be able to weed them out,' he continues. 'I know their hiding places and mentality. I know how to win a fight.'

'Oh, Mr Bonnet. I absolutely agree,' Ella says, holding her hands to her chest like an awestruck bimbo.

'And I can tell who is going to slip down the Score ladder with the new algorithm.' He raises one eyebrow, a coquettish expression that makes Francis fan herself.

Francis flicks her hair, then rolls her shoulders back to push her tits forward. 'What a clever man you are, Norman.'

Ella scowls at her friend, and by some anti-gravity miracle, gets her bosom to almost touch Norman's chin. 'You and your son. How inspirational you are.'

What Norman or any of them do in the statistics department is beyond Iris. She gets the statistics and tells them. They send the information on; paper pushing, that's all. And feeling important.

'Thank you, ladies,' Norman says. 'How about we all go get lunch?'

He's not even being subtle, such is the arrogance of the high Scorers. Even if Iris had no clue about what was going to happen, she'd have a damned good idea now. This makes her worry more that there's no escaping it. They don't know about their hack, she reminds herself. That'll catch them off guard. The high Scorers have no clue how prepared they are.

You have the upper hand. They're too self-absorbed to see you coming.

The voice is right. Iris and her friends are sneaking up on the Eyes Forward. They have no idea what's coming.

A lot has been going through Iris's mind since she found out about her ancestors, and Georgie's theory — them holding her in this job to keep an eye on her. Maybe they gave her internet access so they'll have better access to what she's doing, to track her more. They likely assumed she was using a home computer somewhere. Paranoia courses through her. She is everything the Eyes Forward wants and everything they hate.

When she couldn't sleep last night, she searched Nebula for references of Joan Porter, and threads there filled in a few gaps. She invented Pres-X, then took it herself when she was too senile and died in a psychotic episode a few weeks later. The Sub 750s who took Pres-X and ended up in asylums were referred to as suffering from the Joan Porter effect. XL Medico discredited her as she wasn't from the right background, but then her husband, the now infamous Lloyd Porter, rose to new heights. Sounds about right, to push the woman to one side and shower the man with accolades. Knowing that formula must have put him in a position of power. Like her mum.

Her fucking mum.

Iris fidgets restlessly at her desk, then sifts through the details on demographics. The sharp incline between 650 and 700 is there, as always, the small step down to 800, and the steep drop after. The wedge at the low Scorer and un-Scorable end is still there, though slightly smaller. That gives Iris chills. No chance that reduction in the lowest Scores is purely a result of citizens striving to Score. The massacre must be causing it. It wasn't just in Berkshire. Un-Scorable dorms were being emptied and their inhabitants killed across the Society.

And Iris knows this is just the beginning.

During the Great Unrest, when Iris was born, the life donation policy was branded a cull.

Ten years later, the Pres-X release to Sub 750s cost many lives, elder citizens driven to madness from the drug, yet XL Medico denied it for ages and continued to give out the treatment. Now Iris has learned that they knew all along, and the antidote was only given to the rich.

That was branded as a cull.

Iris always scoffed at such a term before — overly dramatic hyperbole for those who yearn for more drama. But when no one is held accountable, no punishment awarded nor apology nor lesson learned, history repeats itself. Citizens of the Society are blindly walking into another cull. Because they refuse to see, refuse to question. That walled-in eye is like Plato's Cave. They can't see past it. They believe those in power have their best intentions at heart. Because their own desire for wealth and all its perks clouds their vision to what's in front of them.

Is this what it's all been leading to? Attempt after attempt by the Eyes Forward to rid the Society of its less well-off, a happy conjoining of the Enough and the Time's Up factions. No one cares which age brackets are slaughtered this time as long as they're poor.

As Iris reviews the demographics, there are still so many poor and so many low Scorers in Berkshire alone who are at risk. She tuts at the stupidity of it; how people have been so blind. Humans are only ever one generation away from forgetting their past. Stories die on muted mouths. Pages rot and burn. Computers delete their cache. It takes effort to pass on knowledge. It takes zero effort to forget. That's what the Eyes Forward are banking on. The innate laziness of humankind. Dull the senses with reports of other problems, and citizens ignore the much bigger issues. Hold the bait of renewed youth in someone's eyeline, and all the true awfulness is obscured. It's as Georgie says: decoy politics.

Iris emails the stats of the demographic results to Ella and Francis. She tells the truth for the first time in a couple of weeks. And then she slowly cycles home, still plenty of time before curfew. The Lloyd Porter story has been pushed back to the tail end of the news. The quarterly demographic results have stolen the limelight for today. Today's decoy.

There's been no progress finding the killer. They mention thoughts for his family. Did he have another family? Iris wonders, despite her hatred for the man. She's glad he's dead. She hopes it hurt, that he knew fear, worse than the fear Iris and Georgie felt that night when they were hunted. She hopes he died in his own excrement, soggy with piss. Perhaps that would have made him feel some shame.

Chapter 38
Iris

Georgie is talking to the mirror when Iris gets home. Iris stops a while, watching her, listening, before she can't stifle her giggles any longer.

'Iris!' Georgie says as she snaps around, her cheeks blushing. 'How long have you been standing there?'

'Long enough. What are you doing?'

'Practising being a news reporter, like I always wanted.' She holds her head a little higher, and there's a glint in her eye, one not brought on by whisky and tears.

'No way! They're giving you a job?'

'Sod them. I'm giving myself one. When we take them down, I'm going to report it all — live from the ground.'

Iris shakes her head. 'You can't, Georgie.' She tries to make the same pleading face Georgie so often does, the one that's impossible to argue with. 'That's so dangerous. If we fail—'

'We won't.' Georgie appears the most determined Iris has ever seen her. Gone are her giggles and tears. Gone is every trace of fear from their ordeal. Her ruby lips form a straight line, her shoulders are back and squared and her eyes unblinking. 'We're going to do this. We have a plan. It's going to work.'

Iris has never talked Georgie down when she's made up her mind, but she tries, she has to try. 'It's too risky. You're adding more danger for yourself. And this is if Tash can make the hack work.'

'She's brilliant. She will. The high Scorers will destroy themselves if it all works. They think they'll be hunting the low Scorers, but they'll be destroying everything. We won't need to get involved with anything. We can just watch them unravel their whole precious Society and all their stupid Life Score points.'

If the hack works; Georgie is right. Only now it dawns on Iris that destroying the Life Score network means destroying her mother. And her dad's medication supply. She's selfish to feel that way. They'll find another way to get her dad's medication, like she said before. If the Eyes Forward criminalised her mum for any screw up, well, she brought it on herself.

'It's all we can do, Iris. We have to do something.'

Iris gives a small nod and walks away. From the privacy of her bedroom, she loads up Nebula. She tries and tries to search for other counties, to see if a hunt has been confirmed in any of them. So many forums are still down, but there are new ones, new chat threads. However much the Eyes Forward are trying to silence people, the chatter won't stop. There are rumours of planned hunts like in Berkshire, other low Scorers have heard. Some are worried their area will be worse since there are more low Scorers, though some think that'll be a good thing since there are fewer high Scorers to go on a rampage. The rumours are more than gossip. People have overheard and hacked and seen evidence. But there is nothing to imply it's happened before. So, either Berkshire is the first, the only, or its Society-wide all at once.

It's only there for a moment before it disappears and gets taken down, but it pops up again and again. Someone is reposting it everywhere. A list, a points list. Someone who calls themselves GT28 has shared it. It's a list of how much each life taken is worth in points. One point per kill. But twenty or more in any one incident, a building collapse, for example, points are doubled and given to everyone who helped barricade and collapse the building. Easier to cover it up, that's clear.

A message at the end reads: *NO GUNS. WE'RE NOT SAVAGES. THESE MUST BE HONOURABLE KILLS.*

Honourable kills. It actually says that.

Iris could so easily walk away, safe with her not-too-low Score. She could lock the doors and watch the world go to shit around her. That would be the easy option, the safe option, an option she's considered more than once — hide under the duvet and wait for all the horribleness to go away. But every time she hears more about it, she feels old Iris Taylor nudging her on, lighting a fire inside her.

If they can get the hack right, it could work so well. The date is on the top of the list. It's 15th March.

Iris manages to take a screenshot of the points list, then shows Georgie.

Georgie does a slow, loud exhale. 'Well, that confirms it.'

'That's a Saturday. Only ten days away.'

As Iris messages the others about the date confirmation, the news reports state the quarterly results are in. The walled-in eye fills the screen and the Eyes Forward anthem plays. There's something alluring about the tune, like it's subliminal messaging. Iris and Georgie sit and watch, out of habit more than interest, out of conditioning and historical duty. Such Eyes Forward announcements are choreographed with expert lighting and just the right amount of pizazz. It's almost impossible not to watch.

It's the Prime Minister. His never-ageing face shows up every quarter and for the most important announcements in between. It's been that way for as long as Iris can remember. She never questioned it before. Why always the same man, what's he doing the rest of the time? It just is how it is, how it's always been. What a damned fool she's been to never question! He's flanked by an Eyes Forward representative on either side. Their almost symmetrical faces appear unsmiling, half concealed by the shadows of their wide-brimmed hats. Iris and Georgie's TV struggles with the black suits and the colours swim.

The Prime Minister's rigid face stares directly down at the camera, the sort of stare that bores straight through you. 'Citizens of the Society, the quarterly results are in. While the Eyes Forward must commend the majority of citizens for their continued efforts in bringing the population down, we are sad to report that we still have not yet met our sub 100 million target. At 110 million, the population is currently still 10 million too high. Rest assured, as a Society we will tackle this. We have an international commitment to honour, and the Society is a shining example of what we can achieve when every citizen knows their place.

'The demographics are off kilter. There are too many low Scorers dragging down our average, but we have high hopes that by the next quarterly announcement our methods will have proved effective.'

That sentence is enough to snap Iris out of the trance, and she picks up the remote to mute it. 'Effective'. That's what they consider mass murder to be. Georgie grabs Iris's hand and squeezes it. They sit in silence, eyes glazed, staring nowhere, the cold licking its way up Iris's spine.

You're going to take them down, Iris. I believe in you.

The voice may have been trying to give Iris some confidence, but it fails. The determination of the Eyes Forward to enact their plan creates a barrier to hope. The Eyes Forward are too strong, too resolute.

Iris's shoulders curl forward. She takes her hand back, opting to hug herself instead as her stomach caves in with the hopelessness of it all.

Without help, the odds are against them.

Chapter 39
Mae

The formula was easy for Mae to reconstruct. The sparse notes Lloyd Porter left behind gave a nudge, though he kept most of his knowledge secure in his mind. Funny that those who control the data don't trust its security. The nudge was merely that, for as much as Mae tried to bury it away in her mind, it resurfaced readily. Numbers and equations never seem to erase themselves from Mae's brain. She still remembers every phone number she's ever had, every postcode she's ever lived at, and even restaurant bills from special occasions years ago.

Recalling the original Life Score formula she slaved over years ago was simple, morphing it into what her father changed it into took a little longer. She had to approach it with his degree of ruthlessness, to put herself in the shoes of someone so obsessed with elitism that he would sit back and let the poorest lose their homes and have nothing but powdered rations to eat. But she has it. She stares at the line of Xs and Ys on her screen. It's shorter than most would expect; certainly theoretical physicists would be surprised. There's an ugliness in its simplicity. That people can be quantified by such an equation is vulgar. To think she was ever naïve enough to help create such a formula, that she was so taken with her desire for logic and order, she never saw the maliciousness in it. Her hypothesis moulded to their own.

Iris had mentioned Plato's Cave, and that sums it up well. She was so enraptured with the writing on the wall, she never even tried to peer out. The cave was bigger back then, there was a little more room to manoeuvre. It's shrunk over the years and now she squashes her arms by her sides and keeps her head low. The rocks creak as they creep in.

The ohm symbol on the left of the equation is a changeable number that has its own separate formula to evolve with external factors, to keep the economy at the required balance. It's what the Eyes Forward refer to as the living part of the equation. Adaptable, they say. The formula strives with the citizens. It's that part she's expected to change.

She knows what the Eyes Forward want. They weren't even subtle when they told her. They were forthright in their demands, as if they were telling her what brand of coffee to buy.

Every Sub 200 is to be demoted. That's their aim, for the lowest to sink lower.

Mae has a pencil in her hand, working on paper. It's safer than a computer, less traceable. She can burn her notes if needed.

Iris's disapproval pulled a chord. Pasha's too, one that she was hoping to ignore. How can she keep her family safe and do what Iris wants? How can she do right by the lowest Scorers and her family? Pasha's protests had come slurred with wheezing breaths, ripping at her heart. She can't sit back and watch him suffer more. He once said he was her armour. Now it's her turn to be his.

She's been working on the formula for seven hours and thirteen minutes today. Four hundred and thirty-three minutes. Twenty-five thousand, one hundred and eighty seconds. Distracting herself with simple sums calms her, but doesn't get the work done. She chews the end of the pencil, wipes down the already clean surfaces, then polishes the mirrors before getting back to work again.

She stares at the numbers, the symbols that were her only friends once, the symbols she knows and understands so well. Usually she works for them, now she needs them to work for her.

She bites her lip, picturing the rearrangement of the formula, subtle changes, an imperceptible tweak.

A small glitch is what she needs. Something easily disguised as an error. Like when she drops a single stitch in her knitting. A tightly knitted scarf takes longer to unravel than a loose one. Any action needs to be artfully applied, deviously altered. The fallout from any change would be subtle. A ratio altered, a little chaos.

She glances at the chess game they've been playing for two days now and moves a pawn one place.

Chapter 40
Iris

On Friday, Iris, like everyone across the Society, checks her Life Score. She doesn't load up the app to the sound of the jingle and mutes her phone before the celebratory music plays. She doesn't check while she's in a high Score bar or café, like so many will, or among the company of friends and loved ones. She's so consumed with digesting the figures for the rest of the Society that she only remembers to check her new Score when she's sitting on the toilet. It's unchanged at 270.

While making herself a cup of tepid, bitter coffee, she leans against the counter, printouts of the charts in her hand, then studies the demographics. There's not been the big shift that so many expected, hardly any Sub 800s getting pushed into the 900s, and not many low Scorers dropping down far. The demographic chart is much the same. But the news tells a different story, as does Ella.

'It must be a mistake,' she cries, hanging on Francis, who bats her away like she's a bug. 'I'm a 900 plus. They can't put me this low. It's a mistake.'

Francis clicks her tongue and steps around her, giving her neediness a wide berth. 'It must be your DNA. You submitted it, right?'

'Yes, of course. But my family goes back generations.'

Francis checks her slowly, more carefully than she ever has before when making flippant compliments, like she's trying to find the hint of a foreigner she's been hiding. 'Look,' she says after her inspection. 'You're still Preserved and sterile. I'm sure they won't sack you.'

'Sacked?' Ella gasps. 'It's not even my job I'm concerned about.' Although it really sounds like it is. 'I've millions in debt that I can keep up with payments easily as a 900 plus. I'm going to spiral now. Where can I even eat?'

Francis rubs her ear and winces. Ella is screechy, but not *that* screechy. 'I really think you should get your life in order rather than scream at me.'

'180. Sub 200. How is that even possible? My neighbourhood is 800 plus. I'll lose my home to this.'

'At least you're not un-Scorable.' Francis's lack of compassion surprises Ella from the shock on her face, though Iris is barely entertained. It's always the way. The high Score's empathy is limited to their wealthy friends' minor aesthetic dramas. Real problems don't even register.

Ella's eyes widen then, fear creating red lines creeping up the whites. She steps closer to Francis, who maintains their distance and steps back. 'They're changing it, you know,' she says. Her voice is not the low whisper she probably thinks it is. 'It's not just un-Scorables to be targeted. There wasn't enough of a shift. Oh my God. It's the Sub 200s. They could hunt me!'

Francis upturns her mouth and nods. 'Well, if you're eligible, then that's what's best. The Eyes Forward know what they're doing. It's about what's best for the Society, not just for you.'

Tears fill Ella's eyes, then cut rivets down her cheeks through her makeup. Iris almost feels sorry for her. Almost.

'Perhaps I could stay with you?' Ella asks Francis.

Francis takes another step away and holds up her hands. 'My neighbourhood is more exclusive than yours. I can hardly have a Sub 200 living with me.' She glares at Ella as if she smells like rotten vegetables rather than the floral musk of her intense perfume.

Iris stops eavesdropping and sits at her desk, feeling quite fortunate her Score wasn't reduced, then inwardly chastises herself for that thought, reminding herself that the whole system is bollocks. She wants to not care, really wants to, but there's a part of her brain that she can't switch off, the part the Eyes Forward have been attaching puppet strings to since she was born.

Soon, Iris, you'll be free of them.

The voice sounds as certain as ever. At least her madness is the self-assured kind.

Ella leaves their office, her hair in disarray and face red and wet with tears. The news is on a loop on the TV across the office, and Iris finds the remote to turn it up.

According to the news, apparently, it's not just Ella. It's not the usual anchor. The one who perved on Georgie isn't working for the channel anymore since he logged his new Score of 200. He's the most prominent 'victim of the Society's continued success,' so the headline reads. The new anchor is grinning like he's swallowed a coat hanger. The shift has been a bit random, with some top Scorers downgraded to almost nothing. The odd un-Scorable is now an 800 plus.

Iris's lips curl up into a smile. Her mum wouldn't make such a mistake. She's not capable of getting numbers wrong. She did the right thing. Sort of. She didn't fix it, but she highlighted how stupid the system is. She threw some nonsense into the mix.

Chapter 41
Ava

Ava stays away from XL Medico, emailing instead to say she's doing new factory site visits all weekend, and she'll be there to oversee the factory start up from Monday. They'll probably assume Mandisa is with her. She can avoid questions for a time, helping her to compartmentalise everything she has to do and everything she's done. Revenge isn't as sweet as she thought it would be. It sits heavy on her chest, and she's not even done yet.

The new factory is taking over the old Butts Shopping Mall. The development has breathed life into the end of town that saw the worst carnage during the Great Unrest and has had the least renovation since. XL Medico was pleased enough; it meant the building was cheap. For the richest company in the Society, throwing a pittance at their biggest scaling-up project to date has made their shareholders very happy. Ava made a brief appearance at the CEO meeting where the development was announced, and all the men sitting around the table literally rubbed their chubby hands together.

Since XL Medico is also the Eyes Forward's most generous financier, Ava's sceptical mind wonders if keeping that end of town rundown was the plan all along. Create poverty and let the fat cats profit. It's the circle of life.

It's test day for the equipment in the factory. The engineers finished the install last week, so this is the last step before they can put it to use. Making Preservation drugs. Angus is already on site when Ava arrives. His logistics company has proven instrumental in sourcing all they need from across the Society, and those skills and contacts Ava's put to use elsewhere.

'Morning, Ava,' he says when she approaches.

They each glance over their shoulders as they shake hands, then Ava offers him the backpack. 'Last couple of kilos.'

'Shouldn't need any more. The date is almost here.'

'Nebula?'

'It's working. The forums are being shut down everywhere, but word is getting out. There are more users than ever. I went to a flat party last weekend—'

'I know.' Ava's tone bites.

'You know?'

'A Society Police took a photo of you handing out Flake. You're damned lucky I intercepted it.' She omits the part that it was Iris who uploaded the photo, and that she only knew because she tapped Iris's phone. 'I specifically told you not to.'

'I had to check to make sure it's working properly. It was a lot of fun actually.'

'Fun is not really the aim here.'

'I know. I'm sorry. And, God, thanks for helping. But listen, everyone there was taking Flake. And everyone was talking about an uprising, disbelieving all the Eyes Forward hype. Some were quoting *ETC*, that bit of coding has spread everywhere. I only painted it a couple of times, others have done the rest. The drug really works. It makes people question everything.'

It didn't take that long to get the recipe right for the drug. Once Ava had gone through the chemical compositions of B-Well and Memorexin, she knew she was halfway there just by mixing the two. Adding the sprinkling of psilocybe was what brought it all together so beautifully and is something the government-controlled pharmaceutical company would never have foreseen. They'd never consider such a heady mix of happiness to be something worth exploring. With the hunt so close though, time has almost run out. 'There's hardly any time now before the hunt.'

'I'll get this out there,' Angus says. 'It'll give the low Scorers an edge. It staves off panic and reinforces logic. It even enhances their night vision. It'll give them more of a fighting chance.'

Angus's courage is admirable. He's only a mid Scorer. It's rare for someone to believe so passionately in a cause who doesn't massively profit from it nor hugely lose out. With his Score, he has a better choice of eateries than the lower, but that's about it.

'You're risking a lot,' Ava says.

'As are you. Well done on passing the no guns rule, by the way. I don't think I ever commended you for that one.'

'It wasn't that hard. I mean, where would they source all the guns? That would only delay things. And in the end, they loved the idea of being honourable.'

They both laugh at that.

'I couldn't stop the explosives though. Grenades, mostly. They were distributed a while ago.'

'A few explosions might not be a bad thing,' he says with a smirk.

Their walk around the factory proves the equipment works. It all hums to life when they start it up with a flick of a few switches. Centrifuges and conveyors run smoothly with minimal human input, and there's robotic arms for the packaging. It's like a dance. If it were making any other drug, Ava would dance too. Preservation drugs warrant no such celebration though. It's brought out the worst in everyone.

The building appears beautifully constructed, reclaimed red bricks on the outside to give it a classic flair that contrasts with the shiny steel equipment. The floors are clean and tiled, reflective glass windows add some light, each brick and inch of render and windowpane look purposeful and strong.

'Rolan did a good job on the build,' Ava says.

'Yeah.' Angus nods. 'Dad's a good architect.'

The times she met Rolan, she was blown away by his sincerity and dedication. It's easy to see where his son gets his moral compass from. But his wife is another matter. She could match Mandisa for snobbery and believes that the Eyes Forward are right in serving the most deserving best. She's only met her once. Her skin was still rosy from the recent Pres-X-2 treatment that left her appearing younger than her son. Moira fawned over Ava, wanting selfies and laughing exuberantly at everything Ava said, as if Ava's a noteworthy comedian. She's not, and she gets rather sick of people's attempts to suck up to her because of her mild celebrity status. It's but another side effect of the Society's model for the population. It's created such fakery, it's impossible to know who your friends are and who's just sucking up for status and pharmaceuticals.

'There're no stockpiles of Pres-X-2,' Ava explains. 'Demand is too high with second doses being rolled out. It sells quicker than we can make it. If this building were to be destroyed, it would cause chaos among the 700 pluses.'

'Wouldn't that be a shame,' Angus says with a glint in his eye.

'Well, the factory seems to be working just fine, so I'll see that all of Pres-X-2 manufacturing is moved here immediately. First thing Monday. It should be in full swing by the weekend, making a hundred per cent of Berkshire's Pres-X-2 and fifty per cent of the entire Society's.'

'Perfect timing.'

Ava has nothing but hate for Pres-X-2, for the drug she was forced to take, for the fact that it made her appear younger, and that was one of the main reasons why she's been so financially successful and why Mandisa fell for her again. She never believed her excuses of their prior breakup being to keep Ava safe and Mandisa's covert Time's Up work below the radar. She wanted perkier tits and smoother skin in her partner. That's the recipe for success.

The Eyes Forward use the promise of youth as a bribe, and so many citizens fall for it. They keep the masses controlled by holding citizens' youth to ransom. Behave and never age. This will be a lesson for them.

Ava and Angus part ways, and Ava walks to the funeral home. On her way, she stops by the Society Police building, turning left down the alleyway where the thick gas pipes are. She's gone over this so many times in her head, checked the plans over and over, mimed the actions in private; it's almost like muscle memory. It takes less than a minute to swap the inflow for the outflow.

For the briefest moment, she considers opening the door and checking on Mandisa, to see that she really is dead. There's no banging coming from the inside, not that she'd hear it from the outside. The walls are thick, armour-level protection for the precious data centre inside. By Ava's calculations, Mandisa would have suffocated from the lack of oxygen hours ago. She tries not to picture her blue lips or her hands to her throat as she gasps her final poisoned breath. No, she wouldn't have done that. She would have sat, a little delirious but without pain. It would have been a nice death — a hit of euphoria before the end. A better death than she afforded the thousands upon thousands who took dodgy Pres-X doses.

There's an old asylum near the factory. She tries to bring the image of that to her mind instead of Mandisa's dead body, tries to remember the sound of the building falling — the screams of insanity were long extinguished by then. Some people say the elders were left chained up to die of starvation like in a mediaeval dungeon. She pictures that: the shackles cutting into bony wrists, their freshly preserved pink skin turning pale, eyes wild and scared with fear and fatigue. She tries to imagine if her Zia had taken Pres-X and died in such a way.

It makes the guilt slide away, tipping the scales back where they should be.

No one suspected foul play when the asylums crumbled. No one said it out loud anyway. Nebula was rife with such accusations, of course. But that's low Score tittle-tattle. It holds no weight when the Eyes Forward press release blames the Great Unrest and reminds everyone how amazing they are for bringing about peace.

The cost of keeping alive such mentally ill elders was unjustifiable, Mandisa had said at dinner one night. This is kinder. Their original plan was to never section them in the first place, but they couldn't deny the situation. The Eyes Forward have to be seen to be doing something, Mandisa had said. It's what's best for the Society.

Perhaps gentle asphyxiation was too kind a death.

Recalibrating the gas flow is easy enough. Now all she has to do is wait. Just one spark is all it needs.

She feels no remorse for the soon demise of the Society Police and has nothing but shame for her devout service for years. Society Police pitted citizen against citizen, people creating hate rather than uniting against the one, real enemy. With that level of animosity among the public, no one notices what the government gets up to. It's just another distraction from the Eyes Forward.

This revenge has been nearly two decades in the making, yet it has sour undertones, like overripe fruit.

She thinks of Zia, their friendship, and the kindness Zia always shared.

Zia wouldn't recognise her now.

When she makes it back to the funeral home, she glances at the photograph of her parents on the wall. They'd turned their backs on their cause for the sake of their personal profit. Sold their souls. From the outside, it would appear Ava's done much the same. The new Life Score algorithm would claim it's in her DNA. She was born to be a traitor.

She goes through the books at the funeral home, checking the staff are doing what they should. It's all in order. They're impeccably trained.

On the list is Lloyd Porter. Another pang of guilt raps at her chest. Mae has signed off on his details as his next of kin. Ava hadn't really expected that. As estranged as they were, she'd assumed Lloyd Porter would have someone else lined up. Perhaps if he knew he was going to die, he would have gotten such affairs in order. His death came as quite the surprise.

Looking at what Mae has signed off for her dad's funeral plans, it's clear that his death hasn't upset her. Perhaps she's coming around to how drastic action needs to be. Perhaps Ava won't be the only one with blood on her hands.

Chapter 42
Iris

They didn't dare meet over the weekend with curfew banning them from leaving their apartments. Iris keeps checking Nebula for news. There are reports of the odd killing but not an all-out mass slaughter. The big event is yet to come.

They arrange to meet at Iris and Georgie's place in the week. Stage one, Georgie calls it, sober this time and has a lot more to say about everything. They've tidied the flat, put out basic snacks, and even flushed the toilet. It's probably the tidiest the place has been in ages.

Georgie pulls on a balaclava, black and knitted, leaving only her mouth and eyes uncovered.

'What do you think?' she asks Iris.

'It looks warm.'

Georgie takes it off, her hair sticking up from the static. 'It's to maintain anonymity for the news story.'

'Oh! I see. Good idea.'

'I'm going to start tonight,' she says. 'We need to warn people. And then later, if we broadcast a story where we say everyone is hiding in the Eyes Forward building, that'll help the hack.'

Iris can't deny the logic. It all makes sense. She just wishes it wasn't Georgie on camera. She watches her practice in front of the mirror for a while, projecting her voice, making every syllable clear and engaging. She's a natural, much better than the entitled idiots the news normally features. If she'd been a higher Scorer, she'd have been in a real TV job for years. Perhaps if they succeed and there are no Life Scores anymore, Georgie will have a shot.

Skylar, Tash, Johan, and Ezra arrive on time. Skylar makes her way to the snacks as soon as she enters the apartment. Like many of the lowest Scorers, she's thin and pale, her blue hair only emphasising her sad appearance. Iris doubts she's ever even tried dried fruit. After they've all had refreshments, Iris shows them the screenshot of the points allocations for proof, just in case there was still an ounce of doubt in their minds.

Ezra's pallor is stark, appearing as if he hasn't slept since they last saw him. There's no doubt now his sister and nephew are dead, along with so many others. And now he knows they were murdered for points like a sick reenactment of a computer game.

'No,' he says. 'We cannot let this happen to anyone else. This has to stop now.' In his broken state, he's also resolute. His anger is fuelling his motivation.

Georgie puts her arm around him. 'We won't. We're going to save them all.'

Iris swallows and hopes it's not an empty promise. Saving them all and doing the best they can are two ends of a very wide scale.

They go through the hack, Plato, as Tash calls it. 'I've run through it so many times. Sorry it's taken so long, but I think I'm there. I've ironed out all the kinks. It's pretty easy to use. Let me show you.'

Iris and Georgie watch, and it's as easy as she says, although the coding behind it must be masterful.

'It's this Saturday,' Iris says when they've learned how it works. 'Just four days. All the 800 pluses are going to be out to kill. They must be exploring our streets now, scouting out buildings and routes.'

'The curfew is playing into their hands,' Georgie says. 'Everyone will be indoors, at home. They'll gas people out like they did with Ezra's family or just collapse whole buildings and blame an earthquake.'

Iris winces at her crass remark. Painting such a vivid picture of what happened to Ezra's family seems unnecessary, although he nods, his expression set like steel.

'We need to hunt the hunters,' Johan says. His broad frame and deep voice make him seem like he could tackle the job solo. 'They won't be expecting any retaliation. They think they'll be catching everyone off guard. I'll bet none of them can actually fight, nor would they want to. They'll be too worried about scarring and ruining their complexions. We don't have to kill anyone, just show that we can cut their stupid faces a bit.'

'Combat is a huge risk,' Iris says.

Johan slams his hands on the table. 'A risk I am willing to take.'

Ezra puts his hands down too, though he's a weed next to Johan. 'I agree. I'm happy to get my hands dirty. More than that — I want to.'

'It says no guns.' Johan snorts a laugh. 'Honourable killings. I find that hard to believe.'

Skylar seems more terrified of Johan than anyone. No, not terrified, in awe, like she's never seen a person so huge, so determined. 'We should watch for people planting bombs,' she says. 'They're definitely going to be doing their homework.'

'You're right,' Tash says. 'Plato needs to be activated before they light the explosives, if that's what they're doing. I can't imagine them attacking the buildings with sledgehammers. We can't move people. They'd get killed in the streets instead. We have to make it appear they're somewhere else before they blow stuff up.'

Georgie steps forward. 'That's where my news reports will come in. I'll make them think we've intervened.'

'So,' Iris says, taking a deep breath. 'We all know what we're doing?'

They nod and mumble a yes, except for Johan, who bellows his response. Not the most resounding voice of confidence, but they're all in uncertain agreement. Their plan has a million holes, so many things can go wrong. Iris can't even quantify.

They have no time to rehearse or change anything. This is what they have. That and their determination.

That counts for so much, Iris. You can do this.

Chapter 43
Mae

The Eyes Forward knock. Odd for them. They usually just barge in, but Mae knows it's them from the rhythm, a steady drumbeat. No one with any sort of personality would knock like that. She and Pasha lock eyes.

'It's okay,' she says. 'I'll get it.'

Three of them stand in the doorway close together, like they're one being. To intimidate, probably. The sort of tactics prey use against a predator, Mae thinks. Except the Eyes Forward definitely aren't the prey, ever. She expects them to demand she come with them but, instead, they stare at her in the doorway for a while, then walk past and enter her home uninvited. She wonders for a moment if they rehearse this, if they discuss intimidation tactics en route, or if they're all just one mind, like starlings or locusts.

They walk through her hallway, then stand in her living room in front of her husband, taking five steps to do so, whereas Mae usually takes six. Pasha doesn't do them the courtesy of standing, though they probably prefer that. They step closer, towering over him, and he flicks his gaze up to them for a second before glancing at Mae. His face of reassurance doesn't help much, and Mae sits next to him and stares at the floor.

She bites her tongue and pulls her sleeves down, wringing them out in her fists. They should have just taken her away like last time. This is worse. It's *her* home. He's *her* husband. Mae thinks of these things as hers, but all could be taken away by the Eyes Forward in a second. Do regular citizens ever really own anything? Is anything ever really owned by people without power, or is life and all of its blessings actually just on loan from the powerful? Any moment, someone higher up the pecking order can simply turn up and collect.

'Pasha Taylor?' one Eyes Forward representative asks.

Pasha stares at all three of them as if they're individual people. 'Yes.'

'Your wife has been disobedient. She has not done her duty to the Society.'

'Erm,' Mae stands up. 'I'm right here.'

'Women, even safe age women, should be adequately controlled. Failure to do so means you are failing the Society.'

'Excuse me!' Mae stamps her foot.

The Eyes Forward turn slowly to face her. 'Your job was to demote the 200s to un-Scorable or near enough.'

'It's difficult. You didn't give me enough time.'

'Clearly, your husband didn't motivate you. He failed to support you in this task.'

She makes eye contact with Pasha. He's unruffled, always so damned cool.

'Look,' she says. 'Just give me another chance. Leave my husband out of this.'

'As such,' the Eyes Forward continues, 'his access to healthcare will be limited until you complete your task. You have until Friday to fix the algorithm.'

'That's four days! I can't possibly—'

'Every Sub 200 will be un-Scorable by Friday night. If you fail, your daughter will lose all of her points and will be ranked as un-Scorable. Is that clear?'

Mae's stomach twists, and she nods as they show themselves out.

'I have to do it,' Mae says, cupping her head in her hands. 'What choice do we have?'

'Mae, you can't,' Pasha says. 'There must be another way. We can't let them get away with this.'

She sits on the seat next to his and he grabs her hand, then leans in and rests his forehead on hers. 'We can't let Iris become un-Scorable. You've seen the rumours on Nebula. What if they're true?'

'You can stop this, Mae. If there are no Life Scores, the hunt wouldn't work.'

She sits forward and rearranges his hair that's smudging up his glasses. It's gotten too long. He needs a trim. 'That's a huge risk. They'd know it was me. They'd know it was us.'

He takes her hand. His shakes are completely gone now. He's her sturdy rock again. 'Doing nothing, just playing along, is a bigger risk.'

She sees so much of his grandmother in him, and Iris. They both have a reckless nature, a belief that if you're doing something for the good of others, it'll all just work out. Mae is a tad more realistic.

'You know you can do it,' Pasha says. 'But I have a plan B, too.'

Mae tenses and narrows her eyes at him. She knows that tone of voice, the tone that means he's planned something stupid. 'What?'

'Don't be mad. . .'

Too late. She knows him too well and might as well get mad now. 'Oh, God. Pasha, what have you done?'

'It's a good idea. Something they can't trace back to us.'

'Pasha,' she says his name through her teeth. 'What have you been up to?'

'So. . .' His face flushes with guilt as he searches for words. 'About that photography course I've been on with Rolan—'

'Oh, no.' She shakes her head and puts her hands over her ears. 'I'm not going to like this. What have you done?' The carpet in front of her has crumbs on it. How did she miss those? She'll vacuum in a moment. That'll make everything better.

'The time we've been spending together. . .we've been planning something. Wait here.' He leaves the room a moment, then returns with a cardboard tube, removing some rolled up paper from inside. 'Look.'

Nope. Vacuuming is not going to be enough to calm her. 'You have documents stashed under our bed labelled confidential — for Eyes Forward and XL Medico CEOs only. Pasha, we just had Eyes Forward representatives in our home! What if they'd found that?'

'It was in the wardrobe. Why would they look there? Rolan couldn't keep them at his place. Moira would go mad.'

'And I wouldn't?'

'You'd understand.'

She bloody well won't, and the face she makes depicts just that.

'Just think, Mae-bug. The high Scorers. All they care about is Pres-X and Pres-X-2. The new factory is making all of it. If that were destroyed, it would create quite the distraction, don't you think?'

'You're going to destroy the factory? You'll get done for terrorism, Pasha.'

'No. Just the Preservation drugs. See, Rolan designed the factory, and all the drugs are stored on this side, in big fridges. All we have to do is cut the electric. There're backups, of course, but if we cut the cables in all these places, open the doors, it'll be maybe an hour before all the drugs are ruined.'

'So? That's vengeance. It doesn't stop anything.'

'Think about it. The factory will be open, the fridges open. We'll put an anonymous post out on Nebula and inform the press. Make sure the alarm goes off. You think that all those 800 pluses awaiting first and second doses will be fussed about hunting when they can fill their pockets with preservation drugs — when they can *save* the preservation drugs?'

That's actually Pasha's plan. They might as well hand their daughter over to the Society Police, send a request in for her to be un-Scorable, and for the two of them to be imprisoned. She can feel the handcuffs digging in already. God, they'd be on the news. Her face everywhere.

'You're going to destroy billions of pounds' worth of drugs and do it by accessing the building Rolan designed?' How is it she's saying these words? It's so ridiculous. She's almost out of her body, staring down at an idiot couple having this conversation. This isn't her. This isn't her husband.

'He told me exactly how to get in the building, where all the cables are,' Pasha says. Still so damned calm. 'He wants this destroyed as much as anyone. He's going to meet me over there.'

They've actually planned this. Mae puts her head in her hands. 'This is your most dumbass idea yet.'

Chapter 44
Iris

Georgie pins her hair back, wetting her hands to get rid of the static flyaways, then flattens it down so it doesn't make her head appear massive under the balaclava. She then applies her usual ruby lipstick and checks her eyelash extensions, since they're the only parts of her face that will be visible on camera. Iris watches every move, in awe of the glam she portrays even though her face is mostly covered, even when they're in a time of crisis. Iris attempts to tame her own locks for a moment, just so she doesn't seem so dishevelled next to Georgie, then resigns herself to the behind-the-camera role.

They play around with lighting and backgrounds for a while to get it just right, and when they're about ready, Iris hands Georgie a cup of warm water with sugar. They were longing for honey but have none, so they hope the sugar is just the same.

They've cleared a wall of pictures and furniture — easy to do when there's so much empty space around the rest of the flat. Now all that remains is bare brick. It was partially rendered when they first moved in, but the damp air from no heating made it flake off bit by bit. One day, in a moment of frustration over the constant wall crumbs on the floor, they hacked away the lot and decided bare brick had a certain boutique feel. Now, it's the perfect background for Georgie.

Iris places her phone on a stand to keep it steady. The others are all behind her, sitting on chairs facing Georgie, becoming her first live audience. They've opted to stay over. There's safety in numbers, and it means they don't have to worry about getting home before curfew.

'I think we can maintain a secure line for two minutes,' Tash says as she loads up the secure Virtual Private Network. It's software she designed herself and balloons with pride as she shows it off. 'It's the most private of private networks,' she said when she showed them. 'Most get traced in seconds, but this one, this beauty, *tens* of seconds.'

Iris admires her, and a flutter moves through her tummy. With someone as smart as Tash on their team, maybe they really can pull this off.

Georgie clears her throat, wipes her palms on her trousers, and gives Iris a nod. Iris presses record, waits a second, then gives Georgie a thumbs up.

Georgie stares straight at the camera, her long eyelashes unmoving under the balaclava. Iris's skin prickles with gooseflesh. Georgie's got this.

'Berkshire. The low Scorers of Berkshire, specifically. We are recording this to get a message out to you at great risk to ourselves. Our personal safety is no longer our concern. This is bigger than us.

'The Eyes Forward want the population to drop by over 10 million as quickly as possible, and they want that loss to be entirely shouldered by the poorest of the Society. Many of you have noticed bodies, and missed loved ones, but the Eyes Forward and their so-called Society Police take little interest. Yet one high Scorer is killed, and they restrain us under curfew with a thorough investigation underway. Why do the low Scorers not warrant such an investigation? Why are our lives so cheap?

'The Eyes Forward hold your youth as a ransom. They only grant the preservation drugs to the richest. Why? They keep you under their control with this. For years we have conformed to this ideal, but now they are going too far.

'We have confirmation that the Pres-X distributed to the lower Scorers eighteen years ago was tainted, that the B-Well given to its users was a different drug, In the high Scorers, B-Well counteracts the drug's hideous side effects. The B-Well given to the sub 750s though, did not. They were meant to lose their faculties. Their mental demise was pre-planned. They were never meant to survive. Cast your memories back to the Time's Up faction during the Great Unrest. The terrorists never went away. They live among us. They have joined forces. They have power.'

Tash glances up from the computer and taps her watch, then spins her finger around in the air to tell Georgie to hurry it up.

'This weekend, those factions of the Great Unrest plan to utilise their power. The Eyes Forward have not only granted permission to the 800 pluses to kill low Scorers, it is being incentivised. There will be points awarded for every kill. A mass killing is worth twice the points of individual killings. This weekend, the Eyes Forward have sanctioned a massacre.

'Please, low Scorers, anyone under 200, if you can, stay with some mid Scorers and get there before Saturday. Do not trust the highest Scorers. Be vigilant. If you see someone you don't recognise, a high Scorer sniffing around your building or scouting out your block, confront them, and watch what they do.

'Do not believe a word that the news tells you. We have been lied to for years. We have been stuck in a cave of the Eyes Forward's making. It's time to escape the cave, to see who the Eyes Forward really are. They have attempted culls before. This time, they're going to more extremes than ever.

'We'll be reporting all weekend to keep you updated. Please, be safe. Stay indoors and stay quiet. Open your eyes to what is happening. They may be wealthier, more powerful, but together we can beat them. We will survive.' Georgie's expression changes. In the gap in the woollen fabric, Iris watches her eyes narrow, and she glares down the camera. 'Now, this message is for the Eyes Forward. We see you for what you are, not just what you tell us. Other counties do too. Berkshire is not the best county there is. They're all great and shit for their own reasons. We are done with your control. We are done with your propaganda. And we are coming for you.'

Tash swipes her hand across her neck, signalling cut, and Iris clicks to end the recording, saves the video, then gives a little squeal. 'Oh, Georgie! That was amazing. I've got goosebumps!'

'Totally. I mean, that was insane!' Johan says.

'We are so fucked if they figure out where that comes from. It was *that* good.' Skylar for once, doesn't sound scared. She sounds excited, powerful.

'They won't,' Tash says. 'We've got Nebula and my own encryption software on my personally designed VPN. Might as well be coming from the moon for all the Eyes Forward know.'

They upload the video. Again and again, to every Nebula chat they can find. As quickly as they can upload it, the forums get shut down. They open new forums, then share it on socials. There are replies, both believing and disbelieving. At this stage, they agree that whether or not people believe them doesn't matter. There are ripples. They've dropped a pebble in the pond, and the waves are spreading.

They walk to the shop in pairs, stocking up on supplies while listening to the gossip. People are talking. They're buying rolling pins, bottles of spirits, rags, matches, and fire extinguishers — all manner of things to defend and fight. Shoplifters are more common. Iris spots several un-Scorables stuffing paraffin and matches in their pockets.

Not everyone knows, not everyone believes, but some are preparing.

A rebellion begins with a few people. No uprising began with an army. Whispers get louder. Truth takes longer to permeate than lies. Why is that? Iris wonders. Because lies are custom made to be believable, to draw you in, to disarm you. No one believes the truth when it punches them in the gut, when it isn't what they want to hear, when it makes them feel weak.

That's the message they need to propagate, they decide. The truth will make them stronger because the Eyes Forward are relying on their weakness.

They walk to the shop past the un-Scorable dorms, the ones still standing and inhabited. They're quieter than usual. Iris hopes they've all hidden well. Their only defence is to run or grab whatever weapons they can steal. Guilt tightens Iris's chest. They should have sent the video out earlier. They didn't want to give too much notice as that would also let the Eyes Forward know in advance. But it's not enough time for the low Scorers. Nowhere near.

The news isn't reporting anything on their story. The usual tactic, ignoring the words of those against them, is their main defence. The Lloyd Porter murder is again dominating the headlines and curfews are tightening. There are various reports of the fallout of the new algorithm chaos. Some high Scorers are distraught. Then, numerous reports of seismic activity on the continent pop up, giving Iris chills. However much she and the others are preparing, the Eyes Forward are too. Seismic activity will be their cover for buildings being destroyed. For the deaths.

Georgie watches the news with a grin, which seems bizarre until she explains. 'They're reacting. We've ruffled feathers. Reactive versus proactive. We caught them off guard. They're panicking.'

See, Iris. You see, don't you? It doesn't take power to be powerful. It takes a cause, for good, for salvation. You are more powerful than you know.

Iris's posture straightens. She stands tall, taller than anyone. She flexes her muscles a little, sticking her elbows out. There's room outside the cave. She's not cramped anymore.

***

Saturday daytime comes all too quickly, and the streets are deserted in a way they never have been before. The six of them peer out the window and spot people in comfortable sportswear walking the pavements or on expensive looking eBikes circling the bike lanes.

The predators are out.

The high Scorers don't even appear cautious. They think they're invincible, scouting out the un-Scorable dorms and low Score blocks in full daylight. That is their battle cry.

Iris and her friends hold hands as they gaze down on the preparations below. Georgie's hand squeeze's Iris's tightly on one side, Ezra's does the same on the other. They're a chain of defiance.

The rebellion is on.

Chapter 45
Iris

Iris mutes her phone, the incessant pinging driving her and everyone else mad. All the messages are from her parents. They're worried about her, fretting, telling her not to do anything stupid: *Darling, please be safe. Please, please come stay with us. Bring your friends. We love you so much.*

Iris knows her mum didn't do exactly as the Eyes Forward wanted, and that's made her contempt diffuse slightly. But there's still a lifetime of lies that can't be excused. She's not ready to face them yet. There's a long story they want to tell, and hearing it right now would serve as nothing but a distraction.

'You should go see them,' Georgie says. 'If things go wrong tonight, and you never said. . .you know. . .goodbye.'

'We're staying here, in our apartment. We're totally safe.' Iris says with such authority even she believes it. 'We're not the Score they're hunting.'

'Still.'

Iris's thumbs twitch over her phone for a while, and she presses her lips together, pondering what to say before she replies: *We'll be safe. Don't worry. Love to dad.*

It's the best she can do right now.

Outside, the sun has set behind the town skyline and highlights the clouds with an orange glow like fire. It's muggy. Storms are brewing, the weather said. The rain will wash away the blood.

Iris pulls her attention away from the view. Beauty is not what she needs to be looking at right now. Unless that beauty is code. 'How're we doing, Tash?'

Tash gives a thumbs up but doesn't turn away from her screen. 'All good,' she says, then pushes her spectacles up her nose.

Georgie has been sure to keep a steady supply of water and snacks next to Tash, and the odd instant coffee too.

'Not too much coffee,' Tash said. 'I can't spare the time for a bathroom break.'

The one toilet trip she did need, she took the laptop with her, navigating her way to the bathroom without even glancing up.

Iris tries to imagine what can go wrong. The hack could fail, the high Scorers could use massive bombs, they might be less indiscriminate, the no guns rule might be a lie, they could have the wrong date, the Eyes Forward might be onto them. And that's all she can come up with in a couple of seconds. Give her an hour and the list will have multiplied tenfold.

I believe in you, Iris.

At least her imaginary friend has something positive to say.

Iris sits in her room for a moment. A few minutes of calm. She hasn't eaten anything in hours. Several sips of water is all she can manage, despite her mouth being so dry she sounds like she's swallowed gravel. All she can think of is that she's led them to this, these people that now sit in her living room. She's inspired action. It was she who called them together after the post-flat-party-massacre. She who told them of the points list. She could have ignored it all and allowed them to mourn in safety. If harm comes to any of them, it's on her.

Over the past few days, she's properly unpacked her belongings from her parents' house. She's binned a lot, but also displayed some old trinkets and memories. Her namesake great-grandmother's picture is on a shelf, her kind and aged face smiling at her. There's something so beautiful about her face, one that has all the evidence of life and laughter, a face that's preserved her wisdom rather than complexion. The woman who founded Sisters and Spies. At least there's one family member who would be proud of Iris right now. Iris scratches her tattoo. It irritates her arm, as if trying to remind her who she is, of how she came about. It's a tragedy that she never knew her great-grandmother properly, that she has no one else like her to speak to. The drop of blood that was used in her tattoo is all that links them now.

Iris can't change the past, but she can seek revenge. She picks up the picture and speaks to it. 'I'm avenging you, great-grandmother, Iris. I'm doing this for you.'

I know, dear. I know.

Iris gasps and almost drops the photo. She has no time to think anymore as footsteps come up the stairs, and Iris rushes out of her room. It's not a stampede, only one person, one heavy-footed person. They all look at each other for answers. Skylar backs into a corner, Johan pushes his sleeves up and walks towards the door with Ezra just behind. Tash glances up from her laptop for a second, then carries on typing. Iris swallows, then steps towards Johan and Ezra, Georgie by her side.

There's a knock, and they all freeze.

A voice comes through the door. 'Georgie?'

Iris sags against the wall and presses her hands to her racing heart as Georgie rushes to the door.

'Sam?' Georgie unlocks the deadbolts and moves the chairs away that Skylar put there in a moment of panic. 'What the hell are you doing here?'

'I'd recognise your voice anywhere.' She pulls her in for a hug.

'You should stay at your apartment.'

'Come with me. My 500 neighbourhood will be safer than here.'

Georgie pulls away and steps back, shaking her head. 'We need to stay closer to the Eyes Forward building. We've a plan, a hack—'

Iris clears her throat.

'It's fine, Iris. I trust her.'

'Maybe keep quiet, just in case?'

Georgie purses her lips and faces Sam again. 'I'm staying here. I'm not cowering in a safe zone.'

'Georgie—'

'It's not up for debate. I'm staying. I'm needed here, to report from the ground. We have to get the message out.'

Sam glances away from Georgie's pleading and resolute face to take in the room, all six of them, as if sizing them up individually. To be fair, they don't look like much. Johan appears to be the only force to be reckoned with. The rest all look like a bunch of underfed nerds. 'Well,' Sam says, 'I'll stay too. Maybe having me here will make them go easy on you.'

'We're not their target hit,' Georgie says. 'We're all over 200.' Georgie doesn't mention Skylar, who backs further into the corner.

Sam takes Georgie's hand as Iris watches the attentiveness. She does seem to genuinely care.

'The things I've heard,' Sam says. 'They're not even bothering to be quiet about it now. It's not even about the points for a load of them. They're out for blood, for kicks, utterly obsessed with getting below 100 million, to not be the world's laughingstock. That's their excuse, but I think it's just a power trip. I don't think even your Score is safe.' It's then she glances at Georgie's implant, the gold glow making her jaw drop.

Iris steps forward and looks at Georgie. She's still pale from her procedure. Her hot water bottle lies idle on the table. 'Georgie, you're still recovering. No one will judge you if you want to be safe.'

'No,' she says so firmly, Ezra jumps. 'Not after what they did to me. They forced this on me.' She lifts her hand for everyone to see. 'I have more reason than any of you to hate the Eyes Forward for what they did to my mum, to Grandpa Eddie. I'm staying, and I am reporting this.'

The streetlights flicker outside as the last of the sun disappears, then they go out completely. The power's cut. The orange sky is extinguished now, replaced with the blackest black. Iris turns on the standby torches they keep for such incidents, and they all stand closer, preserving the warmth.

'I'm in!' Tash says from the table. 'Plato is working, guys. I'm in their system.'

They all smile and air punch, except Johan, who bares his teeth and cracks his knuckles. 'Game on.'

Chapter 46
Mae

Mae rubs the back of her neck, refusing Pasha's offer of a massage. He was a physiotherapist once, he's good at massages, but she doesn't want to give in to this tension. Now is not the time to relax. She takes a painkiller for her headache, paces the living room, then snaps the band on her wrist.

Her second attempt at the new algorithm has supposedly gone live, and it's not what the Eyes Forward want. In fact, she left it almost the same. That would be enough to make her nauseous with worry on its own, but she just saw a video on Nebula, confirming Iris does take after her dad in the dumbass ideas department.

'Try to stay calm, Mae,' Pasha says, although his pacing almost matches hers. If he was back to full strength, he'd be worse.

'You saw that video? That was Georgie. I'd recognise her voice and bright red lipstick anywhere. Which means Iris was behind the camera. Those girls are doing something really stupid.'

'They're trying to help people.'

'Don't you imply this is going to be fine. Our daughter is standing up against the government, The Eyes Forward. She's starting a rebellion. Do you have any idea what they'll do to her? All we've done is try to protect her.'

'Maybe she's past the age where she needs protecting?'

If looks could flay flesh, Mae's would do it. Heat rises from her toes all the way to her head as she stares at him. 'And I wonder who Iris gets her stupid ideas genes from? Do they even know the danger they're in? This hunt is happening.'

He takes her shoulders, resting his forehead on hers. He's so cool, she's surprised he doesn't give her brain freeze. 'That's why they're doing it. Be proud. She's the best of us, Mae.'

Mae pulls away. She'll be a hell of a lot prouder of an alive daughter than a dead one. 'I should have done it, should have done what they said. She's un-Scorable now either way.'

Pasha heaves a breath and sits down. 'Iris can look after herself.'

'She can't climb her way out of this.'

Pasha takes her hand, his dark eyes like a begging puppy's. 'Once we destroy the Pres-X—'

Mae scoffs at him.

'The panic about the loss of preservation drugs will make the high Scorers go crazy. It'll be all over the news, for sure. But it doesn't even need to make the news. We'll get word out everywhere. Everyone knows that the whole of Berkshire's stock is there. They'll panic about that more than they'll give a toss about the hunt.'

There will likely be chaos. Will that be enough of a distraction? She's not sure.

He drops her hand and with his touch gone, it's like someone has turned off an electrical switch inside her. Her inner fizz runs flat. Mae steps back and gazes at him a while, at that face she loves so much. He's a lot stronger than he was a couple of weeks ago, but not up to full fitness. Not by far. She can't lose him.

Mae leaves the room, rummages for what she needs in the bedroom, then changes. She's dressed all in black and offers a similar outfit to him. 'This doesn't mean I approve or that I think this is anything more than a stupid idea.'

His dark eyes light up. 'You're coming too?'

'I can hardly leave you idiot men to do something on your own.'

Pasha's grin reaches both ears as he takes the clothing from her. 'Admit it, Mae. You love the idea.'

'Oh, just get dressed. We've got billions of pounds worth of drugs to destroy.'

Chapter 47
Iris

The hack is simple. Well, as simple as taking over the phones of everyone in Berkshire. To Tash, it's like a ten-piece jigsaw puzzle, so she says. It's clear the Eyes Forward are tracking everyone with the Society Police app, so all Tash's hack does is make it seem like every Sub 200 is hiding out in the Eyes Forward building and the Society Police headquarters and Iris's workplace, just for good measure. The hunters won't be able to track them, and there's a chance they might even destroy the government buildings trying to kill them. If that's the case, every data centre in the county could be destroyed. That seems like a stretch, but possible.

The first hole in their plan: about half a million people in Berkshire are Sub 200. Only a quarter of those live in Reading town.

'Nothing we can do about that,' Tash says. 'Reading is the biggest town by far. And literally no one but you, Iris, knows the population of Berkshire and Reading. The stat reports are always Society-wide. I can't make it appear people are in buildings that are out of range. The top Scorers mostly live in or near

Reading, so they'll likely hunt locally. This is the best we can do.'

It's a tough pill to swallow, the 'it's the best we can do' pill, instead of the 'hundred per cent guaranteed all low Scorers are safe' pill. That would slip down her gullet like ice cream.

Those towers and buildings in the town centre are big enough to house that many if they all squished in, probably. They also seem sensible places where people would think they could be safe. Again, probably. But the high Score hunters might destroy those buildings trying to kill all the low Scorers hiding out in there, and hopefully, in their efforts they'll destroy the data centres. All the Life Score data, facial recognition, Society Police data. All of it will be gone or, at the very least, damaged. And the low Scorers will be safe.

Probably. Actually, now that she thinks about it more, 'probably' is optimistic. Maybe, perhaps, if pigs could fly.

Iris has managed a sip more water and gagged back half a biscuit. Georgie has been staring at herself in the mirror for the last twenty minutes, practising her voice and posture. Georgie will be on camera, but it's Iris who's getting stage fright.

You've got this, Iris. Trust your team.

The voice has gone back to speaking crap again. Iris sweats, itches, fans herself, and paces.

'Jesus Christ, Iris. You're making everyone nervous.' Johan doesn't sound nervous, just his usual angry self.

There are so many holes in their plan, Iris can't even count them. But she keeps telling herself it's the best they can do.

At least they're trying. That's what she repeats when she needs talking off her mental cliff. If it saves even one person, it's worth it. It should give the low Scorers a bit more time at least and may make the high Scorers doubt the competence of the Eyes Forward and Society Police app. There are too many maybes. . .but right now, destroying the Eyes Forward is second place to saving thousands of un-Scorables and low Scorers from being slaughtered. Hide them in the tech. The hack is camouflage.

There's no convincing Johan and Ezra to stay inside and out of trouble. Johan looks like he might be good in such a ruckus, Ezra, not so much. He makes to leave, unconcerned with his own safety. His desire for self-preservation ended when they killed his sister. He's out for revenge and doesn't care at what cost.

'Are you sure, guys?' Georgie asks. 'No one will think less of you if you wait in here with us, help with the hack and the reporting.'

'No,' Ezra says, for the hundredth time. 'This is for Jasmine and Otis. I have to do this.'

Johan grunts. 'Don't even try to convince me to sit tight while all those poor fuckers are in danger. No way. I'm shit with computers, and the camera stuff just isn't my bag.'

Tash leaves her laptop for a moment to give him a hug. 'If it gets too bad, come back. Okay?'

'You know me, bud,' Johan says.

Tash tuts. 'Yeah. I do. That's the problem.'

They have crowbars as weapons and Johan says, 'See you in Wales, bud,' as they leave.

'To Wales,' Tash says, still glued to her laptop screen. 'It's just his way,' she says to the others after the door closes behind them. 'Never been one for formalities.'

That doesn't reassure Iris much. It just means Johan is reckless.

'Wales?' Iris asks.

'It's where we're going. When we're free. Honestly, I don't know how it started. We started saying it as kids and it just kind of stuck.'

'He called you bud? You guys not a couple?' Iris asks. The way they're always together, she'd assumed as much.

'Johan and me? Nah. No chance. Been mates since we were kids. Right, let's get this show on the road.'

Plato loads up. The rest of them crowd behind her, staring at the screen. She has a separate monitor that's currently black. The laptop shows a map of Berkshire. She zooms into the Berkshire map until it only shows Reading town centre. The black monitor then fills with pages and pages of code, thousands upon thousands of lines. Tash is linked to every phone in Berkshire, and after typing in instructions, she filters down to the lowest Scorers. Hovering the cursor over the screen, she selects a third of them, then drags their location across to the map, and dumps them in the Society Police building.

'Okay,' Tash says. 'First step done. So far, so good.'

Iris steps back and tilts her head to the side, cracking her neck. She glances across to Georgie, who's bitten her thumbnail down to the skin. Next to her, Sam's clenching and unclenching her fists. Skylar's pale complexion appears greener, and she swallows like she might throw up.

They all jump as screams outside ring through the apartment. A bang, then another. A rumble that makes the cups on the table jingle.

The hunt has begun.

No one rushes Tash, verbally anyway. No one wants to pile on the pressure, but from the sweat trickling across her hairline and her foot tapping out a rapid beat, she's feeling tons of it.

'You're doing well,' Iris says.

Another third, highlighted, then dumped in Iris's work building. They all heave out a breath, and Tash takes a sip of water. It's then Iris notes how much her hands are shaking.

'Take it easy, Tash,' Iris says. 'So far, so good. That's nearly two hundred thousand people you've just saved.'

'Just the final third to go,' Tash says as she almost spills the dregs putting the glass down.

Nearly two hundred thousand low Scorers are now apparently holed up in government buildings. This has to at least buy them time. The high Scorers won't know where to look. As long as they stay indoors and quiet, the hunters won't know they're there. They'll think the un-Scorable dorms are deserted. The video was released, and everyone will surely be sitting inside, quiet as mice.

And if the high Scorers take the hunt to the government buildings and destroy them, if it topples the entire system, well, that's going for gold.

The final third.

Tash highlights, drags, then drops into the Eyes Forward headquarters. They all watch as their locations move, then stay, now showing as visible in Eyes Forward HQ. They're there. All low Scorers accounted for, safely tucked inside government buildings.

Iris exhales a shuddery breath, her hands go to her mouth. They've done it! They all cheer and hug and high-five for the briefest moment.

The screen goes grainy. They all know a Nebula glitch when they see one and they stare, not daring to breathe, willing the screen to stay as it is, with that final third all still safely tucked away in the Eyes Forward headquarters. The grainy screen intensifies. It's all snow now, stripes in the snow. Then, both screens go dark. Except for a few words that form across the bottom: *All Eyes Are Our Eyes.*

The Eyes Forward are onto them. They're trying to take over.

'No, no, no!' Iris says.

Georgie starts on her other thumbnail as Sam punches the wall. Skylar runs to the bathroom, retching as soon as she gets there.

Tash is typing in code, trying to override whatever the Eyes Forward are doing. She slams at the keys and curses, then screams at the screen until she's done. She sits back, holding her cheeks, and watches a moment.

The screen shuts down.

'Shit,' Tash says.

'Crap,' Georgie says.

Iris rubs Tash's shoulders. It's not her fault. She did more than any of them could have managed. 'Oh, Tash. You did so well. Two-thirds. That's amazing.' Her tone is light, but her stomach churns with disappointment. A third of the low Scorers are still vulnerable.

'It's not good enough,' Tash says, rubbing the tears from her eyes. 'It's not enough.'

Iris crouches next to her and holds her hand, her reciprocating grip weak and cold.

'We have to save them,' Tash continues. 'I can do it. I could make Plato work if I was there. From inside the building, I can do it.'

Another rumble shakes the windows, the sound of a building collapsing drowning out any screams.

Iris swallows. 'You want to go across town? All the way there?'

'No. But it's all I can do.'

'You want to go inside Eyes Forward HQ?' Georgie's practice earlier does nothing to stop the quiver in her voice.

Tash nods. 'If I go alone—'

'Not a chance,' Iris says. 'I'll go with you. You can't do this alone.'

'Well, I'm not staying up here while you're down there,' Georgie says, her voice stable now.

Sam shakes her head. 'Georgie—'

'I can report from the ground. We can get footage. Expose all of this.'

'I'll call Johan and Ezra,' Iris says. 'We could use their help.'

Screams ring out from outside, a deep boom they feel in their feet. They all pause a moment as the rumble settles. The streetlights outside flicker on for a split second before it all goes dark again.

'How far is it from here?' Sam asks.

'Two miles,' Iris says. 'That's all. Just two miles.'

Chapter 48
Iris

Tash packs the laptop into a padded bag with the USB, then slings it over her shoulder. She's burned two other copies of the hack on separate USBs.

'It'll be slower to do it on the Eyes Forward computers,' she says. 'I'm not even sure if it will be possible, but worth a shot. So take these. . .you know. . .just in case.'

She gives a USB to Iris along with the second monitor, putting it in a rucksack. A backup. Georgie takes the other USB, staring at it as if it's something so delicate she might snap it, then wraps it in tissue paper and puts it in her pocket.

Iris turns the dining room table upside down to unscrew the metal legs, giving one to Georgie, one to Skylar and Tash, then keeps one for herself.

'What about me?' Sam asks, and appears genuinely disappointed.

'You're a 500 plus. That's weapon enough.'

Sam nods, pleased with the flattery, and they leave the apartment, pad down the stairs, and loiter by the external door for just a few moments. The storm is rumbling in the distance, the mugginess turning into a fine drizzle as a slow and terrible wind snakes its way down the street.

From her pocket, Tash takes out a bag of Flake.

'Erm,' Iris says, 'I don't think now is the time for a party.'

Tash tips it out onto her phone, and using a card, makes five little lines. 'It heightens senses. Makes you more alert, panic less, vision is sharper—'

'My vision was weird,' Georgie says.

'It's a bit sparkly, but contrast is better in the dark. Trust me. This could give us an edge. It's all over Nebula. People say how much more alert they are, that their night vision is better. It's like it was designed for this.'

'She's right, G,' Iris says, recalling her time on Flake. 'It makes sense.' She inhales a line, wincing as it stings all the way up.

Georgie's lips twitch a moment, then she has one too.

Skylar backs away. 'I don't want any, thanks. I've not done it before, and I don't want to start now.'

'You were sober at the flat party?' Iris says, her voice pitched with surprise.

'It obviously doesn't make you that astute then.'

Tash has her dose. 'Fair enough. Whatever you want.'

Iris notices Skylar's face is grey and clammy, fear and nausea blotting through her features. 'Actually, Skylar, you should probably stay here. We need someone to look after the apartment. There's a good view from the window. You could tell us if any trouble comes this way.'

'You. . .you don't want me to come with you?'

'You're a 120,' Tash says flatly. 'You're a liability.'

'120!' Sam whistles. 'Yeah, that's not good.'

Skylar's brows lower, looking them all in the eye. 'No. Everyone is always telling me what I can't do or shouldn't do. I can be useful here. I can help protect Tash and the laptop. I'm not a waste of space low Scorer. This means more to me than any of you.'

'Okay, okay!' Iris says. 'We're all doing this of our own free will. Whatever happens, happens. We all understand the risks, right?'

Everyone nods.

'Our aim is the Eyes Forward HQ,' Iris continues. 'If anyone gets lost on route, tough. Try to get home and send us a message to let us know you're okay. If you're in trouble, we'll come find you after, but we can't delay getting to HQ. Understood?'

They all nod again.

'Good. Okay, so I guess we all try to stay together, and hopefully we all make it.'

'So,' Georgie says, 'what route are we taking?'

They glance out at the street; the darkness making any direction seem as welcoming as a dungeon. The wind carries screams from the direction of town.

'There's the un-Scorable dorms on Gosbrook Road. Several of them,' Iris says.

'The Sub 200 housing around Amersham,' Georgie says.

Iris ponders this. 'We can cross the river at Caversham bridge to avoid that.'

'That means a longer stint in the town centre though,' Georgie says with a wince. 'I don't know what's worse.'

Iris looks to the others for ideas, but they stare blankly. 'Depends on where the trouble is,' she says. 'I guess we'll have to wait and see.'

Johan and Ezra arrive back, their eyes stare straight through them. 'We saw a high Scorer who looked like they were arranging explosives on one of the dorms.'

'Shit, really?' Iris then glances over his crowbar, stringy blood hanging from its tip. She doesn't ask any questions.

'Some are definitely in it for the more personal approach,' Ezra says, his crowbar is equally tarnished.

'I told you,' Sam says, 'they're doing it simply because they can. The points incentive hardly matters. They just want to kill.'

'Come on,' Iris says. 'Let's hurry.'

Sam, Ezra, and Johan finish the Flake as Iris runs back upstairs to grab a torch. With a last-minute idea, she also grabs a bottle of vodka — it's the most flammable thing in the apartment — and also some rags and a lighter in case they have a need for a Molotov cocktail. She stuffs it all in her bag, and they head out. They mount their bikes and ride down the hill, freewheeling, no brakes, as fast as they can. Georgie, wearing her balaclava, holds her phone in front of her and does a piece for the camera.

'It's quiet this far north of the river now, but we can feel the vibrations of buildings collapsing and hear people screaming. Some high Scorers were spotted laying explosives. Those high Scorers have been dealt with. Open your eyes, people. There are no earthquakes or whatever excuse the Eyes Forward will use to explain the destruction. This is an incentivised slaughter. Please stay indoors if you can. Be quiet. Don't let them hear you. And high Scorers, you are not going to get away with this. The time of the Eyes Forward is over.'

Georgie pockets her phone, and the others give her a thumbs up.

A few screams in the distance fade away as the wind rushes past. From the bottom of the hill, they slam their brakes as the building opposite shakes, then collapses, spilling rubble across the road.

Georgie films and narrates. 'Another housing block, destroyed. How many innocents were in there?'

There are no cries from that block at least. It must have been an empty one. They wait until the debris has settled before they dismount to carry their bikes over the rough edges. From the other side of the rubble, they cycle again.

Chapter 49
Iris

Their old bikes all squeak with rust and age, except Sam's, whose electric function works. Iris curses herself for not charging their bikes. A daft oversight. This is an occasion that would definitely have been worth the extra electric usage.

The streets are deserted, quieter than they've ever known, and Iris swells with pride. The only explanation for the abandoned state of the road is that their message must have gotten out, or everyone is obeying the curfew. That seems so unlikely though. There're always a few chancers. They scan alleyways for high Scorers planting explosives but see none in this part of town.

'Cleared this bit out earlier,' Johan says, and Ezra nods, still with that faraway stare.

Their bike lights flicker to almost nothing, except for Sam's, who rides in front to light the way. The streetlights come on sporadically. They're mostly in near darkness until much brighter lights come up behind them. Iris glances back. Those silhouettes are familiar. Too familiar.

She looks at Georgie, whose wide unblinking eyes tell Iris she has noticed it too. 'Iris. ..again!'

Iris stands up on her pedals, forcing her weight into each stroke. 'Everyone, they're after us. Go, go, go!'

They pedal hard, but Iris knows they'll be no match for the hunters' bikes as the blinding lights get closer and closer. Coming up on their left is the old school, Oak High, which they all attended once.

'The school!' Georgie says. 'We can corner them there.'

They make a hard turn into the school driveway, then ditch the bikes at the top of the concrete steps and run down, taking two or three at a time, stumbling as they descend the final few. Iris is sure there used to be more, like the world is shrinking. Everything seemed bigger back then, or rather, she was smaller. At the bottom of the steps, she glances back. Those bike lights at the top switch off as the riders dismount.

They race towards the building that Iris hasn't entered in a decade before slowing their pace, treading carefully and quietly. The grunting breaths from the hunters are coming down the concrete steps. Iris's heartbeat thumps in her ears. She scans her surroundings. The building is so rarely frequented now that no one bothers to tend the playground. In the minimal moonlight, the swings cast a shadow hanging limp on one chain, the other long lost to rust. Grass has forced its way through the rough tarmac, blurring out the hopscotch and painted chess board. They're just a mess now, like the collapsed building to the east of the site that no one has bothered to clear. It's been that way since Iris was at school. What's the point of rebuilding when the building has no use, when there's so few children to fill it?

The benches are still across the playground, probably the same as they were years ago, more chewing gum than wood.

In the ditch in which the school sits, the darkness is blacker, the moon eclipsed by their surroundings. Iris switches her torch on, then thinks better of it as it could give them away and turns it off again. The Flake is helping, as Tash said. Their night vision is slightly enhanced, all except for Skylar, who places each foot down like she's barefoot on drawing pins. Tash takes her hand and pulls her along, yanking her up as she stumbles over the uneven ground.

Huge banners for the Society Police flank either side of the doorway. The white background shines in the fresh torchlight coming up behind them. Their hunters are closing in. Ava Maricelli's face on the banners peers down, below the walled-in logo of the government.

Iris faces Johan, Skylar, and Tash. 'You two, hide behind that wall.' To Georgie, Sam, and Ezra now, she says, 'You, over there. Duck down.'

She's eyed up a bench for her own hiding place and goes to run when the voice resounds: *Iris, duck!* It comes too late. A hard whack clips her on the top of her head, knocking her to the floor.

She reaches up to her head. A tiny spot of blood, not too bad. She looks up, and standing over her are the two hunters, their long metal swords catching the moonlight.

One of them steps forward. 'Hello, Iris.'

Chapter 50
Iris

She'd know that grunting voice anywhere. 'Jason Bonnet,' she says, not a trace of fear in her voice. 'Didn't know you could ride a bike.'

'Smart mouth, this one,' he says to his partner. Norman, Iris realises. 'Doesn't like to give up without a fight.'

Iris bites her lip, sure she's never fought or even talked back to either of them. She just hasn't been the cooperative pushover they'd prefer.

Norman glides the sword through his hand. 'Lucky me. I like a fight.'

'Seems a shame to cut her up before we've had some fun with her. Pretty thing like that shouldn't go to waste.'

Norman slaps him on the back. 'You do what you've got to do, my boy.'

Jason steps closer. Even from the floor, Iris can smell that same rancid breath, like the vape he always smokes is garbage flavour.

Norman shines his torch around and Iris searches in the beam. 'Seems all your low Scoring friends have deserted you. Never mind. We'll find them soon enough. You, though, are our priority. Gonna wipe that Taylor gene off the planet. Especially one that's tainted the Porter lineage.'

Iris fails to keep a deadpan face, her eyes widening at their words.

'Been on our radar for a while, this little reprobate,' Jason says. 'Sick of having to keep an eye on her now. I don't care if she's over 200. She's no good for the Society.' Jason passes his sword to his father and removes his jacket as he speaks, then steps closer and unbuttons his fly.

'Actually son. . .' Norman peers at his phone and his lips curl up into a sinister smile. 'She's un-Scorable now.'

Iris doesn't argue, just assumes he's lying. She isn't un-Scorable. She can't be.

'Really?' Jason says with a pitch of excitement. 'Always wanted to fuck a filthy un-Scorable. Glad we didn't succeed last time. This is going to be a whole lot sweeter now.'

It was them last time? The sick fucks. They almost got Georgie. Iris clenches her fists as Jason reaches for her ankles. She kicks them free, then lands her foot right in his Desirable nose.

'Ow!' he says as the blood pours. 'Fucking bitch. This nose is worth more than everything you own.'

He goes to grab her again, but Iris backs away. Norman steps closer, pointing one sword towards her. When she stares up at him, his wobbly chin catches the torchlight, a sliver of drool collecting in the corner of his mouth. 'Best hold still, un-Scorable trash.'

Jason kneels in front of her, licks his horrible lips, and then takes his trousers down. There's a dull thud when his blood splatters Iris's face.

She startles, then watches, for a brief, beautiful second, as Jason's face appears more confused than pained. That's a shame, she thinks as his body sags, then falls to the side, his father landing directly on top of him, his dented skull cracking on the pavement.

Ezra and Johan lift their crowbars again, belting them across the skull a few more times for good measure. The noise is glorious.

The others all come out of hiding, and Georgie runs over to give Iris a hug as Iris takes a breath for the first time in at least a minute.

'It was them who chased us?' she asks, burying her head into Iris's shoulder.

'Yep. But it's okay. They won't do that again.' She wipes Georgie's tear with her thumb.

'I got it on video,' Georgie says with a wry smile, then faces Johan and Ezra. 'Thanks, guys.'

Johan smiles and wipes his hands on his jeans. 'No problem.'

Ezra's eyes twinkle, his face fixed in a grin. 'No problem at all.'

Chapter 51
Iris

Iris gives the torch to Skylar since she needs it most.

'Thanks,' Skylar says, and Iris realises how calm she is. It's almost eerie, especially since she hasn't even had any Flake. She'd have thought Skylar would be in bits from that confrontation, from those men's brains spilling across the tarmac, but she isn't even shaking. In the torchlight, her normally forlorn eyes have a spark of vindication about them, a razor-sharp focus they lacked before. She has some colour in her cheeks.

They walk back up the stairs, collect their bikes, then cycle away from the school and towards town. They ride in silence, the deserted streets a shroud of stillness. Iris has never known such peace, and despite the attack, the peace brings serenity, like she's exactly where she's meant to be.

You were born to fight them, Iris.

The voice is louder with the Flake in her system and in the quiet, it surprises her. She lets the words sink in, for their meaning to permeate her bones. She was born to fight them. She was born to make things right.

She thinks she should feel remorse for those men, a sadness for their lives lost. Killing shouldn't be this easy, this forgivable.

She may not have swung the crowbar, but she approved it. Saying their deaths weren't her doing, is like saying the Eyes Forward aren't responsible for the low Scorer massacre.

Killing them wasn't murder. It's saving others.

Iris takes a deep breath, smiling as she exhales. She takes a quick glance at those cycling next to her and knows they just saved so many people.

Perhaps it's the Flake keeping her so calm. It gives perspective. They were going to rape and kill her, to kill all of them.

Fuck them.

When they arrive at Caversham bridge, they slam their brakes. Streetlights are working at the moment, dim but enough to give them an impression of what's ahead. There are so many footsteps they can feel them through the ground. In the dusky orange glow, a few torchlights shine, wavering with their footsteps.

They're so close to her parents' now. They could go there, hide away, wait for the weekend to be over, then live with the aftermath. It's so tempting to cower away, to let the Eyes Forward get away with it. Fear creates a longing for the status quo. But she forces all such attitudes out of her head. They've come so far already. The odyssey of equality isn't without hurdles. She tenses her muscles, ready to jump.

As Iris's eyes adjust, she realises it's a solid wall of people walking towards them, denser than any usual pedestrian lanes, no order to it, like a creeping fog. A moment later as Iris's vision clears more, the jerky movements of the torchlights highlight legs not walking but running. Some people are carrying a few possessions, and many women have small children strapped to their fronts. They must be un-Scorable. Most un-Scorables don't even have bikes.

They watch for just a second, Skylar shining the torch towards them, then they inch closer to the crowd to get a better look, the hammering of their footsteps echoing. Georgie has her phone up, silently filming. The heads dip on one patch, a pit forming in the crowd as so many fall over each other. Screams resonate above the footsteps and the stampede continues.

They won't get through that crowd. Not a chance.

Iris turns her bike a hundred and eighty degrees, then cycles back the way they came, shouting for Georgie, for Tash, for all of them to follow her. Cries of fleeing people drown out her voice. They're right behind her now, so close their breaths are as loud as hers, the stench of their body odour and paraffin. Behind, flames shoot up to the sky.

'Georgie!' Iris glances around, wide eyes frantic as she searches for Georgie, Skylar, all of them. They've been separated in the throng of people. 'Georgie!' she screams again, and in the din she hears other cries, indiscernible sounds of panic. So many in front of her now. People to the side knock into her bike and she sways, struggling to stay upright. There's another dip in the crowd to her right; someone goes down, then is trampled.

Please don't let that be Georgie! Please don't let that be any of them!

The smallest of openings forms ahead of her and she cycles faster, eating up the space. When she arrives at the river path, the crowd splits. It's just as dense as the path is narrow. Water splashes up from people falling in the Thames. She can hear the cries now, the names they're calling for, the fewer people making a more audible panic.

'Georgie!' she shouts again.

'Iris!'

Where did that come from? Somewhere just a little way behind, behind a hundred running footsteps and as many other screams and shouts.

'Iris!'

Closer this time. As the river path opens up to Christchurch Meadows, Iris darts to the side, letting the crowd pass, then waits, checking each face for someone she knows. The clunk of bikes follows shortly after her. Georgie first, thank God, followed by Sam. Then Tash, still with the laptop bag, Johan to her side and Ezra the other. Iris shouts them over, and they all wait together, shivering despite the heat of the crowd, panting their breaths. Iris feels for her bag. It's still there, and Georgie confirms it's zipped up and the monitor is safe. Tash checks the laptop bag and finds it intact. They're all okay. Everyone is okay.

The stampede has thinned now. Most people have gone ahead, though to where they don't know. Nowhere is safe. Safety in numbers doesn't even work when the numbers are so huge. Low Scorers are still being hunted no matter their efforts.

'Is it working at all? Are any of the high Scorers falling for it?' Iris asks.

'Look,' Tash says. 'The low Scorers have all gone now, and no one is following them because they can't track them. It's helping. It must be.'

She's right. Iris knows she's right. When they've all caught their breath, they go to move again until Ezra speaks and they all freeze.

'Skylar? Where is she?'

Chapter 52
Iris

They search the immediate area for Skylar. They've no torch now, just their Flake vision. A pit lodges itself in Iris's stomach. Skylar's only a 120. She's prey.

'Skylar?' Johan shouts.

The last of the stragglers from the stampede stare at him a moment, then keep walking.

'She could be anywhere,' Georgie says. 'Crushed, in the river, or gone back — maybe.'

'Let me try her phone.' Iris dials, but it goes straight to voicemail.

They spend precious minutes searching along the riverbank. Being underwater seems like the most logical explanation for her phone not ringing.

Then Iris's phone pings, and she picks it up. 'Hey, guys wait. Maybe this is. . . Oh.'

'What?' Georgie asks.

'It's not Skylar. Just a Life Score update. It turns out I really am un-Scorable.'

They all gasp, then hold their hands to their mouths.

'It doesn't matter,' Iris insists. 'We're taking down this system tonight anyway, right?'

'Sure,' Georgie says. 'But in the meantime—'

'I'm no worse off than Skylar. We still have a job to do.'

'I'll go back and look for her,' Johan says.

'No!' Iris says. 'Getting to that building is more important — more important than any individual. She knows that. We all know that. It's what we agreed on. We can't waste any more time and we can't spare anyone. We can look for her after.' Her words sound confident, but it pains her to say them. Iris told herself if they save even one person, it'll be worth it. Now they've failed the one person they'd promised to keep safe.

No one argues. Only Ezra looks like he disagrees, but he keeps his mouth shut.

'Okay, if everyone agrees, let's keep going,' Iris says. 'We still need to cross the river.'

In silent agreement, they pedal, and as the cycle bridge comes into view, they see it's quiet enough and seize the opportunity, turning a sharp right to cross it. Once on the other side, they carry on along the narrower path, not pausing to catch their breath until they reach King's Meadow. The old lido, half-collapsed with its empty pool, filled with bricks rather than water, is a good place to hide for a few moments. Iris does a quick headcount. Minus Skylar, they're all present.

'I wonder if we're better off on foot from here,' Tash says. 'It's not far to the Town Hall Square. And we can sneak around the alleyways and skirt the buildings much better on foot. We'd be quieter too.'

Iris glances to Ezra and Johan for an answer. She doesn't know why. Because they're men? Because they wield a metal pipe much better than the rest of them? More likely, she doesn't want to take the responsibility of such a decision.

The men look at each other for a few moments, then Ezra nods. 'Okay. That's probably a good idea.'

The resounding lack of confidence makes Iris bristle.

They lock up the bikes, then set off, hurrying towards the Town Hall Square. Forbury Gardens isn't a large park yet compared to the snake-like roads and alleyways it's a terrifying, vast, open space. They skirt the brick fence that encircles it in single file, keeping their heads ducked below the top.

Voices ring out, and they freeze. Iris holds her breath, her eyes streaming as she dares not even blink. The voices sound male and are punctuated with guffaw-type laughs that make Iris grind her teeth. They remind her of a couple of Normans.

'I prefer the individual points rather than the mass ones.'

'I agree. It feels more personal, like more of an achievement.'

'I just want more un-Scorables. The Sub 200s are fine, but all those un-Scorable women and their brats need taking out.'

'Fucking tracking though. How have so many legged it? This is so typical of this government. Give us a whiff of success and fun, and they screw it up by pandering to those beggars. If I don't hit 900 tonight, I'll be pissed.'

'I say we do what Craig said. Destroy the fucking building. There's thousands cowering in there. We'll hear their screams, and we'll hunt down the ones who escape.'

'Rain's coming anyway. Be good to get a load of kills done and be home before the storm to have a pint. Let me check the thread.'

Their footsteps stop just on the other side of the fence. They can only be a metre or two away. There's a rustle of coat pockets.

Rage glints in Johan's eyes, and Iris grabs his wrist when he moves to stand. She shakes her head and mouths, *No*. That would be way too dangerous. They can't see what those men are armed with, and the commotion could make things much worse. The best revenge would be to stop this madness.

'They're headed there now,' one man says. 'The statistics building in town. Same idea as us. They've got more explosives than we do.'

'Great stuff. Let's go spill some un-Scorable blood!'

They all wait, Iris holding Georgie's hand so tightly, Georgie has to give her a nudge to ease up. They stay crouching until those voices pass and the footsteps disappear into the night. The air around them fills with steam as they all release their held breaths at once.

'Fucking hell,' Georgie whispers. 'Can you believe that?'

Iris shakes her head. 'Shows the plan is working though, right?'

'I wanted to cheer when they talked about the tracking,' Tash says.

Johan and Ezra stand straighter now and look around for any more people. 'Coast is clear,' Johan says. From his pursed lips, Iris can tell he's annoyed. He wanted to beat those guys shitless. She can hardly blame him. 'This way.'

They skulk further along the fence, treading softly. Iris winces as she steps on a crisp packet, the crackling noise as loud as a building collapsing. Ezra glares at her as if it was intentional and she shrugs. He holds his finger to his lips, as if she didn't know to keep quiet. She silently huffs and they carry on.

Just a couple of small streets to go. There aren't many hiding places now, just open streets ahead of them. They haven't heard or seen a soul. Surely, they're safe.

'Let's make a run for it from here,' Tash says. 'We can run all the way to the Eyes Forward HQ.'

'Town Hall Square is so exposed,' Georgie says.

'That's why we have to run.'

They both glance at Iris, like she has the right answer. The road bends to the right, and they can't see beyond that. In the silence, she strains her ears. There's no sound, nothing at all.

'I say run for it,' Johan says.

There's a reluctant pause. With their backs pressed against a building, they tilt their heads forward to gauge everyone's reaction. Georgie nods. Johan gives a thumbs up.

'Okay,' Iris whispers. 'We'll run all the way. No stopping, just keep going, and we'll stop when we get to HQ. You ready?' She waits for them all to nod. 'On three. One, two, three. Go!'

Iris pushes away from the wall with her hands, then sprints. She's alongside Johan with Georgie and Sam up front. A few paces in, and her lungs are burning. She looks back to see Ezra and Tash just a little way behind.

They round the bend and ahead is open road. There's a body off to the side, its eyes still open, one arm bent underneath and a pool of blood around its head with what look like arrows piercing its torso. Iris rubbernecks as she runs past and nearly trips over Johan. A second later, something flies past her ear, screaming its way through the air. It's a long metal spike, like something from a crossbow. Such weapons don't discriminate. Their bolts puncture the hearts of anyone in their way.

It lands somewhere in front, missing them all.

A squeal comes from someone. There's no time to see if anyone else noticed it. No time to stop. She ups her pace, gaining ground on Johan, who's a few paces ahead, yet every step seems to take an age, like time is coming to a standstill. Another bolt. It whistles as it cuts through the air like a child's toy, though the metallic clang it makes on the ground proves it's definitely not a toy.

Iris keeps running, her veins pulsing and peripheral vision clouding.

Georgie and Sam still run ahead. Iris isn't sure they've noticed the bolts. Another comes but scuffs against the ground in front of her as she runs past.

There's a thud, a person hitting tarmac. Johan dives to the side, yanking Iris with him and they stop in a shop doorway, hidden from three directions. Her heart hammers, and she holds her hands over her mouth to try to silence her breathing. Through vision smudged with tears, she searches for Georgie. There's a food cart across the street, and Georgie and Sam are waiting behind it. Thank God, Georgie's okay. But she's exposed there, three sides facing out into the open. The bolts came from the right, so Georgie should be safe from that direction. Johan leans forward, then peeks out the side of the doorway. Iris can't look. She hangs off his jacket, willing him to be okay. He gasps and leans back.

'Shit. It's Tash. Tash is down!'

'No!' Iris leans out now. Tash is lying face down on the ground. There's no blood, no bolt sticking out of her back. Iris watches her hands clench and unclench, a subtle move. 'She's okay. I think she just fell.' The laptop pack is still around her shoulder.

'She's such a fucking clutz.' Johan glances out again. He's poised, ready to pounce.

'Wait,' Iris says. 'Where's Ezra?'

They're both staring out now, Johan shielding most of Iris. Just a few metres away, Ezra comes out of a shadow, rushing to Tash, then lifting her. Her bloodied face is clogged with loose gravel, her right arm hanging lifelessly by her side. But she's alive.

Ezra puts his arm around her and supports her, heaving her forward. One foot then the other, Tash wincing with every step. Ezra mutters something in her ear.

He doesn't seem to notice when the next bolt pierces him through the chest.

It's two more paces before he yields, his body going slack. He never looks down at the blood pouring from his wound. Perhaps he feels no pain. Another bolt hits him and passes straight through like he's made of butter, this time accompanied by a shower of blood. He glances down, his knees buckle, then he collapses face-first onto the tarmac.

Iris doubles over, her scream coming from within, but it's muffled by the strong hand against her mouth. She glares up at Johan, wide, wild eyes staring ahead, every muscle of his face protruding from tensing his jaw. His grip around Iris's mouth pushes into her cheeks.

When her scream is done, he releases her, and she sobs silently into her hands.

Chapter 53
Mae

Pasha hasn't had a bike in a year or so now. Since his mobility deteriorated, there seemed no point, and Mae sold his bike when they moved. So, Mae and Pasha walk to the factory, Mae carrying a small bag of tools over her shoulder. It's not far, usually just fifteen minutes when there's pedestrian traffic to pull them along. Tonight though, it's deathly still. The air carries a story of commotion at the other end of town, a deep boom and intermittent howls, like a strong wind whipping past buildings. There's panic somewhere.

There's no un-Scorable dorms between them and the factory, and closer to the factory, no residences at all. Just ruins and rubble.

Mae logs on to the Life Score app while they walk. The Eyes Forward hasn't docked her Score or Pasha's — yet. She searches the database for Iris's name. No one's Life Score is secret. Anyone can know anyone's if they want to look it up. It confirms her fear. Iris is un-Scorable. They're taking out her misdeeds on her daughter. Iris will be hunted.

She pockets her phone and doesn't tell Pasha. There's no point panicking him too.

They keep to the shadows, which are plentiful since the streetlights only come on in bursts. There's the usual litter across the streets, swirling in eddies across the tarmac: food wrappers, vape cases, and bottles. All signs of life, clues there are usually people here. Mae's chest inflates with warmth. Iris and Georgie's video is surely the reason the streets are so quiet. They warned people, and people listened.

Pasha still tires quickly, despite his improvement. He has months and months of inactivity to make up for, and he's a long way off from full fitness. They pause occasionally but only for a few seconds before Pasha insists they press on.

When they arrive at the factory, it's deserted. The red brick building stands eerily perfect among the dilapidated ruins around. The facade is crimson in the moonlight, like it's painted with blood.

'Rolan should be here by now,' Pasha says as he checks his phone. He tries calling him, but it goes to voicemail. 'Come on, Ro. Pick up.'

'You sure you got the time right?'

'Certain.' Pasha taps his foot as he redials. 'We can't wait any longer. We need the attention drawn from the hunt now.'

'Can you do it without him?'

'Yeah. Yeah, for sure. It'll be fine.'

His tone isn't entirely convincing. Pasha saying something will be fine is hardly a vote of confidence. Still, he gets to work, unlocking a series of doors with codes he knows by heart. He must have rehearsed this, gone through it meticulously. He and

Rolan must have practised it a hundred times. The devious dumbass.

Inside, there's an entire wall lined with chrome fridges, and they get to work opening all the doors. A cool blast escapes with each one, the shelves jingling with bottles and bottles of both original Pres-X and its successor, Pres-X-2. The drugs that have changed the world, that ruined Mae's life but gave her a second chance. The drugs that ripped the Society in half, giving youth and opportunity to the rich while the less well-off are put out to pasture. Mae hates these drugs, yet has so much to thank them for. In these cupboards is her mother's life's work. The work Joan Porter loved more than Mae herself.

'Pass me the cutters, Mae,' Pasha says as he holds out his hand.

She obliges, and he takes it off her, then cuts through wires. He goes to another end of the factory, cutting through more. He takes pictures of the open fridges and his simple vandalism, creating a post ready to share. It all takes maybe ten minutes. When he's done, he takes a step back and grabs Mae's hand.

'Are we actually doing this?' Mae asks.

'It's done. Can't undo it now.'

Too late for regrets or second thoughts. They've just committed a crime so big it would have them locked up for life. Mae's head throbs like she's got a hat on too tight. They leave, not shutting the doors behind them.

The wind picks up and carries more screams from not too far away. Mae stares up and above the skyline. Smoke catches the moonlight.

‘Okay,’ Pasha says, ‘just uploading to Nebula first.’

They walk back before he clicks send, then a great orange blast comes from the building.

It’s like it’s in slow motion. The blast is the brightest light, and the building bulges, like a chest inflating. There’s a second of stillness, as if the world is holding its breath before bricks, and shards of concrete and glass, burst from all angles, showering them as they’re thrown through the air.

The blast sends Pasha and Mae flying back, forcing the air from Mae’s lungs. A deafening roar, so loud, it rings inside her head. Her vision goes grey, the whole world deathly white except for an image out of her eye. A figure. Angus.

Then everything goes black.

Chapter 54
Iris

A cloud of black shoots up to the sky and the ground shakes. That's the biggest explosion they've ever felt.

'Shit,' Iris says, then swallows.

She glances at Georgie, still half-hidden behind the food cart, Sam's arms around her in much the same way Johan's were around Iris. Johan's whole body trembles like he's struggling to contain rage, or fear, Iris isn't sure. The two emotions look the same: scarlet face and huge eyes.

'I have to get to Tash,' he says.

Iris dares to peek out for just a moment. There's blood, but it all looks like Ezra's. Poor, poor Ezra. Tash's fist is still moving as it was before.

'She's alive, Johan. I think she's fine. Just staying down. I don't think a bolt got her.'

'I'm going to kill every one of those fuckers. I'm going to rip their heads off.'

Definitely rage, a feeling Iris knows all too well. She lowers her pitch and steadies herself. 'Shh. Listen. We have to think clearly. We need to get Tash and see if Ezra is alive, then get to HQ.'

Johan punches one hand with his other, grinding his fist into his palm.

'Johan, listen. You're not going to help Tash by getting yourself killed.'

He takes a couple of breaths and presses the heel of his hands into his forehead. 'Okay. I'm fine. Okay. Your rucksack safe?'

She nods.

'Go on to the Eyes Forward building. Go with Sam and Georgie. I'll wait back here for a bit. I'll get Tash when I think the coast is clear. If we split up, we may stand a better chance anyway. You do the hack if you can. Tash and I will be right behind as backup.'

Ahead is the small alley that leads to the Town Hall. The old-fashioned building's spire pokes above the closer buildings like an ancient castle. Society Police headquarters isn't too far, less than a minute's run.

'Take my crowbar,' Johan says. 'You might need it to get in.'

Iris glances at Georgie. She's on the wrong side. She still has to cross the street, the street where Ezra just had his heart punctured. She doesn't want Georgie to come. It's too dangerous. But she's so exposed where she is. Who knows if having a 500 plus with her will actually help. She makes eye contact with Georgie, hoping her eyes are telling her the right message, that Georgie will somehow know what to do where Iris doesn't.

Georgie gives her a little nod, then, holding hands with Sam, runs across the street towards Iris and Johan.

The bolts fly with such power they pierce the brick of the building. But Georgie and Sam make it to them.

'They don't even care who they're shooting,' Sam says. 'I'm a 500 plus, for God's sake. I don't deserve this.'

Iris scowls. 'No one deserves this.'

'I didn't get a good look,' Georgie says. 'If they're alive, they're staying down. Playing dead sounds sensible.'

'I just hope Tash is playing,' Iris says. 'I don't think Ezra is.'

'I'll do what I can,' Johan says. 'I'm not leaving Tash. You just go. Now. Carefully. Quickly. Start that hack, and I'll be right behind you with Tash.'

'Just a minute,' Georgie says, getting out her phone.

Iris scowls. 'Now? Seriously?'

'Two seconds.' She pulls her balaclava on, then films Ezra and Tash lying there and zooms in on the blood pooling beneath them before turning the camera back to her. 'There are hunters everywhere, using crossbows and arrows, and God knows what. Please stay indoors and remain quiet. We're doing everything we can.'

She keeps the camera rolling, pointing at their feet as they nod, then they run.

Iris's legs eat up the pavement with every bit of strength and adrenalin she has, Georgie still giving commentary behind. They fly down the rest of the length of Forbury Road, not stopping to see if the coast is clear as they turn right down the alleyway towards Blagrave Street. The Town Hall is so close. They just need to make it to the entrance. They pause for a second as the road opens up onto the Town Hall Square, backing into another shop entranceway. It's so open. They're easy prey.

'You lot wait here,' Iris says. 'I'll go first. Then, well, if I don't make it, you can follow.'

Georgie grabs her arm. 'You're not cannon fodder. We go together.'

'I'll go,' Sam says. 'I'll walk down the Square with my phone held up, stating my 500 plus status. They wouldn't dare shoot a 500 plus.'

'That's very noble of you,' Iris says, and regrets the heavy sarcasm. 'But they would.'

'They wouldn't. And I'll prove it.'

'Unless you're 800 plus, I reckon they're shooting,' Iris says.

'You're just jealous of my Score. You always have been. I worked hard for it. I only started as a 400.'

Iris huffs. 'Fine. You go, and I'll follow with the USB. If they think I'm with someone as important as you, they may not shoot.'

Sam smiles at this, a smug grin.

'What do I do?' Georgie asks.

Iris gives her a hug, then pulls away. 'Wait here as backup.'

They walk off, Sam loudly declaring their presence by stating her Score while Iris uses her as a shield. From behind, Georgie's whispered commentary comes through. 'The bravery people are showing tonight in standing up to this massacre is mind blowing. This proves that low Scorers can be the best of us. You don't have to be a high Scorer to be worthwhile.'

When they reach the entrance to the Town Hall building, Iris tries to decide if she's pleased or angry they made it; that Sam's tactic of showing off helped. She is pleased but gutted. Fucking elitists.

Georgie joins them seconds later and gives a thumbs up. 'We made it!'

Iris rattles the door. 'Shit.' How did they not think about how to break into such a secure building? The doors are shut, obviously, and barred. A quick peek around the side, and it's clear all the lower windows are much the same. She tries to wedge the crowbar between the doors and pry them open, but she'd need something a lot tougher. She takes a few tentative steps out into the open Square, then tilts her head up, peering skywards. The tower at the top has unbarred windows.

She's going to have to climb up.

Chapter 55
Mae

Mae coughs as her winded lungs heave for breath. A puff of dust blows out of her mouth. She's covered in debris and ash. Her gritty eyes see nothing but grey, and they stream as she blinks. Pasha? Where is he?

'Pasha?' She wheezes. 'Pasha!'

She turns her head to the side, and her vision clears slightly, but her view is partially blocked by bricks and debris. She tries to sit up, but she's too heavy. There are bits of building on her, and both arms are pinned. The world goes dark again, but she fights against it.

'Pasha!' It's quieter than a whisper. Her lungs can't force air out properly. Her ribs hurt too much to try.

She turns her head the other way and takes in the carnage. The factory is totally gone. A few of the lowest bricks are in their original position, a blackened hole in the middle. Twisted metal and mangled concrete are in place of everything else.

There's a bulge in the debris, and it moves. There's an arm reaching out, the hand moving bricks, render, and metal.

'Pasha!' She manages a bit more volume.

His head appears. He's sitting up, hair white from dust. Mae's vision blurs more as tears flood her eyes. The silhouette of him walks over, then kneels beside her. His mouth moves, but Mae's ears aren't working properly, and his voice sounds distorted. There's a whooshing echo inside her head. He grabs at the debris, brushing it off her and throwing it to the sides. She blinks and his face is there, sporting a few cuts, only little ones. His eyes appear okay, but his clothes are ripped to shreds. He grabs her limbs as she lies there and pulls them about. They all seem to work.

He gently helps her sit. 'You okay, Mae?'

She lipreads more than hears him, but she understands. Her teeth chatter as she reaches for his face, stroking his cheeks. He's okay. That's all that matters. 'I'm fine,' she says. 'I told you this was a dumbass idea.'

He huffs out a laugh, then hisses and holds his ribs. 'Can you move?' he asks.

'Yeah. I think so.'

She tries to sit a little straighter, and the darkness swirls with the little colour there is. Pasha holds her steady. They sit next to each other and stare at the black hole where the factory once was.

'Did I cut the wrong wire?' Pasha asks.

'I think. . .' Mae strains as she recalls, rubbing her forehead. She saw someone. 'Angus. I saw Angus.'

'Angus? Really? What was he doing here? Shit, is he all right?'

Mae's hearing is still bad, only getting every other syllable. She turns around, but the world turns faster, and she grabs onto Pasha. 'He was here. Close by. I'm sure I remember that.' Is she shouting? It's hard to tell. Pasha's voice sounds far away.

'I don't see him. Why would he be here?' Pasha's over pronouncing his words, his mouth moving in an exaggerated way. Maybe his ears are bad too. 'Rolan was careful to leave him out of it. We should look for him.'

Mae glances over her shoulder, her neck cracking as she does, the clicks running all the way up to her scalp. She points. 'He was over that way, further away than we are. Or, maybe that way, I think. I don't know.'

Another voice comes through, a gurgling sound, as if they're underwater. 'Pasha! Mae!' Angus runs over, eyes wide and wild. 'Oh, my God!'

Pasha cranes his head around. There's blood matting the back of his hair.

'I'm so sorry,' Angus says. 'I didn't see you until it was too late. I'm so sorry.'

Pasha smiles at him, the dust collecting in his eye creases. 'We're fine, Angus, really. What are you doing here?'

'Blowing up the factory. There wasn't supposed to be anyone here. What are you doing here?'

'Destroying the drugs. Stopping the fridges working.'

Angus snorts a laugh. 'That's a less newsworthy way to do it.'

Mae glances from one of them to the other, and her head throbs.

Angus offers his hand and gently lifts Mae to standing. Every vertebrae, her knees and hips, click and creak as she stands, every breath hurting her ribs. Her vision has cleared now, no longer whitewashed everywhere, but her surroundings still spin. She can see the scorch marks and the orange flames, black soot jutting from their tips. Mae squints from the brightness of it. There's a ton of glare, like a migraine. She hadn't noticed the heat before, but the fire is spreading. Vibrations still rumble through her feet.

'You hear that?' Angus asks.

Mae makes a face, then shakes her head and points to her ears. 'I can't hear much. My ears aren't working.'

'Mine too.' Pasha gestures to his ears.

Mae looks again at the back of his head, picks through his hair to find the source. It's a small bump and no longer bleeding. She reaches around the back of her head, and her hand comes away wet and red. It's hard to focus, and her vision blurs again as nausea gurgles through her stomach.

Angus points. Mae can't think. What's that way? She doesn't recognise anywhere properly. 'High Scorers, look. Over Castle Hill way.'

'They must have heard the explosion,' Pasha says. At least she thinks so. Everything sounds distorted now, like white noise. 'That made quite a show.'

'This isn't good for us. We need to get away.'

They're talking so fast it's hard for Mae to take it all in. They should just go home. There's probably a bus somewhere. Why are they out so late anyway? Mae struggles to remember. Her head pounds like her skull is on too tight. Her stomach lurches, and a fresh, hot wave of nausea rides its way up to her head. She bends over and throws up on the ground.

'Shit! Aunt Mae,' Angus says as he tries to keep her upright.

She's tired now and sure it's past her bedtime. 'Let's go home and have a nap,' she says.

Angus says something to Pasha, but Mae doesn't catch it. Their faces are serious, all knitted brows and tight lips.

'Caversham bridge is impassable now,' Angus says, though he doesn't explain why. What is he talking about? 'Let's head east and try to get back over Reading bridge. Can you walk?'

Pasha winces as he takes a step. He always makes that face. Mae should do his physio with him. She will once she's had a nap. He shouldn't be outside. Why did they come all the way out here?

They walk, Angus dragging Mae along. Rude. Her legs aren't as quick as his. Her head is banging, and her legs are wobbly. The ground keeps moving like they're on a boat. She retches again, but it's just a dry heave.

'The high Scorers are going to catch us up,' Angus says.

Mae sees fear in Pasha's eyes. Why is he worried about high Scorers? They're high Scorers now, she remembers and laughs. There are more people now, lots more, lots of pedestrians like always.

'Come on, Mae,' Angus says. 'We need to walk quicker.'

Her chest hurts from Angus dragging her, but Pasha's no quicker though. He's behind them, limping.

Angus's phone rings. It's the new Life Score jingle as his ringtone.

'Ava?'

Ava. Why's he speaking to her? Did he say *Ava*?

'Iris?' he says. 'What about her?'

Despite her brain fog, Mae hears her daughter's name. She'd hear her name in the loudest racket. Iris! Is she okay?

'Iris. . .' Pasha is close now, alongside Angus. 'What about Iris?'

Angus doesn't reply but keeps listening to the phone for a while, an excruciating time as scenarios play out in Mae's mind. Angus doesn't seem happy, his mouth twisting in concern the same way Pasha's does.

Angus pockets his phone.

'You two, you're high Scorers. 900 now, I understand. When did that happen?'

'Long story,' Pasha says. 'What about Iris?'

'This is good.' He leans in closer and dips his voice as Mae angles her head to his ear. 'This lot won't suspect you. I think you should be safe.'

'Iris?' Pasha asks.

'She's un-Scorable.'

Mae knew this. In the back of her mind, it was there.

Pasha shakes his head. 'The bastards actually did it.'

'There's more,' Angus says. 'She's out. In town. Ava tapped her phone a while ago. She was worried about her.'

Pasha winces as he gasps. 'Where is she?'

'Not far. Near Town Hall Square. What the hell is she doing there?'

Pasha limps to Mae, then takes her face in his hands. 'Mae. Angus will look after you. Do you hear me? I need to go get Iris.'

'No. I'll go,' Angus says. 'I can be there in thirty seconds. You take Mae and find a safe place to hide for a bit. There, between those shops.' He points into the darkness; a shopfront to one side says 800 plus health foods, and the other says Cuppa-Go.

Angus lets go of Mae. She hadn't realised how much he was supporting her until her legs go limp. Pasha only just catches her.

Angus says a goodbye or something. Mae can't make it out. They walk to the alleyway as Pasha says something about Iris and it being fine.

He might go on to say something about ice, but she doesn't want ice. She feels cold, so cold. Her swimming vision is like a kaleidoscope and the world a centrifuge. She's light, walking on air, and it all just fades away.

Chapter 56
Ava

Ava spent the day fidgeting, pacing, and clock-watching, then finding things to do that don't need doing. She checked this morning with the OGI camera from L.M. funerals. She didn't need to look, but she wanted one more walk around the funeral home. The place her dad built, the business that gave her a physically comfortable life, money in the bank, where it all began. It's unlikely to survive a significant fire from the Society Police building — if the fire happens. As riddled with doubt as she is, it seems unlikely it won't. The temperature in there will be heating up significantly. It's only going to take one stray spark.

The OGI camera shows the Society Police building's air is over seventy per cent oxygen. Too late for Mandisa, whose corpse must be rotting in there by now, turning to mush in the heat. She'll be written off as a victim of tonight, along with others who are bound to be killed. Being a high Scorer, she's not the Eyes Forward's target kill, but every cause has its casualties. Or so Mandisa always said.

Ava checks her phone. Angus hasn't been back in touch. After all he's done to aid the cause, trying to help his cousin is the smallest courtesy. Iris has also done a great deal to get the word out. And she is Mae's daughter, after all.

From her living room in a nice and safe part of town, Ava logs on to the security camera at the funeral home. One is directed outside, offering a clear view of the Society Police building. To her relief, the streets are quiet. The warning on Nebula, coupled with curfew, has kept everyone inside. There shouldn't be any casualties from a single blast. No low Scoring casualties anyway. She taps her feet and twitches her lips, impatience making her restless. She wonders what the temperature is in there now. It must be stifling with no air con, only flammable gas and tons of heat-producing computers.

Just one spark.

Her phone pings. The CEO from XL Medico is calling. She cancels it, again and again. He's persistent. This must be interesting. She can't talk right now. She hasn't practised her surprise, denial, or her what-the-hell-are-we-going-to-do response yet. She texts: *Sorry. Busy. What's wrong?*

The reply is quick: *Factory explosion. What the fuck? Tell me we have stockpiles of Pres-X and Pres-X-2 elsewhere!!!*

She replies simply: *It's all there. Are you saying it's gone — all of it?*

Shit. Fuck. FUCK.

Ava grins as she reads his message. Angus actually did it. Now she regrets not answering the phone to hear the CEO's voice pitch with panic. She should have video called to see his temporal vein throb. She wishes she could be in a board meeting with them all right now to witness the mental turmoil, wishes she could see the people craving their first or second dose, and their dismay when they realise their wrinkles are going to remain.

She puts her hands behind her head and leans back in her chair, taking a deep breath, allowing satisfaction to permeate every inch. But it doesn't. Not quite. The factory blowing up is one thing, but the Society Police building still stands. If it needs a spark, she'll give it one.

She gets dressed, all in black, as always, then ties her hair back and unlocks her bike.

It's not enough to see it on her phone or hear the reports second-hand. She wants to smell the freshly charred buildings, see the collapse of the Eyes Forward, hear their bones break.

Before she leaves, she sends an anonymous text to the press about the factory. Revenge will be as sweet as she hoped.

Then, her phone rings.

Chapter 57
Mae

It's cold when Mae wakes, the wet ground soaking through her trousers. She comes around on hard tarmac, propped up against. . . what is that? A bin. She's been sleeping next to a bin — in an alleyway — as rain sprays in a howling wind. The acrid smell of damp concrete fills her nose. She blinks, her vision hazy, like a fog.

Huh?

'Mae!' Pasha's face is close to hers, her name filtering through her wooziness. His brows are knitted together, and her head throbs like her brain is trying to break free.

'Pasha. What are we doing here?'

'You hit your head, Mae. I think you have a concussion.'

That explains the splitting headache. She rubs her temples, and even her arms hurt. Her chest aches with every breath.

Iris! The thought hits her like another blow to the head.

'Iris!' She sits up straighter and pain rips through her. 'Angus said Iris was in trouble.' She can't remember why they were with Angus, but she knows there was something about her daughter. Mother's instincts can cut through any head wound.

'Angus went to help her. He's been gone a while though. He said he'd call.' Pasha looks at his phone, then dials. 'Just voicemail. Dammit.' He checks the time, twitches his lips, then dials again. 'Ava?. . .'

Ava! Mae tries to scowl at him, but it's not much different from her painful headache face. Why the hell is he calling that woman?

'Can you see where she is? Eyes Forward headquarters! What the hell? No, we've not heard from Angus. It's been too long. . .Okay, I'm going there. . .Mae has a concussion. I need to leave her here. . .You can come? Great. Thank you. She's down an alleyway on Minster Street.'

He pockets his phone, then takes Mae's hands. His eyes are bloodshot, a contrast to the dusty white of his face. 'Mae, I'm going to get Iris. Wait here, okay? Just don't move. Ava's coming to help you.'

She pulls away and shakes her head. 'Not Ava.'

'Mae, now is not the time for you to worry about your quarrel. You just need to stay here. Promise me you'll stay here. She'll be ten minutes, maybe fifteen. I have to go help Iris.'

Mae takes his hands as firmly as she can and doesn't release when he tries to pull away. She doesn't want him to go. She can't lose them both. 'Please.'

His head dips, and he lifts her hands up to kiss them. 'You know I have to go, Mae. I'll be back as soon as I can. Just wait here.'

The warmth from his hands vanishes as soon as he's gone. She's left alone and cold, with little recollection as to why.

Chapter 58
Iris

Iris's phone vibrates in her pocket, and she takes it out. A message from Angus, of all people: *the Pres-X factory just exploded. Where are you?*

Iris frowns and pockets her phone. 'Guys, that explosion was the Pres-X factory. That should distract the high Scorers for a bit.' Georgie isn't paying Iris any attention. Instead, she's touching up her lipstick. Iris rolls her eyes that she actually brought it with her.

'Now, Georgie? Seriously?'

'I won't be a minute. I haven't uploaded anything yet, only filmed it. I just need to turn the VPN on.'

'You look gorgeous, Georgie,' Sam says.

'Thanks.' Georgie smiles and puts on her balaclava, then hands her phone to Iris. 'Keep it steady.'

'Sure. Please excuse my hands shaking from multiple near-death experiences.' Iris loads up the camera and gives Georgie a thumbs up.

'Low Scorers of the Society, I can confirm the hunt is on. I've been hiding in the shadows, filming what's going on. I'll load up some videos shortly. Be aware, they're harrowing. The high

Scorers are shooting people with crossbows, are armed with swords, and are keen to kill as many low Scorers as possible.

'They cannot trace or track you, so please, stay hidden and quiet. I have it on good authority that the new Pres-X factory has exploded, along with the entire stock of preservation drugs. Excuse us if we have no sympathy. Perhaps if the high Scorers are allowed to age as we are, they might have appreciation for how short life is. How life should be cherished.

'Please low Scorers, stay safe. And Eyes Forward, I hope you enjoy your last minutes in power. Tonight, your reign ends.'

Iris stops recording and hands back her phone. 'All done? Can I get on with the mission now?'

'Yes.'

Sam grabs them both. 'Shit, look! Someone's coming.'

They all jump back to the corner of the doorway, then Iris leans her head out. It's pouring with rain now. The person coming is soaked, limping, and they've no weapon. It doesn't look like a hunter. Iris squints in the lowlight, the Flake and sporadic streetlights helping, but it takes a while to focus.

'It's. . .it's not a hunter, I'm sure. . .' she says, disbelieving. 'That's. . .my dad. *Dad*?'

Pasha runs right through the Town Hall Square, totally exposed. A bolt flies through the air and hits him in the shoulder, sending him tumbling forward.

'Dad!' Iris tries to run towards him, but Georgie and Sam hold her back. 'Dad!'

He stays standing, running slower, still making his way towards them, his right hand holding his left shoulder.

'I'm a 900, arseholes!' he shouts into the night. A dark trickle of blood stains his jacket. Iris watches the sky for more bolts or swords. He's running right through the centre of the Square like an idiot, not even sticking to the shadows.

Please be okay. Please be okay!

When he's but a couple of metres away, Iris shakes free and reaches for him, heaving him into the safety of the doorway.

'Dad! Oh, my God. Are you okay? Shit. Shall I take it out?' The bolt sticks out of his shoulder still, its metal body gleaming in the half light.

'It's fine, sweetheart. No organs hit. Hurts, that's all.'

His hair, skin, everything is covered in red and white gunk — dust turned to paste in the rain. His sodden clothes are ripped, and he has little cuts everywhere. 'What the hell are you doing here?'

'I was going to ask you the same thing.'

'You look like you've been in an explosion.'

'Well—'

Iris's hands go to her face. 'Shit, Dad. The Pres-X factory.'

He winces. 'Long story.'

'Where's Mum?'

'She's safe. She's okay,' he says this with a groan as he inspects the bolt some more, while Iris fetches a rag from her rucksack, then tries to pad out the wound. 'So,' he says, 'are you going to tell me what the hell you're up to out here?'

Iris chews her lip for a moment, then tells him everything. 'It's working, Dad. They can't track the low Scorers. And we heard a few high Scorers say they're going to destroy the Life Score building where I work. This is the last one. We need to get the final third of low Scorers hidden in here. And then, maybe, if this building gets destroyed, and the Society Police building, that's all their data centres for Berkshire. Even if they don't destroy the building, they can't track the rest of the low Scorers. I need to get in there for Plato to work. I'm going to climb up.'

Iris checks on the USB and monitor in her bag. They're in there, still dry, and she tucks the crowbar down her jacket.

'Look after him,' she says to Georgie.

'Of course.'

She looks all three in the eye. 'You lot need to get out of here. Don't wait for me.'

'Shut up, Iris,' Georgie says. 'We're definitely waiting for you.'

'No. The high Scorers might come and bomb this place as soon as the hack starts. So you have to get away before that happens. I'll text you when Plato loads up.'

Pasha grabs her wrist. 'There's no point in me convincing you not to do this?'

She shakes her head, then kisses his cheek. 'No chance, Dad.'

He slumps against the doorframe, and Iris gives him one glance back as she makes to leave. 'Be careful, darling. Go make your great-grandma proud.'

Chapter 59
Mae

Mae drifts off for a moment — or longer — she can't tell. In her mind, she's cradling baby Iris. She never held her much, not as much as she should have. They spent a year locked in their apartment, just Pasha running out for groceries occasionally. The Enough supporters killed babies, and even the tattooed ones weren't safe. New mothers were killed. Any moment someone could charge into their apartment and take baby Iris away.

So Mae tried not to love her too much. She saw a gruesome end more than she saw a bright future. Is this the gruesome end now — finally? Would it be harder for her to cope if she had been more affectionate?

Mae did love her, still does, so much it scares her. Every part of parenting she finds terrifying, as much now that Iris is an adult as when she was a baby. A hug from Iris makes her feel like she's going to explode with love, that she's holding on to something so unbelievably precious and she's worried she'll spoil it. Mae's imprint on anything can dent it.

She can't lose her now, not with Iris never knowing how much she loves her. It makes her bones heavy — her love for Iris — and fills her with an unsettling warmth.

The ground is too cold to sit on for long, and Mae shifts her weight, her head banging with every movement. Rain pours into the alleyway now, and the wind whips cold air right through her. Her jacket is too thin, or it's too cold. Aren't they the same thing? She tries to count bricks and paving slabs, but it's hard to focus, and all the grey swims with the rest of the grey. Her stomach lurches. No vomit comes up, but there's old puke in the corner. It smells like rotten milk.

What's taking Pasha so long? What if he fails and doesn't make it to Iris? She heard him talk to Ava. What did she say? Eyes Forward headquarters. Her memory is like jigsaw pieces and she has to assemble the puzzle. She rolls onto her side, regretting it instantly as rib pain stabs through her, but she gets a quick glimpse outside. She knows where she is. It's not far to that building.

Pasha and his dumbass ideas. Iris is no better.

Supporting herself on the jagged brick wall, she stands, slowly, and after a moment the spinning eases. She tries a couple of practice steps down the alleyway. Bit wonky, but not too bad.

Iris, I'm coming.

She steps out, one wobbly step in front of the other, feeling her way along the shop wall for balance. She blinks, then rubs her eyes. Everything seems so far away, like looking through binoculars backwards.

She trekked the width of the country for this kid once. She can make it a few hundred metres across Reading. She tightens every muscle as much as she can without the pain tearing through her, grits her teeth, then walks a little farther.

The rain hammers, but over the din is a voice, one she knows, calling her name.

'Mae!'

Chapter 60
Iris

The climb is tricky, every brick slippery from the rain. Iris tries to be quiet, stifling her grunts from the effort, wincing from the clank and scratching noise from the crowbar hitting the brick. She's having to use it a lot to hack at the brick and make deeper hand and foot holes. The brickwork crumbles less easily than she hoped. Of course this building is one of the few the Eyes Forward actually look after. The jagged edges cut her hands even through the callouses from years of climbing. She maintains her three points of contact as much as she can, keeping her weight close to the wall. Her jacket isn't that waterproof. Little trickles of cold rain water wiggle in through the seams.

Occasionally, she pauses, bracing for a bolt to fly at her, but it's silent out. The others are hidden in the doorway. Iris dressed all in black and snug against the wall would be hard to spot. Unexpected. The streetlights dim, and she has to blindly grope for the next hole to grip. Every time she swings the crowbar back to hack more holes in the brickwork and chips a bit away, she imagines it's the face of an Eyes Forward representative.

You're doing so well, Iris. Keep going.

The voice doesn't startle her. It's comforting and encouraging, like someone holding her hand.

Going over the windows is easy. The metal bars across them actually help give her some lift, though they're slippery underfoot. She tries to glance inside the windows, but they're blacked out or boarded up. No one in there can see out. It seems weird the Eyes Forward representatives don't want any view at all. She slips as she skirts across the tiled roof but finds her balance, then it's just a brief climb up the tower. Iris orientates herself around the other side so she isn't exposed to the Town Hall Square below. In the shadows, she creeps up.

She's hanging on with one hand, a foot in hastily made supports, then uses her left arm to swing right back, utilising all the momentum she can to smash the window. The noise it makes is incredible. If anyone didn't know she was there, they do now. She's going to have to work fast. She climbs through the gap, scoring her skin with the pointy shards as she does so. No time to care. No time for pain. She lands, body rolling to soften the impact, then catches her breath, leaving a damp trail across the floor.

She's done it. She's inside the building.

For the hundredth time, she checks the contents of her bag. It's all okay.

No time to waste. Keep going, Iris!

Where? She looks around and there are no computers in sight. The tower floor is deserted. Bare brick walls hold nothing except a shoddily constructed handrail. She runs the length of it, her footsteps echoing, then pauses, slows, and treads softly. She has no idea who's going to be in this building. She hadn't thought that far, one of the many holes in their hastily constructed plan. If she comes across an Eyes Forward representative, could she fight? It was easy to imagine when she was chipping away at the brick, but flesh is something else.

You can do whatever you need to do.

Easy for an imaginary voice to say.

On tiptoes, she descends a narrow staircase, feet squelching in her wet shoes as she walks to a barred window on the side of the Square. The blackened boards have left a small gap down one side and she can see out to the open Town Hall Square.

She can see the very moment in slow motion, like an old film playing before her eyes. In infinite detail, Georgie runs at a tall stranger, but she's running like she's going to embrace him. Only she doesn't. She dives to his waist, tackling him to the ground, Georgie screaming as they both hit the tarmac. They stand, and she kicks him in the crotch. Iris can do nothing but watch as the grenade rolls from his hand while Georgie stamps on his face.

The grenade rolls towards the doorway of the Town Hall. It pauses there for a second, then it's blindingly bright, shaking the ground and the building, its epicentre exactly where Pasha and Sam are waiting.

Chapter 61
Iris

Debris blackens her minimal view from the window, the thick rain drops turning it to sludge, and the building shakes. Iris slams her fists against the glass, calling their names.

'Dad! Georgie!'

There's nothing to see below except a cloud of dust streaked with rain. The floor bends under her feet and cracks creep up the wall. She turns to run back to the window she came from, but one step in, she stops. The rucksack on her back. If they're dead, it can't be for nothing. It just can't.

She led her dad here. She led Georgie here.

Use that anger. You have to complete this.

Iris hesitates, torn between her mission and her family. She wipes some sodden hair off her face, then goes to the window again. There's no one there now, no people, just ash settling. The building groans.

The building could be demolished, but the un-Scorables are still vulnerable.

Do this, Iris! Hurry up!

She turns back and pads across the room, down more stairs. The walls are covered in dusty relics from the past. There isn't a computer in sight. Also, no Eyes Forward representatives. The place has the damp smell of neglect. Perhaps she'll find more signs of life downstairs. She grips the crowbar, holding it up as she walks. She finds another staircase and steps down, coming across a metal door and her heart skips a beat as she recognises the hum of air con.

She uses her hip to push against the metal door, then squints as the sensor lights spring to life. Beyond life. It's blinding. She shields her eyes with her free hand and the hum intensifies. Stupefied from the glare, she waits to adapt. It's freezing. She shivers from the cold and the dampness of her clothes, then takes a step forward. The main room lights dim and above, strip lights of green flicker along the ceiling.

Adapted, she can see without her hand in front of her eyes now and she peers around. Either side, floor to ceiling, servers buzz, little blue lights flashing up the length of them. It occurs to her she might be in a tad over her head. The USB is rattling in her bag, but where to put the damned thing? That's about the millionth hole in their plan.

She takes a few steps forward. In patches the air con doesn't reach, there are hot corners around the chilly centres. The narrow room opens into a central, larger one. From the middle, suspended from the ceiling like a chandelier, is a four-sided monitor, the face of an Eyes Forward representative adorning the screen. It's eerie, unmoving. Though, like a painting, the eyes stare straight at her. As she steps closer, the screen flickers, the image blinks, and from the monitor it speaks.

'Iris Taylor. Welcome to the Society.'

Chapter 62
Iris

Iris blinks a few times. She must be in shock, or dehydrated, or both. But it speaks again.

'Iris Taylor. Welcome to the Society.'

She glances over one shoulder, then the other. The voice is coming from the monitor, from the image of the Eyes Forward. Half his face is obscured by the brim of his hat, the monitor struggling with the blackness of his suit.

Another monitor to her side flickers, followed by her image filling the screen. Not a live image, but her ID photo that's used for facial recognition purposes. Next to it are all her details. Everything. Granddaughter of Lloyd and Joan Porter. Great granddaughter of the rebel, her namesake, Iris Taylor. Her movements every day, a screen below showing a montage of video clips, her sitting at her desk, her riding to work, her in a shop. Ordinary, mundane things, along with a statement: *Considered high risk and a valuable asset.* In big bold font across both screens it says, 'UN-SCORABLE.'

The central monitor speaks again. 'Iris Taylor. Welcome to the Society.'

'Shut up!' she shouts back. 'I live in the Society. I've been here my whole life.'

She pulls her gaze away from the screen with her details on, then walks around the circle to another screen. Endless streams of data ripple down the monitor, numbers and symbols spinning past at a rate Iris can't follow.

Another monitor a little further down is playing Eyes Forward press releases, population reports, all at super speed. Many of them, Iris recognises from recent times, although they all look the same. The date in the corner flashes past with the videos. Some from this year, some from last, a jump again to this year, then longer ago. The Prime Minister bookended by the representatives on either side — always. They never change, never age. But then, in the Society, age is an abstract.

Another video plays, the same layout as all the rest, the date flashing past so quickly she almost misses it, but it's there, and she flinches when she sees it. Not this year, not last, but next. She tilts her head and stares a moment longer as the dates flash by. Another, for a couple of years' time, another for the next quarter. How to slow the damn thing down? She explores buttons and dials, then finds it, the speed button, and slows it until she can catch each frame. She fumbles for a volume dial and turns it up. It's the press release population data from last week. She's seen it before, just the same. Then the next video begins, a quarterly population update for next quarter. It's already recorded.

'Reporting on the latest population statistics. The Society has hit its population target of less than a hundred million citizens. . .'

Iris rubs her forehead. How is this possible? She's not submitted the data yet.

'Iris Taylor. Welcome to the Society.'

You know the answers to your questions already.

The voice sounds a lot more certain than Iris feels. And if it's right, she just needs to know the questions. Her dad could be dying outside, but using her brain is like walking through treacle. She shakes, then pushes her fists against her temples. She knows this tech. Voice activated, ask-any-questions tech that was popular a hundred years ago, a souped-up version, by the looks of it.

'Iris Taylor. Welcome to the Society.'

She claws at her head and screams, 'What is the fucking Society?'

The computer repeats her question, the words forming across the screen: *What is the fucking Society?*

Monitors opposite hum and flicker and images appear while the computer keeps talking:

'The Society is a way to manage a population. The Society is a construct born of necessity. The Society is where everyone knows their place. The Society is leadership. The Society is where all citizens are quantifiable. The Society has a numerical value of somewhere between 0 and 1000. The Society is a management system. The Society is here.'

Despite her damp clothes and the cold air con, Iris's body temperature rises. She steps a few paces one way, then the other as the computer repeats its answer. A few phrases tug a nerve more than the rest.

The Society is a construct born of necessity. . . The Society is a management system. The Society is here.

Iris casts her mind back to Nebula, to the gossip on forums, to the theories and outbursts and ramblings she's heard so much of recently. One sentence from those times rings in her ears, a tinnitus of realisation.

The Society isn't real.

Someone said that. Georgie, and others on Nebula. Iris scratches her head, her memory hazy. She turns around to glance at all the computers, all the hardware blinking at her like some Morse code telling her what's so damned obvious now that she's standing there.

'Iris Taylor. Welcome to the Society.'

Her jaw goes slack, and she rubs her clammy palms on her clothes. She walks around the monitors, the reams and reams of data, the press reports on a loop, and she shudders. The Society isn't land, borders, or people. It's not what Britain used to be. It's not some remodelled country with a government and laws and people.

The Society isn't real.

She searches, and the branding on all the hard drives confirms it. *The Society, model 300.*

The Society is just some shitty hard drive?

She rubs her temples some more as heat ripples through her, and she swallows in her dry throat. There's no time to figure it out. She inhales slowly, attempting to breathe in some calm, to let some oxygen make her brain work faster.

With steady hands, she plugs the USB into the nearest hard drive. It seems as good a place as any. She plugs the monitor in next to it. The hack, Plato, comes across the screen and she clicks execute. Coding fills the screen, Tash's ornate code. She can't let her mind dwell on Tash. Iris has no idea if anyone she cares about is still alive, let alone the vulnerable low Scorers. Their only chance is for this to work. They've come so far now, they're all totally fucked if it doesn't.

You've got this, Iris. I am so proud of you.

It doesn't help. The voice is a distraction, and she tries to shake her mind free of it. The Flake is still in her system, all the coding and lights shine brighter than normal, her heart rate is steadier than it should be.

The building dips a little, another rumble, distant or close, she can't tell. She grabs the desk and widens her stance, then sends a message to the group: *I'm in. Is everyone okay?*

The face on the central screen flickers a little. Her text forms across the screen: *I'm in. Is everyone okay?*

Dammit. They can monitor everything from inside here. She checks on the hack. It's still whirring around the code. She runs for the exit, but the front door isn't that way. She's still a couple of floors up from the ground, and there's no way in or out that she can find except the way she came. Cracks are fingering their way up the wall from floor level. The grenade did some damage, but there's still no way out from here. She runs to the windows, but they're blackened and barred all the same. The others need to flee, to get away in case this works and the hunters bomb this building. She texts again: *Go. Get out of here. Plato is loading. I'll find my way back. GO!*

Her text appears on the screen again, and she bares her teeth. Fucking tech.

It's then it dawns on her. There's no way in or out. Ever. Eyes Forward HQ isn't attended by any Eyes Forward representatives at all.

She runs back to another computer, clicking on files. She finds a list of Eyes Forward representatives for Berkshire. The people who all look the same. There's ten of them. Only ten. All are old Preserved bar one in training. All their photos are the same. Hair cut in the same style, black buzzcuts, the same expressionless faces, any differences concealed by the shadow of a wide-brimmed hat. Their duties listed as. . .nothing. To walk. To patrol.

No ministerial positions. No public service roles.

They do nothing.

She clicks Lloyd Porter's file. He was named keeper of the Life Score algorithm, as Mae said. But that's all. It seems like he was the only one with an actual job. She searches under job titles and the computer draws a blank. There are no ministers or parliament or anything. Nothing. It's just faces, the same face that's still on the central monitor.

'Iris Taylor. Welcome to the Society.'

She groans and tugs on her hair. This is it, the whole Society? There's not even a Prime Minister. He's not listed, and in every newsclip ever he's the same. He's just an image. Drawn up by AI.

It's just a computer system. AI software. A load of men, a couple of women, probably chosen because they look similar enough. The news of the future has already been pre-decided. It's not just the Life Scores that are governed by an algorithm, the whole Society is. Algorithms within an algorithm. Plato's Cave isn't a physical thing. It's just code.

Plato pings to say the hack is loaded. She checks on the monitor and begins dragging the final third of the Sub 200s into the Eyes Forward building. The Eyes Forward building where no human ever steps foot, some data centre that was built and boarded up. Not that the high Scorers will know that. Well, some might, yet she has no choice but to gamble right now. The mainframe for the entire county is just a load of 0s and 1s, like life is just binary choice after binary choice.

Get out of bed, 1 or 0

Drink the coffee, 1 or 0

Say good morning, 1 or 0

Like it's ever that straightforward.

But it is. It's here in front of her, the coding that governs them. For that's all the Eyes Forward are. Coding. Like a computer game. A teenager's plaything.

The Eyes Forward, with their whiter than white skin and their blacker than black suits, they're the personification of binary.

She gets out her phone and films the computer telling her welcome to the Society, then the name of the hard drive, the Eyes Forward roles, and all the evidence she can get.

She scrolls through more files until she finds one that makes her freeze. It's the manual for the Society AI software. She clicks and reads through the headlines. She's no time to read it all, but she films it, taking in the chapter headings as she goes.

The Society is an AI programme that endeavours to create the perfect balance of human population.

Humans require distractions from their perils. The AI will prioritise such vanity schemes to keep the population entertained and busy with trivial matters.

The AI is designed to create a perfect economic system.

The AI is designed to unburden humans from needless thought processes.

Humans require the illusion of choice. They do not require genuine choice.

The AI is designed to create perfect conformity, and thus, every citizen knows their place and purpose.

Every human has a numerical value. The AI can quantify every citizen this way.

In the event of the AI making miscalculations, it is possible to reset the system.

That makes Iris stop, then re-read. It is possible to reset the system. Iris pores over those instructions. It's not as simple as the ctrl:alt:delete, but it's not far off. She could do it. She could unplug and reset the entire Society.

But it's an illusion. She can reset, but it'll still be there.

Unless the high Scorers destroy the building.

What did those hunters say — home for a pint before the rain? It's raining now. They may never come. Reset isn't enough. She needs to take the whole damned system down herself.

You know what to do, Iris.

Iris absolutely does. She reaches for the crowbar.

Fuck it.

She swings at the monitor, at the hard drive, then another. She batters server after server. The top Society Police will be here any minute to take her away. She doesn't care. The hack isn't enough. She can't rely on the hunters to destroy the building. She needs it pulverised now.

She swings again, screaming as she does, the jolts ricocheting up her arms and shoulders. The building dips, a bang louder than she heard and felt before. She lands on her backside, then stands again, finding her balance on the newly tilted floor. The explosion outside did some damage, and the building is swaying. It's surely going to crumble, but she needs to make sure. Nothing about the Society can be allowed to survive.

She swings again. Sparks fly from one server, and she smashes more until little flames flicker up. She finds the air con unit and smashes that up too. Let it boil in here. Let everything fry! She drops the crowbar, grabbing the bottle of spirit and rag from her bag. She lights it, throwing it into one corner, standing with a smile as the flames catch.

Footsteps come from the stairs. Somehow someone has come in. That last bang must have blown a hole in the side. The building is dipped towards the entrance where her dad is. Was. Is he still alive? There's a small crack in the blackened windows. Outside are flashes of light, and the groaning rumble vibrates through her feet.

There's an explosion from inside, sending Iris falling backwards, a hole blown through the wall where her Molotov cocktail was. The rubbery smell of burning electrics fills the air as she picks up her dropped crowbar, then swings at every bit of equipment she can.

'Iris Taylor. Welcome to the Society.'

'Fucking die!' She jumps and swings at those screens. When that fails to destroy them, she pulls a desk over, and stands on that. She smashes and smashes and smashes. Shards of plastic and metal rain down, covering her as she screams and batters them until she falls from the desk, landing badly on her knees. She doesn't feel any pain. Even the shards that cut her don't register. All she can feel is the heat from her rage.

When nothing remains except the fire sprouting legs by the blown-out wall, she glances up. Sweat and tears fog her vision, but standing there is a woman who looks like her mum. The single, central monitor still working through its cracked screen tries to continue to show an Eyes Forward representative, but it looks like a Picasso impression, split and warped. The speaker strains and scratches out its message.

'Joan Porter. Welcome to the Society.'

Chapter 63
Iris

Iris stares, rubs her gritty eyes, then takes a step back. 'You look just like her.'

'Well, she is my daughter. We took Pres-X at the same time, so we're visibly the same age.'

Iris's fingers retract over the crowbar like she has talons instead of hands. She wants to scratch this woman's eyes out. She's paler than Mae, slightly. Her red hair as fiery, her build a little heavier. But that's it. Otherwise, all Iris sees is a monster. This monster is her grandmother, her supposedly dead grandmother.

'Why are you here?' Iris asks.

'To finish this if you couldn't.'

'You're meant to be dead,' she says through her teeth, snarling like a dog.

'I opted for a blank slate. I'm a chemist. There are drugs you can take to give the illusion of death.' There's an aloofness to her tone, like she's discussing some TV programme instead of her own twisted existence.

Iris's skin crawls like there's a million insects breathing the same air instead of one Preserved bitch. She looks pathetic, really. This old woman disguised as a middle-aged coward. 'I guess the Eyes Forward figured it out.'

'They know everything,' she says, loosely folding her arms over her chest. 'All Eyes Are Our Eyes is an understatement. Turns out they needed me. Pres-X was just the beginning. I also invented Pres-X-2.' She lifts her chin higher as she says this, an air of superiority in her expression.

'What an achievement,' Iris says, recoiling her nose. 'Am I meant to be impressed? You could have cured cancer or a disease.'

Her mouth lifts in the corners. There's no warmth in that smile. It's sinister and cold. 'Age is a disease. Though you're too young to know that, too young and too beautiful. Let me just look at you for a moment.'

'Piss off.' Iris backs away. 'You abandoned my mum, your daughter, but not your evil government.' The Flake is totally worn off now, like her adrenalin has ejected it from her system, and her heart rate spikes. The crowbar feels heavy, yet she lifts it higher. She's not ready to quit yet.

'She was always an oddball,' the monster says, with a voice so snide, Iris could imagine Moira saying it. 'Better off without me. But you, my dear. You are quite extraordinary. You make her existence worthwhile.'

Iris scoffs. 'Me? I'm nothing. No one.'

'You are *everyone.*' She steps closer, and Iris's grip on the crowbar tightens. 'You are what the Eyes Forward always feared. You and your friend were the first of your generation to try to find out about another county. You are proof that their conditioning methods aren't enough. We scientists embrace failure, politicians do not.'

'Politicians? It's just an algorithm.'

'Algorithms also hate anomalies. You can code, you understand that.'

Iris's face pinches with annoyance. She does understand.

'That's why they had to ban women using computers.'

'Wait,' Iris snaps. 'That was because of us?' Georgie was right!

'You are proof that women will always gossip, always stir up trouble, not do what they're told. The Eyes Forward will fall. It's just software,' she says with such nonchalance it's as if Iris's efforts were a piece of cake. 'Software always gets out of date eventually. This is the blank slate the country needs. Leadership is going to be needed, and what team could be better? Me, the protector of youth, with Iris Taylor by my side.'

Iris swings the crowbar in front of her, hitting cables above that rain down sparks. 'I am no one!'

'You, maybe. But your lineage…' Her voice doesn't vary with any sort of concern. This annoys Iris more. She wants her scared. She wants her backing away into a corner like a terrified little rat.

'Every government has its critics, its rebels,' the monster says. 'But your namesake, the one who donated her life for you, she was the name behind the Shadownet, inventor of Nebula. She founded Sisters and Spies. Lineage is ninety per cent of what people think of you. You can control, I mean, *convince,* the sceptics. You can unite Britain again.'

'Joan Porter. Welcome to the Society.'

The monitors dangle from a cable, Joan standing underneath as the cracked screens display only static and emit a crackling sound from the speaker.

You are as important as she says, Iris. You can end this.

'I don't want to control or convince anyone,' Iris says. 'That's not why I'm here.'

'You want to destroy the government. What do you think will happen afterwards with no one to take charge?'

'No one is in charge anyway. It's not a government. It's just AI. Algorithms.'

'It keeps order.'

Chills creep over Iris and she laughs like she's as insane as this woman. 'I hardly think the massacre out there is order.'

'And what will happen with no Society Police, no algorithms?' She marks her list off on her manicured fingers, the pink polish too girlish for such a person. 'Just people with no purpose or punishment. With me in charge, the promise of Pres-X-2 will maintain order.'

Iris cracks her neck and her nostrils flare. 'Because that's all people care about. Looking a little younger.'

She gives Iris a tight smile. 'Give it time. You'll feel the same.'

Iris holds the crowbar in front, her hands growing clammy around it. She swipes the air, as if warding off Joan Porter's ideals. If the citizens of the Society are anything to go by, her obsessions are contagious. Iris returns the monster's smile. 'The Pres-X-2 is all gone. The factory exploded.'

The monster shrugs. 'A little scarcity isn't a bad thing. People will do what they're told more then. Another reason why I am so important. My recipe is protected.'

Iris shakes her head, mind reeling. The preservation drugs are all destroyed, but here is the woman who created it, who helped create this bribe they all live by. Joan Porter being the only one who knows the recipe seems so unlikely. But what if. . .what if that is true? With her gone, there would be no more Pres-X or Pres-X-2, ever. That monster thinks she's so valuable, but Iris pictures her snapped in half, broken, under rubble, the last of the Eyes Forward wreckage.

The floor dips some more and Iris bends her knees, absorbing the shift, keeping the crowbar in front of her. The monitors sway until they hang from the centre, directly over where Joan stands, attached only by a cable that tracks along the ceiling and reaches the desk next to Iris. Her knuckles blanch from the tension around the crowbar.

'The Eyes Forward were never strict enough, Iris. We can do it better. You and me, we can run the Society.'

'There is no you and me! There is no Society! None of it is real!'

Finish it, Iris!

Iris lifts her crowbar, and with a cry, slams it onto the cable. Joan takes a step forward as the monitors and their casings come crashing down, shattering into a million pieces.

Iris lifts the crowbar again, smashing everything left. Any piece of plastic or metal that isn't broken, she crashes down on.

Her vision is white with rage, complete tunnel vision except for what's right in front of her. She slams the crowbar into the furniture, then more monitors, followed by whatever fragments are left of the hard drives. She'll turn it all to dust. Burn the lot to the ground. No part of the Society will survive. She's going to pulverise it all.

When her arms are too weak to continue, she stands, panting, whole body shaking, tears streaming, her ears ringing.

Joan stands, arms folded across her chest, holding a neutral expression as Iris takes the final steps towards her, her crowbar raised. The final piece of the Society and the Eyes Forward needs to be destroyed too.

'You're not a killer, Iris.'

Iris screams in her face, her hands gripping the metal so tightly, her arms tense to bursting.

She lets the crowbar fall to her side, her neck bowing, then stares at the floor. The inferno within flickers as if attacked by a brisk wind.

'Join me, Iris. Let's rebuild the Society how it was meant to be.'

The buzzing has almost stopped. There's a crackling from the corner where the fire licks its way through the electrics. Iris lifts her chin and looks her grandmother in the eyes. Despite appearing so much like her mother, she's a stranger. There's not an atom in her body that wants to join her. But she's right. She's not a killer.

Iris takes a step back. The knife flies past the left side of her face, so close, the whoosh vibrates her ear. Joan Porter's expression changes from neutral to confused as the dagger embeds itself in her neck, another in her chest. Another dagger clangs to the floor, missing, but the final one hits her in the stomach, creating a dull thud. Blood spurts, hitting Iris in the face. Joan reaches out to her, but Iris steps back as Joan falls to the ground.

Iris stares, wide-eyed for a second, confusion glueing her to the spot. Then she turns, and in the doorway, holding another knife, is Skylar. She stares at Iris, a manic face that Iris can't read.

'Skylar. . .what. . .'

Iris's racing heart pounds, and her mouth moves, but she can't think of the words. Joan Porter lies on the floor, blood seeping out, dribbling out of her mouth that is opening and closing like a guppy. Then she is still. Totally still.

Iris looks at Skylar, who doesn't say a word but gives Iris a little nod, then cuts her own throat.

'No!' Iris screams, but it's too late. All the sadness in Skylar's face has gone. As blood drains from her, it takes her malaise too. In death, she smiles. She looks at peace.

The building dips again, another rumble from outside. Iris stands in silence for a moment, a dead woman in front of her, another behind. The wreckage of the servers and monitors litter all around as flames take hold.

There's nothing left. It's all destroyed. Iris's breath is shallow as she glares frantically from side to side. She's alone. More alone than she ever has been. Where's the voice to reassure her?

Cloudy spots form in her vision. It's hard to remember the way out. It all looks so different now. Smoke collects across the ceiling, snaking its way closer, lower, the temperature spiking, yet she's frozen to the spot.

Is what Joan said true? Chaos will ensue now there's nothing to govern. Nothing in charge. Iris's hands go to her face, then she hugs her trembling body, doubling over as tears stream and all her muscles lose their strength.

There's soft footsteps crunching over the debris. In the doorway is her mum.

'Mum,' she says as Mae steps forward, standing among the carnage. 'Mum, I'm sorry. Shit, I'm so sorry.'

What have I done?

Chapter 64
Iris

'Iris?'

Iris hasn't been paying attention for a while, instead she's been still in her mother's arms like a child, letting her mother's embrace soothe her shaking. She tightens her hold as Mae sways on the spot. Or is that the building rocking?

'Iris?'

Ava Maricelli beckons her over.

'We need to go. Now.'

Iris glances behind her at the body of the woman who looks so much like her mum it's unsettling. Her face is ashen, the blood that dribbled from her mouth now dried.

The smell of burning rubber is intensifying; Iris hadn't noticed the flames getting angrier. She leans away from her mother, holding her hand instead as they make to leave. Stepping over the body of Skylar hits Iris with a pain in her chest. She has so many questions for her that will never be answered.

Leaving the server room, the rest of the building is blackening with smoke and damage from explosions. The building groans with every movement. They don't go up the tower but climb down the rough edge of a damaged wall, out of a hole in the brick and into the pouring rain.

'Carefully, Mae,' Ava says as she guides Mae down each brick and step.

The back of her mum's head is matted and deep red, contrasting with the pallor of her face.

Iris climbs down with ease, jumping the last metre to land with a splash in a puddle. Mae stands silently and Iris links arms with her. They walk a few steps and turn around the side of the building where the entrance is — or was. Where Georgie, Pasha, and Sam were waiting. There's charred blackness on the ground and around the door, but no bodies, no people waiting. The emptiness makes Iris freeze.

'They're okay,' Ava says. 'They've all gone back to your parents.' Let's get there now.'

Iris scans the windows, the skyline, then the open Square ahead of them.

'No one's shooting,' Ava says. 'The hunt is definitely over.'

Iris still doesn't move. She's rigid on the spot and glares at Ava. 'The hunt you organised.'

Ava takes Mae's hand firmly and pulls her along. 'There's a lot you don't know. Come on.'

There's something in Ava's voice, in her expression, something that implies sincerity and kindness. Iris saw it in the old church. She found it hard to believe that Ava's the same sort of heathen that Norman and Jason are, so she follows both of them, holding one of Mae's hands. Lightning flashes in the sky, intermittently brightening their way. Balloons of smoke billow upwards from wrecked buildings, the odd pop and bang like fireworks from somewhere across town. It's hard to tell where the smoke comes from. The wind brings with it wet ash and dust, catching in the sparse light like snowflakes.

There's a thunderous rumble that comes from the ground, and Iris turns as the last of the Eyes Forward HQ collapses, and Mae throws up on the ground.

'Mum! What's wrong?' Seems like a stupid thing to ask. What's right would be more concise.

'She has a concussion,' Ava says. 'Come on, let's get her home.'

The streets are still mostly quiet. A few people run past them, while some cry outside a collapsed building, but no bolts fly, so no new bodies on this route.

Angus answers the door, and Iris goes rigid at the sight of him, taking a step back.

'Iris,' he says. 'Thank God you're okay.' He reaches for her, but she takes another step back.

She turns from Ava to Angus and narrows her eyes. 'You two,' she says without relaxing her jaw. 'You two did all of this.'

Her dad limps over to the doorway, his bloodied shirt padded with bandages, then steps out in the rain to greet them. 'Iris!' He wraps his arms around them, holding as tightly as he can, one arm around each of them. A little sniff in her ear. She's never heard her dad cry before. He pulls back and sniffs a little louder. 'Come in,' he says as he wipes his eye. 'Let's get you dry.'

Georgie is making tea in the kitchen, and she squeals when she sees Iris. 'You did it, Iris! We did it! Society Police building, Life Score building, The Eyes Forward HQ, all of it. Even the factory is gone.'

Tea won't cut it, so Iris opens the fridge, hoping for beer but finds none.

'Come on,' Georgie says and hands her a cup. 'You've got to hear what everyone has to say.'

***

Pasha cleans Mae's wounds, then puts her to bed and checks on her every couple of minutes. Everyone else is too wired to even consider sleeping. The stories go on late into the night, Ava explaining the years she's been plotting, Angus helping her with the Flake. It was always meant to help. He got delayed dodging hunters when Iris scaled the Eyes Forward building. Pasha says it's what he and Rolan planned, though Angus took it further. They did it, all of them. High, mid and low Scorers, all working towards a common goal.

There are no more vibrations of buildings falling, no screams from outside. The Eyes Forward headquarters was the last building to fall. The twenty-four-hour news channel has been silent for a while, the camera only showing an empty desk. Georgie keeps circulating her videos, and they stay online. There are no bots taking them down, no one censoring anything. In a moment of bravery, she uploads it to the main internet.

No one has heard from Tash and Johan yet. Iris and Georgie texted and told them to come, but there's no news yet.

'I took a picture of that blue-haired woman,' Ava says. 'I have the database on my phone. Facial recognition names her as Skylar Harrison. She was a 650 who took Pres-X nine years ago. She was ninety-four years old.'

'No!' Iris says, her hand going to her mouth.

'She was admitted to an asylum shortly after,' Ava continues. 'One that fell down. She and her husband, though it sounds like her husband was the one who was the worst affected. Looks like, somehow, she survived the building collapsing. She must have escaped, I guess. Maybe she had family. I can only speculate as really there's nothing to say where she's been all this time, or how she survived.'

'I'll bet she'd been plotting revenge on XL Medico the whole time,' Iris says.

Ava nods. 'Haven't we all.'

Chapter 65
Iris

The next day, the storm is over and a blue-sky warmth covers Berkshire. Iris checks on her mum as soon as she wakes up, and she's woozy, weak, but okay. She cries when she sees Iris, when they hug again, and when they tell each other how much they love each other. That's all Mae remembers from the latter part of the night, her fear for Iris. Her need to get to her.

'I'm all right, Mum. We're all okay.'

Iris isn't sure if Mae remembers or even noticed Joan in the building. She's not sure if she'll mention it. Despite her injuries and concussion, her mum came for her. Among all the chaos, Mae was there.

Georgie wakes a little later, and they load up Nebula. Her videos have been viewed nearly a hundred thousand times. Iris adds her own to it, the video she took from inside HQ. It's hard to articulate to the others what she saw, or rather, what she didn't see. Across the Society, Life Score apps and Society Police apps are failing to load. There are no Eyes Forward representatives anywhere. Hunts took place in many counties, according to reports on Nebula, as did rebellions with mixed degrees of success. But demolishing Berkshire's HQ, the county with the highest concentration of 800 pluses, cut an artery.

Ava slept on the sofa last night, Angus in Pasha's reclining chair. They're all awake now and turn the TV on.

The news desk is still a mess, but no longer unoccupied. The dishevelled anchors are hysterical about the loss of preservation drugs, that terrorists have destroyed the lives of the most important.

'The war on ageing has been lost,' one of them says. 'Even the best of us are mortal again.'

They don't mention the real news. They report on an issue with the Life Score system and call for calm, but their voices shake with panic. They remind everyone they must trust the Eyes Forward. They'll sort out this blip soon.

Iris and everyone all laugh at that.

Georgie leans into Iris. 'I have an idea.'

***

Iris, Georgie, and Ava leave the apartment, stepping out cautiously, quite unsure of how bad the streets will be. There isn't the chaos Joan Porter predicted, not yet anyway. There are several damaged buildings, weapons abandoned in the street, though no bodies that they can see.

They first head to the spot where Ezra went down and find his body where they left it. They roll him over and close his eyes. Iris and Georgie take his hands and sit with him a while, allow their tears to fall and say their goodbyes and thank yous. Iris hopes he's at peace. They'd packed sheets in a bag, and they cover him, unsure what else to do. Ava says she doesn't think her funeral home was too badly damaged. She's checked the cameras and it's likely the crematorium is still functioning, then she leaves to get the vehicle to collect the body. She promises she'll give him some dignity.

There's no sign of Tash and Johan. Iris messages them again and hopes. She kicks herself for not at least knowing their address when Georgie suggests they probably went home.

They make it to the newsroom just as all the usual staff and anchors are in full-blown panic mode. First doses of Pres-X-2 aren't going to be possible, let alone second doses. They're not sure if any preservation drugs will ever be possible again. The phones are ringing off the hook, a couple of office staff are crying, a couple more walk out. Iris wonders if what Joan Porter said was true and there's no recipe. That seems unlikely, just the over-inflated ego of a Preserved. Once this has all calmed down, they'll find a way to restore youth again. Who gets access is the big question.

With the newsroom floor in a state of disarray and the anchors too preoccupied with their own dismay, Georgie turns the cameras on, then walks up to the news desk, boldly, like she's meant to be there. She applies her ruby lipstick and gazes straight down the camera.

She tells the truth. In its entirety. She's no script. She speaks from the heart to the ordinary people, to those who most need to know the truth. She plays the videos she circulated on the Shadownet, Iris's included.

It's only a Berkshire channel. The news like everything is devolved. But she knows from the Shadownet word is getting out. Her report is just one step.

When they get back home, past the building that fell the night before — was that only a night ago? To Iris, it seems like a lifetime — they make it to their apartment door and taped to the front is a note: *Gone to Wales. Tash and Johan.*

Georgie squeals with delight and air punches. 'They made it! They're okay!'

'She did say Johan isn't one for formalities.' Iris's voice cracks as she speaks, and she holds the note to her chest, blinking away tears. They're okay. And they've done exactly what they said they would. Iris wishes she could thank them. If it wasn't for Johan, she'd have been raped and killed at the school. If it wasn't for Tash, they wouldn't have achieved anything. A warmth spreads through her chest, a warmth she can only attribute to gratitude. She hopes they know how grateful she is.

Iris sits on her bed a while, trying to take it all in. It's Sunday. She should go to work tomorrow, but that job doesn't exist anymore. The entire department where she'd worked for the last six years, and its ethos, doesn't exist anymore. She's spent so long wanting to take the Eyes Forward down, she's given no thought to the aftermath, to what it meant for her or her future.

On her shelf is the picture of her great-grandmother, her namesake, Iris Taylor. She hasn't heard the voice since she smashed up the Eyes Forward building. Her tattoo hasn't itched. It's like a part of her is finally at peace. She stares at the photo, the kindness of her eyes, the joy of her smile. You'd never guess from that face that she fought against the government until her last breath all those years ago. She gave her life for Iris, and now, Iris has helped complete her task. She picks up the photo and kisses the glass. 'I hope I did you proud.'

Her phone pings with a message from her dad. Mae is up and about, and do they want to meet for coffee? Iris gets Georgie and they go.

Iris and Georgie arrive first, and for a while, loiter outside the café. It's a 700 plus, but that means nothing anymore. The sign has been half sprayed over, but it's still readable. It's still meant to say 700 plus. They stand in awkward poses, hands in their pockets as they rock on the balls of their feet.

After a while, Georgie gives her a nudge. 'Come on. Let's just go in.'

A 700 plus café. Neither of them has ever been to such a place. It appears quite modest, considering, homey decor and comfy seats. The coffee smells inviting. They sit at a table and can't relax, expecting any moment for someone to tell them they don't belong, to tell them the likes of them shouldn't be in such an exclusive café. But no one does.

Pasha, Mae, Angus, and Ava arrive a few minutes later. Ava's the only one who walks in without a shred of insecurity, and they all sit at the table. Ava orders the coffees, and they arrive in pretty china cups with ornate patterns swirled into the foam.

'How's the funeral home?' Iris asks.

'Some damage to the front from the Society Police building burning down, but not as bad as I thought. Your friend is resting there now. Let me know what you want to do for a funeral.'

'Thanks. And good news — our other friends are okay.'

Everyone grins at that. Wales, though, is the bit Iris still can't comprehend. She wonders if they've really gone.

Mae is still pale, but after a cleanup and the blood washed out of her hair, she looks much better. She and Pasha have grazes everywhere and bruises, though they each wear a smile. 'How are you, Mum?' Iris asks.

'Not bad at all. Just need some painkillers. I'm more worried about your dad's shoulder.'

'It's fine.' Pasha waves it off. 'I think all in all, we've come off all right.'

'No thanks to me,' Angus says, biting his lip.

'Hey,' Pasha says. 'You did what you had to do. Your dad and I should have told you our plan.'

'We all should have been more open about our plans,' Ava says to Mae. 'Friendships shouldn't be allowed to slip aside so easily.'

Mae nods. 'We're okay. That's all that matters now.'

'How's Moira?' Iris asks, trying not to grimace.

Angus shrugs. 'Less than impressed, but she'll get over it. She realised what Dad was up to. That's why he was late meeting

Pasha. He's keen to start rebuilding the county as soon as possible. He's pretty mad at me for blowing up the factory. But he's going to rebuild everything. Lots of affordable homes, he says, not just the rich areas. No more rubble.'

'That's great,' Pasha says.

'Not sure Mum and Dad will stay together,' Angus continues. 'I dunno. It's their business, I guess. I'm leaving them to it. Think I'm going to cycle to Scotland.'

Iris almost spits out her coffee. 'Scotland!'

'Yeah. Visit Edinburgh and stop by all the counties on the way. I mean, why not? The Eyes Forward never wanted us to travel to other counties. I want to see what all the fuss is about.'

Pasha has a twinkle in his eye. 'Maybe we should go back and visit Cornwall, Mae? That beach, remember?'

Mae nuzzles into him. 'Yeah. Why not?'

'Well,' Georgie says. 'I am going to stick around here for a bit. I reckon I could actually get a job as a news anchor now. What do you think?'

Everyone agrees she'll be great.

'What about you, Iris?' Mae asks.

Iris fiddles with the sleeve of her jacket. 'Me? What about me?'

'Your plans for the future now?'

Iris sits back for a bit, gazes out of the window, and exhales slowly. 'I guess. . .' she thinks a moment longer. 'I don't know, if I'm being honest. Without someone telling me what to do, I'm not sure what to do.'

'I think the great thing is, you don't need to decide, right?' Georgie says. 'No borders, no Life Score classist system, no Eyes Forward watching our every move. You can think about things for a bit.'

Iris smiles her broadest smile. 'Yeah. I can choose.' Pinpricks trickle over her body as it sinks in. 'I can choose,' she says again. 'We can do what we want now, be who we want to be. We're free.'

A note from Emma

Please scan QR code to leave a review.

Rebel is the third book in the Eyes Forward Series. If you enjoyed it, please consider leaving a review on Amazon and Goodreads. Reviews are so vital for indie authors such as myself and knowing you enjoyed my work makes it all worthwhile. Check out my website and Facebook page for updates on my next releases.

If you are in the mood for some more twisted dystopian, my first series, The Raft Series, is available now.

The Society came about from my own alternative way of living. I've been a nomad for a few years now, spending most of my time dawdling around the mountains and coastlines of Europe. Dystopian literature plays on our fears, our what ifs. I have lived all over Britain, including a fair chunk of time in Reading and Cornwall. The counties across Britain are all wonderfully unique and I love exploring them. If it became taboo to cross county borders, I think I'd go insane. There is so much to see in this little world.

In this world I would be about eligible for Pres-X-2. Would I take it? I like to think I wouldn't. I'm quite happy being and looking forty, though I swear my knees are at least sixty. Original Pres-X though, to be young again when I hit eighty years old. . . I don't know. I'll tell you in forty years.

What about you? Let me know!

Acknowledgements

Rebel would not be in print without the help of my wonderful betas and critique partners. Thank you to Maggie, Barry, Joan and Julie. Their time and honest feedback made this book what it is today. Thank you also to my editor Shannon K. O'Brien, for being so incredibly thorough, and Natasja Smith for her proofreading skills.

Thanks especially to my partner, John, for giving me the space and time I need to write, for his support, patience, and encouragement.

And thank you for reading it.

Milton Keynes UK
Ingram Content Group UK Ltd.
UKHW032329221024
449917UK00004B/275